NIGHTCHILD

A Clans Novel

J.A. Cummings

Kresnak

www.kresnakpress.com

ISBN 0-9670668-0-8

First Printing, June 1999
1 2 3 4 5 6 7 8 9

Kresnak Press, Ltd.
PO Box 3581
Dublin, OH 43016-0291
sales@kresnakpress.com

PRINTED IN THE U.S.A.

To everyone who believed in me,
But even more to everyone who didn't.

Part One

One

France, 1744

The guitar strings vibrated beneath Tobyn Reyes' hands as he played, the passionate Spanish gypsy music rising around him. From his seat on the hitching post in front of yet another French tavern, he could watch the outsiders, the *gadje*, money in their hands, gathering to listen and watch. His twin sister danced in the yard before him, and the *gadje* circled around while Araminah swayed and seduced with every step, her green eyes flashing. Tobyn's gaze locked on one man who watched the gypsy girl with salacious glee. When he noticed that he was being observed, the Frenchman quickly tossed a coin into Ara's outstretched hand, then scrambled into the tavern. The young man chuckled and kept playing.

Dusk was falling on this autumn day, the sounds of the harvest dying with the light. A chill bit the air and turned his sister's breath to grey-blue clouds as she completed her final dance. Their uncle Tito, the youngest of their father's two brothers, passed through the crowd of onlookers, soliciting their coins, liberally picking pockets as he went.

Ara came to her brother, breathing heavily. "That was good," she said in Romany, their native tongue. "I think we made some money."

"Good." He handed her his instrument. "It's getting dark. I think you should go home with Tito."

"What about you?"

"I have some business." He smiled. "I'll meet you back at the *kumpania* when I'm done."

She hesitated, then asked, "This doesn't have anything to do with that rich Frenchman we saw last night, does it?"

"Mostly, it has to do with his horse." Tito joined them, and Tobyn carefully counted out his share of the money, passing the coins to Ara for safekeeping.

"His horse?" she echoed.

"Yes. I'm going to steal it."

Araminah ran a slender hand through her black curls, then crossed her arms. "I don't think you should stay."

"Why not?" their uncle asked, looking from one twin to the other curiously.

"It feels dangerous," she explained. "The night air...it's active. This isn't the time. Wait for another night, after *samhain*."

Tito snorted. "Your mother taught you that. Forget that Irish shit. It's no good for a Rom girl to be thinking like a *gadja*." He looked ruefully at his nephew. "If she keeps it up, we'll never be able to marry her off."

"*Tio*," Tobyn sighed, "shut up." He turned to his twin. "And as for you, we've talked about this a hundred times. I know what I'm doing. Go home with Tito. I'll be along as soon as I get my horse."

"Make sure it's a good one," his uncle advised.

"Of course." He smiled and puffed. "I deserve nothing but the best."

Ara rolled her eyes. "Oh, God..."

The eldest Reyes clapped her on the shoulder. "It's getting dark, *chavi*. If your brother is staying here, then it's up to me to get you back to the *kumpania* and your father's wagon before you lose any more value from your bride price."

"If Tobyn is staying,—"

"I said go!" Tito barked, exercising the authority of age. "Night is not the time for a good gypsy girl to be out among the *gadje*. Tobyn is a man. He can handle himself."

"Yes, I've noticed that." She shook her head. "Fine. Just once, I'd like to be listened to."

Tito chuckled and set about preparing their recalcitrant old mare to pull their cart back to the caravan. "You're a woman, Araminah. Who would listen to you?"

She bundled up her things and untied her shawl from her waist, wrapping it around her shoulders. She looked into her brother's blue eyes. *//Don't be long,//* she warned, speaking to him, mind to mind, through their twin link. *//I'm worried about this. Tonight feels...unlucky.//*

The younger man shook his head and replied, *//You and your omens. You know, just because you're a witch, it doesn't mean that you know everything.//*

She gave him a glare that could have scorched bark from the trees. *//I know enough.//*

Tito grabbed Ara's arm and all but threw her up onto the cart. He cast one last grin at his nephew, tipped his hat, and then they were gone, leaving Tobyn alone in the yard. Behind him, the tavern was noisy, full of the sounds of raucous harvest celebration; he could almost taste the ale that awaited him inside. He counted out his coins once more, then squared his shoulders and prepared to brave the crowd.

No matter how much the *gadje* might watch his sister dance and listen to him play, there was still no love lost between the French and the gypsies. On more than one occasion, he had heard of hunting parties of French men who murdered gypsy men and raped the women. He had no illusions that he would be welcome in the tavern, but he knew also that the French would never turn away his *sous*.

He walked into the tavern, jaw set pugnaciously. The barkeeper barked, "Get out of here, you! We don't serve your kind!"

Tobyn held up a gold coin. "Ale," he called back, his voice clear. It carried over the noise in the room, attracted attention. He liked attention. "Now."

"He said get out!" One of the burly crofters who sat near the door rose and towered over the gypsy youth. His companion, a one-eyed farmer, spat at Tobyn's toes. The young man bristled, his hand moving down toward the knife he wore tucked into his belt. The tavern keeper caught his hand.

"Here is your ale. Now go and drink it outside."

Tobyn considered ignoring her, but he had always been a soft touch when it came to women. He flipped his coin into her hand, accepted his pewter tankard, and stepped back toward the door. His smile was cold as he addressed the crofter. "Another time, *monsieur*."

"Count on it, you little gypsy rat!"

He sat on the hitching post again, sipping at the ale. It was a weak brew, barely even burning on its way down his throat. *How disappointing*, he thought. Turning his back to the cold easterly wind, he crossed his arms over his chest and waited.

Hours passed, during which he spent his time earning money by sharpening knives and tool blades for the tavern's clientele. It was long after dark when the sound of hoofbeats caught his attention. He slid down from the hitching post and sneaked around the corner, watching stealthily as the rich Frenchman rode into view.

The Frenchman, tall and elegant in dress and motion, dismounted smoothly, tethering his steed to the post before the tavern door. His brown hair was swept back and neatly tied at the nape of his neck; with an imperious glitter in his cold grey eyes, he looked like a man who thought he owned the world and all the people in it. He was handsome in a regal way, but with an air of repugnant arrogance. As he passed Tobyn, the young Rom's senses reeled with a jolt of pure danger. For a moment, he even thought he saw the man look his way, but he consoled himself that he was in the darkness, and no man could have seen him where he stood. The Frenchman stepped into the tavern without a word.

The horse whuffed at him as he approached, stamping one of its great hooves. It was a stallion, and a large beast, well-muscled and impeccably groomed. Its hide glimmered in the light from the tavern, and it side-stepped ever so slightly, made nervous by the approach of this stranger. Tobyn held up both of his hands, palms up, and shushed the horse, his eyes locked with the animal's brown gaze. There was a hesitation, then honest contact, and the horse ducked its head docilely, stepping forward into the Romany youth's embrace. Self satisfied and excited, Tobyn untethered it.

He sensed the Frenchman's presence behind him a moment too late. He had only enough time to drop the reins before a crashing blow chased him into darkness.

He awoke feeling cold. Tobyn groaned softly in the back of his throat, aware that he was stretched out, spread-eagle, on his back. His head hurt terribly. He tried to bring his hand up to check for blood or breakage, but the motion was stilled before it could begin. Alarm crept into his mind, banishing the fuzziness and making him more alert.

He was naked, lying on a hard, flat surface. Experimental tugs told him that he was bound hand and foot with harsh rope. A cloth, soft and almost slimy with cold, was tied firmly over his eyes, depriving him of sight. He strained against his bonds, the first nasty finger of panic dipping down his throat.

"Michel," a woman said, her voice an icy soprano. Tobyn froze. "I do believe he's waking up."

He swallowed the lump in his throat, then asked in heavily accented French, "Who are you?"

A robust bass laugh reached his ears from somewhere to his right. "He speaks the language! How odd to find civilization in such an unwashed heathen."

Another man, standing directly over Tobyn's head, spoke in a voice smooth as silk and as dangerous as poison. "He has been washed, Roger." He leaned closer, and the Rom could feel breath, strangely cold, close to his ear. "You're very beautiful for a horse thief, my lad."

"What are you going to do to me?" Tobyn asked, his heart pounding in fear and a strange excitement.

Thin fingers stroked his face, and the Frenchman whispered, "Patience."

The gypsy started violently as a strange hand brushed over his exposed hips. Another woman commented, "He's so...physical, Michel. How very human." She caressed him, touching him like a lover. "How beautiful."

"He is gypsy," Roger told her. "Everyone knows they have no morality. He's probably willing to lay with any one of us."

The first woman laughed like breaking glass. "He's certainly ready to."

Tobyn flushed in shame at his body's unconscious reactions to the second woman's hands, but anger followed the embarrassment. "You have no right to judge me!"

A round of general laughter broke free, then faded away. The Frenchman stroked his head, fingers tangling in his hair. "Ladies and gentleman," he announced, "welcome to my home. I hope that you enjoy this evening, something that I truly believe we shall not soon forget. The pantry is stocked, ready to slake your thirst, and your accustomed rooms are at the ready. You need never fear the sun in the home of the Vicomte Michel Dumas."

Tobyn listened closely, searching the urbane and somewhat theatrical words for some clue to his fate. A hand settled onto his leg, a large hand that was cold as ice. Roger asked, "And what of this, Dumas? Is this to be our entertainment or our aperitif?"

Realization dawned and the Rom shuddered. "*Mulle*! Vampires!"

The soprano laughed again and clapped her hands in delight. "Oh, very good! You are a clever child after all."

"Roger, Elisa," Dumas said, "be calm. Our gypsy friend is indeed our appetizer and entertainment this evening, but I must ask you to control yourselves. Take only a taste of him tonight; Romany blood is a fine wine and must be savored."

"A constant supply?" the second woman asked.

Roger laughed like a braying donkey. "Blood on the hoof!" Elisa joined his mirth, and Tobyn fought his ropes with renewed vigor, his mind screaming in panic. A firm hand grasped his shoulder and pushed him back down onto the dinner table.

"Be still, boy," Dumas ordered. Frightened, left with no options, Reyes obeyed.

"Start him off!" Elisa urged, far too eager. "Open his blood to us!"

Tobyn could feel Dumas smiling. "No, *fraulein*, that is an honor I relinquish to our distinguished guest, Doña Isabella."

"Thank you, Michel," she whispered, her hands reluctantly leaving the hot flesh she had been stroking. Isabella's fingertips traced a line up from Tobyn's groin to his sternum, tickling over his trembling flesh. "Where?"

"Amuse yourself," Dumas, ever the gracious host, replied.

"We can all choose our favorite spots," Roger suggested, his voice thick with excitement and emotions Tobyn did not want to identify.

Dumas sounded entertained. "Absolutely."

Isabella joined Tobyn on the table, kneeling over him. He could feel the satin of her skirts as she eased down, draping his body with her own. She, too, was cold, but her entrancingly gentle touch against his throat was almost enough to make him forget what she was. Her finger traced his lips.

"Such a pretty mouth," she whispered to him in Spanish. Gently, smoothly, she turned his face away from her. He could not have resisted her if he'd tried. Her breath touched his ear, and tears sprang to his eyes, making dark spots on the blindfold.

"*Ay, dios...*"

Isabella descended as his whisper died. Pain lanced through him as his throat was impaled with ivory spikes, but it was quickly replaced by a bone-numbing pleasure he'd never known before. He was distantly aware of Elisa laughing and of Ara, frantic on the other end of their twin-link, but all that mattered now was the feeling of Isabella's tongue and lips against his skin. He moaned softly, passionately, and the ecstasy ended as abruptly as it began.

Isabella sat back as Tobyn gasped for breath. Her voice was husky as she whispered, "You are right, Dumas. It is a fine wine."

Gentle hands stroked Tobyn's hair, and Michel Dumas breathed to him, "Easy, my love." More loudly, the Frenchman said, "Elisa...your turn."

"So much blood collected here," she purred, her frigid hand clutching at his groin. "What a shame to waste it."

Her fingernails scored the sensitive skin, and he cried out in terror and in pain, convinced that he was about to be gelded. Dumas' hands clamped onto the sides of his head, holding him still as Elisa's teeth drove into his flesh. As pleasurable as the first bite had been, this one was agony. A ragged scream tore from his throat, and he writhed beneath the heavy hands of the four assembled vampires. On the edges of his mind, he could feel his sister screaming with him, and the pressure from the pain and the double cry sent him reeling into blissful oblivion.

Still stroking the unconscious youth's black curls, Dumas clicked his tongue. "Elisa, really. You amaze me."

Roger frowned down at their captive. "Swooned quite away. How disappointing. Still...I believe that I shall take my turn."

"By all means," Dumas nodded. "But please remember—do not take too much."

With a smile of reassurance, Roger bent to press his toothy kiss to the gypsy's throat.

～✥✦✥～

Sunlight dragged him to a reality full of dull, throbbing pain. His body was an enemy, torturing him with lingering reminiscences of the vampires' attentions. He tried to deny the truth of his situation by keeping his eyes stubbornly closed, but the aching was unaltered.

His head seemed to explode as a furtive message reached him from his twin. *//Tobyn...//*

Using most of what little strength he could muster, he replied, *//Here//*

Araminah's fear and anger echoed through their twin-link. *//They've hurt you! Tobyn, tell me where you are. I'll come for you//*

//No!// The effort of his mental shout cost him dearly. Sagging into the softness of his heretofore unnoticed surroundings, he continued, *//Not here. Don't come here.//*

//But they'll kill you!//

//I...I don't think so. They don't want me dead.//

//Tobyn...//

He closed the link on her anguished protestations. Hearing her troubles would not help him here and now. Taking a deep breath, he forced himself to open his eyes and take a look at where he was.

The room was the richest he'd ever seen, ornate and fit for kings. Rich Persian carpet stretched the width of the chamber, a room which was larger than Tobyn's family wagon. He was nestled in a huge bed built of fine wood and covered with delicate linens and satins. Thin muslin curtains hid half of the bed chamber from his view, and he rested against a veritable mountain of soft pillows. The bedside table bore a tray of food and a pitcher that he dearly hoped was full. His thirst was raging.

So now you know the room, he thought. *Time to have a look at yourself.*

His wrists were livid with rope burns, and a series of puncture wounds marred his inner elbows. A hesitant touch to his aching throat revealed twin sets of puncture marks. He could not remember receiving all these bites. He was reluctant to lift the covers and look lower, but a dreadful set of wild imaginings pushed him farther on. The damage from Elisa's torment was less than he would have expected, and he was more than relieved to see that everything was present and accounted for. He presumed that he was still functional, but somehow he was currently less than eager to test that theory. As he had anticipated, his ankles bore the twins to the rope burns on his wrists.

The door, he thought, looking at where it stood blankly closed across the room. *I have to get out of here.* He swung his legs over the edge of the bed, but when his bare feet touched the cold air, his head swam dangerously. He nearly fell from the bed, and when he caught himself against the bed poster, he could see how badly he was shaking.

Food. I need food. He turned to the tray and pulled a handful of bread from the loaf that waited there. His dry mouth made it difficult to swallow, so he seized the water pitcher and gulped at it, emptying it at once. He fell back onto the pillows, gasping for breath. *It's going to be a very long day.*

※※※

He awoke with a start, wondering when he'd fallen asleep. The window looked out into darkness, and Tobyn's skin prickled with anxiety as he realized what that meant. Years ago, his grandmother Beti had placed a spell on him and Ara, a spell intended to protect them from vampires and the evil eye and ghosts and all the other dangers of the night. He had laughed at her then, but now he recited the final words of the spell to calm himself.

"From now until the end of time, from day into night, they shall not become one of these."

"One of what, my little horse thief?"

He started and cried out in surprise. From a wing-backed chair near the fire, Dumas watched him with an amused smile on his face. Tobyn showed his rebellious spirit with a fierce glare. The Frenchman solicitously rose and came to the bed, his elegant hands smoothing the satin comforter over the gypsy's knees.

"I will send you clothing. The cold may make you ill. We can't have that."

"Why? Won't I taste as good then?" the mortal snapped.

"Oh, come now, my lad. Surely you don't believe that I mean you harm."

Tobyn flared. "No harm? What the hell do you call that dinner party last night if it wasn't harm?"

Dumas' eyes went cold. "I could have let them kill you, my little *bohemièn*. Never forget that fact."

"Go to hell!"

The Rom expected anger. Instead, the French vampire chuckled. "You are a stubborn one, aren't you? Wounded and run to ground, and still you snap and snarl at the hunter. Amazing."

He reached out to touch Reyes' face, but Tobyn pushed his hand away. His blue eyes were accusing as he echoed, "Hunter? I'm not your quarry."

"No?" Dumas raised a thin eyebrow. "You are certainly my prey. You are mine. As my horse would have been yours, so you are mine. I have stolen you away from your wretched gypsy life. I have given you the chance for an eternity of civilization."

"I don't want your civilization," Tobyn protested, his strength flagging once again.

The vampire ignored his words. His hands cupped the Rom's face, and Dumas stared into his eyes. "Mine to touch, to Change, to control. Mine to save or destroy. You are in the company of gods, my gypsy child. And I can make you one of us."

"No."

"Yes."

Before Tobyn could react, moving too fast for the mortal to see, Dumas leaned forward and presented his lips with a heated kiss. Images of tenderness and passion sprang to life in Tobyn's head, created there by the vampire. Reyes fought against him ineffectually, sacrificing the last of his energy to the struggle; finally, he slumped into Dumas' hands, unable to resist more.

The vampire sat back, his gray eyes warm with lust. "You are mine, little gypsy," he told his captive. "Forever."

※※※

Dumas stood aside as the tavern keeper's daughter measured the unconscious gypsy, her eyes cast away from his nakedness in something like maidenly modesty. He had never had much patience for the Christian morality the girl displayed.

"I expect a full set of clothing altered to fit him and returned here by morning. If you succeed, you will be rewarded."

The girl didn't ask what would happen if she failed. She had lived in the shadow of Dumas' *chateau* all of her life; she knew very well the price to be paid for disobedience. "Yes, *m'sieur*," she murmured, praying to God for protection one more time.

Beside her host, Isabella watched the gypsy sleeping. "It's astounding," she whispered. "He reminds me so much of—"

"Yes, I know." He could not bear to hear her say the name. She understood and fell into silence. Dumas looked sadly at his prisoner. "Very much, indeed."

※※※

The morning found him stronger and in an exceedingly foul mood. Clothing, expensive and finely tailored to his exact proportions, waited on an armchair beneath the wide window. Although he disliked the thought of accepting Dumas' gifts, Tobyn disliked being naked to the man's sight even more.

"Now how the hell do I put this on?" he wondered aloud. His talent for mimicry helped him decipher the morass of ties and buttons, and he went to stand before the floor-length mirror that stood on carefully-carved lions' feet, inspecting his appearance. He finger-combed his hair, adjusted the cuffs, then bowed sarcastically to his own reflection. "*Señor,*" he mocked himself. He bore little resemblance to the Rom youth he'd been two days before. A part of him doubted if he'd ever be that man again.

Tobyn banished the dire thought with an enthusiastic assault on the replenished food and drink on the tray beside the bed. To assuage his pride for accepting the vampires' handouts, he told himself, *I'll get out of here or die trying. That's a promise.* He tore into an apple. *I never make a promise that I can't keep.*

After he had decimated the fruit and bread his captors had supplied, he rose and wandered through the room, investigating his opulent prison.

The carpet was thick and plush beneath his newly-booted feet, and he was not surprised to find the door locked from the outside. *So much for that escape route,* he thought. *What about the window?*

He pressed his face to the beveled glass and looked down. He was on the third floor of the *chateau,* and even if he'd thought he could survive the drop, the window was tightly sealed and barred from the outside. He thought it best not to speculate too hard on how Dumas had managed to accomplish that little feat.

Tobyn poked through the rest of the chamber, opening drawers and looking under furniture. There was little to comfort him. Dumas had been careful to remove everything remotely resembling a weapon, eliminating both possible attacks and suicide attempts, depriving Tobyn of his only plans. All that remained was the pewter water jug, but Tobyn knew he could do little damage to Dumas with such a thing.

There was precious little that he could do to occupy his time. With no one to talk to and no fresh air to stimulate his mind with the scents of life, Tobyn was left with staring at walls and a tenacious grip on his slipping sanity. There were books on the divan, but he could not read; there was a music box, but he hated the repetitious tinkling of its waltz the first time he heard it. It was lovely, though, gilded on the edges, and probably worth quite a bit; only his thief's appreciation for value prevented him from hurling it against the window.

He sat and stared through the long and lonely day. The silence of the room weighed on him, and he did anything he could to break it: he sang to himself, told himself bedtime stories he usually reserved for his young cousins, fantasized about freedom. He kept himself occupied as well as he could, but still his skin began to crawl with the unfamiliar closeness of the room and the hated confinement of the locked door.

Finally, there was nothing left to do but sleep. With some sense of resignation, Tobyn followed the call to dreams, rationalizing that he would have to be alert once the sun went down.

It was as good an excuse as any.

He jolted awake as the bolt slid open on the door. Setting his jaw, he rose to face the newcomers like a man.

Dumas led the way, followed by his three guests. Roger was an unattractive lump of a man, brown hair hanging limply beside his round face. His dark eyes glinted as he examined the defiant posture of their unwilling toy.

"So this is what he looks like when he's dressed."

"He looks almost French," commented the taller of the two women, an ascorbic blonde whose voice made Tobyn's skin crawl. Elisa swept closer, her slim white fingers reaching out to play with the curl that flopped onto the gypsy's forehead. He flinched away from her touch, hating this woman with all of his soul. She shook her head. "But no manners. Tell me, how is our little gypsy feeling today?"

He set his jaw. *Puta.*

Doña Isabella, a petite brunette with the face of an angel, sat on the divan with regal grace, like a woman accustomed to sitting in thrones. Her deep brown eyes studied Tobyn in a way that was less predatory, more curious than the frank gazes of the others. He remembered the way she'd touched him, though, and he could not meet her gaze. Blushing furiously, he looked away.

"I feel the time has come for introductions," Dumas said, taking up position in the armchair. "I am the Vicomte Michel Dumas, your host. This is Roger, Earl of Huntingdon. He is English, but we can forgive him that." The vampires laughed; Tobyn, not sharing their humor, merely crossed his arms and waited. "Our feminine companions are Doña Isabella Oñate de las Cruces and Fraulein Elisa Dieter."

They looked to Tobyn expectantly, waiting for his response. He simply stared back stubbornly, keeping his silence.

"What is your name?" Elisa prompted.

"He won't tell you that," Isabella told her softly. "Names are not easily revealed by the *gitanos*."

Roger snorted. "How rude. I never could abide gypsies."

Tobyn turned a baleful glare onto the English vampire and emphatically spat into his face. Roger reacted violently, wiping at his cheek in disgust. The Rom chuckled without a sound, keeping his pleasure at his good aim strictly to himself.

Elisa smiled at him, her wicked teeth gleaming. "I could loosen his tongue."

This time, he could not contain himself. He grinned at the English vampire. "She's more of a man than you are." Huntingdon's jaw set dangerously, his teeth flashing for just an instant. Aware that he had hit a sore spot, the gypsy needled, "I just don't understand why *you're* not the one wearing the skirt."

The vampire flung himself at the impudent Rom. Tobyn fell back onto the bed as Dumas bodily caught Roger and pulled him away. The Englishman's fingers came just close enough to leave livid scratches on Tobyn's cheek. Elisa stepped closer, drawn by the blood that welled up on his skin. Isabella gently but firmly interposed herself between the vampire woman and her intended victim.

Roger fought against Dumas, his eyes still fixed with murderous rage at the gypsy who was creeping to the other side of the bed and the most distant point in the room. Dumas shook his English guest. "Enough of this! I warned you both to contain your tempers and your appetites.

This mortal is *mine*. I shared him with you only in friendship. Do not abuse that sentiment now!"

Huntingdon glared from Dumas to Tobyn, his anger carrying an all-but-physical weight. "Yours, eh?" He stepped back and made a show of brushing off his coat. "Well, you're welcome to him. I hope you kill the little bastard."

Dumas stiffened. "Roger, I must insist that you and Fraulein Dieter leave my home immediately." He escorted them both to the door with understated malice, giving them no chance to step nearer to the shaken gypsy. "I warn you now that if either of you touch one hair on this mortal's head, then you shall answer to me."

Elisa turned a disdainful sneer onto Tobyn, who tried to present a brave face. "Frankly, *monsieur le vicomte*," she minced, "I can't see why you'd want him. His taste is not that fine."

Without another word, she followed Roger out into the corridor. After a brief silence, Isabella left as well. Dumas took a deep breath and swept a hand over his face in the first gesture of agitation Tobyn had seen him display.

"I apologize, little love," the *vicomte* said softly, turning to cast a wan and unconvincing smile in the Rom's direction. "They will not be allowed to harass you so when you are mine, I promise you that."

Tobyn shook his head slightly. "I don't want your promises."

Dumas smiled again, more brightly than before. Something had amused him. "Perhaps you are more prudent than I," he said. "I've always rather liked promises."

"Promises are lies with friends' faces."

The Frenchman raised one brow. "Indeed. You sound wise beyond your years, my love. You will be a fine companion." He went to the double doors and bowed to Tobyn in what may have been honest respect. As he backed out of the room, locking up in his wake, he said, "I will return shortly."

"I'll try not to get too excited." The doors closed on Dumas' smile, and the gypsy groaned before telling himself, "Oh, Tobyn, what are you going to do now?"

Outside the door where his captive could not see him, Dumas silently mouthed the name his preternatural hearing had detected. He liked the feel of it. *Tobyn.*

Knowing that Dumas intended to come back soon did little to calm Tobyn's jangled nerves. He paced through the room, ignoring the pain from the fresh wounds to his face, trying to find something, anything, to use in self-defense. He didn't know what Dumas wanted; he only knew that he fully intended to disappoint him.

As before, no weapons presented themselves to him, and the furniture resisted his efforts to splinter it into something he could use. Exhausted from his panicked search, he returned to his seat on the divan where he'd spent so many long, dull hours the day before.

Why did he protect me? He thought hard on the matter. *Maybe he wants to do the honors himself. But, no, that doesn't make sense. Why be so nice? Why all the tenderness, the little names, if he only wants to kill me?* He fell still, amazed. *Can he really mean it when he says he doesn't want to hurt me?*

He shook his head. There had to be another reason. *Maybe he kept Roger from hurting me because he's got something else in mind, some sort of grand scheme...Jesus!* He shuddered at the thought. *It has to have something to do with the 'ownership' nonsense that he keeps spouting. Nobody, not even the* kris, *owns me! A gypsy belongs only to himself.* He imagined himself playing a part in a Dumas-written drama, and his skin crawled. He didn't want to know what the Frenchman's schemes would entail.

Yes, well, my boy, he thought ruefully, *I think you're going to find out.*

Isabella hesitated at the door of the *chateau*, her lace wrap gathered about her shoulders as if it could offer protection against the cold of the approaching winter. Roger and Elisa had already rumbled away in their shared coach, leaving Dumas' anger in their wake. Now the French vampire was playing the role of gracious host again.

"Really, *mon amie*, you needn't go simply because they have left. I have no quarrel with you."

She smiled up into the handsome face. "I must return to Spain eventually, Michel. You know I do not care to spend too much time away."

He gallantly kissed her hand. "A pleasant journey, then. You are always welcome here."

"Thank you, Michel. I'll remember that. With your permission, I will call again at the next new moon."

Dumas smiled. "The two weeks of your absence will be dark, indeed."

Isabella laughed musically, the sound round-toned like a clarinet. "Sweet talker. But you will have your gypsy to keep you company." Seeing the strange cast that appeared over the French vampire's face, she cocked her head and asked, "Do you love him, or do you love a memory?"

He sighed. "I don't know yet. I love him, I suppose, as much as one of us could love any human." He shook his head. "There is a quality about him, something mysterious, that I find irresistible. Something that goes beyond a physical resemblance to..." He choked on the name. "To someone else."

Isabella kissed him on the cheek. "He is *gitano*," she told him. "Powerful, too. It is common in Spain for our people to be enamored of the gypsies. But I must warn you, if you plan to make him yours: they make poor vampires. And he will never be Alexei."

Dumas flinched from the sound, then smiled superficially. "I shall consider myself warned. I have no intention of making him mine until the time is ripe."

She smiled. "Don't wait too long, *cariño*. He is too beautiful to lose."

"Don't worry for me, Isabella," Dumas said, walking his friend to her waiting equipage.

"I don't," she assured him, taking her skirt in hand in preparation for the climb into the carriage. "I worry for him."

~⟡⟡⟡~

Hours passed, and still Dumas did not return; Tobyn let himself drift off into sleep, a confused vision of vampires and his twin's distress. In his dreams, he could see Araminah, touch her, stroke the soft skin of her shoulders, kiss her, let his fingers dance in her long black curls...

A hand resting lightly on his shoulder intruded into his fantasy, half-waking him to the sensation of another body on the bed with him, curled around his back. A strong arm snaked around his waist and pulled him closer as soft lips gently nuzzled his ear. Tobyn moaned softly in his half-sleep, shifting slightly to allow those lips to continue on their entrancing way down his neck.

He realized his mistake too late. Dumas' teeth found his vein, tapping deeply into his bloodstream and draining the precious elixir away. The pain of the vampire's penetration was brief; as with Doña Isabella, pleasure like none other flooded his senses. Breathlessly, Tobyn surrendered to the feeling, his delicate hand coming up to cup Dumas' head and hold him to his throat. He knew that he should be fighting to get away, but he'd never been good at resisting temptation, and this was the sweetest seduction he'd ever known...shuddering beneath Dumas' attentions, Tobyn fell away into a delightful darkness.

Dumas sensed his mortal lover's slip into unconsciousness and he broke away with reluctance. Leaving the wound with one last wet pass of his tongue, he rolled the young gypsy onto his back, arranging the slender limbs. He studied the youth's face, stroking his brutalized cheek, gently kissing his forehead. Even in repose, Tobyn was a treasure, an artist's masterpiece, as finely turned as any Michelangelo sculpture. He traced the exotic lines of Tobyn's jaw and cheekbones, remarked upon the perfect shape and proportion of the gently parted lips. His body was lean and muscular, but almost child-like in proportion. For all that his personal charisma made him seem larger than life, in reality, he was quite a small man. Never had any mortal inspired such devotion in the Frenchman's heart.

I should make you now, Dumas thought, *but your blood is too sweet to waste too soon. I will keep you here, my Tobyn, and I will have the taste of you. After all, mortal or not, it's all the same. I will never let you go.*

He pressed another kiss to the gypsy's mouth before whispering aloud, "You belong to me, Tobyn *Bohemièn*. Only to me."

Two

Araminah cried out in her sleep, trapped in a dream-like limbo from which she could not escape. Her grandmother grasped her shoulders and tried to shake her into consciousness, but to no avail. As far as Araminah was concerned, the only reality in her world was her link with her brother.

Somewhere, Tobyn was being preyed upon. She could feel it as surely as if she were the one whose blood was being drained away. Waves of pain and distress disguised as pleasure, a pretty trap, broke upon her mind, rip tide on the connection with her twin. She tried to call out to him, to warn him, urge him to be careful, but something powerful blocked the way. She all but screamed in frustration, and Beti took extreme action to silence her with a slap.

Ara blinked, dazed, and sat up in her bed to face her grandmother's stern eyes. "Hush!" the old woman commanded. "Do you want the whole *kumpania* to hear?"

The younger woman shook her head and hugged herself in protective desperation. "The *mullo*...he was..."

Beti stroked her granddaughter's back soothingly, trying to keep her own grief and worry from showing on her face. "Hush, child. There is nothing we can do to help your brother now."

"I don't want to lose him, Grandmama," Ara sobbed into the older woman's comforting arms. "I can't lose him, not this way."

The aged gypsy pulled the girl into a tight embrace, wishing that she could say something comforting that didn't feel like a lie.

❦

Morning broke to a forest clearing full of fog and heavy dew. Araminah took her place with the other women, building campfires and beginning the job of cooking the morning meal. The moisture on the ground was cold against her ankles, soaking the hem of her brightly-colored skirt and weighting the fabric. She wished she could wear boots and trousers without causing a scandal; the men looked so much more comfortable than the *kumpania*'s female population.

The fire was difficult to light and smoky from the dampness of the wood. The food was spare, and she was expected to make it stretch enough to feed four cousins, an uncle, her grandmother, and herself. Tobyn usually took care of keeping them supplied, but he was gone, and nobody knew where he was.

Thoughts of her twin threatened Ara's public face, and she poked at the fire to cover her inner battle for control. The lifeline that led to Tobyn was quiet this morning; he was weak, probably sleeping, and very far away from her now. She realized with a start that she was weeping and hurriedly wiped away the evidence with a quick and angry hand. She tossed her hair back and shifted mental gears, eavesdropping on the three members of the *kris* who sat around a fire at the next *vardo*.

David Dera belched and scratched his chest. "We're the only ones of the council left. It's been a horrible trip. Those damn Reyes..." Manuo Moreno hissed at him, pointing at Ara. Dera's voice dropped in pitch, but she could still hear him. "First those damned Reyes men got nabbed for theft in Spain, then all those others got caught and hanged outside Paris. We have lost more than half our number." He spat at the fire, narrowly missing his wife, who did not look up. "Now that *chovihano* has been taken, and God only knows who's next. We have to move on."

The third man, Pedro Almovar, chuckled. "I don't know why losing Tobyn is a bad thing. He's always given me the creeps."

"Men aren't supposed to have *chovihani* powers," Dera agreed. "It's unnatural."

"Everything about those two is unnatural," Almovar opined. He cast a quick look at Ara, who pretended she didn't hear. "Their mother was a *gadja*, you know. Anytime you mix the blood..." He shook his head. "Very bad."

Manuo stretched, then accepted a cup of birch bark tea from Dera's wife. "Well, I'll agree, losing the boy was not something I'll lose sleep over. He was a pain in all of our sides. But his sister...now, there's a charm."

Dera snorted. "Headstrong, proud, temperamental..."

"Powerful, respected," Moreno finished for him. "Think of it: she's *chovihani*, from a long line of *chovihani*. She's a seer, a healer, and beautiful to boot. And think of the money she brings in! When she dances, the *gadje* throw in twice as much as normal. Once she's married, her husband can sell her to them for gold. And they'll pay!"

Ara could feel her face burning with an angry flush. *God damn him!*

"Ah, she'll never get a husband. She's too old to be unmarried now, and that brother of hers keeps throwing away every offer."

"True," Moreno said, nodding. "But her brother isn't here."

Dera cleared his throat. "Which brings us back to the point. It's too dangerous here. God only knows what Tobyn did this time. The whole country is going to be after us. We have to move on."

Almovar hesitated, then allowed, "We should discuss this with Tito. He's a member of the *kris,* too."

"Bah," Moreno grumbled. "He's too stupid to know anything, and if he did know anything, he wouldn't care. There are only four of us left. Three of us are ready to move on. That means that we move on."

Ara slammed the cook pot onto its hook above the fire, the clang catching their attention. She rose, unable to hold her peace any longer. "How can you just desert him?" she demanded.

"Desert who?" Moreno asked, amused. "Your brother?"

"Yes, my brother," she snapped. "You said yourself that he's *chovihano*. That's rare! You can't just throw that away. A *chovihano* is so much more powerful than a *chovihani*...everybody knows that. He's a treasure. Any *kumpania* with a *chovihano* has prestige. You should be looking for him, but no, here you are, ready to throw him away!"

Dera ran a hand over his hair. "Tito needs to beat you more often. You have a big mouth."

"If Tito beat me, I'd kill him in his sleep, and he knows that." She strode toward them. "We are not moving on until my brother joins us!"

Almovar rose, his eyes stormy. "No woman gives me orders!"

"No? Well, this woman just did."

He slapped her, hard, knocking her to the ground. He kicked her in the side before she could rise, knocking her breathless. His fist rose again, but this time Moreno grabbed his wrist.

"Wait. She's just concerned for her brother. That's not a crime."

"Talking that way to a man, especially one she's not related to or married to, *is* a crime!"

"For a normal woman, yes." He leaned closer to his friend's ear. "*Chovihani...*"

Ara rolled to her knees, coughing, ready for another blow; Almovar, however, relaxed, listening to the sense in Moreno's words. No man really understood the power of the *chovihane*, and he didn't want to be the first to find out what mischievous magic she could wield. He stepped back, letting Moreno go to Ara's side.

The old man helped her to her feet, his hands deceptively gentle on her waist. She was still reeling, blood trickling from her nose; he wiped the scarlet trail away and smiled sweetly. She could tell from looking at him that he was up to something.

"We need to move on, Araminah, for the safety of the *kumpania*. Your grandmother is an old woman. She can't run from the *gadje* the way she used to. You wouldn't want her to get hurt, would you?" He patted her on the unbruised cheek. "For her protection, we have to move on. But we can leave our usual trail so Tobyn can find us if he looks."

It was the best that she could hope for, and she knew it. Silently, she nodded her consent, as if her agreement were an issue. Moreno looked pleased.

"I knew you would understand. You're clever, for a woman."

She pulled away from his hands, straightening and standing upright, albeit unsteadily. "I'm all right now. You don't have to hold me up."

He smirked. "You're welcome." He turned and cast a bright smile to Tito, approaching from the river with a net full of fish. "Ah! Tito...let's talk."

As the men walked away, Beti emerged from the vardo, a cool, wet rag in her hand. She gently tended to her granddaughter's wounds, watching as the inevitable took place.

"Grandmama," Ara said, her voice a quiet whisper, "what are they talking about?"

"Marriage," she answered simply, as if that said it all. She took a deep breath. "You know that you are too old to be without a husband. Twenty-one and still no children...you will wither and dry up. You need..." She sighed. "*Chavi*, your uncle Tito has no daughters to collect dowry for. Your father is in jail, and your brother is never coming home. The dowry that Tobyn commands is too high for anyone to pay, and he is keeping you from a normal life."

She sniffed. "I don't want a normal life." She wiped at her eyes as more tears threatened to fall. "I want Tobyn."

Beti ignored her. "It is for your own good to be married. A husband can take care of you, give you children, give you a home. Give you a purpose. A woman without a son is just...wasted. Nobody. You need to be married. You need to stop living with Tobyn the way you have, and now that he is gone, you can have a future. A *proper* future."

"Oh, Grandmama! This is terrible," she sobbed, distantly reflecting that she'd done more crying in the last three days than in the last three years. "I don't want to marry anyone. All I want is Tobyn, and Europe to travel through, and peace and freedom and privacy. Is that so wrong? Can't I wish?"

"Women's wishes aren't made to come true." Beti held her close. "It will be all right, *chavi*. You'll see."

She pulled away, too distraught to be held. "Who is it?"

"Manuo Moreno is talking to Tito today, asking for your hand for his son, Nikolas."

Nikolas Moreno had leered and played at her for years; she could envision his lecherous grin, his dirty hands...the thought of that oafish man touching her made her shudder in revulsion.

"Beti, no!"

"He is the only one who still wants you." She shook her head. "You have chased all the others away, you with your mouth and your temper, and your brother with his demands. This is your last chance."

Ara shook her head. "No. Please, anybody but a Moreno. They..."

Beti's expression turned firm, and she rose. "Think about it, Araminah. You are not a stupid woman. Think about it, and you will see that we are right."

She turned and scowled into the fire, stabbing it with her stick, hating the old men in the *kris* and all of their rules and prejudices. Not for the first time, she wished she had been born a *gadja* like her mother.

To make matters worse, when she looked up, Nikolas himself was bearing down on her, his round and greasy face split by a snaggle-toothed grin. He sat beside her, poking her in the ribs like a playful boy. Ara slapped his hands away.

"Good morning, Araminah," he greeted jauntily, not in the least put off by her nasty mood. "I heard you last night. Did you have a bad dream?"

Unfortunately, it had been entirely too real, but she wasn't about to tell him that. "Yes," she grumbled.

"Was it about your father? Are you afraid for him?"

Ara pinned him with a harsh look. Everyone in the *kumpania* knew that there was no love lost between Chavo Reyes and his only daughter...everyone, it seemed, but Nikolas Moreno.

"Don't be so stupid."

She walked away, intending to leave him behind while covering her rudeness in getting food for the pot. He scrambled after her, not willing to be shaken so easily.

"Was it about Tobyn?"

Araminah slammed her hand against the side of her family wagon and turned an angry face onto the unflinching man at her side. "What difference does it make, Nikolas? It's none of your business."

He shrugged, then trailed along behind her as she stomped back to the fire. "I was just thinking that you'd probably sleep easier if you had a husband there to protect you."

She snorted derisively. "Yes, I've heard that you're volunteering for the position. Just, honestly, don't talk to Tito. He doesn't know his head from a hole in the ground. Wait for Tobyn to come back, then talk to him."

Nikolas shook his head. "But Tobyn might never come back. The French jails are hard to get out of. He's as good as dead, especially if they caught him stealing a horse. They're going to hang him!"

Anger flashed on her face, giving her beauty a dangerous air. She pounded on his chest, hard, with both fists; he staggered backward and tripped over a rock, landing splayed on his back before her on the ground. "Don't say that!" she ordered, enraged. "Are you trying to wish it to happen? Don't bring bad luck!"

Tito and Manuo reappeared from their discussion, and her uncle called out, "Here, now, what's going on?"

"Nothing, Tito," she told him through clenched teeth. "Nothing is happening here, and nothing ever will."

She stormed off, not certain where she was going except away from them. Behind her, Tito gave Nikolas a hand up, chuckling at the smitten gleam in the younger man's eyes.

"She's a wildcat," Reyes commented with barely-hidden disapproval. "Too much damned trouble for any man. Are you sure you want her?"

"Of course," Nikolas answered, shaking his head. "She's wonderful."

"She'll never make a wife, not unless you slap her down a good bit." Tito clucked his tongue. "Chavo ignored the girl, and Tobyn just coddled her. They spoiled her."

"I don't think so," Moreno said, staring at Ara's retreating back. "They only made her a challenge."

She went into the woods just far enough to lose sight of the caravan. She hated it today; the whole *kumpania* could go to hell, taking every person with it, and she wouldn't care. How dare they talk about her like some brood mare when her brother was in serious trouble somewhere and in need of their help?

And how dare Tobyn enjoy the *mullo* so much?

He groaned as sunlight awakened him with cruel brightness. He rolled over to bury his face in the crook of his elbow, avoiding the light as much as possible. His brain seemed wrapped in a warm, constrictive fuzziness that disoriented and confused him. His fingers were cold, and his toes; taking advantage of the rich bedding, he rolled himself up in the thick comforter and tried to make his head clear.

The door to the room clicked and rattled as someone unlocked it from the outside. Tobyn barely had the energy to work up a decent level of curiosity about his visitor. A pale blonde in a pin-neat maid's uniform, wearing an expression that somehow combined mystification and terror, entered the room, carrying a tray heaped with food and water. She quietly placed her burden on the divan, carefully keeping her eyes turned away from the bed, then moved back toward the door.

"Don't go," Tobyn said, his voice little more than a croaking whisper. "Please."

The maid whirled at the sound, startled out of a year's growth. She stared at him, wide-eyed and gasping. The fear she wore as she faced him upset and disturbed the young man.

"I'm sorry," she blurted. "I didn't mean to..."

"You didn't do anything wrong," he told her as gently as he could, struggling to sit up, ignoring the way his head swam. Even breathing was an effort. "Please...stay and talk to me."

She shook her head sharply. "No, I can't! The *vicomte*..."

"Is probably asleep," Tobyn finished for her. "He doesn't need to know."

"He will," the maid insisted. "Oh, but he will!"

The Rom sighed. Of all the companions he could have asked for, a panic-stricken, addle-pated serving girl was not high on his list. "At least bring that tray over here. I don't think I could reach it if I tried."

After a hesitation, the girl obeyed, bringing the food to the bedside table. She scrupulously kept her eyes turned away from him, behaving so skittishly that Tobyn began to wonder if his clothing wasn't simply a hallucination on his part. *What is she so afraid of seeing?*

"Thank you," he said, and she hurriedly stepped away from the bed as if he would have grabbed her if she hadn't. He groaned inwardly, wishing the maid would relax. He needed either an ally or a friend; neither position was likely to be filled by this fearful child. "Why won't you look at me?"

She forced herself to glance at him, almost in a gesture of appeasement. Her eyes touched him for no longer than a heartbeat before she looked away again. Tobyn would have physically coerced her into actually treating him like a human being if he'd had the strength.

"Will that be all, sir?"

The appellation felt strange; no one had ever applied an honorific to him before. "You could leave the door unlocked, or give me the keys."

"I can't do that, sir." She shook her head. "Don't ask me to do that."

He sighed. "Then, yes, that's all. You can go back to hiding, or whatever it is that you do all day."

Her cheeks reddened, much to Tobyn's amazement. *Can it be that she actually feels something other than fear?* He doubted if he'd ever know for certain. The maid dropped a quick, shallow curtsy to him before she all but bolted from the room, locking the door behind her.

He was absolutely ravenous, and made short work of the provisions on the tray. The water went fastest, sacrificed to his demanding thirst. While he was left unsatisfied, the edge was mercifully dulled. The food and drink did much to make his head stop spinning, and he felt reasonably able to break free of the cotton wrapped around his mind.

Memories of last night's weakness touched him and self-directed rage reared up within him. He had given Dumas exactly what he'd wanted, shamelessly, as wantonly as a cheap Paris whore. He recalled the sensation of the vampire's touch, the mad pleasure of his feeding, and the despicable ease with which Tobyn had so readily submitted to Dumas' desires. How could he call himself a man, a Rom, with such a terrible habit of surrendering to vampires?

His hand covered the rapidly-healing wound on his neck, and he shuddered. *What else could I have done? No matter how much I fought him, he still would've gotten what he wanted.* No mortal could resist the powers that a vampire wielded, and the way the debasement came hand in hand with pleasure was part of the trap. Vampires were equipped to make mortals falter in the face of temptation, equipped to capitalize on human weaknesses; that was what made them so very dangerous. *He could kill me, and I wouldn't mind at all...*

Questions began to spin inside his brain, the whys and wherefores of his situation that he refused to actively contemplate. Thinking about things only made them worse, and for as long as he could deny the walls of his prison, he was free. It was staring at those walls that made them real, and thinking over his dilemma only made him see the trap that he was in.

Burrowing into the bedding in search of a little warmth, Tobyn closed his eyes and concentrated on seeing only wide, open spaces.

~≈≈≈~

Dusk made the campfire look unreal. Dozens of tiny sparks flew up in a glittering cloud as Araminah tossed a handful of kindling into its roaring heat. On the other side of the field the *kumpania* had claimed for the night, a lone man played his guitar, his voice grating out its song. The music and the coming darkness weighed heavily on her heart; crossing her arms to rub her shoulders, she sat back with a sigh.

The anger she had harbored for Tobyn's perceived betrayal in the vampire's arms had flown, leaving only bottomless frustration in its wake. She didn't know where her brother was, or how to help him. Completely unwilling to give him up for lost, she nevertheless had to admit that the chances of his safe return to the *kumpania* were very small, indeed.

Behind her, within the Reyes wagon, Tito and Manuo Moreno were haggling over her dowry, bickering like breeders at a horse show. Nikolas, whom she presumed was soon to be her husband, watched her from his own fire with barely-concealed proprietary delight. She wished that she could work up enough energy for at least a show of disdain, if not open rebellion against the way her uncle so cheerfully sold her life away to a man she could barely stand, but she was just too tired. Nighttime dragged at her, Tobyn was gone, and she could spare no strength to care about anything else.

The guitarist changed his song from a lament to a dancing tune, and somehow that only depressed her more. How could he celebrate, even if only with a song? It seemed so wrong. Gathering up another handful of wood chips, she threw more fuel to the fire and stared morosely as it burned.

Shuffling footsteps, light and hesitant, approached from behind, and Ara acknowledged her grandmother's presence silently. Beti eased down next to the young woman, her gnarled old hand seeking Ara's soft one in a reassuring squeeze. Without speaking, she joined her son's child in watching the flames glow against the encroaching darkness. It was telling, to the old woman, the way Araminah clung to her hand like a frightened girl. Beti smiled sadly; that was exactly what her granddaughter was.

"What are they deciding?" Ara finally whispered.

"I'm just an old woman. I'm not invited to their dealings."

"That's a nice story, Grandmama, but I know you were listening at the door."

Beti patted the girl's slender knee. "It's not so bad, being married..."

Ara closed her eyes against her sudden tears, clenching her teeth on the injustice. "When will it happen?"

"Manuo wants to see it done by a priest in Spain, a Romany priest he used to know. It will be a long time yet."

"Romany priest? Who..."

"One who stopped moving and turned *gadjo*," Beti explained, her voice carrying a dismissive tone. "No real Rom, that's certain."

"And how much do I cost?"

The bitterness in Ara's voice made Beti hesitate. "Two horses, a blanket and a pair of goats." The young woman let out a short, sharp cry that could have been a laugh. "Hush, *chavi*. There's no fighting now. The deal's been struck. Now you must learn to live with Nikolas as your husband."

Araminah pulled away, drawing her shawl more tightly around her shoulders. "But Tobyn..."

"He is a memory now." The old woman shook her head. "He's not coming back, Ara. Not ever. And even if he did try, he's so unclean now...you can't want for him anymore. Leave him to the past, don't even speak his name." Beti rose slowly, not looking into the girl's grief-stricken eyes. "You have a future to think about, now."

The wagon door opened with a clatter, and Tito and Manuo emerged like victorious hunters returning from the forest. Making her face blank, holding herself still, Araminah turned to receive the news.

"Tobyn."

The softly-spoken word penetrated into his dreams, nudging him toward despised wakefulness. Groaning, he snuggled deeper into the comforter and clenched his eyes, wishing that the voice would just go away and let him sleep.

"Tobyn," Dumas repeated, his tone colored with amusement. He reached out and brushed a stray curl from the gypsy's forehead, and the glancing touch of his icy finger sent shivers through the mortal's body.

Reluctantly, Reyes opened his eyes and looked, wary but cautious, at the Frenchman perching beside him on the bed. Dumas smiled with surprising tenderness and sat back, lounging decadently across Tobyn's legs.

"How do you know my name?" the mortal asked softly, his voice little more than a whisper.

"I have ways of learning all of your secrets, my friend."

Somehow, that smug statement was more unsettling than an admission of mind-reading could have been. Uncertain how to react, Tobyn drew his knees up under his chin, freeing them at least from the vampire's weight.

"I don't want to wrest your secrets from you, though," Dumas continued conversationally. "It's far more interesting to see them slowly emerge, rather like watching flowers bloom."

"How very romantic for a man who serves dinner while it's still alive."

The biting tone of Tobyn's words was far more acidic than he had intended, but he no longer cared about mitigating his reactions. Dumas drew a deep, sad sigh. "Ah, Tobyn. Someday you will understand me."

"You keep talking about the future," Reyes said evenly, sounding amazingly calm for all that Dumas' proximity made him want to vomit. "How long do you plan to keep me here?"

The Frenchman blinked, as if he were surprised by the question. "Forever, of course."

"You can't."

"Why not?"

The answer was the most truthful thing Tobyn had ever said. "Because I'll go mad."

The unquestioning confidence behind his words gave them weight in Dumas' view. "It's that simple, is it? And why is that?"

The mortal took a deep breath, then replied, "I'm a gypsy. I'm not like ordinary people. I need to be free to roam around with my *kumpania*. If I can't, it's only a matter of time before I go insane. And after that, I die. It's that easy."

Dumas tried to scoff, but Tobyn so clearly believed what he was saying that his story could not be completely dismissed. "Nonsense," he said finally, his voice redolent with a lack of conviction. "You're only human."

"No. The Rom are something more than human." He swallowed hard, forcing himself to present the kind of unpleasant proof that Dumas would understand. "Why do you think gypsy blood...tastes...better than regular human blood?"

The Frenchman pondered that for a moment. "I suppose there is some basis to what you say. But I assure you, my Tobyn, that I will never allow you to go mad and waste away."

Tobyn froze as Dumas gently touched his cheek, gliding his hand back to cup his dark head. The Frenchman leaned forward to steal a kiss that Tobyn refused to give up. Sighing again, the vampire pulled back.

"What will you do?" Reyes asked quietly, dreading the answer.

The cold fingers trailed down to caress his throat, pressing in to feel the pulse beneath the skin. "Make you one of us, of course."

Held in place by Dumas' hand and the knowledge that struggle was useless, Tobyn remained motionless as the vampire pressed close to him again. The Frenchman replaced his fingertips with his lips, gently kissing the gypsy's neck. The sensation was pure pleasure, it was true, but experience was beginning to let him see past the glamour of the trap to the voracious hunger that lay beneath it. Given the opportunity, Dumas would devour everything that was Tobyn, stripping him of identity until only a shell remained. The threat of losing himself entirely nearly sent him spinning into panic. He was caught in a foolproof snare.

"What if I refuse?" the gypsy asked. "What if I resist your making me one of you?"

The words came out in an impassioned sigh, followed by the now-familiar sensation of the vampire's teeth piercing his flesh. "You can't."

It lasted only a moment, barely long enough for the pain to metamorphose into pleasure, before Dumas withdrew. Tobyn blinked twice, regaining a sense of who and where he was. As the vampire began to speak, he realized that he was trembling, and he fought to still the shudders.

"Life with me won't be so awful, Tobyn. There's no need for you to be afraid or to even consider denying me, because every time I touch you, I'll make it feel so very good that nothing else matters. I'll take care of you, give you fine things, teach you everything I know."

Tobyn shook his head slowly. "You want to control me, don't you?"

"It is inevitable."

"Nothing is inevitable. Can't you see that I don't want to be here?"

Dumas smiled patronizingly. "Ah, but can you honestly say that, when I touch you, you don't want me?"

The gypsy's clear blue eyes locked onto the vampire's grey ones. "Yes," he lied.

"I don't believe you, my love."

"I don't give a damn what you believe. Truth is truth, and you'll know it when I'm a raving lunatic by the next snowfall."

"Stop saying these things!" the vampire ordered imperiously, a nervous edge in his voice. "They are lies designed to trick me into freeing you!"

"I'm not lying to you now."

The command carried a strong telepathic component. "Do not attempt to deceive me, Tobyn!"

"And don't you try to frighten me into obeying you!" Tobyn returned in kind, his considerable anger concealing his equally considerable fear.

Dumas sat back, eyes widened in surprise. He stared at his mortal companion for a long, silent moment, then whispered, "Very interesting. What other tricks do you have in your repertoire?"

"I wish to God there was something that could destroy you!"

The vampire laughed and rose fluidly from the bed. "Oh, you are a jewel. Threats, little one?"

The look in the gypsy's eyes gave the vampire a nasty shock of genuine uneasiness. In an icy growl, Tobyn replied, "Not threats, *monsieur*. Promises."

"I thought you disliked promises."

"I'm changing my mind."

Dumas laughed off his temporary fear. "You are in a bad humor tonight. I understand. Perhaps tomorrow you will be better company." He went to the double doors and opened them, then turned to face his prisoner with a mocking bow. "*Bon soir.*"

Reyes' temper flared beyond his control as the doors were slowly closed and bolted. All but screaming in his tormentor's wake, he shouted, "With luck, I'll be dead tomorrow night!" In his rage, he hurled the music box at the closed doors, deriving at least a small measure of satisfaction from watching it shatter into dozens of silent pieces.

I'm going to find a way out of this room, even if I have to die to do it. At the moment, he had to admit, death really didn't look so bad compared to living in Dumas' shadow.

The sunlight smiled with unseasonable warmth as the *kumpania* retook the road, traveling north through heavy French woods. Araminah sat stoically on the bench between Tito, who guided the team pulling the Reyes wagon, and Nikolas, who slavishly held her hand like a treasure and prattled in her ear.

"It won't be so bad, once you have a little time with me," he told her, wanting desperately to see her smile. "Our horses are very healthy, and this year's foals are strong. By the time we marry, I'll be one of the richest men in the *kumpania*."

"You already are," she reminded him flatly, intending no compliment.

Unfortunately, Nikolas took it as a sign of warming. Excitedly, he barreled on. "Exactly! Think how happy I can make you, Ara. I can give you so much gold to wear, pretty things to make you even more beautiful. Does that sound good to you?"

Tito glanced at her harshly, issuing a silent order. Too tired to fight, the young woman sighed and muttered, "It sounds wonderful."

Nikolas bounced in his seat like an over-eager lapdog. "Oh, Ara, we'll be so happy!"

You will be, she thought.

Tito clucked to his horses, then said, "Come nightfall, we'll be with the Carago *kumpania*. Lots of music, dancing. You ought to make your announcement then, at the party. Maybe even get married."

Moreno squeezed his fiancee's lax hand. "I'll make the announcement, but the wedding has to wait until we reach Seville in the summer. My father has rules about church weddings."

Tito shrugged. "Why not just get married twice, once tonight and again in Seville?"

The oafish young man hesitated, clearly taken with the suggestion. Sensing an approaching tragedy, Ara quickly said, "If Manuo wants us to wait until we reach Seville, then we should wait. There's no sense in rushing things, and Manuo is a bad person to offend."

Her uncle opened his mouth to speak harshly to her, but he was cut off when Nikolas chuckled. "My Ara is too clever for you, Tito. She's right. My father would never stand for something like that. With her intelligence and mine, our children will be geniuses!"

It took a conscious effort of will to keep her from laughing in his face.

When Tobyn awoke to daylight, he was surprised by a bud vase bearing a single red rose, sitting in place of the music box he had demolished the night before. A note rested against the vase, but that did him no good for so long as he could not read. Setting his jaw pugnaciously, he shredded the note in steady, systematic motions, leaving the pieces in a heap in the shadow of the flower. *So much for stupid letters.*

He slid from the bed and walked to the doors, trying ineffectually to open them once again. The carpeting around the doorway, which last night had been strewn with shattered porcelain and glass, was fastidiously clean; not even the tiniest shards of ceramic remained to hint at its former existence. Kicking the books roughly to the floor, Tobyn sprawled on the divan to contemplate the ramifications of the disappeared fragments and the newly-arrived rose.

The answer his brain gave him was unpleasant: Dumas had returned to this room after Tobyn had succumbed to his solitary escape, sleep. He had picked up the broken box and left the flower behind while the gypsy had been completely oblivious to his presence. *How long did he spend, watching me?* Tobyn wondered. *What else did he do while I was sleeping?* He did not recall any touches in the night, and surely he would have awakened to the Frenchman's bite. Had Dumas simply stared, watching him, smirking, perhaps, at the defenseless way he dreamed in the company of the enemy?

Anger and hatred welled up in his heart, and Tobyn vowed again to escape or to destroy the vampire who fed upon him and humiliated him at every turn. *What did he see? Did he enjoy the show?* His mind whirled obsessively around the image of the smug vicomte calmly observing him for hours, and his face flushed with shame. He had been caught with his guard down, the ultimate offense to Tobyn's sensibilities. He had failed his *kumpania*, and worse, he had failed himself.

Tobyn shook himself from his bitter contemplation. *He wants you to be this upset,* he told himself firmly. *He does nothing without an idea of how you'll react. And so far, you haven't disappointed him.*

His eyes trailed over to the rose, and he fell into a different sort of pondering. Dumas wanted him to be angry; it would never, ever do to give in so easily. *What can I do to go against what he expects? What can I say to turn the mind game back on him?* Memories of Dumas' kisses gave him a clue, and a plan began to form.

The best part was, the more he thought about it, the more he believed that his plan just might work.

Three

The long day passed uneventfully, the silent solitude of his prison broken only twice by the arrival of the maid, who brought him his customary tray. Tobyn let her go without trying to force companionship out of her, instead concentrating upon the plan that whirled in his mind. By the first ominous hint of dusk, he knew what he had to do.

He knew that Dumas would return that night, although he was uncertain exactly when to expect his visit. The nervousness of waiting kept Tobyn from feeling fatigue, even as the moon rose higher in the tiny patch of sky he could see between the bars over his windows. The gypsy crouched before the wide white marble hearth, staring into the tiny fire the maid had built. He was cold to his soul, chilled by this waiting, and he dearly wanted the warmth of the flame.

Two hours after sunset, his anticipation was rewarded by the turning of the lock bolt. He rose from his seat near the fireplace and faced the French vampire as he entered the room.

"I expected to find you asleep," Dumas greeted, his handsome face lightened by a smile that would have been endearing if Tobyn hadn't known better.

"I think I've slept too much."

The Frenchman raised an eyebrow and sat gracefully on the divan, ignoring the shambles Tobyn had made of the books. "Hidden meanings, my love?"

Reyes shook his head and debated moving closer to Dumas. His feet rooted to the floor at the thought, so he remained motionless. "No."

The hushed tone of his voice alerted Dumas to a change. Cocking his head, he asked, "Are you all right, Tobyn? You sound...different."

"I'm tired," he answered simply. "And being locked in here with nothing to do really is making me insane."

Dumas rose and walked to Tobyn's side. "And what would you like to do?"

The quality of the whisper made the gypsy shudder. "Anything to pass the time." The Frenchman's hands rested lightly on his shoulders, pulling him closer. With leaden steps, he obeyed, his reluctance impossible to hide.

"Read," Dumas suggested, gently tracing the outer shell of his mortal's ear with one cool fingertip.

"I can't."

"What *can* you do?"

Tobyn closed his eyes tightly as the vampire teased his throat with moist breath and a flickering tongue. He trembled but stood his ground, forcing himself to take Dumas' attentions when all he really wanted was to push him away in revulsion. He turned his head slowly, deliberately, allowing his captor to continue the path of his trailing lips to the pierced lobe of the previously-traced ear. The intimate sensation made him shudder violently, and he covered it with quavering speech.

"Guitar."

Dumas paused, pulled away enough to mumble, "Hmm?"

"I play...guitar..."

The Frenchman took Tobyn's face in his hands and gazed into blue eyes held intentionally wide with feigned innocence. There was gypsy glamour, as well, just as powerful and deceptive as that of vampires. Tobyn was betting his life on it.

"I'll get you one," Dumas promised, before bringing his mouth down on Tobyn's.

Reyes forced his lips to soften to the kiss, receiving the invasion of the vampire's tongue with a monumental effort of will. His stomach lurched against the caress and for a moment he feared that he would be sick; with a tiny sound of desperation that was nearly indistinguishable from passion, he pushed the other man's tongue out of his mouth, offering a deep kiss of his own. The vampire crushed him to his body, strong arms like iron bands clamped around him, trapping Tobyn in the embrace.

After what seemed an eternity, Dumas released him gently, surprising the mortal with his breathlessness. The Frenchman touched Reyes' lips with his fingertips, a look of passion and curiosity in his cool grey eyes.

"Yes, you are different tonight." Telepathically, he added, *//What has changed you?//*

Tobyn knew better than to try to lie during such psychic contact. Wavering slightly where he stood, he whispered a change of subject. "Did you leave the rose?"

The vampire smiled. "Yes. Did you like it?"

"It helps to have something real in the room with me, something from outside."

"It reminded me of you," Dumas breathed, slowly opening the fastens of Tobyn's shirt, testing the limits of his mortal's new-found passivity. They were not difficult to exceed. Unable to hold himself to the act any longer, the gypsy pulled away from the possessive hands, turning his back to Dumas to hide the disgust he could no longer keep from his face.

"In what way?"

"A thing of beauty, born wild on the earth and reared beneath the open sky, plucked in its prime and saved the indignity of fading into old age and gradual death." Dumas watched the careful, measured way his captive crossed the room to the arm chair. "It symbolizes you, I think."

Tobyn did not face him as he said softly, "But the rose will be rotting tomorrow. It died when it was taken from its bush." He closed his shirt once more, moving slowly so that his shaking fingers could do the work. "Do you want the same to happen to me?"

"It won't."

"You don't know that."

Dumas crossed the room in less than a heartbeat, moving without any visible motion at all. Suddenly, he simply appeared behind Tobyn, pressed to him with an arm looped possessively around the youth's trim waist. He breathed his promise, his cheek to his captive's.

"I will not let you die, my Tobyn."

Reyes' mind screamed against the ownership of the word and the vampire's arm, but he bit back on the storm that roiled within him. *Don't lose it now,* he coached himself. Tears of panic and desperation filled his vision, and he closed his eyes against them, fighting to slow his speeding breath.

"But I will," he choked out. "You're already killing me. I'm dying inside."

"You lose only what you don't need, my love. Let me replace it."

"With what?"

"With myself." He grazed Tobyn's skin with the shining tips of his feral teeth, squeezing him tighter when he shuddered in response. "I will recreate you in my own image and we will rule the world together as gods. Don't you want that?"

The word sounded like a sob. "No."

Apparently, Tobyn's reply was irrelevant to the vampire's plans. Gripping the gypsy like a snake, Dumas again raped the mortal's vein with a thrust of his fangs. Tobyn cried out in desolate defeat, tears spilling onto his cheeks. He had never felt so lost, so completely ensnared. For the first time, he believed that there may be no escape for him.

Dumas drained him, taking him until Tobyn's legs could no longer support his weight. As Reyes fell to his knees, the vampire stayed with him, following him to the floor. The Rom could feel more than blood being stolen away by the hungry kiss; pieces of his spirit, tiny parts of his mind and soul were being torn loose and consumed. Frantically working against the tides of shameful pleasure Dumas' feeding gave and the looming shadow of approaching unconsciousness, Tobyn held on to his soul with both hands, erecting as many psychic shields and protective barriers as he could. His body tremored with the loss of blood, his heart weakly pumping a depleted supply. The desperate spinning of his mind was slowing to a stop, and the encroaching darkness held serenity for him. Praying that somewhere there was a deity who would smile upon murdered gypsies,

Tobyn tried to take his soul and plunge into that sea of black. Dumas released him abruptly, horrified. The spell of darkness was broken, leaving the mortal blinking feebly into the Frenchman's concerned expression.

"No, Tobyn. Not that way. Promise me: not that way."

The blue eyes, glassy with fever and the brush with death, drifted shut. Dumas held him tightly for several moments, listening to the thready pulse and feeling the shallow breaths. So close, too close...he refused to lose his gypsy prize to either his own greed or Tobyn's desperation.

Gently gathering the fragile mortal into his arms, Dumas carried him to the bed and laid him upon the pillows, covering him with blankets and comforter before taking up a position of vigilance near the head of the bed, watching, listening. If Tobyn lived to morning, he would survive; the *vicomte* fully intended to make certain that he did.

Araminah twirled in the dance, taking the opportunity of the music to disconnect her brain from its melancholy preoccupation. Nikolas had publicly announced their impending marriage when they had met up with the Carago caravan, and then the party had begun. Ara had long ago learned that any excuse was good enough for a party where gypsies were concerned, and the noise and activity of it helped distract her from the disquieting silence on Tobyn's end of their twin-link.

Standing beside his distinguished father in the ring of men who watched the women dance, Nikolas smiled at Ara with a gleam in his eye. Manuo looked up at his future daughter-in-law, clearly pleased with his son's choice; Ara knew the elder Moreno well enough to know that he would never dream of refusing a chance to bed her, himself. Both father and son wanted her, and badly. *Fine, then...I'll make them feel every bit of it.*

Altering her dancing slowly, subtly, Araminah began to move for the benefit of the men who watched her. She could enslave the Morenos, make them want her until they ached with the force of it, and laughingly tell them no...she would give them the misery they deserved, the only misery that was hers to give them. After the wedding, of course, the game with Nikolas would lose its bite, but she could play with Manuo forever if she chose.

Pain struck her suddenly, blinding and white-hot, arcing to her from her distant brother. The protections he had erected to keep her from him through the link had been shattered, and she could feel the lifeline that connected them become possessed of a greedy hunger. Agonized, she could feel herself being shredded from the inside out, one piece of her soul at a time. She could do nothing to stop it or slow the decimation of her spirit before she crumpled to the dirt of the dance space, motionless and still as death.

When he finally opened his eyes, the room was dark and silent as a tomb. He had no idea how long he'd been unconscious, but the air was heavy, as if it had not been stirred by movement for a very long time. Tobyn lay still and pondered this, in no hurry to change the situation.

His eyes saw clearly in the moonlit chamber, showing him that things had changed in his prison. The arm chair had been pulled out of position and placed near his bed; the books had been cleared from the floor by the divan. A guitar stood against the wall near the window, a beautiful piece of work with a gleaming finish. A fresh rose blushed from the bud vase beside his pillow.

Tobyn considered his options. His plan had been so simple: be nice to Dumas, gull him into complacency, and run at the first open path. But now, he could see the danger. *The nicer I am to him, the more he takes. I won't live through this.* He sighed deeply and threw an arm over his eyes. The movement took more energy than he cared to admit. The loss of blood he had suffered so continually since his imprisonment dragged at him, and beneath the fatigue and weakness was a disturbing emptiness. *He's stealing my soul.*

He didn't know how to take his spirit back, and worse, he wasn't sure he cared. *If I fight, if I don't, it doesn't matter,* he thought pessimistically. *He'll just keep on taking no matter what I do. He'll take it nicely, or he'll just take it. He's in control.*

He heard his own thoughts, and he frowned. *No! Stop it. That's exactly what he wants you to think. If you give up, he wins. And he can't ever win.* He clenched his teeth. *I can act like nothing matters, but the minute I feel it, I'm dead. The only question now is: do I keep it up, or do I fight?*

He ran scenarios through in his mind, envisioning his own actions and Dumas' responses. Every time he saw himself resisting, fighting against the vampire, he saw his own demise. The plan, with its humiliating submissions and nauseating intimacies, would be his best bet to see another sunrise.

Tobyn took a deep breath, suddenly aching for sunrise in the mountains. It had been too long since he'd seen the sky change colors over the Pyrenees, and he would give anything for the feeling of a living tree beneath his hands. The real world, the living world, called to him, its vital energy something that he sorely missed. *That's what's so wrong with this place,* he realized. *Everything here is dead. Nothing is alive, except for me.* He could feel tears rise, and this time, with nobody to witness, he let them come. *God, I miss Ara! I miss Beti. I want to go home.* Loneliness choked him; even a visit from Dumas, dangerous though it was, would be preferable to this silent, solitary darkness.

He took a deep breath and tried to bring his emotions back under control. He had to protect what was left of him, to save his soul from his vampiric keeper before the plan could continue. Only through the plan could he gain his freedom. Concentrating the last of his strength, Tobyn built walls and figuratively tied his spirit into place. It could not be stolen now without all of his defenses falling away, and Beti had taught him how to build defenses that could never crumble. Thinking of his grandmother made him stronger, and he whispered the words of her protection spell as he wrapped his soul with glowing shields as hard as masonry.

"From now until the end of time, from day into night, they shall not become one of these."

There has to be a way out of this. I just haven't found it yet.

⦿⦿⦿

Nikolas was beside Ara as soon as she moved, clutching at her hand with a dedicated concern that impressed Beti. The love Moreno felt for her granddaughter was real; it was a pity that it had been wasted on a woman who would never return it.

The young woman moaned breathily as she drew closer to wakefulness. Nikolas stroked her hair, looking up at Beti with a question in his eyes.

"She will be fine," the old woman informed him. "The illness has passed."

Moreno's thick face split with a grin, and he leaned close to Araminah, whispering her name. After a moment, he was rewarded by the opening of her green eyes. She peered up at him, letting his reality chase the cobwebs away.

"Nikolas..."

He nodded joyfully, his ardent attention sending him back into the role of the fawning puppy. "How do you feel?"

"Weak," was her honest answer. "Grandmama...do you know what's happened?"

Beti rested her hand on Nikolas' shoulder. "Why don't you tell Manuo and Tito that she is awake and well? They'll probably want to know before Tito gives back the bride price."

The young man looked from one enigmatic woman to the other before nodding his obedience to the aged healer. "All right. I'll be back soon."

"Don't hurry," Ara muttered after him as he clattered from the Reyes wagon. Beti closed the door behind him as her granddaughter said, "Tell me, now. What's happening with Tobyn?"

Beti sat down heavily and considered the things the more esoteric of her senses were telling her. "I would say that the vampire is destroying him, slowly and from the heart first. He is lost to us now. I've tried to cut the thread connecting the two of you, and I think I finally managed it. Can you feel him?"

Ara searched for her brother and came up distressingly empty. "No," she admitted, blinking back frustrated tears. "Oh, Beti, I don't want to lose him!"

"It's too late, *chavi*. There is no choice, now. He is gone." Beti sat quietly for a moment, then said, "You've slept for a long time, Araminah. This is the third night after you fell."

"Third night?" she echoed in disbelief. "How could it have been so long?"

"I don't ask those questions. I only say what is." She took a deep breath. "The Carago *kumpania* is heading back to Spain. We will be in Seville for your wedding in a few weeks."

The young woman took a deep breath, unwilling to react to the dispassionate telling of the bad news. Her brother was lost, her formerly distant marriage was inestimably closer, and she felt that even Beti had ceased to be an ally. Somehow, drifting unconsciousness was vastly preferable to this kind of waking nightmare. She closed her eyes tightly.

"A few weeks," Ara whispered.

"It is time for you to grow up and leave your games behind," Beti told her flatly. "This is not an easy world for a woman to live in, but it is easier when you do what they ask. Even though men can control your body, your soul is always yours. Nothing can take it away from you."

Araminah's thoughts went to her brother, and she shuddered. "I don't know about that, Beti. Maybe something can."

⁓⊱⋅⊰⁓

Tobyn held the guitar in experienced hands, his head bowed close to the strings to listen as he tuned the instrument by ear. Although his sense of pitch was quite good, he had a devil of a time trying to get the tuning right without the aid of another guitar. He'd fought with the thing for what felt like hours, and the blend was finally coming together. He stroked a chord and listened to the resonance, turning the screw until the note fell into place. There; now he thought he had it right.

He straightened in his seat on the divan, staring between the bars on the windows at the moon beyond the glass. His fingers took up position on the frets and strings as his brain went wandering; with a slow crescendo, hands and mind began to dance to the song he played. The escape it gave was sweet, and he needed the memories that rose to meet the music. Dancing and playing and firelight in countless night camps shimmered in his head, and he could still hear the bright tinkling of the charms Ara had sewn into her skirt when she'd danced to his playing for Bavarian money. They had been so excited by the dancing, so happy with each other...like a hundred nights before, they'd taken their time getting back to the *kumpania*, each enjoying the company of their only friend. They had always been outsiders, the Reyes twins; the other Romanies kept a superstitious distance. They had never had any children to play with but one another, and when their bodies had matured, it had seemed only natural to continue the game in a new, more interesting direction. He could still remember the night they danced in Bavaria, the night they made love in the woods on the way back to the *vardo*...

He was lost in the hypnotic swirl of sound, and the quiet applause from the doorway startled him out of his dream-state. He blinked and turned to face Dumas, who leaned, smiling, against the closed doors.

"Very good, my love," the vampire complimented. "You are a talented musician. How long have you been playing?"

Tobyn put the guitar aside with a deep blush of something like pleasant embarrassment. He was dismayed by how pleased the compliment had made him feel. "Since I was very small. All of my people play or sing. It's nothing special."

"Everything about you is special."

Dumas strolled closer, then sat beside the gypsy on the divan. Tobyn held himself still with an effort, reminding himself of what his plan dictated. Over the protestations of his insides, he allowed the vampire to take his hand and hold it gently, like a lover. Casting his eyes away in a show of docility, mostly because he couldn't bear to look Dumas in the face, Reyes suffered the Frenchman to pet his face and stroke his hair.

"How do you feel, Tobyn?"

"Very tired," he answered honestly. "Being dinner is an exhausting thing."

The vampire smiled, and the Rom could sense him searching his soul. Striving to project nothing but apathy, he merely waited for Dumas to react. Finally, the vicomte said, "I will allow you time to recover, then, before I come to you again. For now, though, I want to know about you. Tell me about yourself, Tobyn."

Reyes balked momentarily, as he did whenever secrets were demanded of him, but he covered it with a bland, "What do you want to know?"

"Everything."

"Ask me some questions."

"Very well." Rocking back with an amused expression, Dumas thought a moment. "Easy ones, first. How long have you beautified this world?"

The courtly romance of the question made Tobyn smile before he could remind himself to do so. Was the plan affecting his reactions, or were his natural inclinations shaping the plan? *Don't think about it,* he told himself firmly.

"I'm twenty-one years old."

"Ah! Still a baby, then."

A laugh that was surprising to both men in its seductive tone rang out from the gypsy's throat. "I wouldn't say that."

The vicomte raised a slender brow. "Do you have a family?"

"You mean children? None that I know of. My sister, grandmother, and uncle are still traveling with the *kumpania*. My father and another uncle are...someplace else."

"Where?"

"In a jail in Seville."

Dumas chuckled. "Is your sister older or younger than you?"

"Neither." A creeping unease filled him; he did not want Ara exposed to the likes of Dumas. "She's my twin."

This time, the vampire laughed in delight. "How wonderful! I've never known a twin before." His eyes were warm with what might have been affection as he said, "You see? You are special. You've been so since birth. Tell me...is your sister as attractive as you?"

Before Tobyn could stop himself, he proudly answered, "She's the most beautiful woman in the world."

Again, the vampire favored him with that piercing look, and Reyes feared that he had somehow revealed too much. *How do vampires feel about incest?* Finally, Dumas nodded to himself and continued with his gentle interrogation.

"Are you married?"

"No, thank God."

The vampire grinned, his teeth clearly displayed. Tobyn did not flinch. "Are you Christian?"

"When I need to be."

Dumas found that answer amusing, as well. "Opportunistic, then, are you?"

"You can't tell me that *you*, of all people, object to that." Tobyn felt his apathetic façade slip, but he could not bring himself to care. Leveling a clear gaze onto his companion's face, brazenly meeting his eyes, he said calmly, "I'm a survivor, *monsieur*. I learned from an early age to do anything it took to see the next sunrise."

"Interesting choice of words, little one, considering your present company." Dumas leaned back from the mortal, his face unreadable, his eyes betraying something very like boredom. "I find sunrises to be...overrated."

"Perhaps it's been too long since you've seen one." Tobyn studied the other man's face. "How long has it been, Dumas?"

"Ah! You remember my name. I thought I would never hear you say it." He took Tobyn's hands in his own and held them tightly. "Your voice makes it beautiful."

"You're avoiding my question."

"You're right." He smiled. "That is because I ask the questions and you supply the answers. Shall we get back to it?"

Tobyn smirked. "One hundred years."

"What?"

He nearly laughed at the confusion on the vampire's face. "Are you one hundred years old?"

Dumas shook his head. "Older. Older by far, little love. But tell me—have you any lovers back in your caravan? Or have I happened upon the only virgin gypsy in France?"

This time, he did laugh. "A virgin? Hardly." He nodded sagely, an enigmatic smile on his face. *How easy would it be to shock you, and how wise would it be for me to do it?* There was only one way to find out, and as Tobyn saw it, he had very little left to lose. "There have been a few lovers."

The vampire regarded him closely. "Women? Or men?"

Reyes hesitated. Romany society greatly frowned upon homosexuality, and for that reason he should have been offended by the Frenchman's words. Still, the thought of breaking that taboo carried a heady excitement. *What difference should* kumpania *rules make to me? Haven't I already shown that I'll break them all?* Slowly, he responded, "Only women...so far."

The vampire raised an eyebrow but moved on to the next question in his bizarre interview. "And was your sister one of these women?"

"What difference does it make?"

"I am intrigued." Dumas smiled tightly, an odd mix of fascination and disgust on his aristocratic features. "From your reaction, I can see your answer. Tobyn, really. Your own twin? It's positively distasteful."

The gypsy shrugged. "Maybe to you. I enjoy it."

"So you are a sexual creature, then? You find pleasure in the act?"

"It's what it's for." Reyes put on a pitying look. "Didn't you ever learn that?"

For a moment, it seemed that the vampire was struggling with his answer. A haunted look came into his eyes, and Tobyn almost felt compassion for him. When he finally spoke, it was in a whisper. "I was taught a different lesson."

"*Gadjo,*" he snorted.

Dumas leaned closer, his body inching nearer to his captive's, his cool eyes peering into Reyes' blue ones. "Do you miss it?"

"What? Sex?"

The vicomte actually looked embarrassed. "Mortals have...mortal needs," he said slowly, obviously selecting his words with care. "Sometimes these...desires...are very powerful, are they not? The lust for the flesh is consuming."

Tobyn's skin crawled with a terrible feeling of apprehension. "What are you getting at?"

Dumas took his captive's hand and held it, fondling the fingers absently. "All this time here in my *chateau*, you have been alone. Have you...needed?"

The vampire's discomfort with the subject was obvious, but Tobyn was just cynical enough to doubt his sincerity. He was torn between the drive to protect himself and the necessity of enacting his plan. After vacillating wildly in the confines of his mind, he steered the course of honesty.

"Yes."

Those icy eyes seized him again, and the gypsy could almost feel himself falling into their shadows. Dumas' voice was a husky whisper as he asked, "Have you needed me?"

Images of the two of them, entwined, rose before his mind's eye, and Tobyn blinked them away. He did not want the vampire to touch him, but he desperately wanted freedom. *The plan*, he told himself, forcing an answer disguised as a kiss.

Dumas clutched him tightly, holding on to the kiss with an inexorable grasp. If the mortal had wanted to escape, he could not; it was just as well that his scheme forced him to return the embrace. The vampire left his mouth, trailing lips and tongue down the tender skin of Reyes' neck. Tobyn trembled at the sensation of Dumas' teeth nipping at his throat, stinging but not pushing through to the vein beneath. The vampire's hands skimmed over him, touching and exploring gently, seeking out the center of Tobyn's conjured desire. The mortal gasped as Dumas found what he was looking for; his frame shook with the effort of holding himself still. A moan of revulsion that sounded very much like pleasure tumbled from the gypsy's lips, and the vampire concentrated his attention.

Unable to restrain his natural reactions, Tobyn responded to the arousing touch of the vampire's hand. Hating himself for liking the experience so much, he pulled Dumas closer. The Frenchman complied, but only for a moment; all but flinging himself away from the gypsy, his eyes wide with a very real hunger, Dumas stepped toward the door.

"You are very physical, indeed. There is much I would know of you, Tobyn, but this—this I cannot do, much to my regret." He turned his back on the panting youth, battling for self-control. Over his shoulder, he confessed, "You enthrall me, little love, but..."

"Dumas..."

The vicomte went to the doors, his hands visibly shaking as he reached for the handles. "No. You do not understand. If I stayed with you now, I would kill you, and that would destroy me." He finally turned to look the gypsy in the face, seemingly unmoved by the flush to Tobyn's cheeks, his eminently regal control restored. "This will not last, my love. Once you are one of us, these...needs...will disappear. And then I could hold you until the end of time with no fear. But this way, you are too great a temptation, and I would not have you hurt." The concern in his voice sounded genuine; Tobyn wondered if it was. Dumas spoke again. "I promised you rest, so I shall leave you to it." His gaze flickered from Tobyn's face to his lap. "I trust that you are not too inconvenienced."

"*Inconvenienced?* That doesn't even begin to cover this..."

"I apologize. Perhaps tomorrow night will show another way. For tonight, however, I bid you a very fond farewell."

Tobyn watched in disbelief as the vampire left the room, locking the door behind him as he went. Flopping backward with a groan, he wondered why nothing in his life made sense anymore, and just how long it would be before he lost his mind completely.

I wanted him, he thought, his hand moving down to solve his current problem. *God help me, I wanted him. I would have done anything he wanted me to.* He closed his eyes and touched himself, and although he would never have admitted it, his fantasies all featured his regal keeper, and as he hit his climax, he cried out the vampire's name.

❧❧❧❧❧

Outside the room, Dumas leaned against the bolted doors, listening to Tobyn loving himself, fighting a pitched battle with the thirst that had demanded his beloved gypsy's blood. He shook with the effort, and it was all he could do to prevent himself from ripping the doors off of their hinges and taking Tobyn there and then.

No, Michel, he told himself, his mind-voice astonishingly clear and calm. *You almost have him completely. He's giving himself to you; it will wait.*

He had never denied himself the luxury of feeding before; the vampire in him shrieked and howled against the constraints he had imposed. He would not see Tobyn destroyed so needlessly, not when he was so close to being brought over willingly into the darkness of Dumas' world.

He heard the passionate cry from the locked room, and he shivered. He could still feel the heat of Reyes' body, the throb of his pulse. He wanted Tobyn very badly, in a way he had not wanted since he had surrendered to Tristan's gentle charms. He loved him.

Dumas smiled to himself. *It is unthinkable. I am the prince of my clan, I am the Prime! Why should I degrade myself for the love of a mortal, especially if the desire he shows is insincere? There should be a test...my Tobyn should prove his love...*

Moving away from the locked doors, he headed to the library to consider the situation.

Four

Tobyn stood, motionless, before the window, watching the rain streak the glass in icy streams. Late October rains like this were always cold, and he hoped that Ara and Beti were keeping warm somehow. He probed the link with his twin and received only echoes of his own message. The silence from Araminah was disturbing, although he could sense no illness or injury as its cause. He only knew that the tiny light that had shimmered in his soul had been extinguished, and that his isolation was complete.

The rain made him contemplative. *What am I gaining by resisting him?* He turned and walked to where his guitar awaited him on the divan. He sat and cradled the instrument in his hands. *Freedom, I suppose. But what would happen if I escaped? He's able to track me down until the end of time, and I can't run forever. Besides, even if I were able to get out of here, where would I go? I can't rejoin the* kumpania *now. They have to have moved on by now, and, anyway, I'm so unclean now...any* chovihani *in any* kumpania *only has to look at me to see how tainted Dumas has made me.* He strummed a chord, then another. *I am cut off from Ara now,* he thought sadly. *She's the only person who's ever really mattered to me. But now, I have to be dead to her. I have to start over.*

Sure. Start over. He absently played a brief melody he'd learned in Portugal. *How? With Dumas?* This time, the thought did not bring the knee-jerk reaction of revulsion. He considered the option openly, admitting to himself that not all of the plan he was currently enacting was a hoax. *He's magnetic,* he allowed, *and there are moments when it's very tempting to take him up on his offer. Eternity...never to get old, to always have him here...not a bad idea. But he keeps saying that he owns me, and* nobody *owns me, not even Ara. And how can I honestly be falling in love with a man who's keeping me locked up in a glorified prison cell, a man who serves me as the main course at banquets for his friends?* He shook his head. *Ara would call this a pleasure trap. And she'd be right. I can't forget the details.*

So, what are my choices? Solitude or confinement. Unacceptable from any angle, and losers all. I can't go back to my old life, and I can't stay here as a prisoner to the end of time.

Something in his mind whispered sweet promises, reminding him of the allure of eternal life.

So why not just take him up on the offer?

Sighing, he put the guitar aside and paced through the room for the hundredth time that day. *It's pointless. I can't make any decisions here. I'm not in control.*

Not in control...he shivered. He had learned the hard way, many years ago, to never let anyone have control over him. His uncle Antonio had taught him that. Memories of the things that man had done to him, the pain, the degradation...he shuddered and stopped pacing. He had been so young, and Antonio so much stronger...*Not too much unlike the way I'm helpless against Dumas.* He shook himself. *Now, stop it, Tobyn. Antonio is in jail with Da all the way back in Seville. One problem at a time.*

His mind could not be so easily ordered, however, and try though he did, he could not chase away the memories, or the fear that the same thing would happen again. He always got hurt when somebody else was in control. The thought that control was comfortably held in the hollow of Dumas' hand made him very much afraid.

〜〜〜〜

Dumas found him pacing the room like a tiger, a look of haunted desperation shadowing his blue eyes. Tobyn wore an air of frazzled nerves, and the sharpness to his motions as he turned to face his visitor betrayed his anxiety.

"Good evening," the vicomte greeted politely. "How are you tonight, my love?"

"Slowly losing my mind," the gypsy replied in an odd mixture of snarl and groan. "I warned you that this would happen. I can't take the locks, Dumas. I beg of you, if you have any feeling for me at all, let me out of this damned room!"

The vampire sat in the arm chair, a king taking his throne. "I wish that I could do that."

"You can. You have to."

"You would attempt to escape me."

"And go where? My people have gone. Even if they were still here, they'd never take me back." He knelt on the rug at Dumas' feet, staring bleakly into the vampire's face. "My life is over. There's nothing left for me, now." To his amazement, his vision swam with genuine tears. "You've destroyed me."

The vicomte's brow puckered, and he bent to him, gently wiping the salt drops from the gypsy's lashes. "No...you are not destroyed. Don't say such things." He gathered up the mortal's hands. "You're trembling."

Reyes shook his head slowly, his eyes fixed, unseeing, on the vampire's boots. "I warned you that this would happen." He turned a pleading gaze to his captor. "Unlock the door. Please. I don't have anywhere to go, so you don't have to worry about escape attempts. Just let me out of here, even if it's only for an hour." He shook his head and whispered, "Please. I'll do anything you want. Just let me out."

Dumas rested a finger against Tobyn's lips, silencing him. "Is it so bad?"

The gypsy laughed sharply. "I've been here for days with nobody to talk to, with the same things to look at. Nothing ever changes, and I hate to be alone, and..."

"Shh. No more. You are upsetting yourself needlessly." He slid his hands up to Tobyn's shoulders, then to the nape of his neck. Forcing Reyes to meet his eyes, he said softly, "You need to rest. Sleep will soothe your nerves."

"I don't want to sleep," Tobyn objected petulantly. "I have nightmares."

"Hush. I will give you dreamless sleep."

He gently pulled Tobyn to his feet, then guided him to sit in the vampire's lap. Tobyn curled up like a child, his body shaking, and wrapped his arms around his knees. Dumas caught his face and turned him so their gazes could meet.

The grey eyes that held the gypsy captive seemed to flare, and the bright flame in their depths drew him instantly. A cocoon of warmth wrapped itself around him, mind and body, and his shaking gradually stopped. He stared, wide-eyed, into the dancing flame, immobilized by Dumas' hypnotic power. A distant part of him deplored the ease of his surrender, but he needed the peace that the vampire could give. His vision swayed, and before he realized what was happening, he slumped into the Frenchman's arms.

Dumas held him that way for hours, gently kissing his temple and rocking him in his arms. Something was wrong with his fearless little horse thief. Moving carefully, he put the unconscious young man on the bed and left him with another loving kiss. He took one last look, pity and affection softening his face, before he closed the doors to Tobyn's opulent prison. He hesitated when his hand found the latch, and, after a moment of deliberation, he left the doors unlocked.

Tobyn would sleep through until daybreak, he knew. That left him plenty of time to appoint a guard. It wasn't that he distrusted his mortal love; it was just that one could never be too sure. And Dumas had always been one to cover his bets.

Ara crept from the wagon with the first hint of greyness on the morning sky, slipping past Beti as silently as she could. The air outside was bitingly cold, and she pulled her cloak tighter about her body as she made her way out of the night camp. It was odd to see so many wagons, but the Carago group was a large, traditional one. For so long as they were traveling together, life for the Reyes-Moreno group, always renegades and outsiders even among the Rom, would be very different. Old man Carago was already watching the newcomers with a policeman's eye. For now, though, the Caragos were of only peripheral concern. Her mind had to be focused on finding her brother.

The link between them had fallen silent, the invisible thread that bound them severed by Beti's well-meaning but misguided interference. While Araminah knew that her grandmother had intended only to protect her from her twin's distress, separating their fates, there were other factors involved. Ara knew Tobyn and herself well enough to know that neither of them could survive in isolation from one another. No matter what it took, she had to reestablish the link.

She found a quiet spot not far from the caravan where she could concentrate without fear of discovery. Sitting down amid the underbrush and tall, frost-browned grass, ignoring the wetness of the morning dew, Ara closed her eyes and reached out for Tobyn.

For a long time, she flailed in darkness, unable to connect with her brother. She would never find the loose end of Tobyn's line this way. Exasperated, she pulled back to try again, this time envisioning what she wanted to find, hoping that wishful thinking could give natural ability an extra push. She knew every inch of Tobyn, knew how he felt in body and soul; surely she could recreate him now! Taking a slow, deep breath, she "saw" the glimmer of white in the darkness that was Tobyn. His light was weak, and she could barely feel it. Determined, she pushed, and in the effort forgot to breathe. Almost there, almost to it...the burning in her lungs faded away like background noise as she refocused her concentration. She would deal with breathing later.

Her extended "fingers" caught the line and tied her brother to her once again. An almost physically visible burst of energy accompanied the fusing of their severed link, and an awareness of her twin flooded her.

//Tobyn!//

She could feel him startle into wakefulness. The mental voice that reached her was heartrending in its vulnerable, wounded tone. *//Ara?//*

She poured as much life and love into their link as she could, reinforcing him. He was frighteningly depleted. *//Yes. I'm here.//*

//My God...I thought I'd lost you.// Tears welled in her eyes; her brother was crying. *//I thought you'd given up and left me.//*

//I'd never do that.// She took a deep breath. *//Are you well?//*

He hesitated, uncertainty clear in his brief silence. She could feel him breathing in her offering, accepting the energy that pulsed to him from his sister. *//I'm better now. God, Ara, I miss you!//*

//Where are you? Can you find your way back to us?// She knew that she was sending him too many questions, but she couldn't stop. *//Has the vampire hurt you? Are you safe?//*

//Ara.// He sounded gently reproachful.

//I'm concerned.//

//So am I.// She shivered. That wasn't what he was supposed to say. He was always the fearless one. *//If I can get away, I'll find you.//*

//If?//

//Nothing here makes any sense. I don't know what will happen from one minute to the next. If things go well, I'll be with you again.//

She felt cold to the very core of her heart. *//And if things go badly?//*

Soft, rueful laughter echoed along their link. *//Don't forget me.//*

//Don't say that! Do you want it to happen?// Horrified, she demanded, *//Tobyn, you have to come back. I need you with me.//*

Ara briefly considered telling him of her impending marriage, but she could see no use in burdening her twin with more troubles. Besides, this form of communication was difficult and draining, and neither of them had the strength for a long, drawn-out explanation.

His reply was quiet and heartfelt. *//I'll do my best. I love you, Ara.//*

//I love you, too.//

They fell out of touch, unable to maintain the connection over so great a distance. The iciness of the morning penetrated Ara's senses, and she shivered; her head swam with the after effects of her fight to restore the link, and she wanted only to sleep in a warm place for a very long time. Standing slowly, she brushed the dirt and twigs from her skirt before she headed back to the camp. While Tobyn had given her precious little reason to hope, he had soothed her fears simply by being alive. Her brother was strong, and clever in a pinch; she believed that he would return to her. She needed that faith in Tobyn to see her through whatever was to come.

Please, Tobyn, she thought, almost in prayer. *Don't prove me wrong.*

<hr/>

He blinked in the silence, reveling in the feeling of the restored link. *Did I really consider giving up?* He shook his head in amazement. *I can't desert Ara so easily. What was I thinking? No matter what happens now, I have to find a way back to her.*

Rising from the bed, he took up his usual routine of pacing and noodling on the guitar. He was surprised that he hadn't started leaving tracks on the carpet. There was no change from yesterday in the room's appearance, or from the day before, but somehow, everything looked brighter. With renewed optimism, he sat down on the divan to think.

I have to make Dumas trust me, that's obvious. Trust isn't easily given by anybody, but I think it's going to be especially hard with him. But once I have it, it can be manipulated very easily. If I can just make him think I love him, I can get the hell out of here. Dumas is a romantic, and the more he thinks I'm responding, the more likely he is to get careless and make mistakes. Those mistakes will get me out of here.

There was only one way to earn that trust, however, and the thought thrilled him even while it twisted his stomach. He had to bow to the Frenchman's whims in all things and at all times. Tobyn knew something of power, and he knew from personal experience that vampires had a way of controlling mortals completely. *So, I need to seem controlled. When he kisses me, I have to kiss him back. When he touches me, I have to act like I want it. Whatever he wants, I have to do.* He sighed. *Unfortunately, I think that's not going to be a problem.*

He could not deny the pleasure he got from the vampire's touch and from his feeding. He was never certain, though, how much of that burn for Dumas was honestly his or created by the Frenchman himself. *As long as I don't know, I have to be careful. Is that pleasure worth losing Ara? Is it worth losing myself?*

Tobyn was confused by the conflicting want for the Frenchman and the revulsion he felt when he saw his captor clearly. *It would be so easy to give in to him, to bend to him, to become what he wants me to be...* Clarity was tied to his sister, and now that they were once again linked, his head was clearer than it had been through the bleakness of the day before. He needed Ara in order to live, it seemed, and that fact guided his decision. *I'll bend for him, but I won't break, unless it's to break free.*

His head hurt, he noticed, leaving off his strategy for the time being. For the first time, he saw that the breakfast tray was absent, as was the pitcher of water that usually stood at the bedside table. He snorted softly to himself, thinking that he wouldn't be a bit surprised if the flighty maid who brought his provisions had bolted out of pure terror. She wasn't what he would call brave, even in his most sarcastic moment.

Without food or drink to occupy his time, he rose and continued to wander through his prison. Out of desperation for something to do, he fiddled with the guitar a bit more, jiggled the loose tile in the hearth that he'd discovered three days before, and rearranged the lighter furniture. He briefly considered trying to open the window despite the bars and the outside latch, but the chill of the glass changed his mind. Fighting boredom, he went to the doors and gave a half-hearted tug.

To his vast surprise, the door opened.

He took a quick step backward, irrationally afraid that Dumas would spring on him from the hallway, prepared to deny any involvement with the opening of the door. He closed his eyes and took a deep breath to calm his racing heart, then stepped out of the room. He'd half expected an invisible barrier to rise up and keep him in; when he found himself standing in the center of the hallway, face to face with a full-length mirror in a glittering frame, he laughed aloud in triumph. He was out!

A movement to his right nearly sent him through the ceiling. Spinning, he faced a surly mountain of a man who quietly regarded him. The man, the same who had menaced him in the tavern below the *chateau*, picked at a ragged fingernail as he stared down at the diminutive gypsy. Tobyn fought his panic reaction but took a step away from the man anyway.

"Hello," he greeted hesitantly, the accent in his French made more pronounced by the pounding of his nerves. "You must be my prison guard."

The man's only answer was to blink his dark eyes in stupid silence. Tobyn was reminded very much of a poleaxed ox.

"Were you sent here by Dumas?" He waited a long time for an answer or a reaction; neither was forthcoming. "Can I explore?"

No response. *Something tells me this is pointless.*

"All right, fine." Switching to Romany, he smiled brightly and said, "You're the stupidest man alive, aren't you?" The guard blinked again, and Tobyn sighed. The fun of this encounter was extremely limited. In French, he said, "I'll just wander off and have a look around. All right? Good. I'm glad you approve."

Turning his back on the uncommunicative lump by the door, he proceeded down the hallway. He had passed four open rooms similar to the one that had been his prison before he realized that the lump was following in his footsteps, watching every move with those unsettlingly expressionless eyes. If he had planned escape, this guard would surely stop him, and Dumas would no doubt know immediately. Tobyn smiled to himself; well, this guard would just have to waste his day. There would be no bolting today.

Ignoring the man to the best of his ability, the gypsy walked on. Passing the open doors that offered more variably-colored versions of his accustomed cell, he focused on the infinitely more interesting prospects of a closed door to his right. The latch resisted him, and his curiosity was piqued. Glancing over his shoulder at the approaching guard, he rattled the handle and tried again to gain entrance.

A huge, rough-palmed hand grasped his wrist firmly. "No."

Tobyn released the handle and stepped back "You do have a voice. Why can't I go in?"

He shook his head. "*Monsieur le vicomte* says no."

A slender eyebrow arched in the appearance of a sudden theory. "This is where he sleeps during the day, isn't it?"

The man, still clutching Reyes' wrist, steered him away from the door. The grip he was held in was not painful, but it promised that it could be with little effort on the part of the guard. Choosing to preserve his wrist rather than his curiosity, Tobyn allowed himself to be conducted back down the hallway. Only when it became apparent that his guard was intending to deposit him back in his prison did he resist. To his great surprise, the man docilely released him and waited for Tobyn to go somewhere so that he could play shadow. Reyes was enjoying this; suppressing a grin, he turned and walked briskly in the direction of the staircase beyond that intriguing locked door.

He paused on the top step, looking down the wide expanse that led to a highly-polished stone floor. Gripping the carved banister, he trotted down the carpeted stairs to the main level, his guard close on his heels. The heavy doors that must certainly have led outside stood invitingly across from the last step, but Tobyn forced himself to showily pass them by without a second glance. *Think about that, if you can,* he silently directed his trailing companion.

He swung around to his right, following the wide, mirror-lined chamber toward a cluster of closed, engraved doors. He opened the way to the first room and stepped in. The walls were lined with what seemed to be hundreds of books, interspersed with portraits of ancient noblemen and their ladies. A generous hearth flickered with a friendly warmth, and a comfortable-looking duo of armchairs beckoned him to sit in the fire's light. Not far away, a writing desk strewn with papers bearing scores of words waited for Dumas' return. For the first time, Tobyn regretted his lack of education; he would have liked to know what a man like his captor could be writing.

Since he could not read, libraries held little interest for him. Closing the doors and flashing a smile at the watching guard, he continued to the next room.

When he stepped over this new threshold, he came face to face with a dinner table he remembered all too well. Dark wood—dark, he presumed, to better conceal blood stains—and enormous, the table seemed somehow malignant in the dim light falling from high, slit-like windows. The room was oppressive, gloomy, and full of memories too painful and far too fresh. With a shudder, Tobyn closed up the room abruptly.

Further exploration revealed a sitting room, a vast salon equipped with a brand-new harpsichord, and a plush drawing room. All were richly appointed, with little treasures lying about that made his thief's heart glad. Dumas was incredibly wealthy, and careless about his money. *If there's way, I've got to figure out how to get free* and *rob him blind.* He cataloged what he would like to have as he continued to wander through the *chateau.*

After making his way through a sprawling ballroom that echoed with his every step, Tobyn found a smaller door in a side hall, perhaps meant for servants. Plain to the point of obtrusiveness in the face of the manor's elegance, the door promised either an anachronistic surprise or something he could understand. With his hulking guard behind him, he pushed through to see what was on the other side.

He was delighted to find a kitchen, with all of the amenities a stately house would require. Gleaming pots and pans hung from hooks, awaiting the next meal, and the wide cupboards were spotless. They were also unused, and the stillness of the air was distracting. Of course, a vampire had no need of a kitchen; he didn't eat food that needed to be cooked. *Very good for Dumas, but I'm hungry, and I do eat food. The maid brought in fruit and bread every morning,* he told himself in an attempt at logical thinking, *so there has to be something to eat here somewhere.* Rummaging in storage bins and boxes, Tobyn managed to scare up half a loaf of bread and a single apple that was beginning to soften with age and bruises. Not top-of-the-line food, but at least it was edible.

Didn't Dumas mention a pantry at the banquet? Yes, he did, and he said that it was stocked. Biting off a chunk of the stale bread, Tobyn set about hunting down the *chateau's* food stores.

The search was not too difficult. Finding the pantry doors, he raised the wooden latch and flung them open with a triumphant smile. The accompanying cry of satisfaction died in his constricting throat when he saw what was waiting inside.

People.

People were strewn around the room like sacks of flour. Some lay still on the floor, others lolled against the walls; here and there, some were propped up against one another. Their eyes stared sightlessly ahead, their limp limbs drooping. If not for the rasp of their labored breathing, Tobyn would have believed that they were dead. He crept closer to what had once been a rather pretty young woman and touched her lax fingers. Her hand flopped to the floor, the knuckles rapping hollowly against the flagstone, and her eyes swiveled slowly toward him. Not a spark of consciousness remained in her, and the marks on her throat and arms told him why. Drawing back in horror, he collided with the solid bulk of his guard, who seized him by the shoulders and hauled him out of the macabre pantry.

"*Monsieur le vicomte* says no," the guard rumbled, dragging his stunned charge out of the kitchen. Tobyn did not resist, and soon he was back in his prison room with the door safely locked behind him.

As Reyes fought to make his hands stop shaking, he asked himself, *What the hell did you expect, Tobyn? It's a vampire's stock room. But...Jesus Christ! Their eyes!* He shuddered and hugged himself, finding no comfort in the pseudo-embrace. Each time he closed his eyes, he could see the girl he'd touched, could see how utterly bereft of spirit his vampire "host" had left her. *How easy it would be for me to end up down there, just another bag of blood in the pantry...*

He shivered again, chilled more inside than out, and he wrapped the comforter around himself. He went to the window to wait for the afternoon to fade into the evening, trying to will the light to stay for a few hours more. He was afraid.

When sunset came, Dumas would come to call, and he had to find a way to keep his horror from showing. When he looked the Frenchman in the face, he would see that girl again. *What was the phrase Roger used? 'Blood on the hoof.' My God.*

His eyes went to the closed door, his thoughts to the guard on the other side. The man was devoid of intelligence and expression; he seemed to retain the capacity to speak only one sentence; his dark eyes were as dead as the girl's. *Is he at some intermediate stage, I wonder? Someplace between fully human and pantry stock? Does Dumas see through his eyes during the day, or is he just a drone?* He shook his head. *Holy Mother, if you ever loved gypsies, start praying for me now. Get me out of this.*

The caravan had been on the move all day, rattling through the village-specked forests and fields of France, drawing steadily nearer to Spain. Araminah rode with Nikolas in the Moreno family *vardo*, unwilling to spend time with her uncle or her former ally, Beti. The precious link with Tobyn had only recently been healed; she would not allow it to be severed again, which was exactly what her grandmother would do, given half a chance.

Nikolas held her hands in his to keep them warm, chattering on about all of the happiness he would give her after their marriage. He spoke so fervently that Ara almost believed him. He clearly meant every word, and the sweetness in his dark eyes when he fussed about her comfort began to draw her attention. *He isn't ugly so much as plain,* she decided, *and his clumsiness is endearing, I suppose.* Ara could almost like him when he was like this; if forced into the marriage, she could probably find a way to be content even if happiness escaped her. She would never love him, though, not for so long as she was already in love with Tobyn.

She sighed softly and looked away from Nikolas' eager face. She didn't care at all for this man at her side, feeling neither hatred nor friendship. He touched her, and her insides were cold and empty. Araminah almost wished she could hate him; that, at least, would have been an emotion, and it might have made things easier. Fighting she could live with. A life full of blank grey was too much to ask of her, and all she would have for so long as she was separated from her twin.

As Nikolas continued prattling on, she noticed his mother watching with anger and distaste. Cristina Moreno and Araminah were old enemies who had seldom maintained civility with one another, and then only with Beti's interference and peacekeeping. The older woman obviously thought her only son could do better, and she was perfectly aware of how her husband watched Ara with lust shining in his eyes. Manuo had never been subtle in his desires, and it had to pain Cristina. Ara, for her part, remembered the Moreno woman's cruelty to Lucia Reyes, born Lucy Kelly, the Irish girl who had married Chavo Reyes and borne his twins. The effort of bearing Tobyn and Ara had injured her, and Lucy had been weak and sickly to the end. The women of the *kumpania* who bore pure Rom blood, Cristina Moreno chief among them, had ridiculed her "*gadja* weakness," and it was they who had broken Lucy's spirit. Ara had watched her mother suffer silently under Cristina's abuses, had watched Chavo ignoring his wife's need. When Lucy died, her daughter had placed the blame squarely on Chavo and Cristina. Ara's father was languishing in a Spanish jail; his price was being paid. Cristina, though, had not begun to atone for her sins. Araminah hoped that she would live to see Cristina's price paid in full.

"You're so far away."

She blinked and faced Nikolas again. Laughing softly at herself, she said, "I'm sorry, Niki. I was thinking too hard."

He beamed at her, and she knew that if he had a tail, it would be wagging. "I like that about you. You're as smart as you are beautiful." Cocking his head, he asked, "What were you thinking about?"

"People. My family."

His face softened compassionately. "Don't worry about Antonio and Chavo. We'll get them out when we get to Seville. And Tobyn is just as smart as you. He'll be just fine. You'll see."

She pulled her hands free and tucked them under her legs. "I hope you're right."

๛๛๛

Tobyn sat, motionless, on the edge of the armchair and waited for Dumas to arrive. Through a concentrated effort, he had choked himself on his own anxiety until he was too tired to feel it anymore. He safeguarded the cold, exhausted spot deep within his soul; when he touched it, it would reach up and cover his face in an expression of nothing. As long as he held on to the cold, he could keep his anger and his disgust at bay. When the vampire visited him, he would greet him calmly, without tremor, keeping a tight hold on the ice inside.

Sunset tinged the sky a violent pink, then faded into a steely grey-black. The clouds on the horizon had been promising a storm all day, and they looked as if they might deliver that night. *Very good, my boy. Think about the weather.* It would probably snow, and there might even be thunder. If the air were warm enough, the snow might turn to rain, and lightning might blaze across the sky, blue and bright. *I hope there will be lightning. I've always liked lightning.*

The door slid open, and he smoothly, slowly turned to face Dumas. The vampire had a secret-keeping smile on his lips, and those cold grey eyes were alive with mischief, malicious or otherwise. Tobyn was certain he would not like what this night would bring.

"There's going to be a storm," he said, his voice toneless and level.

Dumas raised an eyebrow. "So there is. But we are safe indoors, now. The weather cannot hurt you here." He drifted to the bed and perched on the edge, one elegant hand lightly gripping the poster. He patted the mattress. "Come here, my love. Come sit."

Docile and unthinking, as if he were halfway to the pantry, he concentrated on his internal ice and obeyed.

The vampire took his hand and kissed the palm, then smiled gently into the gypsy's pretty eyes. "You explored the *chateau* today."

It was not a question. "Yes."

"What did you think?"

"It's beautiful," he replied truthfully. "I was surprised that there were so many mirrors. Aren't they useless to you?"

The French vampire laughed. "Lord, no! Gypsies and their superstitions! No, little one, I can use looking glasses as easily as you. My kind, it may be, use them more than mortals. We are a vain lot."

Tobyn looked silently at their hands, feeling strangely disconnected from the contact, as if it were not his hand Dumas was holding. Unable to think of something useful to say, he held his tongue. Dumas broke the silence.

"Do you really like the place? Could you live here?"

"I am adaptable, *monsieur*. I can live anywhere."

The vampire smiled sadly. "So I am *monsieur* again, am I? I would have thought that our intimacy would merit the use of names."

"Intimacy?"

He leaned in and stole a kiss that Tobyn returned with little urging and less real sentiment. Drawing back, the vampire said, "Don't tell me you've forgotten."

Tobyn's hands clutched Dumas' shoulders as he turned his head to allow the Frenchman access to his throat. This was an old routine, and he closed his eyes, arching into the touch and waiting for it to be over. Dumas took his time, nuzzling and licking his earlobe, lightly nipping at his skin as he trailed down to the hollow of the gypsy's throat. His hands were exploring again, and Tobyn was betrayed by his body as before. Squeezing his eyes tighter, he brought one hand up to cup Dumas' head, fingers burrowing into the soft brown hair as their breathing quickened. A soft groan filled Reyes' throat, and Dumas pulled back slowly, staring into the mortal's eyes.

"Call me by my first name," the vampire ordered in loving tones. Tobyn shuddered to hear it. "Use my given name. I know you've heard it."

Trembling at a skillful touch, the gypsy complied in a heated whisper. "Michel..."

Dumas actually shivered; releasing his hold on Tobyn, he eased back and breathed, "Oh, very good, my love. Very good." Cupping Reyes' face, he kissed the young man's lips and pushed him down onto the bed with a steady, gentle pressure. The gypsy gasped for air as Dumas' weight settled onto him and his mouth found its usual place on Tobyn's pulse point. While one hand tangled in the gypsy's black curls, the other smoothly stripped the French shirt away, opening the buttons and pushing the fabric down over Reyes' smooth shoulders.

The mortal sighed brokenly in both shame and pleasure as Dumas mouthed a trail along his sternum. For a little while, the vampire's hands and lips were never still, moving with practiced ease until Tobyn was quaking beneath his fingertips. For a moment, it seemed that the caresses would move farther down his body, but Dumas skimmed over him to kneel at the mortal's bare feet. Their eyes met, and the vampire smiled with warmth. He spoke in a voice meant to recite love poems.

"You are beautiful, *mon bohemièn*."

The mortal sat up slowly, hand extended to touch Dumas' cheek. The Frenchman caught his fingers and held them firmly.

"Finish what you start, Michel," Tobyn breathed. "Don't leave me like this again."

The vampire pushed him back down with only a gaze. Unable to resist, Reyes stretched out again, his eyes heavy with lust and a distant, absent-minded ennui. His grasp on the coldness was sliding away...Dumas busied himself with Tobyn's breeches, unlacing the stiff fabric and pulling them free. When the gypsy was once more lying naked before him, he whispered, "You will be satisfied, my love, and more. Do you love me?" The young man smiled, which Dumas took as an affirmative. "Will you prove it?"

"I'll do anything..." His body was taut, quivering; Dumas could smell the blood beneath his skin.

"Good." Barely raising his voice, Dumas called out over his shoulder, "Matthieu."

The door opened, and Tobyn's guard lurched in, dark eyes as blank as before. He stripped off his jacket and homespun shirt as he came closer. Tobyn, alarmed, lost his grip on the ice he'd been treasuring, and his eyes grew wide in fear.

"What's he doing?"

"He will do what I am no longer capable of," the vampire replied with a beatific smile.

Dread and nausea fought for control as he struggled to sit up. "But Dumas—Michel, I—"

Dumas grasped his wrists and held him down, his superior strength nullifying any fight the gypsy could have offered. Shifting to kneel behind his captive's head, he asked, "Does this not please you? It pleases me."

Tobyn closed his eyes tightly as Matthieu's naked weight fell upon the bed. Biting back the curses he wanted to hurl at his tormentors, he somehow maintained his silence. The guard's callused hands were rough as he wrestled the gypsy's limbs into position. Tobyn struggled against him, the first hint of panic coloring his expression while that precious inner nothing slid further and further away.

Dumas smiled up into Matthieu's dirty face, his pointed teeth clear to see, his eyes bright with the mind-control link that let him direct and experience everything the mortal peasant did. "Slowly, now. Let him feel all there is to feel. The second time, you may go fast."

Second time? "Oh, God..."

The vampire gazed down into Tobyn's terror-bright eyes. "You act as though you love me, and yet you do not tell me the truth. Why did you not tell me of your trip to the pantry?"

"I...please, if that's all this is about, yes, I went, I..." He shuddered as he felt Matthieu getting into position. "Don't let him do this! I never lied to you!"

"But silence is as good as a lie. You act as though you love me. Now is the time to prove it. Do this thing, and I will know that you are true. You said you would do anything." Looking back at the clumsy, mindless guard, his eyes glinted. "Remember, Matthieu. Three is the charm."

Reyes bit his cheek and swore himself to silence, eyes screwed shut. He would deprive Dumas of the satisfaction of seeing a reaction. As the first pain of this violation by proxy came, he heard the vampire who held him down begin to laugh in pure delight.

Tobyn would remember that laughter.

It was just prior to dawn when Dumas dismissed his in-house rapist. The vampire sat on the divan with a look of bland disinterest, watching as Tobyn wrapped his bruised form in the rumpled sheets from the bed. Canting his head, he mildly noted, "You're bleeding."

I'm not surprised, he thought, but he did not reply aloud. He kept his eyes cast down, unable to look Dumas in the face.

"Is there anything that you would like before I go?"

He found his voice somehow. "Clean clothes. New bedding. A way to wash."

The vampire laughed, and Reyes wanted to murder him for it. "Anything else, little love?"

Pulling the bedclothes tighter, he nodded. "Wine. Lots of it."

Hiding beneath her covers, her back turned to Beti, Araminah knew. She tried to touch her brother through the link, but was not surprised when she saw how completely he'd withdrawn. His pain, physical and otherwise, echoed to her in endless waves, shadowed by an unsettling, confusing feeling of detachment. Tobyn needed her badly, needed comfort and rescue, but she could offer him no aid.

Clutching her blanket in her fist, she clenched her teeth and silently wept.

Five

He spent hours after sunrise scrubbing himself raw in the heavy porcelain bathtub that Matthieu had placed by the fire, attempting to wash away his violation. He scrubbed and scoured until he bled, and still the feeling of filth remained, like grit beneath his fingernails that he could not remove. Even after the water was cold, he sat and washed desperately, but he knew that he would never be clean again.

After pondering the logistical difficulties of drowning himself without attracting the attention of his guard, Tobyn left the water and toweled off on the hearth, feeling the warmth that had no chance of penetrating to that icy spot in his soul. The coldness was bigger than it had been before, far too big to ever leave him again. He tossed the towel aside and pulled on the new clothes Dumas had given him, expensive black fabric hugging him with uncomfortable intimacy, then turned to stare into a mirror that had been brought in from another room. He did not recognize the face that looked back at him. Where was the young Rom that he had been? *Dead and gone*, he answered himself. *Dead and buried.*

The door opened, and the pale, nervous maid scurried in with breakfast and a bottle. Tobyn cared little for the food, but he was very glad to see the wine.

"Your morning meal, sir," she said, bobbing in an anxious curtsy. "Is there anything you need?"

He took the wine in hand and gestured with it. "Another of these."

"Yes, sir. Are you finished with your bath, sir?"

"Yes." Tobyn uncorked the alcohol and took a hearty swallow. "Feel free to get it out of here."

Another curtsy, and she replied, "Yes, sir. I'll send one of the stable hands up to get it momentarily, sir."

His lip curled and his voice was a sneer as he asked, "Where is Matthieu?"

The maid blanched. "M-Matthieu?"

"Yes, Matthieu. You know, big man, ugly, covered in filth, stinking. Matthieu."

"He—oh, *monsieur*—"

"Isn't he standing guard on the door?" He glared at the skittish girl. "Isn't he?"

"N-no, *monsieur*." She licked her lips and glanced about as if looking for eavesdroppers. Leaning closer, she husked out, "Matthieu is dead, *monsieur*. Master k-killed him just after they drew your bath."

He nearly dropped the bottle. "Killed?"

The girl nodded, her eyes wild with madness and terror. "Master bit him. On the neck, he bit him. He...he drank—"

"—his blood," the gypsy finished for her. He pinned her with a piercing look. "Has your master hurt you? Has he bitten you at all?"

"Oh, no, sir! Sweet Christ, no! I'm only here in the day. He pays my father a franc a day for me to come and see to his *chateau* while he...while he sleeps. But I'm always gone by sundown."

He eyed her suspiciously. "I remember when you couldn't bring yourself to speak to me. What loosened your tongue, *gadja*?" He shook his head. "Never mind. It doesn't matter. Have you got a name?"

"Rachel."

"All right, Rachel. I am afraid that you've caught me out of a talking mood. Bring me another bottle, or maybe two, then go home. This is no place for you."

"Nor for you, neither," she responded. "If it wasn't that Master knows who I am and where we live, I'd get Papa to help you run away."

Rachel stopped short, literally biting her tongue. She had gone much too far, and the shyness crept over her again. Tobyn nodded slowly, watching her with cool appraisal. She fidgeted with her apron, then bobbed again.

"More wine, *monsieur.*"

Without another word, she scuttled away, closing the door in her wake. He almost began to scheme, but he'd had enough of plans, and nothing but bad luck with them. Sitting gingerly in the armchair, mindful of his bruises, he turned again to the bottle he clutched. A bad plan poorly executed had brought him to this point, and he was tired of thinking. It never came to anything. He was sick of the entire situation.

The first bottle brought only dizziness to his exhausted brain, and while he drank to forget, every detail was blazing in his memory with cruel clarity. The second bottle might have been tasteless, for all he knew. He simply swallowed mouthful after mouthful. The aching in his body seemed to fade away by the time he uncorked the third, and the ice in his gut had spread all through him. He would not have been surprised to see frost upon his arms, if he had cared enough to look.

Sleep stole him before he found the bottom of bottle number three, and Tobyn gave in to the darkness of it, inwardly wishing that he'd never wake up again.

<hr/>

Dumas slipped into the room and smiled to see his mortal prisoner sprawled face-down across the bed. Stepping around the empty wine bottles on the floor, he went to Reyes' side, sinking down lightly on the mattress to stroke the firm young back.

At the touch, Tobyn jolted into wakefulness, whirling to face Dumas while simultaneously putting a healthy distance between them. The vampire smiled benignly into Tobyn's wide-eyed stare, patiently waiting for him to settle down. The gypsy swallowed hard, forcing his breathing and pulse to slow to reasonable speeds.

"You startled me," he vastly understated.

Dumas arched an eyebrow in a familiar look. "You thought, perhaps, that I was Matthieu, hm?"

Tobyn looked away, pulling himself into a huddled and self-defensive ball. "I don't know what I thought."

"Last night...you enjoyed it, yes?"

"No."

"Your body said differently."

The Rom's temper flared. "My body is a liar." He fell quiet again, the coldness inside making him unable to sustain the emotion. "It's like it isn't even part of me anymore."

The mumbled words seemed to please Dumas. "I, for one, found the display...fascinating."

You would, Tobyn commented silently.

The vampire took advantage of his mortal's silence to study the shambles of the room. The empty wine bottles drew his attention. Dumas was no fool; he knew perfectly well that Reyes had been less than happy with his ploy the night before, just as he knew that the wine had not been requested for celebration. He also knew that the gypsy hated him with every bit of the soul that was left to him, which he believed was little enough. No amount of acting or game playing could hide the quiet loathing that danced in Tobyn's eyes with every look, or the shudder that coursed along his spine whenever Dumas entered the room. In a way, that was good, and a quality that he hoped Reyes would never lose. There was little appeal in gentling the Rom into an adoring slave full of emptiness, with no fire; what Dumas wanted was a companion to make the years less dull. It helped that Tobyn was beautiful. That, added to what the vampire hoped would be a sincere and well-cultivated despite, would make eternal life more interesting.

Of course, it would be all right if Tobyn ended up loving him a little, too. But the only thing Dumas asked was that he would be broken just enough to offer only a token resistance. A little fighting was nice, and even exciting, but in the end, Dumas always had to win.

Tobyn sat in the heavy silence of the room, waiting for his captor to say something, anything. Each minute that passed pressed harder than the last until the gypsy was convinced that he would have to speak himself or go mad with waiting.

"You're very quiet," he offered lamely, glad just for the sound of his own voice.

Dumas smiled at him. "I'm thinking, that's all."

"About what?"

"You. I think you're ready."

The words chilled him. "Ready for what?"

"To be mine."

The gypsy sat stock still as Dumas drifted closer, his eyes locked to his captive's like a predator to its prey. Powerful hands seized his shoulders in a painless but unbreakable grip, and something inside of Tobyn snapped. Howling like a wounded dog, he fought against Dumas with every ounce of his strength, both physical and otherwise. Though surprised by the telepathic attack, the vampire easily overcame him, turning the struggle against him. The more he fought, the more thoroughly he was ensnared, until Dumas wrestled him to the floor and pinned him there. He roughly pushed Tobyn's head to the side, laying bare his throat, and without preamble or glamour plunged his pointed teeth into the vein.

Unable to fight, unable to escape, Tobyn wept openly as he felt his life being stolen away. This was unlike the gentle taps Dumas had made before into his bloodstream; it went deep, ruthlessly seeking out all of his heart and mind and soul and ripping them away. Rapidly, he lost even the strength to cry; his vision collapsed upon itself, and breathing was an effort that required all of his attention. The coldness inside of him had not been touched, and it owned him now. He was cold, so very cold...

The rapacious parasite at his throat released him, and Tobyn was distantly aware that he was dying. His coldness shivered indignantly at the thought, and as an act of rebellion, he managed to shove his eyelids open.

Dumas hovered over him, face ruddy with Tobyn's life. The gypsy wished that he could strike that thieving smile away, but he couldn't locate his hands, much less make them useful.

The vampire's lips moved, and his voice reached Reyes out of synchrony. "Now I will make you mine. I will give you everlasting life, and you will be my lover and nightchild until the end of time."

His eyes began to close, but he fought them open again in time to see the blotch that must have been Dumas produce a tiny blade from somewhere and slice open his own wrist. Confused but weak past caring, Tobyn watched the vampire husband his wound to profuse bleeding.

"I give you the Gift," Dumas told him from a hundred miles away.

He felt a warm, sticky moisture press against the lips that had begun to go numb and cold, and then a torrent ran down his throat as if of its own volition, igniting his tongue and raging its way into his gullet. It was living, somehow, and pulsing with an alien power, coursing into his body like a pack of wolves intent upon seeking out his heart and rending it to bits. The taste was sweet, too sweet, and it was thick enough to choke him. He tried to refuse it as the vampire's blood brought consciousness back to his brain, but his traitor body was caught in the spell and would not obey. The blood poured in and it seemed that it would never stop, and his throat opened and closed for it, swallowing by itself, greedily taking all that Dumas was willing to give. His weakness fled, and his limbs trembled with strength not their own; the power in the blood stabbed through him and wrapped itself around his center, setting off a titanic inner battle as the differing energies fought for preeminence or harmony. His body took the blood, accepted it, drew strength from it. His soul, though, sloughed it off, despite the tendrils of the foreign energy that wrapped around it, insinuating into his spirit's depths.

His inward screaming became outward as Dumas ripped his wrist away from Tobyn's lips and sat back to observe, waiting for the tell-tale change from mortal to vampire.

Tobyn stopped screaming and started sobbing, gasping for breath.

Dumas waited. And waited.

The signs of Change never appeared.

Reyes rolled onto his side and curled into a fetal position, his cheeks red and sweat-damp with fever. He was shaking from head to toe, clutching his stomach as nausea rocked him. He moaned softly to himself and pressed his head, pounding with pain, against the floor. He felt poisoned.

Dumas retreated, gray eyes huge with disbelief and a measure of fear. The change should have been complete by now! What manner of man was this, to drink vampire blood and remain a mortal?

"Impossible!" he breathed, stumbling for the door in a complete loss of composure. "Impossible!"

Tobyn did not watch him as he left the room and slammed the doors shut behind him. Crawling to his knees, he hung his head and tried to remember to breathe. Cramps rose like fire in his abdomen and in his chest, and his stomach convulsed, expelling the blood onto the floor. When the last spasm left him, he crept, shuddering and sick, to the bed, where he collapsed.

~❧~

Daylight was a cold cruelty when he opened his eyes again. It seemed too hot; it burned his skin without leaving a mark. Tobyn groaned and somehow managed to turn onto his back, where he lay for a long, silent moment. His mind gradually cleared its fog away, and he began to think as rationally as he could.

Something had gone wrong with the transfer of power, and he silently thanked Beti for her protection. Dumas could not have known about his grandmother's gypsy magic, and the lack of transformation had dumbfounded him. Tobyn half-smiled at the thought; so, now *monsieur le vicomte* felt a little fear, as well. Good. Perhaps that fear could win Tobyn some time.

Dumas would not stay away forever, though, he knew. The vampire was not the sort to bear denial gracefully. He would return, perhaps that night, and try again. And he would keep forcing Tobyn to take "the Gift" until he had his way. Time, for obvious reasons, was on the Frenchman's side. He could afford to make a thousand nightly visits with a thousand failed attempts; Tobyn could not. He would age, he would lose his mind, he would die. It was inevitable, all of it. The gypsy shuddered at the thought of spending the rest of his life in the *chateau*, fighting for his very soul every single night, enduring Dumas' whims and sadistic games until he finally found his escape in death. It was something he could not, would not bear.

To hell with the plan, miserable and misbegotten thing that it was, and the same with Dumas and his *chateau*. Tobyn would not stay here another hour, if he could help it. He had suffered two rapes here, one physical, one vastly worse; he had suffered injury and illness here. He hated the place, hated Dumas, hated the night. He was beginning to hate himself, especially the weak part that made his body betray him. He was going insane, and he had very little time left before he was completely mad. He had to make his break today or lose himself forever.

He struggled to his feet and straightened his shirt, letting his head get used to him standing up before he tried anything so radical as moving. After a wobbly moment, he made his way to the door with even, determined steps. Grasping the handle, he took a deep breath before tugging the door open.

As he had hoped, there was no guard; striding out into the hallway, he checked along the corridor for signs of life. He was the only person moving around the *chateau*, it seemed, and he thanked the gods for that favor. In another of the rooms, he found a warm frock coat and put it on, ready for the cold he could feel through the walls. He was already mostly ice, so the weather would daunt him very little.

The door to Dumas' room was bolted, so he could do nothing to sabotage his captor. He took the time to push a heavy desk from the hallway in front of Dumas' door, expending both precious time and energy. It was the best he could do to protect his back.

Tobyn trotted down the stairs and hurried to the kitchen. While scrupulously avoiding the pantry, he hunted down a reasonably-sized knife with a good, sharp edge and put it into the coat's pocket for future use. He deserted the kitchen then, returning to the front entrance. He was not surprised to see the main doors barred from the inside; undoing the lock, Tobyn let himself out into the glaring brightness of the day.

Temporarily blinded by the sunlight in his eyes, he breathed deeply of his first fresh air in nearly two weeks. As his eyes adjusted to the light, he saw something that made his chest tighten in anxiety.

Snow.

The ground was covered in a thick blanket of white for as far as he could see. It reached almost to his knees, and it reflected and intensified the sun until it was almost painful. Stooping, he gathered up a handful of the powdery-fine stuff, feeling the chill and realizing that even a gypsy raised on stealth would leave clear-cut tracks that anyone could follow, night or day. He needed to go south, across a wide open field that abutted a distant, thickly forested swath of land. If he could reach the forest by nightfall, he could hide his tracks up against the tree boles; he could lose himself, if the forest were deep enough. More importantly, if the woods were thick, then he could lose Dumas, as well.

He squinted up into the sky and judged that it was well after noon. There was no time to lose. Squaring his shoulders, Tobyn made a bee-line for the sheltering forest.

He kept moving for what felt like hours, never looking back despite a nervous urge to watch for shadows. A trail appeared, going in the direction that he was headed, a trail as covered by snow as the rest of the valley. He chose to stay among the trees, hugging the bark as much as possible.

The sun was punishing, its heat contradicting the cold of the ice around him. The light made him squint, the heat made him want to melt. He could barely move; he was weak, too weak for this mad scramble. Unable to continue, he slumped against a giant oak and fought to catch his breath. Closing his eyes against the sunlight, knees turning to water, he slid down the tree to take an abrupt seat among its damp, white-covered roots.

Six

When he opened his eyes again, the sun was sitting very low in the western sky. A chill crept along his spine, and he scrambled to his feet. Too much time had been lost.

Clutching his stolen knife, Tobyn abandoned the tree that had sheltered his unconsciousness and ran south for all he was worth. In the darkness, he had energy; he didn't want to speculate on that just now. Rather, he took advantage of that fact, flying from the vampire who even now was floating muzzily toward wakefulness.

He ran until he could run no more; as he stopped to slow his racing heart, he could see the wide expanse of a farmer's field stretching endlessly just beyond the trees. Tobyn panted and fought down the urge to scream. Dumas would surely find him in that field! He would have to wait to cross it by daylight, for he certainly could not skirt its vastness in the dark. But that meant spending the night here in this forest, crouching under trees and waiting for Dumas to find him.

Perhaps, though, the trees would hide him well enough; perhaps the wind that had arisen to tug at the gypsy's hair could blow away the scent of his mortal blood. Perhaps that part of his soul that told him that Dumas had found the furniture blocking his door, the part that said Dumas was furious, was wrong.

Tobyn really wished he could believe that.

His only hope was to make himself invisible, and to stay alert. Silently mouthing half-remembered prayers, he burrowed under the snow-fringed bushes and held on to his weapon as if he were holding on to his life.

Dumas burst from his rooms with a roar of outrage, shattering both the desk and his doors to kindling. He did not need to look in the windowed room to know that Tobyn was gone. He could feel it in his heart, in the blood that boiled now in fury at his would-be lover's betrayal. Gnashing his teeth in his anger and thirst, Dumas stalked to the glass doors at the end of the corridor. With a careless jerk, he wrenched the doors open and went to the railing of the balcony beyond. He glared into the moonlight, gripping the worked marble, seeing the clearly-outlined marks of his mortal's escape.

His shout was loud and clear, physical and psychic. "TOBYN!"

In the forest, the gypsy heard the call and shuddered in fear, his fist closing spasmodically on the grip of the knife. He closed his eyes against the tears that flooded them. He was not ready to die.

But Dumas was coming, whether Tobyn was ready for him or not.

The wind spiraled through the treetops, howling above him like an angry demon, then fell ominously still. The snowy canopy of bushes shivered once, then shook more intensely as twigs rained down on them from a nearby tree. Tobyn rose onto his hands and knees, ready to defend himself.

His nerves shrieked with awareness of Dumas' presence, and the bushes were suddenly uprooted and tossed aside. Tobyn straightened as quickly as he could, his eyes frozen onto the sight of Dumas' face twisted with rage. The vampire seized him with rough hands, and Tobyn buried the knife to the hilt in Dumas' stomach.

The Frenchman hissed with pain, but his grip on Tobyn's shoulders did not slacken. "Bastard!" he growled, hauling his prey to his feet. "Damn you!"

With a shout, the gypsy pulled out the knife and stabbed again, this time striking him in the chest. He could hear a rib cracking beneath the impact of the blade, and the flash of fear on Dumas' face pleased him to no end.

Angered now beyond words, the vampire grabbed Tobyn's wrist and squeezed until he dropped the knife with a cry of pain. Dumas' other hand came into play, smashing into the side of the mortal's head, stunning him. The Frenchman gathered up the now-unresisting Tobyn and clutched him to his bloody front, holding him tightly as he rose into the air for the return flight to the *chateau*.

Reyes was just beginning to come back to himself as Dumas alit on the second floor balcony. The gypsy struggled bitterly as his captor dragged him down the corridor and into a different room, much smaller and less ornate than his usual cell. With a snarl, Dumas hurled him inside, unmindful of his extraordinary strength. Tobyn hit the far wall, his skull and spine taking the brunt of the collision, then slid down to the uncarpeted wooden floor where he lay, gasping.

The vampire stalked to his side and hauled him up by the collar, flinging him onto a narrow four-poster bed.

"Did you think you could escape me?" he hissed, furious. "After all I've given you, this is how you repay me!"

Tobyn was still too logy to answer. Taking advantage of the mortal's incapacity, Dumas tethered him, spread-eagle, using the cords from the bed curtains as restraints.

"Ungrateful child! Don't you realize what you've tried to throw away? Power! Immortality! I would have made you one of us, one of the Prime, my consort! Ignorant, foolish boy!"

Tobyn tugged at his bonds and replied by spitting into the *vicomte*'s face. Dumas flinched back, revolted, and wiped the spittle away with a trembling hand.

"Mortal," he snapped. "Filthy, heathen gypsy!"

Anger flared in response, hand-in-hand with bravado. "Monster!" Reyes fired back. "Parasite!"

Dumas' eyes went cold, and the ice was more dangerous by far than the heat of his rage. "What words from a lover."

"I am not your lover! I despise you!"

"And I you, little one." He rose and pressed his fingers to the now-healed wound on his stomach. "And yet I will have you. You are already of my blood. We are connected."

Tobyn shook his head sharply. "You're insane."

"Perhaps. But you will be mine."

"I'd rather die."

"That is your other option. Run again, and I assure you that you will get your wish." He took another step to the door, bowed in a mockery of courtliness, and left Tobyn locked into the silent, lightless room.

Still full of anger and fear, the gypsy howled curses after him until he could no longer speak.

In his own room, Dumas heard the aggrieved, wild shouting, but chose to ignore it. He stripped his ruined clothes away and washed the healed wounds of their blood stains. His fingers hesitated over the scar on his chest, gently probing it to feel the lingering pain. If Tobyn had known how close he'd come to freedom...only one more inch to the left...

A particularly virulent stream of abuse poured from Tobyn's cell, and Dumas smiled, amused in spite of himself. If he had wanted a companion to make life interesting, he had certainly chosen well. He would simply have to remember to keep knives away from him.

His thirst roared crazily, inspired by the weakness of his body and impatient for satisfaction. No doubt he would be dining in tonight. Dressing in new clothes, he headed to the pantry to select his evening meal.

In the sullen silence of his cell after his voice had been whittled down to less than a hiss, Tobyn concentrated on freeing his hands from their bonds. He could not reach his wrists with his teeth, and the knots were probably too tight, anyway. His only hope was that the silky material of the ropes could slip over his fists with a little encouragement.

He pulled and writhed until his shoulders ached and his skin was raw and bleeding. He fell back against the hard mattress, out of breath, and stared wide-eyed into the impenetrable darkness. If there was a window, he couldn't tell; either it was boarded up, or he'd been imprisoned in a closet. All he knew was that the black around him was total, deep and soft and cold. He felt like he was in a grave.

That thought made him shudder in quiet dread. He did not like to think of death; he was afraid to die. He had never quite decided what happened after life ended, and where a person's soul went when the body refused to hold it any longer. The Christian ideals had always fallen flat for him; Heaven and God and all of His churches had always been very far from the life that Tobyn knew. Beti's "magic" had also failed to convince him to believe. Perhaps there really was no afterlife, despite the angels, saints and ghosts he'd heard about for so long. Perhaps men had no souls, no matter how much an invisible force seemed to move hands and legs for him. Perhaps he'd end up living forever, Dumas' blood-sucking creation, and never learn the answers. Perhaps he'd find out sooner than he'd like.

And no matter how much he thought about it, he couldn't decide which "perhaps" was most appealing.

Dumas spent the quiet time after his feeding playing the harpsichord in his library. A bright fire on the hearth helped warm him, and as he played, he let his mind wander back to the subject of his mortal "guest." He had always known that Tobyn's love was a lie; why, then, was he so disappointed to learn that he was right? It was a mystery, and only one of the many that the handsome gypsy had brought into his life. Dumas would never know why he felt as he did for Tobyn, why he was willing to accept so much trouble when he could easily kill him and be done with it.

He had not lied when he'd said he hated Tobyn. He despised his duplicity, his guile, his thievery, his very mortality. The way his body reacted to Dumas' feeding, and to Matthieu, was shocking, disgustingly carnal. The Prime, his personal clan of vampires, had risen so far above the physical that they could not bear it any longer. It was so...human.

And yet, beside the hatred and its equal in power, Dumas loved Tobyn. He could happily spend all of eternity watching the firelight dance in his eyes, or the way his full lips moved when he spoke. The young man's perfect form reminded the vampire of the Greek gods, an Endymion come down just for him. He even loved the way the gypsy loathed him in return.

Making Tobyn an immortal would be both a favor to the world and his worst mistake. A favor, because the young man's beauty would not be lost. A mistake, because the two of them would drive one another to madness within a century, dancing their half-dance of love and hate, matching their steps but never quite connecting. It would be no way to spend eternity, but Dumas could not suffer himself to make a different choice.

With a sigh, he closed the harpsichord and returned to the second floor, boredom pulling at him as it always did. The silence from Tobyn's room was oddly unsettling, and after a moment's consideration, he unlocked the door and stepped inside, bringing a lamp from the corridor.

Reyes was slumbering uncomfortably, his limbs splayed at awkward angles and held securely by the curtain ties. Dumas could smell the blood from where the mortal's wrists were rubbed raw, and he gently inspected the wounds, trying not to wake him. The gypsy was a light sleeper tonight, though, and he jerked to consciousness with a gasp of surprise and fear.

"Shh," the Frenchman soothed, petting his hair. "It's only me."

Tobyn blinked in the light from the lamp, then asked in a voice almost painful in its scratchiness, "What do you want?"

"I wanted to check in on you, to see if you were well."

"To see if I was still here, you mean."

The vampire smiled. "That, too." Tobyn looked away in disgust, and he continued. "I see that you failed to escape the ropes."

"Does that amuse you?"

"Vastly."

"Bastard."

With a laugh, Dumas kissed the gypsy's forehead. When he pulled back, he saw Tobyn staring at him. "What's wrong, my love?"

"Early this evening, you tried to smash my brains out on the wall. Now you're kissing me."

He shrugged. "As they say, I am mercurial."

"You're mad."

"Perhaps. And perhaps someday we shall be mad together."

Tobyn set his jaw and stared at the foot of the bed. "That will probably happen tomorrow if you don't put some damned light in here soon."

"You're never happy," Dumas said with a theatrical sigh. "Always complaining. Get used to the darkness, my darling. It's where you will spend the rest of your life."

～✣✦✣～

The next sunset found Dumas fully recovered from his wounds and determined to bring Tobyn, kicking and screaming, into immortality. He was still uncertain why the first attempt had failed; perhaps the mortal had spoken truth when he'd said that gypsies were something more than human. Even if Tobyn were enchanted, Dumas was sure, he would eventually succumb to the effects of the blood transfer. There was no power greater than that of a vampire.

He brought a single lighted candle into the locked room where Tobyn lay, drifting in half-sleep. Apparently, he had spent the daylight hours attempting to escape. One slender wrist, ragged and rope-burned, was free of its bonds. Dumas wondered briefly why Tobyn had not brought his suddenly-useful hand to bear against the other knots; only the mortal could answer that. For safety's sake, the Frenchman decided to keep his distance for the moment.

Resting the candlestick on the sill of the bricked-up window at the foot of the bed, Dumas silently probed at his prisoner, nudging him into wakefulness. Tobyn started, his eyes snapping open to stare blearily at the vampire at his side.

"Good evening," the Frenchman greeted. "You had an eventful day, I see."

Reyes ran his liberated fingers through the unholy tangle that was his hair, then dropped his arm down onto his stomach. He offered no conversation.

"You look a bit pale, my love. Is there anything I can do for you?"

This time, the gypsy made a show of ignoring him, sliding his arm underneath his pillow in a casual posture that would have been convincing if the ropes on his other limbs weren't so obvious.

Dumas laughed quietly to himself, amused by his mortal's bullheaded behavior. "You're so obstinate," he commented, abandoning his self-defensiveness and strolling closer. He sat beside the youth and gently grasped his elbow. "Come on, now, Tobyn. Give me your wrist."

"Why?"

"It speaks!" Smiling, he replied, "So that I might secure it again."

Reyes shrugged and gestured with the benumbed fingers of his tethered right hand. "I don't think you need to. I'm not going anywhere."

Dumas turned to rearrange the silken rope for Tobyn's free arm. "I want to be sure of that."

The gypsy moved suddenly, almost too quickly for a mortal, and a metallic glint was the only warning that the vampire had. A blade crashed into his back, just shy of his spine. Dumas roared in pain and fury, twisting to grab at the youth who was trying to hack through his bonds. The vampire easily wrestled him down, disarming him and delivering a slap to the face that nearly broke Tobyn's neck. Behind him, Dumas heard the wardrobe door burst open, and Rachel, the heretofore timid maidservant, clattered desperately for the door.

The vampire was upon her in an instant, wrenching her arm painfully behind her back, dragging her closer to the gypsy.

"What is this? An accomplice?" he demanded, forcing the whimpering girl to her knees. "She gave you that knife to help you escape!" Betrayed and enraged, he accused, "You have soft feelings for her, perhaps? You prefer her to me? I can kill her here!"

"Go ahead!" Tobyn snapped back. "She's nothing to me. But if you think that killing her in front of me will make me want to stay with you, then you really are a fool."

Dumas snarled and hurled Rachel aside, smashing her into the wall with a sickening thud. He seized Tobyn's throat with both hands, squeezing, choking off his air supply. "Never insult my intellect, you filthy child! I will take no more abuse from you! Do you think I offer the Gift to everyone? It is an honor you have forsaken, ungrateful wretch!" He tightened his fingers, enjoying the panic and the pain that danced in Tobyn's features as he gasped vainly for breath. "I would have made you a king. Now I will make you a corpse!"

The constricting hands were gone, then, and Tobyn managed to draw one breath into his burning lungs before a new agony shot through him.

Dumas had pierced him once again, terrible fangs sunken deep into his neck. The vampire pulled his life avidly, feeding to deplete, feeding to cause pain. Horror sang its screeching aria in the gypsy's brain, counterpointed by a strange calm certainty that emanated from the ice wrapped around his soul. Death was coming for him, and he welcomed the silent darkness that approached him swiftly as a storm.

The vampire broke away just in time, his lips stained with the carelessness of his angry attack. He would not let Tobyn die, not when he wanted him here, not when it was so clear that death was all that the gypsy wanted. Slashing his wrist with his own teeth, Dumas released the blood that throbbed in his veins. He forced the pale, sweat-sheened youth to open his mouth, and then the river of life eddied in to entrance Tobyn's tongue.

This time, Reyes accepted the Gift eagerly, voraciously, without a hint of inward struggle. The vampire felt the delicious heat of his lover's mouth against his skin, and he moaned in pleasure. Their heartbeats merged as one, their thoughts dovetailed into a seamless whole. Dumas could feel nothing from Tobyn but the need for blood, the raging thirst that the vampire's power quenched. There was no consciousness in Tobyn, no thinking, nothing but the madness of feeding. Dumas' spirit convulsed, and power mingled with the blood that coursed down Tobyn's throat, forging a glowing bond that connected them, heart to heart.

Weakness filled Dumas now, and he pulled away from Tobyn, who was hunched over his wrist like a wild beast, greedily seeking more. For a moment, Tobyn was stronger, holding the Frenchman to him; with a frantic tug, he freed himself from Reyes' hold. Tobyn fell back, gasping, eyes wide and staring in the candlelight as Dumas wrapped his wound with a handkerchief. The transfer was complete.

Pain from his back and the dreadful smell of death from Rachel called Dumas' attention away, and he gathered up the servant's body like a rag doll. One last glance at Tobyn showed an odd stillness on the gypsy's face, and then the Frenchman spared no more time before returning to his private rooms for badly-needed rest.

Tobyn heard the door close and lock, and a single tear trailed down his face, glittering in the light from the taper Dumas had left behind. He could feel the acid-like heat of the vampire's blood twisting in his stomach, seeping through him, permeating every inch of his body. The coldness was almost total, now, and he felt imprisoned in a tiny corner of his soul, shivering and surrounded and desperately trying to stave off the encroaching alien-ness that had taken over his limbs.

Was he Changing? He could only feel the creeping ice, could only feel the fear that throbbed within him. Another hot tear left its glistening trail on his cheek, and a wave of nausea and vertigo swept over him. He shuddered and moaned in his misery.

"Oh, God," he whispered, not really expecting a reply. "Oh, God, please help me."

His mouth felt dry, his tongue swollen; he tried to moisten his lips and failed. He could see shapes dancing through the darkness, hideous faces that leered in the corners, and a shiver of terror raced through him. Tobyn closed his eyes tightly and tried to find a new way to pray for mercy, but his mind was whirling out of control, and all he could see was Rachel flying into the wall to die. He was sorry for that, very sorry; she had tried to help him. But a part of him dismissed her as a brainless girl whose stupidity had earned her doom. She could have helped him during daylight instead of dusk; she could have stayed hidden until Dumas was gone. Her death was not on his hands. She had been nothing to him.

Still, he was very sorry that she had died.

Another shudder shook his arms and legs, and the ice crept a little closer to his corner-fortress. In desperation, he grasped his end of the twin-link like a life line, leaning on the solid warmth and humanity that flowed to him from Araminah. Her being, her comfort held the ice at bay, and he "sent" her a rush of gratitude and love. She returned the emotions, tinged with confusion, and he clung to the bright cord between them as he slipped away into dreamless sleep.

Seven

At some point during the indistinguishable blackness of empty days and nights, Tobyn was awakened by a clattering of footsteps in the corridor outside his room. He sat up as much as he could with his right arm still bound, the knot resistant to his every effort to untie it. Straining his ears, he could make out the sound of gruff voices chattering in city-gutter Spanish, with the silken tones of Dumas' French lilting about it in counterpoint.

Well, then, he thought. *It must be night time, and we have visitors.*

We? Since when did he start thinking of himself and Dumas as a unit?

He was saved from the unpleasantness of that question by the sound of a key in the lock. Preparing himself for company, he settled back down and watched the door open.

Two shadows appeared against the painful and unaccustomed intrusion of light from the hall, and he heard Dumas saying, "The first transfer failed, but I believe that now the change is complete. Forgive the bonds, but he is quite unmanageable."

Doña Isabella's warm contralto responded, "Has he been confined the entire time?"

"In one way or another, yes," Dumas told his fellow vampire. "He was—my God!"

Tobyn squinted into the light from the candles they carried, keeping his silence. He knew why his captor was shocked.

"The transfer failed," Doña Isabella whispered. Dumas faltered, but the Spanish vampire stepped closer, her beautiful face a study in contemplation. She sat lightly beside the gypsy, dark eyes scanning his features. In her own language, she breathed, "You are an amazement."

Behind her, Dumas had recovered at least a semblance of aplomb. "My lady, I cannot explain this. This is impossible!"

Isabella clicked her tongue. "Nothing is impossible, Michel, especially when it is sitting before you." Her tone took on a scientific air as she touched Tobyn's cheek and asked, "How do you feel, *gitano mio*?"

"Cramped," he answered truthfully. "Untie me."

"Why hasn't he Changed?" Dumas asked, hushed. "Why is he still mortal?"

The woman rose and smoothed her midnight-colored skirts. "I don't know," she answered thoughtfully. "It could be that his power rivals yours, or that it is impossible to make a gypsy vampire."

Tobyn cleared his throat, trying to ignore the thirst that ached in him. He would do almost anything for a little water. "I've told you before," he rasped. "The Rom aren't like ordinary people. We're different. You're wasting your time with me."

The Frenchman's face darkened with a fierce glower. "That cannot be."

"There may be no other explanation," Isabella mused. "But we will talk more on this elsewhere, Michel. You should untie him now."

Dumas stared at her in open confusion. "What? He cannot be trusted if—"

"He can't get through a locked door and bricked windows," she cajoled gently. "Besides, he's mangling himself on the ropes. You want him undamaged, don't you?"

The Frenchman hesitated, then freed Tobyn's arm and legs. The gypsy changed position immediately, alleviating the pressure in his aching joints. Dumas stared at him as Reyes tried to massage some feeling back into his booted feet.

"I do not understand."

Isabella smiled like a Madonna at the other vampire's whisper. "Come, then. Perhaps we can puzzle out an answer together."

Looping an arm around Dumas' elbow, she led him away, taking the candles out with her. At the door, she turned to gaze silently into Tobyn's face, looking very much as though there were something she wanted to say. The door closed on her silence.

In darkness once again, Reyes rose to pace away some of his numbness, giving thanks once more for Beti's blessing. There had been an uncomfortable time after his second taste of Dumas' blood when he'd feared that his grandmother's spell had failed; now, though, still firmly entrenched in his precious mortality, he felt stronger. A long night, or possibly a long day, spent clutching his link with Ara had melted some of the ice inside his soul, and he was much more certain of himself. He had come very close to losing his grasp on what he was, and that had given Dumas power over him. Now, however, he had his identity in a list, and he chanted it to himself like a mantra. He was Romany; he was a Reyes; he was son to Chavo, oldest heir; he was brother to Araminah. He was her twin, her friend, and her lover. He was Rom, he was Reyes...

This litany of self may not have given him magical protection, but it kept him grounded, and repeating it helped to fill his time.

❧❧❧

Isabella sat beside Dumas on the divan in the library, taking his hand in her own. He was one of her oldest friends in her vampire existence, and she disliked seeing him in such distress. He obviously loved his gypsy prisoner, and wanted him desperately. She did not doubt the strength of his emotions, but she also could not deny the blinding effect they had on him. For as long as Dumas so single-mindedly pursued the goal of bringing Tobyn into their night world, he would not see the stumbling blocks that barred his way.

She, however, had no such misapprehensions.

"You still love him," she told Dumas. "That is plain to see. But, tell me...what does he feel for you?"

"Not love," he admitted. "I wish he did, but he seems to run between mild interest and hatred."

Isabella sat back. "If he hates you, then why do you want to keep him beside you?"

"He will learn at least to tolerate me," the Frenchman said firmly. "And a measure of animosity is essential to maintain intrigue in a relationship."

"You don't want a lover so much as a debating partner," she observed. "I fear that you will get neither in your gypsy. The two of you will only hate one another more each year, driving each other mad in time. Is that what you want?"

He stubbornly clung to his first ideal. "I want Tobyn to be completely mine, Isabella. I don't care what it takes."

"He will never be completely yours, Michel! If two transfers have failed, then—"

"Then a third will succeed. The last one almost worked. If he takes only a little more..."

"Oh, *cariño*," she sighed. "It is not meant to be. He will not Change, and you will be forced to watch him age and die like all other mortals."

"I don't believe that. He is too beautiful to be lost that way."

"It will happen." She caught his eyes with her earnest gaze. "You can never own a gypsy. You cannot chain him like a pet. Captivity will break his spirit and his mind, and the beauty you so love will follow. Don't you see the way he is even now? Pale and thin, barely a hint of what he was before. Your love is killing him by holding on too tightly."

Dumas' gray eyes glinted like polished steel. "You're asking me to give him up, aren't you?"

She took a deep breath, refusing to be cowed by the older vampire's growing anger. "Yes."

"You presume too much upon our friendship," he rumbled warningly.

"Not at all. Don't you see? This Tobyn has become an obsession for you, and you are wounding yourself with it. I do not like to see you unhappy."

The Frenchman pulled free of her grasp, standing to pace the room. "I will decide how best to fulfill my needs, Isabella. I do not require your assistance."

She sighed and sat back. "Of course. Forgive me, my friend. I do not mean to impose."

Dumas stood by the hearth and studied the flames, then said, "If you must meddle, then help me find a way to bring him into our life. That is all I ask."

The night wore on in silence until Dumas excused himself from his guest with courtly manners. "I fear I must attend to manorial business, Isabella," he said, rising from his seat by the library fire. "If you require anything, merely alert the servants in the stable. The pantry is full if you have thirst."

She smiled graciously. "I have already supped this evening, Michel, but I thank you for your hospitality." Holding up a book she had taken from a nearby shelf, she said, "I have this to occupy my time until you return."

Not yet over his anger with her, Dumas nodded curtly. "Excellent. I shall return before dawn."

Isabella watched him go, regretful of his anger and the slow waning of their friendship. After tonight, she was certain that the *vicomte* would be more than happy to be rid of her. Beyond the window, she could see the Frenchman swing up into the saddle of his best horse. He took one last look toward the *chateau* before spurring his mount toward the village.

She waited until he was well away before she rose and left her seat, deserting her book in favor of the gypsy in the locked room at the head of the stairs. The Romany clans of Spain had long been an interest of hers, and she had spent many years trailing the caravans through the countryside. Isabella had at one time been something of a collector of gypsies, keeping her beloved specimens in special rooms in her *hacienda*. Her warnings to Dumas came from personal experience. Without exception, every one of her beautiful *gitanos* had been lost to madness, suicide, or a simple will to die. She had learned not to wrap gypsies in chains, even if those shackles were allegorical, and she would not allow the same fate to come to Tobyn.

As quietly as she could, she slid the bolt aside and opened the door. Bearing a lamp from the hallway, she stepped into the stillness of the room.

Tobyn's voice startled her in spite of herself. "Where is Dumas?"

"Overseeing his estate, I believe," she replied. She put the lamp down onto the bureau and watched the Rom step slowly, gracefully from the shadows by the useless window. His pale face gleamed in the soft light, offset by the black clothes the *vicomte* had given him, and for a moment he looked so like one of her kind that she wondered if the Change had come during her talk with Dumas. "Are you more comfortable now?"

He answered her question with a pugnacious one of his own. "Why do you care?"

Isabella shrugged. "Because I do."

"That's no reason." He stepped closer, the heels of his boots clicking quietly against the floor. "To what do I owe the honor of this visit?"

"I have questions to ask you," she told him, sitting on the rumpled bed. Looking up into his cool eyes, she asked, "Can I trust you to answer them honestly?"

"Trust is earned."

"Fair enough. But so too is distrust. Have I earned that?"

He leaned against the wall, arms crossed over his chest, and raised one slender eyebrow. "What do you think?"

She considered this for a moment, then decided to let it go. "Tell me, Tobyn, what do you feel for Dumas?"

"He disgusts me."

"Have you any love for him at all?"

This time, he hesitated before responding. "No."

"I see. And what do you think of vampire immortality?"

"It's unclean and revolting."

She smiled at the stubborn firmness in his voice. "You don't want it?"

"I'd rather die."

She rose and came closer to him, studying the pleasing angles of his face, aware that he was as attracted to her as she was to him. "Would you take it from me?"

He looked her in the eyes and smirked. Giving a little shake of his dark head, he answered, "No."

Isabella cupped his cheek with her small hand and took a gentle kiss from his lips. Tobyn, never one to object to the amorous attentions of lovely women, returned the caress immediately. She pulled back with a chuckle.

"Oh, you gypsies."

He grinned. "You vampires."

The Spanish woman drifted away from him, pushing down the blood-lust the kiss had aroused. "How has your sanity been during your time here?"

Tobyn shrugged. "It comes and goes."

"Where is it now?"

"It's as 'here' as it ever was."

"You react differently to me than to Michel. Why? Do you like me?"

Her question was worded with naïveté, but Reyes was not fooled. "I wouldn't say that I like you. Better to say that I dislike you less than Dumas."

"Why?"

"You've never really hurt me," he replied pensively, his moment of levity over. "Dumas has."

"He's hurt you?"

Tobyn nodded gravely. "In many ways. He has a lot to atone for."

"I see."

He smiled again, watching her as she walked. "It doesn't hurt matters any that you're a woman."

Isabella pursed her lips flirtatiously. "You don't like men the way Michel does, then?"

"I'm not entirely certain," he admitted. "I only know that I don't like him at all."

She faced him solemnly, dark eyes full of shadows. "Do you want to leave this place?"

Suddenly suspicious, Tobyn narrowed his eyes and asked, "Why are you asking this? Are you doing this for him?"

"I'm doing this for you, *querido*. I do not want to see you suffer any longer."

He stepped toward her, stopping just short of grasping her white hand. "Then help me get away," he urged, eyes searching her face. "Please...I'll bargain with you. I'll give you—"

She silenced him with a finger to his lips. "I will take nothing away from you, Tobyn. I want to help you to escape. You can help me atone for my own sins this way." She grasped his fingers and pulled him toward the door. "There is little time. My coach can be prepared within moments, and we can get away from Dumas. I will take you back to Spain with me, and we will find your caravan."

Tobyn followed her into the corridor and watched in disbelief as she rousted her servants from their beds. Isabella sent them scurrying to pack her things and ready her team, then returned to the gypsy's side.

"Why are you doing this?" he whispered.

She kissed him once again, then smilingly replied, "Because I am in love with gypsies." A servant brought him a woolen cloak, and Isabella draped it over his shoulders. "Come on, then. It's time to go."

He followed her down the stairs. "He'll come after us."

She opened the main door of the *chateau*. "I know. But I will protect you." Stepping aside so he could leave the building, she added, "We will go so quickly and by such frequently traveled roads that he will never be able to find us. One mortal is difficult to find in a crowd of hundreds."

The coach rumbled up to the door, and Isabella urged him into the cab. With the barest of hesitations, wondering if he was getting himself into more trouble than he could handle, Tobyn stepped inside.

"Where in Spain are we going to?" he asked as she settled beside him with a rustling of skirts.

"Anywhere you would like to go."

He thought back to the shadows of the life he'd almost lost, finally coming up with a proper destination. "Seville," he told her. "I have to go to Seville."

She rested a fond hand on his slim knee and smiled. "Then that is where we'll go." The coach lurched into motion, speeding recklessly into the night, and Tobyn tensed beneath her touch. "Relax, *querido*," she advised. "You are free, now."

Peering through the window at the dark sky, he muttered in reply, "I'll believe that when the sun comes out."

They drove at breakneck speed until a thin band of pink appeared on the horizon. Isabella tapped against the driver's back board, then settled back against the plush cushions of her seat. Tobyn studied her quietly, holding the silence he'd observed since leaving Dumas' grounds.

With eyes closed in creeping weariness, the Spanish vampire said, "I can tell that you want to ask me something."

"Well...yes. What will happen to you at daybreak?" He canted his head, peering at her. "Do you...do you die?"

She glanced at him for a heartbeat, then replied, "In a way, yes. Vampires, as you know, are dead already; or, if you like, undead. We cannot live in the sunlight, so—"

"Why?"

"You're full of questions," Isabella teased. "Sunlight destroys us."

"How?"

"I don't know. I've never done it." She shifted in her seat. "At any rate, each morning at sunrise, we must find a dark shelter away from daylight. We do not die, although we appear to. Rather, we sleep...very, very deeply."

He hesitated. "Does it hurt?"

"No."

Tobyn looked out the window at the lightening skies. "Where will you sleep today?"

Isabella smiled. "I will be safe, *cariño*. Do not fear for me. My men, Serrano and Juarez, will act as your servants today. They will take you to an inn to spend the daylight hours in peace and safety while I go elsewhere. I will return for you at dusk."

The gypsy licked his lips, then asked, "How will I pay the innkeeper? This village doesn't take very well to gypsies."

A small bag of coins passed from her hands to Reyes'. "That is good French money," she said, her voice quiet and lazy with fatigue. "It is enough to have them treat you like visiting royalty. In the clothes you're wearing, and with a comb taken to your hair, you'll certainly look like a prince." She smiled, offering him the comb he needed. "Speak Spanish, if you know it, and use my name. Say you are my brother, Don Tomas Oñate de las Cruces, and they will treat you elegantly. I am well-known here."

He wrestled the comb through his mangled curls, allowing Isabella to help him achieve the proper rich-Spaniard look. She adjusted his clothing for him, taking a jeweled brooch from her breast and adding it to the ruffled cravat at his throat. As the coach slowed to a halt, she gently kissed his cheek.

"Mama is proud of you, Tomas," she joked softly. "I have such a handsome brother."

He grinned at her as one of the servants opened the door at his side. "*Naturalmente, mi estimada hermana,*" he replied.

Serrano and Juarez closed the door to the carriage as soon as he was out, locking it and pulling thick wooden screens over the windows. Juarez, a stocky man with a pockmarked face, gathered up a heavy trunk from the ground and led the way to the inn's open door. Serrano bowed low to Tobyn, one corner of his mouth turning up in amusement. Reyes nodded with affected hauteur, well fortified by his natural attitude of Rom superiority, then followed Juarez into the welcoming warmth.

The innkeeper met them at the threshold, wiping his hands on the apron tied about his thick middle. He bowed quickly, speaking in a steady stream of obeisances. "Greetings, my lord. Welcome to my inn. I am honored by your presence here."

Tobyn nodded to him, mimicking every haughty gadjo he'd ever seen. "Thank you, *m'sieur*." Serrano took the cloak from the gypsy's shoulders and Reyes added, "My sister highly recommends your establishment."

The innkeeper bobbed again. "*Merci*. Your sister, sir?"

"The Doña Isabella. I am Don Tomas Oñate de las Cruces."

Tobyn smiled in genuine amusement as his words sent the Frenchman into another round of frenetic bowing and scraping. "Of course, *monsieur*. Your sister is a beautiful lady, and our greatest patroness. Please, sit by the fire and warm yourself. The night was cold for traveling! Is there anything you would like, Don Tomas?"

Serrano took the reins. "Don Tomas will require a private room, a hot meal, and your finest wine. Do not trouble my lord with the arrangements. I will handle all transactions."

"Of course, of course," the innkeeper responded to the symbolic rattle of coins in a leather pouch.

"Immediately, *monsieur*," Serrano urged archly.

Tobyn allowed himself to be led regally to the finest table, sitting near the hearth to feel the heat. Serrano took a chair across from him, watching in quiet mirth as his gypsy charge dismissed the fawning peasant. Juarez hauled the trunk up to the second floor, led by an attractive young maid.

"Well," Serrano said, "I'm sure that we won't be seeing those two for a while. Juarez is a weak man when it comes to beautiful women."

"Like Isabella?"

"Doña Isabella."

"Whatever." He leaned back in his seat. "What's in the trunk?"

"Clothes and belongings. Doña Isabella's things. She thought it best if you had luggage, if only for appearances."

"I see."

The innkeeper returned with plates of steaming food, serving his distinguished guests himself. "If there is anything else—"

"I will call for you," Tobyn said, waving one hand in a noncommittal but regal gesture.

"Of course, of course."

They waited for the man to leave them before resuming their conversation, speaking softly in Spanish. Serrano commented, "You're very good at this business of aristocracy. Or perhaps it's the business of lying."

Tobyn shrugged, concentrating most of his attention of the food before him. "Well, you know what I am, sort of."

"I suppose that you're going to claim to be King of the Gypsies."

"Not at all. God forbid! Rom aristocracy, maybe, but there's no such thing as a gypsy king." He grinned slyly. "Lying, though? I'm very good at that. I've pretended to be a lot of things over the years, and I've never been caught."

Serrano smirked. "Boastful pup, aren't you?"

"And a curious one, too." He fastened a frank gaze on the Spaniard's face. "Why are you with Doña Isabella, if you know what she is?"

The older man sighed thoughtfully. "I think you believe that all of her kind are alike."

"Of course. It's like a clan, isn't it?"

"I suppose. But even clans allow for variation. Doña Isabella is a merciful woman, unlike the Frenchman we stole you from. Dumas is a creature of cruel excess, but my lady is fair. She does not kill. She takes no victims, only willing donors." He shifted his position, making himself comfortable. "As for my service to her, I am continuing a family tradition. For five generations, the Serrano men have been Doña Isabella's retainers and protectors. We are well-paid for our efforts, and kept comfortably into old age. When I am gone, my son will take my place."

Tobyn swallowed some wine, nodding slightly. "I see. Then she is very old?"

"Over three hundred years in this life, I believe. But that is young among her kind."

"Are there many vampires?"

"I don't know. I imagine so. She has many immortal friends throughout France and Spain, and I know of at least one in England. The rest of the world, I am sure, has its own number."

A rough-edged woodsman stalked into the inn, stomping snow from his boots and heading straight for the fire. In a booming voice, he shouted for the innkeeper. "Luc! Luc, for God's sake, get me something hot to drink!"

Serrano sighed. "*Monsieur*, I must ask you to be considerate of other guests. My lord—"

"Spaniard," the man spat.

"Marcel, please!" Luc said earnestly, pressing a mug into his friend's hands. "Don Tomas is very important. Don't bother him."

"Bah! I'll bother who I want to on a wretched day like this one."

"Wretched?" Tobyn asked. "The sun is bright, *monsieur*. The day is beautiful."

Marcel snorted. "Not when you see what I seen coming this way."

"And what is that?" Serrano asked.

The woodsman sneered in open hatred. "Gypsies."

Tobyn's heart skipped a beat, but he kept his face expressionless. "Indeed."

"Bloody thievin' bastards," Marcel opined. "We don't need their kind. Looks like they're headed in your country's direction, Spanish," he told Serrano. "Well, you can keep 'em. We don't need their kind here."

"Nor do we, *monsieur*," the servant told him in a smooth voice.

"What we should do is like the old days," the woodsman mused. "Gypsy hunts. Kill the bucks and take their women for the whores they are. We'd have to burn the witches, of course."

Tobyn rose from his table, face covered with a fierce glare. Hatred danced like fire in his eyes. "Barbarian!"

Serrano grasped his wrist and said warningly, "Don Tomas, do not upset yourself for his like."

Marcel had turned to face the enraged youth. "What's this, your lordship? Are you a gyp-lover?"

"Don Tomas," the Spaniard repeated.

Tobyn shook off Serrano's hand and drew himself up straight. "You disgust me," he told the woodsman icily. "Innkeeper, my room. Now."

"Of course, my lord. Of course. Right this way."

Reyes was not through with Marcel. Before following Luc up the stairs, he growled at the woodsman, "May you have ten-fold pain for every pain you give!"

"My lord, please!" Serrano interjected, nearly frantic. "Your room is waiting."

"Yes, my lord," the innkeeper supplied. "This way."

After sealing his curse by spitting at the man's boots, Tobyn turned his back on Marcel and followed Luc up to the second floor, a relieved Serrano in his wake.

Once Juarez and his companion were wrested out of his room, Tobyn spent the day in solitude, alternately sleeping and plotting horrible fates for Marcel and all of his ilk. From time to time, he went to the window to watch for the arrival of a caravan. He felt torn by his need to see his sister among the gypsies the woodsman had spoken of and his desire to recenter himself before they met again. As he was now, he could never rejoin his *kumpania*; dressed as a *gadjo* nobleman and starting at shadows, he would offer too many reasons to be expelled as a fallen Rom. And if they ever learned of his time with Dumas, or about Matthieu, or the blood he had swallowed, his *kumpania* would shun him completely. Certain things went beyond unclean and straight through to untouchable.

He would have to think up a plausible story to explain away his absence and his clothes once he met with his people again. It had been common knowledge that he had been setting out to get a horse; he could certainly tell them he had gotten caught and imprisoned. As for the clothes, well, they were all a tool in his plan to rescue his father and uncle.

Ara would know the truth, as, most likely, would Beti. His uncle Tito would know nothing but assume that Tobyn was lying. That left the Morenos to convince. Nikolas would be an easy job, since the Lump, as Tobyn had named him without any affection whatsoever, barely had the brain power to think two complete thoughts on the same day. Manuo would be harder to win over. The old man was smart, and he had a strong dislike for the Reyes men, coupled with an unfortunate taste for the Reyes women. Bringing old man Moreno into line would take some truly fancy dancing.

After what Tobyn had been through, though, he doubted that any of his *kumpania* could give him problems he could not handle.

Isabella woke him after dusk with a gentle touch on his cheek and a spoken, "Tobyn."

He opened his eyes and blinked at her for a moment before he remembered where he was. Alarm spread into his consciousness, and he turned to look out the window at the blackness of the night.

"Dumas—"

She smiled soothingly and stroked his back. "He will not find you. Come, we must go. We have many miles to travel tonight."

He slid from the bed and tried to make wakefulness permeate his legs. Serrano and Juarez were gathering together the lady's trunk and the traveling food they had obtained for Tobyn from the innkeeper. Isabella took the gypsy's hand and led him down to the waiting equipage in the yard.

"Serrano told me about the scene you made with the woodsman," she said, amusement coloring her voice. "Spanish royalty doesn't spit."

He blushed. "I lost my temper."

"I quite understand. His sort is a superfluity to the rest of the population." They climbed into the coach, closing the door behind them. She turned to him as Juarez thumped and rattled the trunk into place over their heads. "I will not suffer your people to be hunted like animals, *cariño*. I swear it."

"Thank you. On the whole, though, we can take care of ourselves."

She smirked at his Romany pride. "It's just when you're alone that you get into trouble."

Her mild teasing kept the sting from the words. "Or when you do stupid things," he agreed, "or when you're a Reyes." He grinned. "Sometimes there's not a lot of difference."

ᔔᕼᕤᕮ

As they rode southward into Spain, Tobyn found himself almost forgetting what Isabella was in the face of who she was. While he still did not forgive her for her part in Dumas' dinner party, he could scarcely hold such things against her in light of all she'd done for him since then. She made no overtures to him, and, unlike with Dumas, he did not feel like a bird in a snare watched by a cat. He could not sense that she wanted anything from him, and that freedom from expectation was a blessed relief.

They rode in comfortable silence for nearly an hour, her hand on his, before he spoke. "Can I ask you something?"

"Of course."

"What is the Prime?"

Isabella hesitated, pulling away from him. Unease was clearly written on her face. Finally, she asked, "Where did you hear that word?"

"Dumas, when he was babbling." Intrigued by her sudden tension, he studied her. "Am I not supposed to know of it?"

She laughed softly, possibly at the situation, possibly at herself. "I don't think it matters, now. The Prime is our group, of which Dumas is the leader."

"A group of vampires?"

"One of them, yes."

"You don't all stick together?"

The Spanish lady smiled at his confused expression. "That would be as impossible as uniting all mortals under one government. People are people, whether they are immortal or not." She took his hand once more, continuing, "There are two groups of vampire, the Prime and the Brethren. They differ only politically. The Prime is by far the larger group, and Dumas is its prince."

"But who—"

He was silenced by a sudden kiss that startled him. Isabella pulled away slowly, her fingertips trailing over his smooth cheek. "Hush, now," she commanded in a whisper. "You talk too much."

Tobyn smiled a trifle sheepishly. "I've got—"

"—An inquisitive mind that will get you into trouble one day," she finished for him, wrapping her arms around his neck and shifting to face him more easily. "Let this one go, love. There are some things that mortals aren't meant to know."

Their eyes met as she moved closer, and the gleam of desire-laced fear in the gypsy's eyes made her pause. She brought one hand to his chest, feeling the thudding of his heart beneath her palm, still looking deeply into him. Tobyn, on the verge of panic, tried to move away from her touch but was held fast by the immortal's arm behind his neck. Blanching, he trembled.

"Don't be afraid," she soothed, shaking her head. "I won't hurt you."

His voice sounded strangled. "That's what Dumas said." He licked his lips, profoundly unsettled by her stare. "P-please, lady...let me go, I—don't do this..."

"Shh." She edged closer, her face softening in a kindly smile. "What are you afraid of, eh?"

With a groan, he tried to shove her away, his mortal strength insignificant against her. Isabella caught one of his wrists and held it firmly, but not to hurt.

"Tobyn, hush. It's all right. I'm not going to take you." She smiled again, as gently as she could; he could see the tiny points of her waiting teeth against her lip. "I only want to touch you."

He shuddered violently at the heat in her tone, the bald passion in her dark eyes somehow resurrecting memories, still so fresh, of Matthieu. Struggling with all of his strength, he cried, "Let me go!"

With an astonished expression, Isabella released him abruptly, watching as he plastered himself against the far side of the coach. She had meant no harm! Surely he could see that.

"Tobyn?"

Reyes ran a quaking hand over his face, forcing himself back under control with some difficulty. How could he have begun to trust this woman? Vampires were vampires, first and last, and all of them were rapacious. More than ever, he wished he were with his sister again.

Isabella spoke again, plainly, all traces of seduction and lust gone from her voice. "Tobyn, are you all right?" She resisted the urge to take his hand, so small and pale against his chest. "What's happened to you?"

"I'm fine," he lied badly, making his arms and legs assume a more casual position disproved by the tension in his spine. "I'm just fine."

She wished she could believe him. "I only want to make love to you."

He laughed harshly, and Isabella felt as if she'd been slapped in the face. "By force?" he demanded in acid-laced tones. "That isn't love. All you wanted was blood."

"No! Not at all. I told you, I don't want to hurt you. And I'd never force you," she said earnestly. "Please believe me, I never thought you'd object so strongly. Perhaps I was misled by the kisses."

Tobyn relaxed marginally, but stayed on his distant corner of the coach bench. Not looking at her, he whispered, "Whatever…"

Isabella sighed, relieved that the stand-off was ending. "I apologize for frightening you. There are times when desire is very difficult to control." Studying his profile, she added, "If you like, I'll not touch you again."

The answer he gave was not what she had hoped to hear. "Thank you. I'd like that very much."

As the vampire wrestled down her lusts in disappointment, Tobyn turned to stare out the window beside him, watching the night rush past. His heart was gradually slowing down to a reasonable speed, and the palms that had been clammy with cold sweat were beginning to dry. His mind dulled with memories and he wondered if he'd see Matthieu's face in every intimate moment for the rest of his life. A shudder passed through him at the prospect. With luck, he hoped, and in time, he would forget. The wounds were still too new; he could still feel the bruises.

In the meantime, he was at the mercy of the beautiful *gadja* vampire at his side. If she wanted to, he knew, she could put him back in Dumas' clutches, or plunge him into a new kind of hell as soon as he displeased her. *Mind your manners, boy,* he told himself, *and you still might get out of this alive…oh, Ara, I miss you!*

With the goal of staying on Isabella's good side, and taking the risk of starting the whole scene again, Tobyn forced himself to reach out and take the vampire's hand.

Eight

Ara left the wagon as sunrise gave way to full morning. Not too surprisingly, Nikolas was waiting for her beyond the door. Suppressing a sigh, she nodded to him and let him take her hand.

"Good morning, darling," he greeted, bright-eyed. "You're beautiful today."

She pulled her hand back. "You say that every day, Nik."

"It's true every day." His grin widened somehow. "You called me Nik! I like it when you do that."

Araminah was spared the necessity of replying by the appearance of Manuo and old man Carago. The two *kumpania* elders broke off their discussion when they saw the young couple. Carago stepped forward, his dark eyes alert and shining in his craggy face.

"Araminah Reyes," he said simply. "Nikolas Moreno. You are to marry when we reach Seville, yes?"

"That's what I'm told," she answered, showing neither regard nor disrespect. Carago was very old, and one of the *kris* in the group they had joined; as such, he called the shots, usually according to ancient ways. She would acknowledge his power, but she would be damned if she would bow to it.

The old man did not react to her female audacity. "Your grandmother is *chovihani*, yes?"

"That's right."

Manuo looked mortified by her attitude. Traditional Rom women were taught to be deferential to their men, and Ara was standing tall and proud before Carago. She had managed to reject her early training in Romany ways; Manuo liked fire in his women, but not in the presence of the leader of the *kris*. She would dishonor his family at this rate.

Carago, however, seemed amused. Scanning her face, he commented, "And you will follow in Beti's footsteps. I can see it." Without looking away from her, he said, "Moreno, the willfulness you warned me about is only *chovihani* attitude. Women with her power must be forgiven."

That wasn't what Moreno was expecting to hear. Gaping gracelessly, he managed to choke out, "But, Carago, I—"

"Nikolas Moreno," the elder continued, ignoring Manuo, much to Ara's delight. "You have a special duty with this woman. Treat her well, at all costs. Enjoy her fire, allow her temper. But keep her within honor and give her many children. Her power must be maintained and passed along."

"I will," Nikolas nodded, reverence in his voice.

Carago looked into Ara's green eyes and grinned, showing healthy white teeth that belied his age. "Don't take advantage of your specialness, Reyes, but I like you. I'd marry you myself, if I were still young. Now, I don't think I have strength enough to handle you."

Ara laughed throatily, pleased to be granted the freedom and respect implied in Carago's words. "I'll remember that."

"When do we reach Seville?" Nikolas asked, grasping his fiancée's hand in gentle possessiveness.

"In three or four days, if the weather is good," Manuo replied.

"Plenty of time," Carago said. "My daughter, Sela, will help you with your preparations, Araminah. She is waiting by the cookfire. Go talk to her."

"My preparations are made," she said, daring to refuse him.

The old man wrinkled his nose. "Go talk to her anyway."

Ara hesitated, wondering why she was being dismissed. Manuo's face twisted angrily as he tried to order her with a look. Wishing she could stay, she freed her hand from Nikolas' grasp and obeyed, leaving the men to their mysterious discussion.

Carago waited until she was out of ear shot before he turned to Manuo. "Tell me all you know about her, Moreno, and about her family. Be sure that you leave nothing out."

The coach rumbled through the cold October sunlight, its speed slowed considerably by the mantle of rock that edged between France and Spain. Isabella was wrapped tightly in her cloak in the sheltered cab, sleeping off the day. Tobyn sat beside Serrano on the driver's bench, leaving the vampire to her unsettling stillness. There had been no suitable place to stop here in the mountains, and Tobyn had not wanted to leave the road. Juarez had complainingly relinquished his bench seat to the gypsy, moving to the footman's position on Isabella's orders. Tobyn didn't mind the occasional nasty look the surly man sent his way; Juarez meant nothing to him.

To fill the time for himself, Serrano prattled on ceaselessly about the trees they passed, the horses before them, and countless memories of his boyhood. Tobyn was certain he would have been bored stiff if he'd been listening. Instead, he concentrated on reaching out to his twin.

After a moment of seemingly futile probing, he was rewarded by her 'voice.' *//Tobyn! Where are you?//*

He smiled. *//I'm on my way to Seville. I'll rejoin you after I have father and Antonio.//*

//How did you get away? You sound so much stronger...are you well?// She paused, almost as if taking a deep breath to calm herself. *//Tobyn, are you really free?//*

He found himself wishing he could take Ara's hand. *//I'm free,//* he affirmed. *//A friend helped me get away. I think you'd like her.//*

//Her?//

The tinge of jealousy in his sister's voice was both amusing and gratifying. *//Relax, lover. She's just a friend.//*

As usual, Araminah saw more than he revealed. *//Is this 'friend' a vampire as well?//*

//Yes.//

//Tobyn, be careful. You can't trust them.//

//Don't worry about me. I can take care of myself.//

Her derisive snort came through loud and clear. *//I've noticed,//* she Sent sarcastically.

Changing the subject, he asked, *//Where are you?//*

//We're headed back to Seville.//

He hesitated, surprised. *//We were going north.//*

//We joined up with the Caragos, and turned south.//

//Well, it's good luck, anyway,// he sighed in satisfaction. *//I'll meet you in Seville.//*

//Good.//

The relief in her tone carried too many layers, and his protective instincts kicked in. *//What's going on, Ara?//*

//Just hurry, Tobyn. That's all.//

//Ara—//

He fell silent as she clamped down on her end of the link, cutting him off. It wasn't like his sister, normally so vocal in her opinions, to be evasive. His instincts told him that something was wrong, something that he needed to fix.

Well, this is a change, he thought. *This time it's Ara who needs help.* Perversely, he saw that as a good sign, and he was glad of it. Not that he wanted his sister to be troubled; quite the contrary. Rather, it was an indication that he was returning to himself. Perhaps he really would be able to put this business of vampires behind him, just as if nothing had ever happened.

At least he could try.

The *kumpania* rattled to a halt at the foot of the mountains, clustering their wagons together to share companionship and protection. After the necessary business of dinner was cleared away, the music began, and Ara was among the first to start the dancing. Carago watched her as Manuo and Nikolas bent his ear, chattering, she had no doubt, about the wedding and about her. She didn't object to being the subject of their conversation. The attention was something that she quite liked.

Nikolas saw her watching them, and he smiled warmly at her. She nodded to him to show that she had seen, then danced away. Gentle he may have been, and sweet, and his devotion to her was extremely touching; but all in all, he was simply stultifyingly dull. She almost liked him, sometimes, but she doubted if she ever really would like him completely. At least she didn't hate him.

The song changed, and she found herself thinking about her brother. The words reminded her of him and his presence, the feeling of him that came to her whenever he was near. She hadn't felt that for far too long. Now, though, he was returning to her, perhaps in time to stop the foolishness of her marriage to Nikolas.

And do what? she asked herself. *Marry me himself?* Such a thing was hardly likely, however much each of them might wish it were. There was nothing Tobyn could do but watch, and she knew it. In a way, she didn't care. It would be enough just to have him back, safe and sound. There would be stolen moments, she was certain, husband or not; Araminah would not consent to being constrained by others' rules. She wanted Tobyn, and so she would have him...discreetly, of course. Romany punishments could be rather severe.

Sela Carago trotted by, angling for a husband in charming naïveté. Although Ara had only recently met her, she was quite fond of the *kris* member's daughter. They were nearly the same age, but Sela seemed vastly younger in her manner. Ara felt almost protective toward the sweet-tempered and rather giddy young woman, like an older sister. Reyes chuckled to herself as Sela flirted with every eligible and reasonably attractive bachelor assembled around the valley field they had occupied for the night. Carago was pretty enough, young and docile. She would have no trouble attracting suitors, especially not since any man who married her would inherit her father's proud position in the group. Sela was an only child, and no woman could ever lead a pack of Rom. Her husband would be fortunate, indeed.

Seen pragmatically, Ara had to admit that her own situation could certainly be worse. In Nikolas, she had a man too in love to beat her, a man who would treat her very well. The Moreno family was wealthy, and she would be free to gather in some of that richness for herself. She had Manuo's lusts to frustrate and Cristina to bedevil. Once Tobyn came back, she would have him and all of his talents as well. All in all, it was a fair deal. For the first time since the arrangements were struck, Araminah found herself not entirely displeased.

Dusk brought them to a stately home, ornate and distinctly Spanish. Isabella emerged from the cab as Tobyn jumped down from his bench seat to land beside her. She smiled to him and took his hand, squeezing it in a familiar, friendly way.

"Welcome to my home, *querido*. You will find everything you need here."

Serrano climbed down to join them on the ground. "Shall I roust Ana, my lady?"

Tobyn raised an eyebrow. "Ana?"

"Please do," Isabella told Serrano before turning to her gypsy companion. "Ana is Serrano's wife, my housekeeper. She will prepare a meal for the three of you and see you to your room for tonight. Juarez, please show Tobyn the way to the kitchen."

The servant grunted something, and Reyes asked, "You aren't coming in?"

Isabella smiled and stroked his face before pulling away. "Not just yet. I must see to other things first."

He saw through her euphemism. "Serrano said that you had willing donors. Is that true?"

The lady laughed. "Violence is hardly my way, Tobyn. I prefer to see it as sharing rather than taking."

The words that came from his own lips startled him. "I'd be willing to share."

Isabella sobered, then shook her head. "No, *mi amo*. You have given too much already to Dumas. I refuse to weaken you."

After a moment, he licked his lips nervously and said, "I owe you something for all of the help you've given me. I don't like debts. Let me repay you somehow."

She studied his face, trying to judge the sincerity of his offer. Like all Rom, he wore so many faces that he was nearly impossible to read. "If you trust me that much, and if you truly wish to repay me, leave your door unlocked tonight. I will take my repayment then, and I swear that no harm will come to you."

Swallowing hard, he nodded. "All right."

Isabella kissed him tenderly, then disappeared into the darkness of the night. Tobyn stared after her, palms slick and cool, rooted to the spot until Juarez called his attention back to the present and the waiting *hacienda*. Shaking himself out of his strange reverie, Reyes followed the Spaniard into the palatial building.

After a filling meal of good, hot food and a courage-restoring tankard of mulled wine, Tobyn retreated to a small but comfortably-appointed bedroom that bore no resemblance whatsoever to the room in Dumas' *chateau*. As he built up the fire and shed his clothing, he pondered the nature of the repayment Isabella wanted. He did trust her insofar as he believed that she wished him no harm. She had denied his offer of blood, which was reassuring; and the only other thing she had seemed interested in from him was physical intimacy. That was a bit of a stumbling block, but he told himself repeatedly that Isabella was not Matthieu, was not equipped to do such things to him, and by dint of her vampire nature probably would never be capable of it, anyway. Hadn't Dumas had to bring in another mortal to do the job, since he was unable to rape Tobyn himself? Of course, it might be easier for a female vampire to use a mortal sexually. They really weren't dependent upon outwardly functional parts. He had never heard of a woman raping a man, but he had no doubt that it was possible. Would Isabella do such a thing? And, when it came down to it, would it be rape at all?

Debt is debt, he thought, *and Isabella is attractive. Maybe it won't be so bad. Maybe that isn't really what she wants.*

There was only one way to find out. Squaring his shoulders and mustering every bit of resolve he could find, Tobyn extinguished the candles and left the door unlocked.

⤚⤙

He awoke to the sound of silk and crinoline rustling to the floor. Uncertain of what to do, Tobyn opened his eyes in the darkness left by the guttering fire and remained stone-still. The covers were lifted as the mattress dipped, and he felt a smooth, cool, feminine nakedness press against his back. Isabella's arms looped innocuously around his waist, holding him tightly, and she dropped kisses on his shoulders. She was cold from the night and her nature, snuggling close to his body heat. He waited for her to do something, to make some demand, his heart thudding wildly in his ears. Isabella only kissed and held him, asking nothing, her hands showing no sign of roaming.

Shifting slightly, he took a deep breath and whispered, "Isabella..."

"Shh," she responded, kissing the nape of his neck around the long curls that brushed his shoulders. "Go back to sleep, darling. I didn't mean to wake you."

He trailed a hand up to slowly interlace with her slender fingers. "Your repayment..."

"Just let me hold you." She hugged him closer, then murmured, "Please. Let me warm myself here."

He considered for a moment, liking the soft feeling of her breasts against his skin. Swallowing his trepidation, he turned in her embrace to look into her face, barely visible in the sparse light from the hearth. With a trembling finger, he traced her lips, then combed through the mass of raven hair that spilled across the other pillow. She allowed the touches, reveling in the mortal life force that raced through him. He was so warm and alive, and so vulnerable...protectively, she clutched him nearer still.

"Oh, Tobyn," she whispered. There were things she wanted to tell him, but words escaped her in the blueness of his eyes.

He sent his hand gliding over the satin of her side. She was so soft, so smooth. So womanly.

So unlike Matthieu.

His voice was quiet and husky. "There are ways of getting warm, if you want me to show them to you." He claimed her mouth gently but not without passion. "If you want me..."

Isabella smiled and released him, lying back and gazing up into his youthfully handsome face. "Are you certain that you want me?"

There was no doubt in his reply. "Oh, yes."

She nodded and opened her arms to him. "Then show me."

And, torn between desire and niggling fear, he did.

⚜

Sunlight found him alone in the rumpled bed, a note on the pillow beside him the only reminder of Isabella. Irritated for the first time by his illiteracy, he went to the basin to wash and dress before hunting down Serrano to make him read the words on the paper.

The man was in the kitchen with Ana, his pleasant-tempered and plump wife, sharing their morning meal. The cook noticed him first.

"Good morning, sleepyhead," she greeted. "You slept in late. Would you like some food?"

"Yes, thanks." He eased into a chair beside Serrano, handing over the note. "What does this say?"

The servant accepted the paper with a raised eyebrow. "You can't read?"

"No." Defensively, he added, "I never needed to."

"Relax, *señor gitano*. Nobody is passing judgments on you." Turning his attention to the message, he said, "Doña Isabella expresses her gratitude for your company last night, and she asks that you remember her. She wants to give you certain gifts to send you on your way to Seville."

Ana returned with a bowl of gruel for him, asking her husband, "What gifts?"

Serrano raised his brows in surprise, looking impressed for the first time in Tobyn's acquaintance. "She has a purse prepared for you, and she's giving you one of her breeding stallions as well."

Tobyn stared at the other man, dumbfounded. "She's what?"

Ana snickered. "You must have done something right. I should say that she enjoyed your company!"

"Hush," Serrano ordered as the gypsy's fair cheeks blushed. "I'll get Juarez to supply you with tack. I'm sure Doña Isabella has every intention of you continuing as Don Tomas. We'll have to be certain that you're properly outfitted."

Tobyn watched Serrano go, then sipped his breakfast while Ana leered jovially. He supposed he should have felt cheap, like a whore; all he could see was the respect he'd get in his *kumpania* when he returned, a conquering hero for rescuing Antonio and Chavo, and very rich, indeed.

It was an appealing image.

⚜

Araminah's pleasure at anticipating her brother's return was more than a little dampened as she and Sela worked on sewing adornments onto the dress she would wear when she married Nikolas. *Just a friend,* she fumed to herself, piercing the fabric with her needle with a ferocity that attracted the other girl's attention. *Yes, I'd say that she's very friendly.*

"Ara, it's a skirt, not a mortal enemy," Sela teased. "What has you so out of sorts today?"

She closed her eyes for a moment, took a deep breath, then let it out in a rush on the heels of a lie. "Nothing. I'm fine."

Sela shrugged. "Whatever you say. I don't believe you, anyway." After another pair of small, precise stitches, she unwittingly said the wrong thing. "I'm told that you have a twin brother. What is his name?"

She said it in a near-growl. "Tobyn."

"What an odd name."

"He's an odd boy."

"Is he married?"

"No." Ara saw the calculating cast that came to Sela's eyes, and she quickly added, "I don't think he'd make a good husband for you."

"Why not?"

"He can't be trusted where *gadja* are concerned."

Sela laughed and waved her hand dismissively. "Oh, so, he's a man. Not one of them is trustworthy. I'd expect that, especially with the way those people raise their daughters." She sniffed with proper Romany disdain. "No morals."

"I wouldn't say that morals are one of Tobyn's strong suits, either," Araminah grumbled.

"Where is your brother?"

"He's—he's been in a French jail."

Carago's face puckered. "Oh, how awful! I hope he can get away."

"He has," the other woman assured automatically, before she could stop herself. Sela was looking at her strangely, and she scrambled for an explanation. "We're twins, so I just know about him, that's all. I can—well, I can..."

Sela nodded sagely. "I understand. *Chovihani.*" She saw the surprise in Ara's face, and she laughed. "Your reputation is spreading. Besides, Father talks a lot."

"I see." She looked back at her sewing, disquieted by this piece of news.

"Since you're twins, does your brother share your powers?"

"I think so."

Sela bounced suddenly, enthusiasm getting the better of her. "Oh, I hope he comes back! I've never met a *chovihano* before. Is he very handsome? Is he tall? Tell me all about him."

"Stop jumping around, Sela. You're wrecking my stitches."

"Sorry."

As the other girl settled down, Ara repaired some messy work and considered misleading Sela in her answers. On second thought, though, it would serve Tobyn right to have Carago's daughter stalking him with marriageability as soon as he got back from his little tryst with the *mulla*.

"He's my height," she began, "but the handsomest man I've ever seen..."

<hr />

Serrano held the reins while Tobyn mounted into the saddle of his new horse, a pure-bred Andalusian stallion of beautiful bay. The animal was spirited and a trifle headstrong, but it accepted the Rom as its rider with only a flick of an ear and a twitch of its long, silken mane.

"Here is the purse," Serrano said, handing over a small leather bag heavy with gold and silver coins. Tobyn put it into a pocket of his great coat, and the servant continued. "See that you spend it wisely, and not all at once. Stay among people if you can, especially after dark. You should reach Seville by tomorrow night."

Reyes gathered up the reins. "Thank Doña Isabella for me."

"I will." Serrano hesitated. "Take care of this horse, lad. He's worth more than your gypsy hide."

"Maybe to you," Tobyn returned without rancor. "But don't worry. I don't intend to mistreat him." He glanced up at the dark windows of the house. "What will happen to all of you, if Dumas catches up to you?"

"If he catches us, we die," was the matter-of-fact reply. "That's why we're leaving before he can find us."

"Where will you go?"

"Italy, perhaps, or England. There are places to hide all over the globe." He turned solemn. "You're in more need of that than we are. Get out of here and put some miles behind you."

The two men clasped hands before Tobyn stirred his mount into action. A click of his tongue and a nudge in the side with his heel sent the animal trotting away from the *hacienda*, following the road to Seville.

Nine

Michel Dumas was livid but frighteningly in control of himself. As he strode into the hastily-called meeting of the Triad of the Prime, no emotion leaked out around his mask of majestic calm. The chattering among the assembled vampiric hangers-on fell silent with the arrival of their prince.

Dumas seated himself at the head of the Triad's large three-sided table, taking his seat like a potentate occupying his throne. With little more than a cursory glance loaded with *noblesse oblige* to the group of extraneous immortals, he spoke a flat, clear-toned command.

"Leave us."

A moment of hesitation was followed by the obedience of the rank and file. Rapidly and in surprisingly organized form, the others left the Triad to their congress.

The Triad consisted of the top vampires in the group hierarchy, each with his own title and prestige. Dumas held the office of the Prime, sharing his name with their confraternity. A quietly malicious Italian named Laurenzo di Giufizi was next in line as Secondary Prime. Seated to Dumas' right, Laurenzo was preternaturally still, all pretenses of humanity absent from his manner. He was the most accomplished killer of their number. The Tertiary Prime sat at the third seat, a jittery and almost hyperactive man named Isa. His swarthy face was blank, but his coal-black eyes glittered with constant watchfulness and paranoia.

Laurenzo broke the silence of the room after the door closed on the last retreating vampire. "What is this about, Dumas, that you have dragged us here to this God-forsaken country?"

The Frenchman's temper was too preoccupied to pay attention to Laurenzo's Florentine snobbishness. "I have called you here to inform you of recent events. One of our members, Doña Isabella Oñate de las Cruces, has broken our most sacred laws. She must be destroyed."

Isa leaned forward, gaping at the Prime. "You aren't serious!"

More pragmatically, Laurenzo asked, "What has she done?"

"She has stolen from me," Dumas replied, his voice icy with rage. "I had a youth here, a man I would have made my nightchild. She took him from me while my back was turned, violating my hospitality."

The Tertiary shook his head in amazement. "This is over a mortal?"

"Ah, but no ordinary mortal," Laurenzo interjected. "Am I not correct, *monsieur*? A young gypsy, exceedingly handsome and well-made. But you kept him as a toy, did you not?"

"How do you know these things?" Dumas snarled, gray eyes glinting dangerously. "I warn you, *signore.*"

"I do not fear you, and I do not respect a Prime brought to his knees with emotion for a mortal. You affronted Elisa Dieter and Roger of Huntingdon for the sake of this gypsy." Laurenzo matched Dumas, ice for ice. "You could have made this nightchild at any time. Why did you wait?"

"I do not need to explain myself to you." He had not anticipated such resistance from the other members of the Triad. "I am the Prime."

Isa took up the refrain. "Yes, and as such, you are responsible for maintaining our ways. Did you love this mortal?"

Laurenzo coughed. "Disgusting."

Dumas gripped the arms of his chair. "This congress was called to discuss Doña Isabella, not myself."

"So she took your mortal toy away," Isa scoffed. "Perhaps she even killed him. That is what mortals are for, Dumas. They are cattle. Have you forgotten?"

"Or perhaps you fancied yourself the bull to this gypsy's cow," the Secondary Prime suggested. "Isabella did not affront your honor. She saved it."

His temper broke loudly. "I will not be insulted! I will not have such disrespect! I demand that she be punished for her crimes against me!"

Isa leaned back from the sheer force of Dumas' rage as Laurenzo pressed, "If you lost, it was your own fault, *monsieur.* You should know better than to play with your food."

With a cry of incoherent fury, the French vampire wrenched the wooden arm from his chair, breaking the furniture with an explosive crack. Before either Isa or Laurenzo could react, Dumas drove the jagged end of the wood piece into the Italian's chest. Years of experience guided him unerringly to Laurenzo's heart, impaling him.

Isa flung himself away from the table, shouting, "Madman!"

Dumas rounded on him and seized his arms, superior age giving him superior strength. Disregarding Isa's struggles, he growled, "Will you support me in this matter, or will you join Laurenzo?"

Unfortunately for Isa, he had never been good at thinking on his feet. "You are mad, Dumas! Age has turned your mind!"

The Frenchman's face twisted with a feral snarl, and he hauled the Tertiary Prime to the hearth's raging flames. Isa howled in terror, doubling his fight against Dumas, but to no avail. Without hesitation or remorse, the French vampire hurled his underling into the fire. Isa instantly became a man-shaped conflagration, limbs surrounded by crackling fire as if he were a dry-twig effigy. He was consumed in a heartbeat.

The door burst open, admitting a shocked cluster of lesser immortals. Dumas faced them proudly, fangs clearly displayed beneath his angry eyes.

"Who here will defy me now?" he demanded, knowing full well that all of those vampires were too young to be any match for him. They knew it, as well, and demurred in all haste, falling over each other in their desperation to prove their loyalty. Satisfied, Dumas issued the order he had called the Triad to endorse. "Doña Isabella Oñate de las Cruces is no longer one of us. She must be destroyed. A gypsy youth named Tobyn is the prize you will collect for me. Do this immediately!"

Bowing and groveling before their wrathful lord, the other immortals backed away, less eager to do Dumas' bidding than to remove themselves from his presence. For his part, Dumas enjoyed their fear. It gave him power.

He would not be denied.

~∽∾∘∾∽~

The ride to Seville was quiet and a little lonely, but in a way Tobyn was grateful for the time alone. It gave him the opportunity to adjust to the new person he had become before he rejoined his *kumpania*. The horse he rode was intelligent, at least as far as those animals went, and lively, but it was an easy thing to let his mind wander while keeping the beast under control.

There had been many changes he'd not yet accepted, circumstances that had rearranged the fibers of his spirit. Only Ara and, he suspected, Beti would really know what had befallen him, and why he was so different now. He could never be the youth he'd been before, could never erase the memories and scars that had created the man he now was. He had never believed in that kind of rapid change, not until he'd experienced it. One week, or two? How long had he been in Dumas' chateau? It had been so brief, and yet it had been eternity. Two weeks, two years, two centuries...he wasn't certain anymore.

He smiled wryly. His people would scarcely know him when he returned.

The wind blowing in from the not-so-distant sea was cold and heavy, and he clutched his cloak closer, feeling the gratifying thud of his coin bag against his thigh from its seat in his pocket. Although he had taken Serrano's advice and stayed at the busiest inn he could find at sunset on his first night on the road, the cost of room and food had been covered by a single one of Isabella's gold coins. The Spanish innkeeper had bought the Don Tomas story with little encouragement, and the hospitality the gypsy had enjoyed had been lavish. Through it all, Tobyn had struggled not to laugh; the same obsequious Spaniard who piled rich foods before him on his plate had not too long ago heaped curses on his Romany head. How a little gold and a change of wardrobe could change a person's mind!

"Do I perhaps know you, Don Tomas?" the man had asked. "Your face is familiar to me."

Tobyn laughed as he recalled the elaborate lies he'd spun. Perhaps the Duchess' hunting party, or perhaps when His Majesty the King had traveled through with his retainers? He had been more than happy to supply names and details to jog the *gadjo*'s memory. Finally they had agreed upon Don Tomas' presence among the Duke of Aragon's traveling companions a winter ago, and they'd shared "memories" of the party's stay in the wayside inn. Those lies had earned him an extra coverlet that night.

Reyes leaned forward to tell his horse, "Rule one for dealing with *gadje*: they're hopelessly stupid."

In reply, and perhaps in agreement, the animal gave an enthusiastic snort.

⌐∾⊷⊶∾⌐

At nightfall, he passed through the gates into Seville, nervously watching the dark sky above him. Clouds were rolling in from the ocean, glowering down on the city and threatening either rain or snow. He wanted the protection of a roof and multiple companions, as soon as he could get it.

Haste compelled him to stop at the first inn he reached, a raucous place bright with people. He knew this establishment; he and Chavo and others of their *kumpania* had come there to buy wine and to have a good laugh at the expense of the *gadje* who flocked around the *buju* women ensconced in the corner with their crystal ball and their Tarot cards. They had been run out of this inn more than once, and had such great fun that they came back every time they hit Seville.

He knew the place well enough to know its prices and the propensity of its clientele to rob one another blind. It was not the sort of place for Don Tomas or his money, but Tobyn knew how to thwart pickpockets. That skill came from experience as a thief.

He dismounted and settled his horse in the stable himself, currying him before leaving him to horsely concerns. Rearranging his money and openly displaying a purse full of stones and dirt as a decoy, he made his way to the tavern.

It took a moment for the serving girl to notice his arrival, but he didn't mind. It gave him more time at the fire's warmth, listening to the loud singing of a bawdy song from a trio of Portuguese sailors in the corner. Once she saw him there, the barmaid escorted him to a seat and brought him what he requested. Tobyn was beginning to like that kind of service; perhaps he should consider getting a traditional wife. Ara would certainly never serve him this way.

The door opened, admitting a babbling horde of noisy gypsies who swarmed in and set up their reign over the tavern floor. A number of the faces were known to Tobyn, and he shrank away, hiding from them. He was not ready yet to be recognized, not ready to go back. Around the comforting but unwelcome buzz of his own language, Tobyn stole out into the night, going to the stable to stand guard over his horse and escape from friends with miserable timing.

The stable was warm and quiet, the only sounds those of the horses who snorted and stomped to themselves. He crept by the sleeping livery hand and let himself into the stall he'd rented for the night. His bay blinked at him sleepily with great dark eyes, and Tobyn patted its muzzle gently, his other hand reaching up to scratch the mane.

"I hope you don't mind a roommate," he whispered, looking into the animal's face. When no objections were forthcoming, the gypsy settled into a reasonably clean corner, his back pressed to the wooden wall. He felt protected by the building around him, and safe in the friendly company of the horse.

"Chal," he told the stallion. "That's your name now. Do you like it?"

Chal wandered closer and nudged his human with his nose, then snorted into Reyes' hair. Tobyn laughed and patted Chal's cheek.

"Hello to you, too, horse. Go to sleep."

Wrapping himself in his great coat, he set about taking his own advice, one hand clutching the knife at his belt for security.

Tobyn started violently, his instincts yanking him into wakefulness as Chal stomped and whickered nervously, churning the straw beneath his hooves. From his spot in the corner, the gypsy could see a small man in a long black cloak creep silently into the stall. For the moment, Tobyn was hidden behind his anxious horse, safely out of the man's view. He was glad for that; every nerve in his body was screaming that the man was dangerous. Choosing to take no chances, he drew his knife and prepared to use it.

The stranger was ignoring Chal for the present, inspecting the tack that hung on the wall. His hands, pale as moonlight, skin stretched almost transparently over a network of stringy veins, searched the bridle and saddle, looking over particular brass ornaments. He knew what he was looking for. A smile spread over the man's face, his thin lips pulling back to reveal the teeth that Tobyn was not at all surprised to see.

Mullo! Tobyn spat in silent fury.

Perhaps he had thought too loudly; the vampire turned his wild smile onto the young man, his cadaverous, desiccated face surrounded by a tangle of gray hair. "Hello, little gypsy," he greeted, his voice a dry rasp. "Are you one of Doña Isabella's friends?"

Reyes stood his ground, his right hand tightening on the handle of his knife. He would not go down without a fight. "Who is Doña Isabella?"

The vampire cackled. "Your name wouldn't happen to be Tobyn, would it?"

Clenching his teeth, the Rom stepped closer, his eyes locked on the vampire's, all of his defenses up. The *mullo* stepped forward as well, his thin arms raised as if to pull the mortal into an embrace. Tobyn took a deep breath, then replied.

"Did Dumas send you?"

The vampire laughed loudly, triumphantly, and seized Tobyn's shoulders. His strength was less than Reyes had expected; weakened from lack of blood, this immortal was an even match for him. Wrenching his arm free, Tobyn stabbed him, his blade striking deep into the other's heart as Chal screamed and kicked at the walls. The vampire fell bonelessly, his weight bearing the gypsy down with him. Not in the least convinced by his enemy's motionlessness, Reyes shoved the knife in deeper. Thick blood, almost black, surged out over his hand and stained his clothes. The smell choked him, and he pushed the vampire's body aside, desperately watching him for signs of life.

Chal screamed and reared, bringing his hooves down onto the vampire's head and chest, trampling him into the floor and snapping the handle from the knife blade still embedded in his body. Tobyn backed away, staring, trying to avoid the horse's flailing legs, expecting to see the vampire rise and come after him again at any moment.

Eventually, Chal tired of pounding the intruder's body into pulp, and in the absolute quiet that followed, the *mullo* failed to move. Tobyn could hear his heart pounding in his ears as he nudged the fallen man's foot. There was no response.

The main door to the stable opened loudly, and the innkeeper stomped in with a lantern and his two strapping sons. The noise had called him. Thinking quickly, even though he was amazed that he could still think at all, Tobyn wrapped himself in his great coat, covering the stains upon his clothing, then stepped out into the light from the Spaniard's lamp.

The innkeeper narrowed his eyes and asked, "Are you all right, my lord? I heard a horse raising a rumpus..."

Suspicion colored the man's voice like a layer of paint. Tobyn put on his best aristocratic *gadjo* act and tried to pretend his hands weren't shaking. "A man tried to kill me and take my horse. We fought, and I fear there's been a terrible result."

One of the young men brushed past Tobyn and into the stall. "Oh my God...Papa, the man is dead!"

The innkeeper fixed Tobyn with a measuring look. "Indeed."

His son reappeared, pale-faced but in control. "The horse stomped him to death."

"He dislikes thieves and murderers," Reyes offered in explanation.

"Pepe, run and fetch a priest," the innkeeper ordered his second boy. Turning back to the shaken gypsy before him, he continued, "It is a miracle that you escaped unharmed, *señor*."

"Yes, it is," Tobyn agreed honestly.

"Your face is familiar to me. Do I perhaps know you?"

"No, I don't believe that we've met. I am from the south. I am Don Tomas Oñate de las Cruces."

The innkeeper nodded, satisfied at some level by the reply. "De las Cruces, eh? I thought I saw your family crest upon the saddle there over the door. Did you have a Crusader for an ancestor?"

Tobyn's heart skipped a beat. Isabella's crest had attracted the vampire's attention. He would have to get rid of it as soon as he rejoined his *kumpania*. Realizing that the innkeeper was expecting an answer, he mumbled, "Yes." He sighed. "I would like a new stall for my horse, *señor*, and privacy. My animal is very high-strung will require much attention to settle his constitution."

"I understand, my lord. David, help Don Tomas to a new stall. A clean one." He grumbled to himself as he turned to peer at the man-shaped lump on the floor. "I'll take care of this mess."

Chal woke him when the sun was high, snorting in his curl-fringed ear with barley breath. Tobyn pushed the horse's nose away and groaned in his usual lack of morning enthusiasm. The events of the night before replayed before his mind's eye, and he shuddered in revulsion, glaring down at his blood-bespattered clothes.

They were clean.

He straightened in confusion, and his eyes fell onto the cloth lining of his discarded coat. It had absorbed the vampire's blood from his shirt and pants, gore stains spreading through the fabric. In the bright morning sunlight, the stains were disappearing, as if the light itself were cleansing it away.

This was something to remember, a graphic demonstration of why daylight was so lethal to vampires. He had learned two important vampire facts: they could be killed by a stab wound to the heart, and sunshine made at least their blood disappear as if it had never existed at all. He held his hand in the light from the window and enjoyed the warmth.

Perhaps the sun could also erase whatever elements of the vampire he had absorbed when he'd swallowed Dumas' blood. Perhaps, he conjectured, he could become ordinary and himself again if he just spent enough time in the sun.

A loud rap on the stall door shook him from his reverie. Buttoning and smoothing his rumpled shirt, he rose to greet his visitor. The innkeeper's youngest son, the one called Pepe, was waiting at the door. When Tobyn appeared, he bowed quickly. "My lord, the magistrate would like to speak to you about last night."

Like any gypsy, Tobyn hated even the thought of dealing with the law. "Is that absolutely necessary?"

"Yes, my lord, I'm afraid so."

He sighed and pulled his coat over his shoulders. "All right," he grumbled. "Where is he?"

"With my father in the tavern. Please, follow me."

Tobyn let Pepe walk ahead of him, watching as the teenager strode toward the inn. As soon as the unsuspecting lad turned around the corner from the stable doors, Tobyn went back to Chal and saddled him with rapid efficiency. He had things to do, and talking to a local official did not fall among their number. He swung himself up into the saddle and headed off in the direction of the jail where Chavo and Antonio Reyes were languishing.

The ride was short and enjoyable, following the winding roads of the city until he reached his destination. Dismounting, he studied the building. Only one small window lightened the front wall, and he had no doubt that the interior was dismal. He took a moment to arrange his appearance into a reasonable facsimile of a proper grandee, then let himself into the reception area.

The deputy at the desk, a chubby man with a bored expression, straightened as he strode in, responding to the cut of his clothing and the money bag bouncing at his waist. "Can I help you, *señor?*"

"I sincerely hope so," he sniffed. "Tell me, have you any *gitanos* in your cells here?"

The guard shrugged, his eyes skimming to the money bag once again. "Why do you ask?"

Tobyn could see how this man could be controlled. Fishing out a silver coin, he replied, "I like to collect gypsies. Are there any here?"

After a moment, the man accepted the bribe. "Only one. We did have two, but one of them died late yesterday."

Tobyn clenched his teeth, fighting not to react. "Will you bring me the remaining gypsy, then?"

"That all depends."

"On what?" he asked, offering another silver piece that disappeared into the guard's huge paw.

"Why do you want him? I don't think he's quite manageable."

"I have my reasons," he said coolly. "That's all you need to know."

After relieving Tobyn of another coin, the guard lumbered off to get whichever gypsy had survived. Tobyn leaned against the desk as soon as he was gone, trembling in restrained grief. He had arrived too late, and the horror of the fact that he could have prevented his kinsman's death was a capping blow to the soul-damaging trial he had endured. If he had been a little quicker, if he had taken one day less to play-act... Almost guiltily, he prayed that Chavo was the survivor.

The guard returned, pushing a surly Antonio before him. The elder Reyes was handsome but sour, his dark eyes flat with constant anger and mean-spiritedness. He was a classic Romany man, prideful and headstrong, more than a little "uncivilized" and full of his own ideas of the way the world should be run. His thick wrists and ankles were connected by shackles to a metal band about his waist, and his mien left no doubt that without those restraints he would have gladly smashed the guard's brains out on the wall.

When Antonio saw Tobyn standing there, pale and thin in expensive *gadjo* clothing, his eyes pinched in suspicion. Tobyn straightened and fixed his uncle with a firmly silencing look.

"Here he is, my lord, even though I'm not sure why you want him."

Antonio growled a virulent word under his breath, and Tobyn said, "Unchain him."

"What? Have you lost your mind? He'd break you over his knee!"

Power and authority he'd never known he had crept into his voice, making the guard disinclined to argue further. "Do it now."

Antonio stared at Tobyn while the Spanish deputy reluctantly freed his prisoner's arms and legs. As the guard bent over the chains on Antonio's feet, the older Rom brought both fists, clutching his former shackles, down hard on the back of the man's head. The guard fell, unconscious, to the floor, and Antonio finished freeing his ankles for himself. Tobyn retrieved his silver plus a little interest from the man's pockets, then faced his uncle.

"There are horses outside."

Antonio followed him out to where Chal and the guard's animal waited, and they mounted up in near unison. "Where is the *kumpania*?"

Tobyn hesitated. "This city, probably in the usual place."

"You don't know? Where have you been?" the elder Reyes demanded, his tone accusing.

"In France," he replied curtly, turning Chal to head toward the eastern edge of Seville. Antonio kicked his own horse to follow, leaving the jail as far behind and as quickly as humanly possible.

"What were you doing in France, nephew? Where did you get those clothes?"

"I took them," he lied, avoiding the first question with determination. "What happened to my father?"

Antonio was silent for a moment, then replied, "A *gadjo* prisoner beat him to death. I could do nothing to help him."

Rage bubbled up inside him. "Did you even try?"

"We were in separate cells," his uncle said. "Now talk about something else. It isn't good to talk about the dead."

Tobyn watched as Antonio took the lead, cantering ahead of him. He did not believe his uncle's story. Fatigue, more emotional than physical, wrapped around him, and all he wanted was the comfort of Araminah's embrace. He wanted to cling to her, to cry on her shoulder, to convince himself that he really wasn't as alone as he felt, to know that she was real. Antonio shot a distrustful glance over his shoulder, and Tobyn set his jaw in obliging anger.

Go ahead and watch me, he thought hotly. *I promise that I'll be watching you*

Ten

The first people to see them coming were a trio of men from the Carago *kumpania* who were arguing amiably over the relative merits of their horses. The youngest of them nodded in the Reyes' direction, muttering a soft word to his fellows, who lapsed into silence until the riders were close enough to be identified.

"Who are these people?" Antonio asked before he shouted a hearty greeting in Romany, calling the attention of the women who were washing clothes in a wooden barrel. Cristina Moreno wiped her hands on her skirt and replied in kind, using the names of the approaching men for the benefit of the Carago people.

Antonio and Tobyn brought their horses to a halt in the center of the clearing, sliding out of the saddle as throngs of Rom gathered about them in a chattering cluster. Tobyn held onto the cinch of Chal's saddle to keep himself upright, his knees going weak as the strength he'd derived from stubborn isolation fled in the face of his reabsorption into the *kumpania*. One of Tito's little sons chattered at him, grabbing at his hand, but Tobyn's eyes were fixed on the crowd, watching for his sister's face.

Suddenly she was there beside him, her arms around him, holding him tightly to her as she wept in relief. He clasped her near, releasing his hold on the saddle strap and leaning on her for support. Beti swooped in and laid claim to him, wrapping his left arm over her shoulder and helping her granddaughter bear him away from the crush of clansmen. They had only walked a few steps before his legs buckled completely, dragging him to the ground.

Old man Carago helped the women carry Tobyn into the quiet privacy of the Reyes wagon, although they required no assistance. As Ara covered her brother with a warm blanket, Beti ushered the *kumpania* leader back outside.

"What's wrong with him?" he asked, gesturing back at the slowly-recovering youth.

"We'll take care of him," was the old woman's nonanswer as she all but shoved Carago out the door. She turned to her granddaughter. "See to him, Ara. I'll go check Antonio and keep people away from here."

"Thank you, Grandmama," she sighed earnestly, clutching Tobyn's hand for dear life. As soon as Beti was gone, she pressed a kiss to his forehead, her free hand petting his hair away from his face. He squeezed her fingers gently and opened his eyes to gaze up at her in shell-shocked wonder. She smiled for him. "Welcome home."

Tobyn tried to return the expression, but the weight of the memories of Dumas' *chateau* pressed down, making it impossible. It had been so easy to deny that any of those things had happened while he'd been playing Don Tomas. He hadn't had to confront his pains while he was on his own. But now he was in the embrace of his people, and he was simply Tobyn once again, the same Tobyn who had been an aperitif for vampires, the one who had suffered Matthieu's loveless touch. He almost wished he could be Don Tomas again.

His silence worried her, and she leaned closer, holding his hand more tightly. "Tobyn, are you all right? I've missed you so much."

Tears rose in his eyes, silver puddles in the blue, and his shoulders quaked in silent sobs. Ara, who had been a long-distance witness to much of his ordeal, understood. Pulling him into a tight embrace, she held him as he cried, giving him the silent comfort of her presence, being strong for him so that he could be weak for a while.

After what could have been hours of bitter weeping, Tobyn straightened and pulled away, putting himself back under the unflappable control he had once possessed, the calmness that she so envied in him. He stroked her hair and let out a short, tear-thickened laugh.

"You're so beautiful," he whispered, shaking his head. "I was afraid I'd never be able to touch you again." He swallowed hard, raised his eyes to her. "Father is dead."

She nodded in acknowledgment, keeping her opinion of Chavo to herself. No matter how little she had cared for the man, Tobyn had idolized him. Out of respect for her twin's grief, she held her silence.

He pulled her close again, rocking her in his arms, inhaling the aroma of her hair. Her reality gave him a clue to his own, and reaffirming his sister's existence helped put him back in contact with himself. The nightmare was over at last.

Ara stroked his back. "Are you hurt? Is there anything that I can do for you?"

He pulled back and kissed her gently. When they separated, he smiled and raised his eyebrows in an endearing, child-like expression. "Food? I'm starving."

She presented him with a kiss of her own. "Fine. I'll be right back."

Araminah left the wagon to get at the cook fire, and Tobyn reacquainted himself with the family's belongings. He sought and found the little wooden box that held all of his clothes and, after a brief moment of deliberation, changed out of his Don Tomas gear and into the things that had been his own a lifetime ago. He was a little sad to see the fine French shirt get packed away; he'd quite liked the feeling of the fabric against his skin. Illusion was more comfortable than reality, he supposed, despite the fact that reality had to be worn every day.

His sister returned while he was changing, and she watched mutely, her green eyes taking note of the healing bruises from Matthieu, the rope burns, the bite marks that were so slow to mend. When he turned to look at her with a jaunty and superficial smile on his pale face, she wanted to weep. *What have they done to you?*

Although she had not intended him to, he 'heard' her thoughts and replied, *//Nothing that I'd care to repeat.//*

Ara held out a bowl of steaming food. "Here," she said. "You need to get your strength back up."

"Any particular reason why?"

The door clattered open before she could reply to his cautiously-probing question. Antonio and Beti came into the wagon, their uncle making a fairly substantial amount of noise in the process. He sat heavily beside Tobyn with his own meal. "I tied your horse up to the wagon. Nikolas Moreno is currying it for you. Nice tack you have."

Tobyn stirred his food and wrinkled his nose. "I'd rather someone else took care of my horse. The Lump might give him fleas."

"Be nice to the boy," Antonio commanded, speaking as if to a tiresome child. "After all, he's going to be part of the family after tomorrow."

He froze. When he spoke, his voice was a rumbling, icy snarl. "What did you say?"

Antonio smiled in great satisfaction, a sentiment doubled, no doubt, by his nephew's displeasure. "Tito got Ara sold to somebody. She's supposed to marry Nikolas tomorrow afternoon in the church in Seville. She got a surprisingly good price, too, considering how old she is." He glanced at his niece. "Of course, with a body like that, it's no wonder..."

Tobyn put his bowl aside with a clatter and rose to his feet in one anger-filled motion. "Where is he, Beti?"

"You're not going after him," the old woman told him sternly. "You're going to sit here, eat your food, and accept the decision."

//Tobyn, please listen to her!//

He turned to glare at Ara, who was sitting across from him now. Reluctantly, and only out of deference to his sister, he obeyed Beti. Glowering into his bowl while Antonio prattled about what he'd do with his share of Ara's dowry, the young man silently demanded, *//How long has this been set?//*

//Since just after you...left. Tito and Manuo struck their deal the second day you were gone.//

//Just waiting for me to get out of the way,// Tobyn grumbled to her. *//Bastards. I'll kill them both.//*

//You'll do no such thing. This is probably for the best. How long did you think you could keep denying the offers before people caught on? At least it's a man in the kumpania, and he's not the type to hurt—//

//You don't know that,// he objected bitterly. *//You can't tell that from a person's face.//*

//Tobyn, please. I think I know him well enough to say.// She watched him poke furiously at the broth in his bowl and sighed. *//I was going to tell you.//*

//When? Tomorrow morning?//

She glared at him. *//Do you think I should have told you while you were with your* mulla *friend? Or maybe while Matthieu was—//* Ara saw the unidentifiable flicker on Tobyn's features and pulled back, knowing that she had stepped too far into forbidden territory. *//The point is that you had enough troubles of your own without adding mine to them.//*

//Well, that's a pretty excuse, anyway.//

//Even if you had known ahead of time, there's nothing that you could have done. You can't alter the agreement, and you can't demand more from the Morenos.// She gathered up Antonio's empty bowl from where he'd put it onto her last-minute mending. *//Our hands are tied, love.//*

Tobyn ran a hand over his face and sat back. *//I don't want to lose you, Ara.//*

//I'll always be around.//

"Why are you two so quiet?" Antonio asked, the uneasiness in his eyes suggesting that he knew what they'd been doing. "You've heard my story about where I've been. Your turn, Tobyn."

The twins exchanged a quick glance and he told himself, *Make it good.* Settling into a more comfortable position and thinking fast, he began to spin an elaborate yarn about French jails and careless Spanish noblemen.

⁖⁖⁖⁖⁖

He left his bed in silence, leaving behind the soft whistling of Beti's sleep and Antonio's rumbling snore. Stepping over his uncle's feet and swallowing his unaccustomed fear of the darkness outside the wagon, Tobyn let himself out and closed the door with a barely-audible click.

He found Ara beyond the sheltering clump of the *kumpania's* wagons, seated on a stone and watching the sky. Quietly, he sank down beside her, his shoulder brushing hers, and he mimicked her posture, folding his arms on his knees.

"I was just looking at the stars," she told him, her breath coming in clouds of white. "They'll probably look different after tomorrow."

Tobyn looked down at his toes, staring sightlessly as he said, "Do you want to marry Nikolas?"

"Of course not." She smiled slyly. "You'd better watch yourself, brother. You used his name."

"It won't happen again."

They chuckled, and he wrapped an arm around her, holding her close. She turned and clung to him desperately, blinking to dispel the tears that threatened her composure. His fingers petted her cheek, calming her, and she pressed a kiss to the exposed skin at the opening of his shirt.

"I'm afraid," she whispered finally. "Isn't that stupid? After everything you went through, I'm afraid of this."

"I don't blame you for it," he told her, dropping a tenderness to her hairline. "I'm afraid for you, too...and a little for me."

Ara straightened. "For you?"

"Yes." He nodded solemnly, eyes full of pain. "What am I going to do without you?"

They held one another for a long time, soothing one another's fears with reassurances they spoke like litanies, trying not to cry but crying anyway. When they finally separated, Tobyn looked her in the eye and said, "If he ever hurts you, if you ever need me for anything, call me. I'm not going to leave you alone in this."

"I will," she promised. "I love you."

He returned the emotion with a kiss, passion for her burning just beneath the surface. Ara combed her fingers through his hair, letting the curls encircle them, returning his embrace eagerly.

"I love you," she repeated. "Let me show you, one last time. Please—"

Tobyn silenced her, his mouth pressed to hers, and with gentle hands began to show his love for her, instead.

Comparatively, being locked in solitary confinement in Dumas' *chateau* was easier than sitting through the brief time it took for Ara to be married off to Nikolas Moreno. Tobyn kept his face utterly impassive as Manuo's priest droned on about a God he could not believe in and would probably hate if they ever met. Antonio and Tito flanked him, keeping watchful eyes on his reactions as the ceremony dragged on; he refused to give them the satisfaction of seeing his discomfort.

Before the altar, wearing the skirt she and Sela had so painstakingly embroidered, Ara wanted to die. Nikolas had taken on a prideful, possessive air, his smile almost predatory as he held her hand tightly in his own. Behind them, she could feel Manuo watching her, staring, probably grinning like the lunatic he sometimes seemed to be. She could feel her hands shaking with the effort of not running away. Even if she tried, there were men aplenty ready to drag her back and see the ceremony completed. More than one gypsy wedding had ended in a bride-wrestling free-for-all.

//Hold on,// Tobyn told her gently. *//Pretend it's me.//*

She had to smile as her brother spoke Nikolas' part inside her head while the vows were taken, and it was easier to make her promises when she could convince herself that she was making them to Tobyn. And then it was done, and Nikolas was pulling her after him out of the church while the party the *kumpania* had been waiting for erupted in the pews.

"Well, that's done," Tito sighed in happiness and relief, clapping Tobyn on the shoulder. "Come on. There's good wine on the corner."

The younger Reyes smiled wanly and stepped away from his uncle's touch. "I think I'll wait a while. I want to eat something first."

"Suit yourself," Tito shrugged. He and Antonio pushed their way out of the church and into the noonday sun, leaving Tobyn in the rapidly-emptying sanctuary.

The coolness of the stone wrapped around him as the last voice chattered its way out of the building, and he walked slowly down the aisle to where the acolytes were cleaning up after the ceremony. Soon, even they were gone, leaving him alone with the silent sorrow of his sister's absence. His face was blank and almost calm as he leaned against the communion rail, studying the sad eyes of the figure on the crucifix. The Mass held a different meaning for him now. Before Dumas, he'd ignored the silliness, lulled by the droning Latin into a vacant half-sleep. Since he had escaped the French vampire's clutches, "cup of my blood" took on a host of subtle shadings, few of them comfortable. He wondered if God knew about vampires, and if their form of communion was holy as well.

He reached out to his sister as he stood there, trying to give her strength as Nikolas, unable to wait so much as an hour more, dragged her into the privacy of his *vardo* to initiate her into her wifely duties. There was nothing Tobyn could do to prevent it; he could only hope that Nikolas would be kind. Araminah did not deserve violence.

A feminine voice at his side surprised him. "What are you looking at so hard?"

He turned a startled look on Sela Carago, pretty and demure in her dark blue dress and parti-colored shawl. Her large dark eyes peered up at him curiously, flirtatiously. He forced a smile, feeling Ara shut him out of the sensations of her unwanted marriage bed.

"Nothing," he told her. "Sela, yes? Carago's daughter?"

She beamed. "That's right! And you're Tobyn Reyes."

He smirked and spread his arms loosely. "In the flesh."

Sela blushed and bit her bottom lip before saying, "I like that."

Tobyn leaned his hips against the communion rail, his hands in his pockets, and asked, "What, the name or the flesh?"

She turned and strolled away, hands clasped behind her swaying hips as she called back over her shoulder, "Both."

Reyes laughed softly, amused by her practiced ease at trolling for a husband. Sela had "traditional Rom" written all over her. Still, she was attractive and rich, and it wouldn't hurt him to be her friend. Cultivating her attentions would also deflect some of Antonio's suspicions. Tobyn wasn't certain what his uncle was thinking, but he felt reasonably sure that it was nothing flattering. The more he acted like an average Romany man, the less reason Antonio would have for watching him so closely.

Shrugging to himself, he hurried to catch up with Sela.

By nightfall, the *kumpania* had taken over the town, many of the gypsies running into trouble with the local law while the party whirled on. Tobyn and Sela stayed in the town square until dusk, listening to the music their fellows played and flirting shamelessly with one another. The Sevillano authorities herded them out beyond the gates as night approached, and the celebration continued without missing a beat, moving to the campground they had claimed and building a bonfire in the center of the circle of wagons. Wine was plentiful and freely flowing, and it was the rare man who was still sober as the last rays of daylight left the sky.

Tobyn was such a man. He had no wish to dull his senses with alcohol, not when the night around him was black and thick. He needed to be on his guard, he needed to be ready for whatever should come his way. He had no illusions about his safety from vampires; if Dumas or one of his kind wanted to find him, he would be found. If he were drunk, the enemy's job would be that much easier. He had no intention of being an easy mark again.

Antonio staggered past the Moreno *vardo*, slapping the brightly-painted wooden side and shouting raucous encouragement to the bridegroom within. The man was thoroughly soused, the wine making him even more obnoxious than he usually was. Tobyn watched in distaste as his uncle joined an equally besotted Tito in the light of the fire. He had a difficult time accepting that he shared blood with them.

Chavo had once told him that he often felt the same, and Tobyn could remember bitter arguments between the three Reyes brothers. Invariably, Chavo would face off against Antonio, behind whom the essentially spineless Tito would throw his weight. There had been violent times, and the young Rom could remember seeing his father returning, bloodied, from a confrontation with Antonio. The number of threats against Chavo's life had been enough to no longer be taken seriously. In fact, only last July Tobyn and his father had laughed at Antonio's blustering.

How very interesting, Tobyn thought, that Antonio was the one to survive their time in jail. And how fascinating that only Antonio's word stood to explain the circumstances of Chavo's death.

His suspicions were interrupted by the clamorous arrival of three young women he had somehow managed to bring together into a personal admiration society. He had never learned their names, but after a day full of finding them dogging his every step, he knew their faces. The warm, starry-eyed looks they wore, three variations on a common theme, gave his ego something to mull over and preen about. He could have done anything to these girls, and they would not object.

"Come and play for us," the smallest, and boldest, of them begged while her companions giggled. "Sing us a song."

Smiling with charm but not enthusiasm, he said, "I don't think so. The men who are playing now are doing just fine. They don't need my help."

The girls pouted, wracking their brains for a way to cajole him, when Sela reappeared at his side, grabbing his hand and pulling him after her toward the Rom dancing by the fire. Tobyn did not resist, grateful to have been rescued from his courtiers.

Just before they reached the dancers, Sela turned to him with a wicked grin. "I've told Papa all about you," she said deviously.

He raised an eyebrow. "Oh? What did you tell him?"

"That I like you." She executed a quick spin, laughing to herself as she faced him once more. "He wants to meet you."

He could feel her weaving her marital net around him, and he silently gave thanks to whoever was responsible that Romany women were not allowed to propose to their men. "I'm sure we'll meet sooner or later," he told her, walking toward the musicians.

She stopped him with a hand on his arm. "You're a pretty man, *chovihano*. I like you. And I know Papa will like you, too."

Tobyn looked to where old Carago sat watchfully guarding his daughter with his eyes, and he wondered exactly what Sela had told the *kris* member. Turning back to the girl, he smiled to her and said, "I hope he does. It would make life difficult if he didn't like me." Disengaging himself gracefully from her grasp, he excused himself by saying, "I have to go talk to my uncle now."

"Of course," Sela replied happily, letting him go, visions of marriage offers dancing before her mind's eye. "I'll see you later?"

"Maybe," he allowed, making it sound more definite than it was. Breaking away, Tobyn went off to find Antonio.

⁓≈⁓

Araminah sighed in relief as Nikolas rolled away from her, his weight lifting as he moved. Her husband had been overwhelmingly eager to consummate their marriage and equally inept at doing so. She was beginning to think that she'd gotten truly spoiled in Tobyn's arms; at least her brother knew how to make her feel important to the act. The way Nikolas made love, she could have been a stand-in for a sheep. She'd never felt so manhandled in all of her life.

"How do you feel?" Nikolas panted, petting her hair.

She offered him a wan smile. "Tired."

He somehow took that as a compliment and puffed up with manly pride. As his hands moved on, demandingly fondling her breasts, he asked, "Are you happy?"

"Nikolas," she sighed, "I'm tired. I want to sleep."

"Later," he objected, shaking his head.

"Now."

He studied her face for a moment, taking in the determined set of her jaw and the no-nonsense look in her eyes before he relented. Araminah turned to lie with her back to him, pillowing her head on her arm and staring at the wall.

Nikolas spoke softly to her, toying with her hair. "I know you didn't want to marry me, Ara. I know you don't love me. But someday you will. You'll feel better about all of this once you get used to me, once we've had sons together. I'll make you happy. I promise I will."

His prating was getting on her nerves. Reaching up, she covered his mouth with her hand, looking at him wearily. "Nikki, be quiet."

He kissed her palm docilely and curled around her, silently snuggling close. His arm around her waist held her too tightly, and she managed to pull free at least enough to breathe. Within moments, Nikolas was asleep and snoring softly, leaving Ara to stare wakefully into the darkness.

~~~

Tobyn found Antonio and Tito sitting beside the Reyes *vardo*, sharing a bottle and speaking in conspiratorial whispers. Silently, he crept closer to listen in.

"...and he fought me on it," Antonio was saying. "He said he'd bring me before the *kris*."

"With his ways?" Tito asked. He spat on the ground. "Chavo was barely Rom in the first place. They'd have never listened to him."

Frowning, Tobyn leaned closer.

"I couldn't take the chance. The *gadje* were giving me good money to turn in troublemakers, and I couldn't let him jeopardize that."

Both of his uncles were drunk as could be, but Tobyn had no doubt of what Antonio was saying. Wine could be better than torture at procuring confessions.

"So what did you do?" Tito prodded like a child listening to a bedtime story.

"I waited until we were alone," the elder Reyes complied, "and then I killed him. I hit him over the head and kicked him until he was dead."

Tobyn's jaw set in cold rage at his uncle's words, coldness spreading through his gut. He would avenge his father, he swore, but not through the *kris*. Antonio had brutally murdered his own kin; he deserved no less in return. This was blood for blood.

"Didn't the jailers ask questions?"

"They didn't care. What's another gypsy, more or less? The most they said was, 'Good riddance.'"

Tito hesitated as his brother knocked back a little more wine, then he asked, "And Tobyn? What did you tell him?"

"*Gadje* did it."

"Do you think he believed you?"

"I don't care," Antonio claimed. "He's no more a proper Rom than his father was. He and his sister both are nothing but headaches."

"But he's a smart boy," Tito fretted. "You know he doesn't trust you."

"I don't trust him, either. I think he's unclean...perverse. I don't know why I think it, but I do." Antonio took another drink. "If he gives me trouble, I'll just kill him like I did Chavo. What's another one, more or less?"

Tobyn made a noisy show out of getting his guitar from the wagon, turning a calm smile that left the ice in his eyes untouched onto his startled, murderous uncles. Their raucous laughter died beneath his gaze. He held up the instrument and said, "I'm going over to join the Caragos at their *vardo*. There's more wine over there if you want it."

Tito fidgeted with the nearly-empty bottle as Antonio studied his nephew's deceptively guileless face. "How long have you been over there?"

"Where? With the Caragos?" Tobyn returned innocently. "All night. I only just came here for my guitar."

Tito bought the explanation immediately, mostly because he wanted to. Antonio, however, failed to be convinced, staring into the younger man's cool blue eyes. Tobyn smiled at him again, but it was a smile with teeth, as if a predator were giving warning to his prey. His uncle faltered but returned the expression threat for threat, his dark eyes narrowed to slits.

Lines were being drawn.

Eleven

Throughout the winter, the *kumpania* hovered in southern Spain, haunting the Mediterranean coast and merging with the other gypsies of Andalucia. Carago kept his group well in hand, not controlling them so much as monitoring their activities to a fare-thee-well. The occasional scuffle with the police was quickly ended and made right through the old man's charm and easy way of manipulating outsiders, and interpersonal squabbles were firmly nipped in the bud before they could get carried away.

This was all very good for the *kumpania* as a whole, but it made life for the Reyes family extremely interesting. Tobyn, who was learning a great deal from watching Carago in action, felt constrained by his unwitting mentor's dislike of gypsy infighting. He and Antonio circled one another like wary wolves, snarling quietly behind Carago's back and looking for the vulnerabilities they would have no hope of exploiting for so long as the *kumpania* elder remained so vigilant. The war between uncle and nephew had quickly settled into the routine of Tobyn acting the perfect Rom and devoted kinsman to Antonio's face while the older man took careful note of everything that was done and said, hunting for a chink in the armor.

Tobyn found that insinuating himself into Carago's good graces was an excellent way to get under his uncle's skin, and that the closer he got into the old man's confidences, the closer Antonio got to having absolute fits. Sela was more than willing to be the ostensible cause for Tobyn's interest in Carago, and she proved so easy to use in that capacity that Reyes began to wonder exactly who was using whom.

Tito, of course, was blissfully unaware of the familial warfare that raged around his head. Beti kept him in the dark, something she had always been good at, even while she kept Antonio and Tobyn separated when the hatred behind their smiles threatened to make itself violently, physically real.

Ara, meanwhile, was enjoying Carago's moratorium on family fighting, since it kept Cristina Moreno reasonably in check and made Manuo keep his hands, if not his eyes, to himself. Carago was not the sort to brook improprieties, and Ara had no intention of being punished for her father-in-law's lack of control.

She also had no intention of ruining her life with a child, and through all of Nikolas' frantic efforts to become a father, she blithely drank the foul-tasting herbal concoction that would make it impossible. She had learned the art of making this and other remedies from Beti, who, with shaking hands and ever-slowing step, had begun the final process of passing on the knowledge of the *chovihani*. Ara was becoming quite well-known among the gypsies in Andalucia, and her purse was growing heavier, much to Nikolas' delight. She was proud of herself, too, knowing that the talents she was using could not be mandated or controlled by anyone but herself. At least that much of her could not be owned by any man.

Marriage had proven to be inconvenient and nothing more. She detested Cristina no more than she had before the ceremony, and certainly no less, and her attitude toward Nikolas had become one of apathetic tolerance. He was gentle, if clumsy, and he doted on her to the point of pampering her more than Tobyn ever did. All in all, it wasn't so bad. She didn't love him, would never love him, probably would never even like him; but, she told herself each day, at least she didn't hate him.

Despite Carago's efforts, radical improprieties did occur, but no one but Tobyn, Ara, and sometimes Beti knew. The twins still found comfort in one another, managing to steal a moment or an hour before they went back to their public role-playing. It was all too short for them, and sometimes late in the night Tobyn would lie awake and fantasize about the two of them running away together to live as man and wife in the open the way they already were in their minds. It was only a dream, he knew, and their few, precious moments were all that they had, but it was enough. Just barely, it was enough. And it was better than no stolen moments at all.

Tobyn was beginning to relax, feeling himself slip back into the rhythm of life in the caravan. Even if he could not quite put together the pieces of the man he'd been before Dumas, he was perfectly capable of refitting his place in his group to suit the person he had become. Vampires seemed distant and a vague unreality to him now, even in the night, and he only saw Dumas' face in dreams. Given time, he was certain that he would forget all about it.

Carago had taken Tobyn under his wing, his friendly nature extended to the small *chovihano* who always wore a wry smile on his face. It was clear to almost all of the *kumpania* that the old man was preening a successor, much to Antonio's vast chagrin; suitors stopped coming to call on Sela, who spent more and more time on Reyes' arm. There was an air of inevitability about the proceedings, and Sela, Carago, and the rest of the caravan were counting the days until Tobyn asked for her hand.

As Tobyn himself saw it, those people would continue to wait until the end of time. He did not want to marry Sela; being her friend, her most constant suitor, was enough for him. He was learning from the old man, who was bound to drop off before too long, and he was getting into a position to slide in and take over. When that happened, Antonio's miserable life wouldn't be worth the gold he took for betraying his fellow Rom. Revenge was what Tobyn lived for now.

Of course, days like this one made life apart from his ulterior motives pleasant in the extreme. December in Almería was beautiful, and the wind that blew in from the south skipped over the water and ran along the beach, dogging his heels as he rode Chal away from the city and the gypsy camps outside of it. The horse had proven to be a wonderful animal, his strength and beauty bringing a number of requests for stud service once breeding season began again. If he played his cards right, Tobyn could forge a proper breeding line from his one stallion. Horse breeders and traders were always wealthy among the Rom. Wealth was a very good thing, indeed; Tobyn liked money.

He turned and looked over his shoulder at Almería and the cluster of brightly-painted gypsy wagons that dotted the land around the city. He was not quite adventurous enough to ride so far that his people were out of reach, at least not today. He disliked being alone, and isolation meant that he was unprotected. It was still too soon to swallow those kinds of feelings, even if the cause of them seemed remote.

Righting himself in the saddle, now devoid of crests and livery markings, Tobyn nudged Chal farther from the sheltering sight of the *kumpania*, heading toward the beach that stretched beyond an outcropping of dark stone. Once he rounded that stone barrier, he would break the line of vision between himself and his fellow Rom, finding a little privacy in the cove.

The shoreline was deserted, which pleased him greatly; he hadn't wanted to have company. Sliding from the saddle, he ground-tethered Chal near a clump of brush. The pure blueness of the water tempted him, and he walked out to the damp tide sand, staring south toward Africa. He had heard fascinating stories about that other continent's deserts and beasts. Perhaps one day he would explore it for himself.

The afternoon sun was smiling down onto his head, its heat and brightness wrapping him in thick, muzzy folds. Tobyn smiled to himself and tilted his face up to receive the light, feeling the wind tug amiably at his hair and the loose material of the shirt that fluttered around him. His bones felt comfortable, and the day and this stretch of beach seemed blessed with an umbrella spell of unreality. Nothing existed but the sun's warmth, the stirring air, and the quiet whispering of the sea as it made love to the land. There was freedom in this place.

He stood at the waterline and watched the boats on the water coming and going from the city's ports, part of his mind rushing into wild imagination of sailing life. He could book passage on a ship and go somewhere new, someplace without memories or vampires, although he kept trying to tell himself that vampires didn't exist. He could go to England, or even to America. Or he could go east, perhaps to Egypt or to India. There was a wide world to explore, a world for him to conquer and come to know as friend or enemy.

For all of his fantasies, though, he knew that he would never go. Without Ara, and even without the *kumpania*, he would be lost, left without even a name to call himself. He needed his twin and his clan, no matter how much a piece of him was always running away from them.

And yet, hadn't he been comfortable as Don Tomas? Hadn't he enjoyed that alter ego, even postponing his reunion with the Rom so that he could hold on to it a little longer?

Come on, Tobyn, he chided himself. *You never played these games with yourself before. Stop second-guessing every move you make.*

The soft sound of footsteps approaching across the sand brought him back from his self-doubts, and he slid his unflappable mask into place. It would do no good to be caught unguarded.

Sela stopped beside him, staring out at the water and echoing his pose. Her skirt billowed around her legs, the charms sewn into the hem jingling merrily. For a long moment, they were silent, watching the ships come and go. Finally, she spoke.

"Why are you out here all alone?" Sela asked quietly, not facing him.

"I was thinking."

"About what?"

He smiled and glanced over at her, breaking away from the hypnotic rhythm of the tide. "About *vardos*."

"Oh, really?" Something had sparked her interest; she cast a sidelong flirt his way. "What about them?"

"I need to get one for myself," he replied, warming to his arbitrary choice of imaginary topics. "I need to get away from my uncles. They drive me crazy."

"Poor Tobyn," she sympathized with a whiff of sarcasm. "You need a little privacy, is that it?"

"Yes, that's exactly it." He felt like an idiot for not having thought sooner of getting a wagon of his own. It would certainly take the edge off of his hiding with Araminah.

"That might be difficult," Sela told him, her tone sly and laden with hidden motives. "*Vardos* are expensive and they take a long time to make."

"I can afford it," he assured her, then mentally kicked himself. *Tell her you have money, idiot, and she'll start thinking about dowries!*

The look on her face told him that the damage was done. Sela seemed to simply file the information away, though, before she turned back to watch the sea birds flying over the water. "Papa could help you, if you wanted him to. He likes you, and Araminah, too."

Tobyn smirked. "Well, I like him."

She turned a brilliant smile to him. "Do you swim?"

"Not if I can avoid it."

"Boring," she accused with a laugh. Pointing toward Chal, she asked, "Can we ride for a while?"

Tobyn could see her angling for something, and he felt just contrary enough to deny her. "I don't want to tire him out. He's got a big season ahead of him."

Sela sighed, putting her hands on her hips and looking down at the sand that pushed between her toes. For a moment, Tobyn almost felt sorry for having disappointed her, but his regret was fleeting. It served her right to try and trap him.

"If we ride together, it'll only be back to the *kumpania*," he told her.

She grimaced. "No, thanks. Not just yet."

The young woman turned and wandered toward where Chal was munching on the bushes. Tobyn followed her, asking, "Why don't you want to go back?"

Sela faced him, her dark eyes frank and astonishingly womanly in her doll's face. "I want to spend time with you," she told him, no hint of shyness in her voice. "I like you, Tobyn. Don't send me away."

On an impulse he wasn't certain he understood, he stole a gentle kiss from her. Her reaction surprised him. After a moment of staring at him, she wrapped her arms around his neck and pulled him into a passionate embrace. Their breath mingled and stopped for a heartbeat as her tongue dove into his mouth, startling him with its knowledge. They were both gasping when they finally separated.

Sela bit her lower lip in a failed effort to keep from smiling too widely, her hands petting his face and hair briefly before they settled onto his shoulders. A trifle breathlessly, he asked, "Where did a nice girl like you learn to kiss like that?"

"I've had a lot of boyfriends," she shrugged, blushing. Her eyes were shining with pride and delight as she wound her arms around his waist. "Just look at what I'm holding..."

While his ego appreciated the comment and his body was pleased with her close proximity, his self-control was taking a beating. Uncharacteristically blushing, he attempted to free himself from the circle of her arms.

"Ah...I don't think this is such a good idea, Sela," he said shakily, considering calling his sister to come to the rescue. "Your father—"

"Papa doesn't have to know." She caught him again, squeezing him tightly. "Please, Tobyn...*chovihano*...I think I love you."

He broke away again, this time managing a step backwards before she came after him. "You've got this all wrong," he told her. "The man is supposed to chase the woman until she gives in."

Sela laughed throatily and stepped closer. "I kept waiting. You wouldn't chase me."

He began to protest again, but she silenced him with a kiss, just as heated as the one before. The embrace counter-balanced their initial momentum, and they toppled to the sandy ground, Tobyn landing on his back with Sela sprawled on top of him. She took advantage of the situation to put him in an extremely vulnerable position, her legs straddling his hips as she straightened up, allowing him to catch his breath...in theory.

"Sela, I don't think—"

"Hush, Tobyn." She kissed him, lightly this time. "You talk too much."

"And you're pushy," he returned, realizing that he could have unseated her a dozen times by now if he'd really wanted to.

"I just try to get what I want."

He looked down with a start as she began unbuttoning her shirt, revealing herself to his wide eyes. Sela knew the moves, that was certain; he wondered if Carago knew what his little girl was really like. She removed the garment all together, then gathered up the hands that had fallen limp at Tobyn's side and pressed them to her softness.

He was in agony; his Rom moral restraint where the *kumpania* leader's daughter was concerned was pitching in its death throes.

"Come on, Tobyn," she breathed, rubbing against the outward sign of his inward weakening. "I want you."

With a groan acknowledging his defeat, a section of his brain rattling about marriage traps, he gave in to her advances. He had to admit that he didn't really mind.

~∽✺∾~

Araminah and Beti sat together on the steps of the Reyes *vardo*, talking quietly about cures and medicines. Antonio hovered nearby, sharpening the blades of his ever-expanding knife collection, trying to seem as though he wasn't listening even though they both knew that he was. Ara soundly disliked him.

In the middle of Beti's description of the perfect combination of herbs to induce sleep, the old woman shifted gears and subjects. "Have you been treating yourself?"

Ara blinked at her, surprised out of her jealous monitoring of Tobyn's activities. "What?"

"You're not a mother, and you aren't with child," Beti said, making the import of her question clear to her granddaughter even if her intrusive son did not completely understand.

"Yes," Ara admitted. "Nikolas is disappointed."

More quietly, the older woman asked, "And Tobyn? Is he disappointed?"

Their eyes met, and Ara suddenly saw what Beti was getting at. Nikolas was demanding children, and sooner or later, a child would have to be born. That child, though, needed to be Moreno's progeny in name only. The thought had crossed Ara's mind before, it was true. Was Beti advocating the fledgling plan, or was she warning against it?

"Tobyn is disappointed."

Beti nodded and patted the young woman's knee. "Good. Talk is that he will be marrying Sela Carago soon."

Ara's face darkened. "I'd say that's a distinct possibility."

"As it should be. It will be a good match. She will be a good wife to him, a proper Romany woman. Normal." The old woman smiled to her granddaughter. "And you have a good husband now. Normal. That's how it should be."

Ara sighed. "Grandmother, I know what it is you're saying. You're wasting your breath. 'Normal' doesn't make us happy."

"You must stop this, child," Beti ordered silently. "I see nothing but harm in it." More quietly, out of deference to Antonio's listening ear, she said, "It is too late for your brother. He is lost. The cards prove it. It is not too late for you!"

Ara rose, irritated by Beti's insistence. "What are you talking about, lost? He's here. He's safe."

"But for how long?" The old woman's face puckered in concern. "Think of yourself, and of your life. You have a husband now. You ought to have a child soon while you are still young." She shook her head and whispered, "Forget your brother."

"You're asking the impossible."

Beti grabbed her hand, preventing her from storming away. "Then be careful. Always be careful. I won't be here to protect you for much longer."

Still angry, Araminah pulled away. "We don't need your protection anymore, grandmother."

Beti watched the young woman stomp back to the Moreno *vardo*, and she shook her head sadly. "Oh, but you do, *chavi*," she told her shadow. "You both do."

～ぁぇℓ℘～

Tobyn lay beside Sela, propped up on one elbow, watching her face as she relaxed and settled her pulse and breathing back to normal rates. With one finger, he traced a line from her hairline down her nose and to the hollow between her breasts. She looked up at him and smiled dreamily, making him chuckle to himself.

"Are you happy?" she asked him.

"Yes. You?"

"Very." She stretched and spread her arms to the side, her fingers toying with the sand. "It was just like I thought it would be."

He kissed her shoulder, then her lips, before he sat back to look into her honest gaze. "In spite of the way you kiss and everything, I was your first, wasn't I?"

"Of course! Papa would kill me otherwise."

"He still might."

"Not if he doesn't find out."

He saw the sly color to her smile, and he narrowed his eyes. "But he will, won't he? You little monster. You're going to go straight home and tell him."

"Not if you ask him for me tonight."

He could see that Carago's manipulative skill was genetic. Laughing in spite of himself, he teased, "Tonight? I can't ask tomorrow?"

"Within two days, then." She sat up, fixing him with a shrewd look she'd never worn around him before. "You can't tell me no, Tobyn. Once he finds out, you'll have to marry me, or else we'll both pay the price. This way, we get the easiest arrangement."

He rose and gathered his clothing, knocking the sand from them as well as he could. "You tricked me," he accused. "You only wanted to trap a husband."

"I told you I always go after what I want," she shrugged, refusing to be dismayed by his sudden anger.

"Why me? Anybody could have been a husband to you. Why me, and not one of these boyfriends that taught you kissing?"

Sela pulled on her skirt and made a list. "Why you? Because you're interesting. Papa likes you—for now. You're Ara's brother, and I like her. You're young. You have money. You're beautiful enough to turn every woman's head. You're *chovihano*—"

"Ah! But that isn't me, that's just something that I was taught." He poured sand from a boot before tugging it on. "What's wrong, Sela? Didn't the Carago family have a healer yet?"

He expected her to wither beneath his glare, but she stood tall, which spoke of either bravery or stupidity. "As a matter of fact, we didn't. And the whole reason, the biggest reason for 'why you' is that I want you. I've wanted you since I first saw you months ago. I promised myself that I would have you, and now I do."

"Not yet."

"You can't fight it. One way or another, we'll be together." She sighed as he turned his back on her to gather up Chal's reins. Sela walked up behind him and put her hands on his hips, murmuring in his ear, "Please don't be angry. I just love you so much."

He stepped from beneath her touch, feeling as if he were locked in a room again, this time in one with invisible walls. "I'm not angry," he lied, although in time it would be true. "I just don't like being used."

"You're not getting a bad deal on this, you know. You'll get Papa's position once he dies, and when we marry, he'll nominate you to the *kris*."

"I'm too young to be in the *kris*," he groaned.

"Not if he says you should be there. And he will." She came to him again, and this time he accepted her embrace. "I'll be a good wife, I swear it. And I've got plenty of gold that you can have. I'll give you anything you want." She sought his eyes with hers, locking a pleading gaze onto him. "I'll always remember today, Tobyn. Please don't make me remember bad things about it, too."

Relenting, he pressed her to him, mumbling into her hair, "I'm sorry, Sela."

Smiling beatifically, knowing she had won, she returned the squeeze. "It's all right, Tobyn. I understand." She laughed and scratched her back. "You'd better hurry and get that *vardo* so we don't have to do this in the sand again."

◦◦◦◦◦◦

Antonio was honing the last of his blades when Tobyn and Sela Carago rode into view, both of them astride his stolen horse. The way she looked at the young man and held her arms around his middle bespoke emotions that he was not pleased to see. All he needed was to have his nephew marrying into the most influential family of the *kumpania*. Spitting onto the ground in irritation, he glared at them as they arrived. Marrying Sela to Tobyn would not only give his nephew too much power; it was also, in Antonio's way of seeing things, a waste of a good woman.

Tobyn dismounted smoothly, then helped Sela to the ground with his easy strength. The girl went back to her father's wagon, a glowing smile on her face, and Reyes walked to his uncle's side.

"We need to talk," Tobyn said simply, his tone emotionless.

Antonio swept his whet stone over the blade once more. "About what?"

The younger man could hear the ice in Antonio's voice, but he did not react to it. "I want to marry Sela, and we need to organize our offer."

As he had hoped, the news did not go over well. Antonio looked up at him in obvious foul temper, threats as clear upon his face as anything could be. "Carago's daughter?" the older man rumbled. "You can't afford her, and I'm not giving you anything."

"I'm not asking for your money," Tobyn sneered. "I wouldn't want to touch it. As eldest Reyes man, though, it falls on you to negotiate this wedding. You should be Rom enough to know that. Or aren't you?"

Antonio narrowed his eyes and glared. "And when will you be making this offer?"

"Tonight."

"Why the sudden decision? I thought you liked your freedom."

The younger man shrugged. "I changed my mind. It happens."

A low growl only vaguely reminiscent of a human voice fell from Antonio's throat. "Did you dishonor the girl? If you did, I swear I'll—"

"You'll do what?" Tobyn demanded, openly scornful.

The knife in his hand was a temptation, but he knew that the boy was under Carago's personal protection. Tobyn's hand was straying to within easy reach of another of Antonio's blades, and he knew his nephew well enough to avoid direct knife fighting with him. Young, quick, and with a mean streak a mile wide where his uncle was concerned, Tobyn was not an enemy to cultivate. Reluctantly, Antonio backed down.

"Just remember your place in this *kumpania*, boy."

"I suggest that you mind your own."

Another moment of hate-chilled silence passed between them, broken by Beti's emergence from the *vardo*. Tobyn turned to look at her, and he was suddenly struck by how wan and old she appeared. His grandmother looked from one man to the other and said, "You're arguing again."

Tobyn patted her shoulder and slid his arm around her, alarmed by the way she leaned against him. "It was only foolishness, Grandmama. It's over now."

Antonio stabbed his newly-sharpened knife into the ground, startling his aged mother. "Tobyn wants to get married," he informed her, his voice dripping displeasure.

Beti grasped her grandson's slender hand, her eyes shining as she turned to him. "Sela Carago?"

Tobyn kissed her temple; she was feverish, and her skin smelled like death. Tears sprang to his eyes, and he blinked them away. "You're a mind-reader."

"No, just a good guesser." She squeezed his fingers. "I'm happy for you. You love her?"

He smiled to her and let her interpret it as she would. She beamed and embraced him.

"It'll be expensive," Antonio complained.

"Quiet. The money will be well spent." She turned to Tobyn. "I hope you'll be happy with her. Mind that you keep only to her. Marriage is special."

"Women," Antonio muttered, gathering up his knives. "Always raving about fidelity."

Beti turned a stern look onto him. "Romany do not commit adultery. Remember when your wife got chased out for that?"

"Very well. I'm just glad I got to beat her first."

He climbed into the *vardo*, blissfully unaware that his nephew was spitting curses at him under his breath. Beti pulled Tobyn's attention back to her.

"Tell me. Why did you decide today to ask for her?"

He shrugged. "She didn't leave me much choice."

"Weak-willed man," Beti teased, her voice lively in spite of her weak look. "Just like your father."

Blushing, he offered his only excuse. "She's very pretty."

The old *chovihani* kissed him on both cheeks, then begged, "Please have a normal life. Stop what you and your sister are doing."

Tobyn patted his grandmother's hand. "Oh, Beti. How can I stop the wind?"

She hung her head, hiding the tears in her eyes. "I fear for you. You aren't prepared for what's coming your way."

He misunderstood the gravity of what she was trying to say. Hugging her briefly, he whispered, "Marriage won't be that difficult. I'll manage."

Beti sniffed and clutched him, then said, "Bring Ara to me. I need to tell her more."

The young man pulled away, looking into her face. "Grandmama, are you all right?"

She patted his hand, then sat on Antonio's vacated stool. "Just go fetch your sister."

Foreboding gripped him with its dreadful claws, but he obeyed, leaving her in the shade of the wagon while he beat a hasty trail to the Moreno *vardo*. Cristina watched him closely as he approached, her usual disapproval of the half-*gadjo* alive in her eyes. She stirred the stew she was cooking and waited for him to speak.

"Where is Araminah?"

"She's in the *vardo* with Nikki," the woman replied stiffly, keeping herself strictly contained as if touching him with so much as a thought would contaminate her. "Why?"

"Beti sent for her," Tobyn answered, invoking the altered status of the *chovihane* to influence Cristina.

"Wait a bit," she advised. "He'll be done with her in a minute."

"He's that good at it, eh?" he asked, not meaning to let himself be heard. Her eyes cooled with her glare, which he chose to ignore. "I don't have a minute. Beti needs her."

"Husbands have more claim on women than anybody, even *chovihane*," she told him firmly. She rose and stood between him and the wagon. "Wait."

He was in the mood to neither argue nor fight her for the door. Cristina Moreno was a strong woman, with a well-known ability to be cruel. Tobyn had seen her work before. Standing still, arms crossed over his chest, he glared back at her and touched the link that bound him to his twin.

She responded immediately. *//Tobyn? What's wrong?//*

//It's Beti. She's sent me to fetch you. I think she's ill.//

//I'll be there as soon as I can.//

He explored the sensations he was receiving ·from Araminah, envisioning her as she sat quietly, ignoring the Lump who spoke to her so savagely. *//What's he on about?//*

//The usual. He wants a baby.// A whiff of anger reached him. *//Did you enjoy the ride? Or maybe I should ask Sela.//*

//Don't start now, Ara, please.// He sighed. *//After we help Beti, we can bicker about this.//* Tobyn looked back over his shoulder at the small form of his grandmother, and he told his twin, *//I'm going back to her. Come quickly.//*

//I will.//

Cristina was still glowering at him as he came back into complete awareness of corporeal reality. Without a word to her, he turned and left the Moreno campsite.

Beti looked up as he rejoined her, smiling affectionately as he took her hand. He clasped it close to his chest, feeling it strangely lifeless against his skin. "Grandmama, if you need medicine, tell me how to mix it. Ara will be here as soon as she can, but I don't know when that will be. Let me help you until then."

"Just sit with me. That's all the help I need." She touched his face. "You look very much like your grandfather. He was a handsome man. Did you know that he was part *gadjo* too? That's where your eyes came from, from Caolo and from your mother. Blue eyes." She sighed. "Not very Rom."

"Sorry," he offered lamely.

The old woman smiled again, but it was a smile with shadows. "You can't help being what you are. Tobyn...what happened in France...it altered you."

He felt cold to his very soul. He had not wanted to admit this, not to Beti, not to himself. "I know."

"Every day, you're different." She began to weep. "You must leave the *kumpania* before it's too late. Break your ties with Ara, be alone." Her shoulders shook. "You're so unclean now..."

"What are you saying? I'm fine, Grandmama." He held her close and let her sob her fears onto his shoulder. Beti was genuinely terrified, sensing something that she was powerless to stop. Tobyn didn't know precisely what she saw—the Sight was limited to the women in his bloodline—or what frightened her about him now, and he knew that Beti would never tell him openly. The secret between them chilled him, and he began to share a little of his grandmother's fear.

"I tried to spare you this," she told him, her voice penitent. "I knew the way *mulle* think, what attracts them. I thought I could protect you from them."

"You did," he insisted, disliking the little voice in the back of his mind that whispered, *No, she didn't.* "I'm still here. I didn't Change into one of them." He frowned in confusion. "Beti, what is it? What are you trying to tell me?"

She shook her head. "You must learn it in your own time. Promise me this: stop being with Araminah. It is so wrong, Tobyn, and it will hurt you both before it's through. I should never have allowed it to begin."

"Shh. You're upsetting yourself over nothing." He hugged her again, looking over her head to see Ara rushing toward them. He sighed in relief, knowing that his sister could help.

Ara reached them, her clear green eyes heavy with concern and empathic reaction to Beti's pain. Tobyn handed their still-sobbing grandmother over into her hands; Ara helped Beti into the *vardo* and closed the door.

//Stay out there, Tobyn. Keep Antonio and Tito away.//
//Help her, Ara. I think she's dying.//
There was a long pause. *//I think you're right.//*

Swallowing his tears only to have more spring up to take their place, he set himself as a guardian at the entrance to the wagon. Ara would have room to work if it killed him.

⚜

Sunset came before Ara left the wagon, her face weary, eyes puffy from crying. She went to where her brother waited, his vigil joined by Carago, Tito and Antonio. She spoke softly to him before he could ask any questions.

"She's sleeping peacefully," she reported, "but she's very weak. I don't think she'll live to morning."

Tito began to weep, surprising both twins with emotions they had never suspected he could carry. Antonio, features twisted more with irritation than with grief, asked, "Do we have to leave her to die in there? I don't want to lose my *vardo*."

The man's selfishness in thinking of Romany funeral customs in the face of his own mother's death infuriated Tobyn. He turned on his uncle with a hiss. "All you care about it your damned money! *Bastaris!* Your mother is dying, and you only care about things!"

Ara rested a restraining hand on his arm, and he fell into still rage. She leveled an icy stare onto Antonio and said, "You can rescue all of your belongings now, if you like. I'm certain that you can buy a new *vardo* before the week is through."

Carago spoke up, his authoritative voice demanding to he heard. "Tobyn, you will come to live with me. You'll marry Sela in the morning."

Surprised but well aware that the arrangement galled Antonio and was therefore desirable, he accepted. "Thank you."

"And you, Antonio Reyes," the old man continued, "you are the most heartless man I've ever known."

Ara suppressed a smile as Antonio purpled and choked in anger. It did her heart good to see her uncle offend people in high places. Tito slipped away from the group, and the look he cast at his brother bore its own verdict as he went to his mother's side.

"I'll get everything out before she goes," Antonio told his nephew, hating the sight of Tobyn at Carago's side with sanctioned anger in his eyes. The balance of power between the Reyes men was shifting, and not in his favor. "You can take your things to your new *vardo* yourself."

"I wouldn't want your help."

Antonio, too, entered the wagon, and the twins looked to one another, their own grief welling to the surface. Their protectress, the woman who had been their staunchest, best, and sometimes only ally, the woman who had raised them after their mother's death, lay dying herself, ill beyond their ability to help or heal. They were alone together against the world, now, and the world seemed intent upon driving them apart.

"Tobyn..."

The fatigue on Ara's face deepened, and Tobyn took her in his arms. They clutched one another tightly, mourning Beti together. Carago wrapped his big arms around the knot they made, supporting both of them, giving them his strength while they needed it. He had always had a soft spot for *chovihane*, and these two were so small and fragile looking against the darkness that crept ever closer. Carago had only sired one daughter, but he was father to many. Tobyn and Ara had come to be his children as well.

He held them close as Antonio unloaded the wagon around his sleeping mother. Carago closed his eyes, rocked the twins gently, made soothing sounds to cover the rattle of their uncle's betrayal.

There was little else that he could do.

Beti died in the darkest hour of the morning with Tito, Tobyn and Ara by her side. The young woman dressed her in her best clothing and jewels while Tobyn and Tito bribed a local priest to perform a burial service that day. Antonio watched sullenly as Beti was laid into a simple coffin and carried away from the *vardo*, which was set to burning, its smoke streaking the sky with black on black. Disgusted at the loss of his most prized possession and with the thought of his mother's finery being buried with her corpse when he could have made money from selling it, the eldest Reyes crushed out his cigarette and watched his niece and nephew huddling together to watch the wagon flame. He did not believe their grief. He did not trust them.

Seeing Carago with the twins, acting so kindly and paternal, set Antonio's teeth on edge. If he could stop Tobyn's marriage to the old man's daughter, he would. He would argue that it was unseemly for a wedding to follow a funeral so closely in the same family. He would argue that Tobyn was tainted and unclean from his stay in France and the mysterious jail that Antonio did not believe in. Certainly Carago would listen to concerns about appearances.

But would he listen to them from Antonio?

The sun was just beginning to rise when Antonio approached the *kumpania* leader, calling him away from the silent group of Sela, Nikolas, Tito and the grieving twins. The old man wore too shrewd a look for a man who'd not slept all night, which did not bode well for Antonio's chances of fooling him with fancy talk.

Even the opening word was denied him by Carago, a practiced Rom politician if ever there was one. "You wish to discuss the wedding," the older man stated smoothly. "Perhaps you mean to stop it."

"I only ask that you delay it. Think of how it will look, so soon after her death. It would be callous."

Carago plainly felt that Antonio was the wrong man to be lecturing on callousness, but his tone remained neutral. "On the contrary, a happy event must follow a sad one, if only to maintain balance."

"It is unseemly," Reyes protested.

"So is letting Tobyn into my *vardo* as a single man. He will sleep beneath my roof tonight, and for that, he and Sela must be married."

"No price has been arranged."

"He is *chovihano*, he is not taking Sela from my *vardo*, and no price was necessary," Carago told him. "No negotiation on this point is needed."

Antonio looked over at where his nephew sat, holding Sela's hands and whispering to her. "Are you certain that he is right for your daughter? Think of the time he spent in French jails. He may be unclean."

"By that token, so might you. All that time in Spanish prisons," the *kumpania* leader returned. "I have come to know you, Antonio Reyes. If anything here is unclean, it is your way of thinking. I don't understand your hatred of Tobyn and Araminah. I don't want to. But know this: I will not allow it to affect me, my family, my decisions, or my clan. I will see you driven out before I will allow you to bring these children down for no reason but your own pettiness."

Antonio glared ferociously, tempted to let his knife speak for him. "He has bewitched you."

Carago smiled with subtle malice. "Be careful of your accusations, lest the crimes you charge to others find their way to you. No, Antonio, the wedding will take place, and Tobyn will be my heir." He chuckled. "That sits poorly, doesn't it?"

His temper was strained almost to snapping. "I'm warning you, old man—"

"No. I'm warning you. You have no friends in this *kumpania*, and no one would cry to see you leaving."

Reyes took a mental step backwards and approached the argument from another angle. "And if I prove that he is unclean and unworthy to be called Romany, what then?"

"You can't."

"But what if I do?"

"Then the *kris* will deal with the crime...and with the witness." He shook his head. "I do not advise it, Reyes."

Antonio smiled a thin-lipped threat. "This is just the start, then."

"Not if I can help it. You're talking nonsense." Turning on his heel, Carago marched away toward his daughter and prospective son-in-law.

Antonio watched him go, his eyes enlivened with the thrill of a challenge. "We'll see, old man. We'll see."

Part Two

Twelve

Germany, 1745

The wind was pleasant and warm, carrying a whiff of recent autumn rain. Tobyn liked the smell of it. Harvest time in Germany was crystal-clear to him, pure air blowing across the meadows and skipping over the countless little streams they'd crossed to reach the village before them.

On the ground ahead of his *vardo*, a recent Italian purchase, his father-in-law was spiritedly arguing with the local burgermeister for the right to stay in the vicinity. The God-fearing folk of this pious place harbored no love for gypsies, but Tobyn rather doubted if any arguments could stand against Carago's diplomacy. He listened to the bickering and idly stroked the leather harness lines in his hands. The *gadjo* was beginning to give in; before long, the *kumpania* would be moving into position and setting up housekeeping for a while.

The German's guttural protestations rose in volume, and Tobyn smiled to himself. "Ach urk ikh ack," he choked mockingly, just loudly enough to send Sela into gales of laughter. He playfully covered her mouth with his hand, quieting her so Carago could finish his negotiations, and she dragged him into a brief wrestling match. The old Romany man put an end to their silliness with a stern look, and they pulled themselves into a semblance of dignity. Unable to resist, Tobyn let out one last "awkh" before toeing the line, sitting straight with a serious face while his wife bottled her giggles.

//Having fun?// Ara teased.

He turned to look over at her where she sat beside her brooding husband, her long legs propped up on the riding board before the bench seat. Her skirt had fallen aside, perhaps with help, and her shapely ankles caught the late morning sunlight.

//Nice legs,// he returned in kind. She winked at him and drew her skirt up to the knee for a brief display. Tobyn grinned. *//My, my, my. Aren't we brazen?//*

//Just you wait, lover. I'll show you brazen.//

Carago returned to his own *vardo* immediately to Tobyn's left, giving the all clear signal. With an explosion of chattering and the jingling of charms and tack, the caravan headed through the middle of the town, parading past the *gadje* and making their way to the meadow on the other side. Someone in the back of the procession started singing loudly, interspersing just enough German amid the Romany to give the villagers a show.

"Who is that?" Sela wondered aloud, looking back over her shoulder.

"Probably David Dera," Tobyn guessed. "Nobody else has that bad a voice."

//Oh, Tobyn,// Ara sing-songed to him.

He sang back. *//What?//*

//You're getting a lot of attention from a gadja *on the corner.//*

He looked toward the young German girl who was staring in his direction and smiled for her. She blushed and hid her face against the arm of her companion, a young man of such similar appearance that he could only have been her brother. The young man watched Reyes as he rode past, his eyes curious, his expression as rapt as his sister's had been. Sela had caught the smile her husband had thrown to the girl, and she kicked him in the ankle, just hard enough to remind him that she was there.

//Maybe you should grab her friend,// he advised his twin. *//We could have a party.//*

Ara's mental laughter was her only response.

"You're a terrible flirt," Sela admonished him softly, her amused look belying the scolding words. "What am I going to do with you?"

"I'm not that bad," he defended. "It was just a smile."

"Uh huh. And what about the girl in Avignon last month? I suppose that was just a smile, too."

He shrugged. "I was trying to talk her into giving me something."

With false innocence, she batted her eyes and teased, "I wonder what that could have been?"

"Money." He tapped her ankle with his boot, and she kicked him back. "Suspicious woman."

"Dirty-minded man."

They genially traded insults and gentle kicks until they reached the campsite. Since their marriage, their relationship had been one of running jokes and chummy rough-housing, not at all the standard husband-and-wife situation. Although Tobyn was as much a part of the patriarchal Romany society as any man in the caravan, he was wedded to an independent, strong-willed young woman whom he could not treat as an inferior if he tried. Sela was like Ara, who had given him his advance training, in that respect; the two women, virtually best friends, were the only people living who could keep him in line. He rather liked that, although he'd never admit it.

Not far away, Antonio drove his own new wagon, his perpetually sour face set into a forbidding stare that he shone at Tobyn. Their war had been at a stalemate for months, and it seemed as though his uncle wanted to renew hostilities. That suited Tobyn just fine. The sooner they got back to fighting, the sooner he could be rid of his father's murderer. One way or another, he would make Antonio pay for his past sins, and pay dearly.

Nikolas brought his wagon to a halt beside Tobyn's, indulging his wife in her desire to be near her brother and her friend. Manuo and

Carago took up position on the far side of the lea, their *vardo*s snuggled together in politically correct companionability. The *kris* members always lined up together.

Tobyn was the exception that proved the rule. Although he had been inducted into the ruling council, he had no dealings with any of his fellows outside of their infrequent meetings. Only Carago and Manuo saw him, and that was because of family ties. A large part of Tobyn's exile within the *kris* lay in his age; most of the others in the council were at least twenty years his senior. There may also have been discomfort at his status as *chovihano*. The skills of prophesy, intermediation between the corporeal and the unseen, telepathy, herbal knowledge, healing...these were almost exclusively the domain of women. Few men were born with the necessary talents to fill that position. Tobyn had been. Worse, he was a closely-bonded twin to the *kumpania*'s reigning healer, who was busily teaching his wife the ways of medicine-making, completing the healer's circle around him. It was no wonder that he made some of the old men a trifle nervous. In all things, he was an anomaly.

Tobyn sent his team to the *kumpania*'s makeshift corral, then untethered Chal from the side of his *vardo* as Sela set about preparing them for a moderately long stay. She raised an eyebrow at him as he saddled his horse, silently asking what he was planning to do.

"I'm going to go investigate the town," he told her, cinching the strap around the animal's middle. "There should be something interesting to do."

"Fine." She wiped her hands on her skirt. "If you come back drunk or after dark, you're sleeping outside tonight."

He laughed at her casual threat. "You're so understanding," he teased, stealing a quick kiss before he swung up into the saddle and cantered back toward the town.

"Men," Araminah observed from the steps of her own *vardo*. "Just try and get them to help out."

Sela laughed her agreement, and the two women began to cooperatively put their things in order. After a short while, they settled down by their common cook fire, gossiping and doing busy work. They were comfortable together, and although each kept her own secrets, they were prone to openly discuss even the most private aspects of their lives.

The topic of today's conversation, as it often was, centered around Ara's frustrations with Nikolas' various inadequacies. Sela listened patiently, amused by her friend's descriptions, but unable to fully sympathize. Her own husband's shortcomings were in vastly different arenas.

"It's awful," Ara grumbled, threading a needle with dark blue thread she'd 'found' in a dress shop in Paris. "Three grunts and he's done. I hardly even have to wake up for it. And after all this time, no matter what I've tried to show him, he isn't improving with practice. If anything, he's getting worse." She shook her head and began to stitch. "I'm going to die of boredom at this rate."

"You're the healer," Sela teased. "Give him a potion that will turn him into a good lover."

"I wish it were that easy. Besides, with Nikolas, it would probably be a waste of time."

The smaller woman laughed. "Poor Ara. No wonder you don't have any children yet."

"Yes...it takes more than ten seconds."

They were quiet for a moment, then Sela looked over at her sister-in-law with aching curiosity. "Can I ask you for a favor?"

Ara did not look up. "What?"

"Can you help me to conceive?"

This time, Ara stared at her for a beat before she replied, "I hate to disappoint you, but I'm not equipped."

Sela threw a thimble at her with a laugh. "That's not what I meant! It's just that, well, Tobyn takes a lot longer than ten seconds, and we're together all the time, but for some reason, I'm not having any luck at all getting children. Is it something wrong with me, something I've done?"

"Why do you want a baby so badly?" she asked. "Kids are a pain in the ass."

"I just want to have Tobyn's child," Sela shrugged. "Papa wants that, too, almost more than I do."

Ara raised an eyebrow. *Oh, really?* "And what does my brother want?"

"He says we have time to wait. I don't think he wants any children right now."

"Then don't rush him."

"I have to have his baby," Sela insisted, putting aside her mending. "That's a wife's primary duty. Please, you have to help me somehow."

Araminah considered her options for a moment, then said slowly, "There is one thing you can try. It isn't always effective, though, especially not if the problem is with him, or if you're just not meant to have babies. If you want, I can make it today and get it to you by tonight."

"Oh, yes! Whatever it is, I'll try it." Sela hugged her briefly, then sat back. "What can I do to repay you?"

Ara held up one hand. "It's no problem. Consider it a gift."

"I have to give you something for it."

The other woman smiled. "How about naming your first daughter after me?"

"It's a deal." Reyes sat back down. "I want sons, though."

"No, you don't."

"Why not?"

"There are too many men in the world already."

Sela laughed. "And they're all weak to the core."

Ara joined in with the cheerful man-bashing. "And their core lives just under their belt buckles."

"And they can't keep their cores to themselves." The *kumpania* leader's daughter dropped her sewing into her lap. "Did I ever tell you about Tobyn in Avignon?"

"Is this a core story?"

"It would have been, I'm sure. Your brother is so spineless when it comes to pretty girls!"

Araminah listened in quiet amusement as Sela told her side of the story Tobyn had already gone over with his twin. Seeing the other woman carrying on such joking outrage at what had been one of Tobyn's most minor episodes, Ara wondered how Sela would react if she ever really did learn the truth about her husband's dalliances. With luck, she would never find out.

Ara and Tobyn had enjoyed one another despite their respective marriages, and although Tobyn truly loved Sela, and although they both knew that what they were doing was wrong and punishable by the most extreme forms of Romany justice, they were unable to resist. As always, the pull between them was overpowering and inevitable, as if the intimacy they shared in their minds and hearts was too much for their bodies to be left out of. Nikolas and Sela were unaware, and Ara and Tobyn were discreet. As long as they could limit the number and length of their trysts, they would not be detected.

While Sela talked, Ara considered the potion that she had been asked to create. It would be easy enough, she supposed, as simple as the one she made for herself. If the herbs did their jobs, then Sela would bear Tobyn's child and Ara would be free of the burden of babies for a little longer. She wanted no part of raising a family, and she had been a midwife far too many times to ever want to go through the sort of pain her patients bore. The more Nikolas pushed, too, the less she was willing to go along with it. Her husband was beginning to get a little violent in his demands, and more than one night had ended with Ara bruised and raw from his single-minded attempts to impregnate her.

But the potion did the trick. And the potion was what she clung to for her peace of mind.

⚜

As German hamlets went, this one was fairly typical. The buildings and the faces could have been anywhere in the kingdom, so uniform were the sights that greeted his eyes. Tobyn dismounted and draped Chal's reins over the hitching post in front of the tavern. He took stock of the place even while the Germans took stock of him; finally, he judged the inn's porch a safe enough spot. At least nobody had rushed up to chase him away from it yet.

Aware that he would never be inconspicuous, he sat on a stool beneath the tavern window and took out his whetstone and his knife. As he honed his own blade, he made clear what sort of service he was offering for the right price. Best of all, he did so without having to speak one word of the harsh language he so disliked. It wasn't that he could not express himself in German; he simply refused to. It was a point of honor for him.

A clot of blond *gadje* gathered around, many of them proffering their own knives and gleaming coins. Gypsies were not essential to the fate of sharp edges in Germany, needless to say, but giving over blades and money legitimized the time the villagers spent staring at him. If these people wanted to pay Tobyn to do something that all of them could have done for themselves, that was their business. He certainly wasn't going to complain.

He sharpened two knives without gracing their owners with so much as a glance, pocketing their coins and moving on to the next. His silence was interpreted as simpleness, and a number of the people around him began to hypothesize about his relative lack of intelligence, counting on his inability to understand. Tobyn didn't really care what they said; what did *gadje* know about intelligence, anyway? He finished his current blade and handed it back to its owner with a sly smile.

"Cut yourself," he said in Romany, his bright expression not dimming.

As the German trundled off, Tobyn could see Tito and Antonio riding by, meeting the village constable in the street. He did not doubt that his elder uncle was setting up the framework for continued betrayals. But what role did Tito play in all of this? Certainly they were not intending to make selling out their *kumpania* to the local police some sort of family business.

They would both bear watching.

"Hello," a voice greeted in execrably-accented Romany. "May I talk with you?"

Tobyn looked up into the pink face of the young man at whose sister he had smiled. Where had a *gadjo* like this learned a proper language? There was a frankness in the blond's eyes that gave him unexplainable pause.

"If you want," Reyes replied, speaking German just to be contrary.

The youth sat beside him on the window sill, watching the quick, skilled motions of the gypsy's small hands. When it became obvious that Tobyn had no intention of speaking first, the German said, "My name is Johann. You are?"

Tobyn tested the edge of the blade he was working. "Yes, I am."

Johann hesitated. "What?"

"Where did you learn Romany?" Reyes was much more comfortable on this end of a question.

"I learned from a lover," the youth replied, speaking the German in which the question had been asked.

One of the men in the watching cluster snorted. "Why don't you tell the gypsy what happened to this 'lover?'"

The sneer in the man's voice shamed Johann into silence. Tobyn raised an eyebrow and asked the observer, "Why don't you tell me?"

He was glad to oblige. "Perverted bastard that Johann is, he got a gypsy boy beaten half to death and thrown out of the caravan. The boy wouldn't stay with him—no small wonder, he was probably being raped the whole time—and he ended up freezing to death in a ditch."

"How pleasant," Reyes observed.

"Serves them both right. Sick bastards."

"Yes," Tobyn grinned, sliding back into his own tongue. "Just like you."

Johann heard and understood even if the loud man did not. Casting a smile and a cautiously flirtatious glance toward the gypsy, he asked in Romany, "Are you a friend?"

"Possibly," Tobyn answered, looking for a new knife to sharpen. "Not that close of a friend, though."

The German took the hint and dropped all suggestiveness from his look and tone; Reyes was strangely sorry to see it go. "Don't worry," Johann assured him, "I don't want a repeat of my first experience."

"That's two of us." He looked up to watch his uncles ride back out of the town. Antonio seemed far too pleased with himself for Tobyn's comfort. The constable came into view, striding purposefully toward where the Rom was sitting, and for a moment, Tobyn was afraid he had been turned in on some trumped-up charge of his uncle's design.

The bulky officer smiled down at the gypsy. "I'm told that your people can sharpen anything with an edge."

"It's true," he replied. "Scythes, hoes, razors, knives, axes..."

"And if you've never seen a type of blade before?"

The crowd sensed a challenge coming, and they began placing their bets. Tobyn smiled. "I'm clever. I can figure it out."

"Care to wager?" the constable asked. "If you can sharpen this, I pay you two marks. If you can't, you pay me two marks and stay out of my city."

Reyes shook his head. "Two marks and freedom to roam this city, no curfew, if I can do it."

A low murmur ran through the watching *gadje*, who apparently disliked the thought of a gypsy being let loose in their streets. The constable, though, was certain of his impending victory.

"Agreed."

Tobyn smiled with every bit of charm he could muster and shook the man's hand. "Let's see this strange thing, then."

The constable grinned widely and unsheathed a knife like none the gypsy had ever seen. The handle was highly-polished wood inlaid with brass, attached to a long silver blade with edges that undulated like waves. Tobyn ran his thumb along the cool metal, feeling the dull sides and fingering the blunt tip. Clearly, this was not a blade meant to harvest or to be used in household repair.

"It's a weapon for stabbing," he observed, all gameplaying gone from his voice, chased away by his fascination. "It's not meant to have a cutting edge. What is it called?"

The constable watched as the gypsy fondled the object, rapt concentration on his face. "It's a *kris* knife. It comes from India."

"*Kris* knife?" Tobyn grinned. *Well, isn't that just an interesting name.* He picked up his stone. "I can do this."

"Prove it."

Reyes worked intently, ignoring the constable, the jabbering crowd, and the way Johann pressed closer to see better. He coaxed the point to needle-sharpness and honed the bottom edges of the curves in the blade. Whatever was unfortunate enough to be on the business end of this knife would surely know it.

"Here," Tobyn said, handing over the weapon. "I think you owe me two marks and the key to the city gates."

The constable tested the blade with the side of his thumb, showing his displeasure at the well-honed sharpness with a fierce frown. He slapped the knife into its sheath and fished out the two marks. Grunting something sour, he threw the coins into the dirt between Tobyn's feet and stomped back to his constabulary.

"You're smarter than you look, gypsy," one of the Germans laughed. "And you won me a lager."

Tobyn ignored the *gadje* as they filtered away, just as he ignored the young man who stayed. Quietly, he repeated the name of the fascinating weapon. "*Kris* knife."

He wanted it.

~✦~

Ara knelt in the center of her husband's wagon, the door shut and locked against Nikolas' intrusions. With a specially-selected smooth stone that she had owned for nearly ten years, she ground dried herb leaves and crushed new green ones together into a dark paste that smeared the inside of a china dish Tobyn had stolen for her when they were children.

She added a few more ingredients, a sprinkle or two of dried medicines, and poured water over the top of it.

This was what she wanted, the thing that would keep her childless. Since she was already busy with medicine-making for Sela, she had decided to replenish her own supply. Nothing would make her get fat and have pain for Nikolas Moreno's pride.

The water dissolved the paste and turned dark as coffee. She stirred it several times to be certain, scraping the bottom and sides of the dish to get all of the herbs into the solution, then poured it into a little glass bottle from France. She sealed it with a cork, tied a blue ribbon around the neck, and put it aside.

She washed the dish thoroughly and began Sela's concoction next, repeating the grinding and crushing and dissolving. The steady rhythm of the mortar and pestle soothed her, and she relaxed into her work. Her mind wandered, and she let herself daydream a bit about what Sela and Tobyn's child would look like, if it were in fact conceived. The baby would probably be very pretty, considering its parentage; both of them were beautiful. Sela's luxurious hair would probably be passed along. Ara hoped that the baby would have Tobyn's eyes. He had such expressive, lovely eyes...

She poured this potion into a glass bottle identical to the first, still daydreaming, and tied a ribbon around its neck as well before she put it to the side. She cleaned up after her craft work, then put the dish and her now-empty case of herbs into her special hiding place under the bed. Wiping her hands on her skirt, she turned to gather up Sela's potion for the delivery.

Both ribbons were blue.

She stared mutely at the bottles lying innocently on the carpet square Nikolas had stolen in Venice. Which was which? She thought she remembered putting hers farther to the left.

"Oh, Ara, you stupid woman," she moaned. "Pay attention!" What would Beti say?

Taking a deep breath, she trusted to her intuition and plucked one of the bottles from the carpet. Praying that she was right, she went to give the bottle to Sela.

✺

His wife was smiling over some secret when Tobyn returned late that afternoon, humming to herself as she went about her myriad chores. No matter how much he tried to pry the words from her, she staunchly refused to clue him in to her happiness. Shrugging it off as yet another feminine mystery, he sat back to plan how to get his knife.

The last time he'd stolen something from an important *gadjo*, or tried to, the results had been extremely bad. This time would be different. Not only did he learn from his mistakes, but he was certain that the knife's current owner was not a vampire. That was valuable knowledge, as far as his nerves were concerned.

The knife was in the constabulary, most likely; according to Johann, the man who had shown it lived in private rooms above the main floor of the little building. If he liked the knife, and he apparently did, it would be in his apartment. If he did not, if the *kris* knife were a mere novelty, then it would be in the constabulary. Tobyn needed more to go on to make the job easier. But easy meant boring, and he disliked stealing when there were no risks. To be honest, all of the unknowns made this the perfect situation for him.

Perhaps he didn't learn from his mistakes, after all.

Sela was unexpectedly amorous that night, and it took some time— albeit time he enjoyed spending—to get her satisfied and asleep. Most of the night was gone by the time she was sleeping soundly enough for him to rise and leave the *vardo*. There was no moon to be seen, and the stars were hiding behind clouds that threatened him with rainfall. Still, he could see clearly enough in the darkness, almost the same as if it were day. Leaving Chal dozing beside the wagon, he headed toward the town.

What he was doing was exceptionally ill-advised, he knew. The timing was terrible if he wanted the *kumpania* to seem blameless, and he knew that Carago would be furious if he were to be caught. Antonio and Tito and their deal with the constable, whatever that may have been, should have given him at least a moment's hesitation. The very audacity of stealing from the local law, especially when the local law had seen his face clearly, appealed to him, and he desperately wanted a chance to point out Antonio and Tito as they played Judas to their people. If the law came directly to his wagon steps, he would have proof for the *kris*, and his uncles would be forced out.

That goal alone was worth any risk he took to reach it.

On silent feet, he went to the door of the constabulary. It was latched on the inside, but only with a wooden bar. A quick and well-aimed wiggle of his knife took care of that problem, and he let himself in.

The main room was spotless, with no knives in evidence. It certainly wouldn't be back in the jail cell area. That meant that it had to be upstairs with the constable himself. Taking a deep breath, Tobyn crept up the stairs into the German's private rooms.

He found the sheathed knife in the bedroom, resting beside the constable's pillow with the man's hand curled loosely around it. Tobyn watched the German as he lay sleeping, the utter vulnerability of his position striking a curiously resonant chord in his soul. It was strange and thrilling to watch him sleeping, so completely at the Rom's mercy. He could do anything he wanted, he could take anything he pleased...

Take the knife and go, he scolded himself, shaking out of his reverie. *What are you doing?*

Concentrating on convincing the man to remain asleep through his willpower alone, Tobyn knelt at the bedside and took hold of the tip of the weapon's handle. Slowly, as slowly as he could, he pulled the prize free of the German's grasp. As the sheath slid away from his fingers, the constable let out a snort and rolled over, flopping beneath his blankets like a fish on a beach before he settled back into peaceful slumber.

Once Tobyn got his heartbeat under control, he reversed his path, easing his way out of the building with elaborate care. He returned to his *vardo* at a dead run as soon as he reached the street, never looking back.

When he reached the *kumpania,* the adrenaline in his blood had him exhilarated and much too wide awake to go to sleep. After stowing his prize in the bottom frame of his wagon, he crept to Ara and the Lump's neighboring *vardo.*

//Ara,// he called urgently.

She responded quickly; apparently, she had not been asleep. *//I'm here. Come in.//*

//The Lump?//

//Asleep. He won't move until tomorrow. I made sure of it.//

Tobyn chuckled. *//Did you drug him?//*

//Absolutely. It's the only way.//

//Good work.//

She opened the door for him, ascertaining that they had no witnesses before she let him in. *//You could stampede a herd of cattle through here and he'd never know.//*

//Wonderful.//

He kissed her passionately, the immediacy in his touch surprising them both. Ara could feel mad energy rushing through him, spiraling wildly beneath his skin. Pulling back, she peered into his shining eyes.

//Are you all right?//

//Never better. Want you...//

Wondering at this change in her brother but not in the mood to object, affected as she was by the echoes through their link, she wrapped her arms around him and returned his kiss. *//You have me.//*

Thirteen

For the fourth time that day, Sela gave Tobyn a good shake, hoping that his brain would rattle hard enough to wake him up this time.

"Get up," she grumbled, shaking him again.

He groaned, reacting more than he had to her other attempts, and pried one eye open to peer at her. "Hm?" he mumbled, not yet capable of coherent speech.

"It's after noon, and there's a *gadjo* looking for you."

Tobyn struggled to sit up. "Fuck him."

"I'd rather not." Sela put her hands on her hips. "Are you going to get up on your own, or am I going to have to get Papa to drag you out?"

"Don't threaten me with your father." He tossed his head to flip a stray curl out of his eyes. "I'm up, I'm up."

"No, you're not."

"I will be, then. Give me a chance, Sela, please."

She frowned, unaccustomed to crankiness from her husband. Something was wrong. "Are you feeling all right?" she asked doubtfully.

"I'm fine." He rose on the third try and dragged his way to his clothes to hunt up a clean shirt. "I could use some coffee, though, if you don't mind."

She snorted. "You look like hell, love."

"Feel like it." He paused in the process of pulling on his shirt. "We do have coffee, don't we?"

"Sort of. I picked something up in the last town."

"Please let me have some."

"Ooh! You're begging." She grinned. "I like that."

"Wench."

Sela only laughed and stepped out to fetch him the coffee, leaving him to improve his temper. In the silence following her departure, Tobyn considered burrowing back under his blankets and going back to sleep. He was tired, unbelievably so, and every muscle in his body ached. The light streaming in through the open *vardo* door was ferocious, doing horrible things to his head. He shielded his eyes from the glare with an aggrieved groan and waited for his wife to return.

Sela came back inside and pressed a stoneware mug of Italian make into his grateful hands. He mumbled something reasonably like "thank you" and took a hearty swallow. Immediately his face puckered and twisted as the quasi-coffee mauled his tastebuds.

"Puts hair on your chest," she told him, valiantly trying not to laugh at his facial contortions.

"I think it's more likely to take it off," he gasped, "but it's waking me up." After taking another shot of the stuff, he asked, "What's this about somebody looking for me?"

"A *gadjo* came around early today, looking for someone with your description. He doesn't know your name, and I wasn't about to let him near you."

He smiled and kissed her cheek, finding the softness of her skin beguiling. His pulse sped up a notch and he said, "You're too good to me."

She wrinkled her nose. "I know."

"He didn't happen to say what he wanted, did he?"

"No, not really. He wanted to talk to you, and he knew Antonio."

Tobyn raised an eyebrow. "Oh, really? Did he tell you his name?"

"The *gadjo*? Ah...it was Johann, I think. Nice enough to look at, if a bit German. He's the one whose sister you flirted with."

He put the mug aside and pulled her down with him into the tangle of blankets. "I was not flirting," he insisted, pinning her to the floor through her giggling shrieks and half-hearted resistance. They wrestled boisterously for a moment, progressing rapidly from play to seduction. He wondered where all of this energy was coming from, but he was in no mood to fight it when it felt so very good.

Sela, at least, knew the difference between a good time and a bad time for such things. Tearing her mouth away from his, she gasped, "What about the *gadjo*? Do you know him?"

Amazingly enough, Tobyn took the hint. Easing off, he fought his body back under control and replied, "Sort of. He seems nice enough."

"What do you think he wants?"

"I don't know."

She rearranged her disheveled clothing and scooted slightly away from him, her instincts insisting that there was something going on inside her husband. "Maybe you should find out."

He sighed and ran a hand over his hair. "Yeah. Maybe I should."

The sunlight hit him with an almost physical force, dazzling him until he could see nothing but blazing light. Wincing, he shaded his eyes and waited to adjust to the brightness. The improvement was only marginal, but it was enough to allow him to function.

Carago came up to him, his old face harsh with tension. "I don't know how you know him, but there's a *gadjo* at the edge of the camp who's insisting to see you. Make him leave."

Tobyn was a bit surprised by his father-in-law's harsh tone, but he knew enough not to cross the man. "Where is he?"

Carago silently pointed to where Johann could be seen arguing with Manuo Moreno. Tobyn nodded to his companion and went to stand before the German.

"What is it, Johann?" he asked wearily. "You're causing a terrible fuss."

"You have to hide," the blond urged without preamble. "I don't know what you've done, but the constable is coming for you tonight."

"The constable?" Manuo echoed, the look he shot Tobyn full of accusations.

"How does he know of me?" Reyes asked, unperturbed.

"From when you were sharpening his knife, and..." He trailed off, distrustful of Moreno. "Can we talk in private?"

The two Rom exchanged a brief glance, and Tobyn replied, "Certainly. Come with me."

Moreno was not pleased. "Tobyn."

"Be quiet, old man," Reyes ordered, pure authority shining in his voice. "This is my affair."

Johann followed as the smaller man led him to his *vardo*. Sela eyed the visitor but said nothing, trusting her husband's judgment. Tobyn ushered him inside and closed the door while his wife waited at the cook fire.

"Tell me now," he requested, sitting back in the comfortable dimness of the wagon's interior.

"You've been betrayed," the German told him gravely. "A man named Antonio Reyes has been taken into Constable Beurling's pay as an informant."

Tobyn was not surprised but still vastly annoyed. "Do you have proof of this?"

"Not enough for a court, no," Johann admitted. "But I know it's true. I overheard them talking this morning."

The gypsy tapped a finger against his knee in a slow beat of frustration. Looking up into Johann's worried eyes, he asked, "Why are you doing this? Why do you care if this Constable Beurling of yours comes after me?"

"I don't want to see you hurt," he offered carefully. "I don't want to see you get locked away."

"And what do you want to see?"

The German's answer was cut off by a clamorous uproar of voices outside. The door to the *vardo* burst open, and Sela scrambled in, eyes wide.

"The constable is here!" she cried. "He's looking for you."

Tobyn was on his feet with a snarl. "I thought he was coming tonight," he snapped at the German in his *vardo*.

"He knows which wagon is yours," Johann said, ignoring Tobyn's tacit accusation. "Antonio told him."

The young woman frowned. "Antonio?"

The door banged open, and a trio of Germans in uniform roughly shoved Sela aside while the constable bickered with Carago at the steps. Tobyn leapt to his feet, ready to defend his wife while she made a show of pain to cover her search for Tobyn's knife. Johann rose to stand beside him, but the police battered him away. The first German reached out to grab Tobyn, but the Rom uncooperatively kicked him in the groin instead. Sela lunged at a second man while the third went after her husband; she was thrown aside, landing solidly against a wooden storage box. The thud of skull on wood was loud inside the wagon, and concern made Tobyn's reflexes slow. The offended first guardsman seized his arms and held them wrenched behind Tobyn's back while another German held his pistol to Sela's forehead.

"No!" Reyes shouted, struggling in his captor's grasp. The man was experienced, however, and he turned the Rom's efforts against him, all but dislocating his shoulders. In a softer voice and flawless German, Tobyn begged, "Please don't hurt her. She didn't do anything."

The officer who held him grunted, "Bring her."

Reyes stopped struggling long enough to make a sincere promise. "If you lay a finger on her, I'll kill you."

Johann staggered to his feet, only to be apprehended by the third guard. The constable called from outside, "Bring me the gypsy!" Obediently, his men hauled Tobyn out into the daylight while Sela was left alone.

The center of the camp was thronged with *gadje*, both uniformed police and volunteering townsmen. If an all-out fight took place, the *kumpania* stood to be sorely wounded. A quick glance at Carago's sputtering, angry silence told Tobyn that he was about to be given up for the sake of the group. Not far away, Antonio looked on with a still face but eyes shining in glee.

Constable Beurling glared at Tobyn; when his size and attitude failed to make the gypsy quail, he scowled even more fiercely than before. "This is the one," he told his men. "Take him back to town and make him tell you where he hid my property."

The Rom on all sides gave an outcry, and Tobyn could see anger flashing treacherously on his twin's face. Ara took a threatening step toward the Germans, but Nikolas held her back firmly, coming to good use at last. As the guards began to drag him away, he urged her, *//See to Sela. She's hurt.//*

//Why are you letting them take you?// she demanded, too furious to really listen to his reply.

//Sela.//

He closed down their link as the German guards bound his hands and shoved him roughly toward the town. The police were likely to be brutal; they always were with captive Rom. A part of him dreaded the onslaught. Still, in light of everything he had been through, they could do virtually nothing to him that would not be redundant. Letting himself be jostled and dragged along, he worried about Sela and plotted Antonio's come-uppance.

⁓⳽⳽⳽⁓

"Where is it?" Beurling demanded, slapping his prisoner's face once more for emphasis as he walked a slow circle around where the bound man had been forced to kneel.

"Switzerland."

His flippancy was rewarded by a guard's crashing fist, and he toppled onto his side. Out of sheer obstinance, Tobyn struggled back up to his knees and smiled coldly at the constable.

"I grow tired of your games, gypsy. You are not important enough to be kept alive, and the knife you stole is worth twelve of you."

Reyes launched a glob of bloody spittle at Beurling, staining his tunic. The German snarled in disgust and backed away. "Take him to his cell! Get him out of my sight! Let Reyes come back and finish him off tonight. I want nothing more to do with him."

His men obeyed, pulling Tobyn to his feet and all but carrying him to a tiny, dank-smelling cell with filthy straw on the floor. After a few parting blows, they left him, still bound, to his own devices and the company of vermin.

Reaching out, ignoring the pains in his face and the insistent itch of blood running from a wound in his scalp, he contacted his sister. *//Ara, are you there?//*

//Yes.// The anger he had expected flooded her 'voice.' *//They've beaten you, the bastards! Hold on, lover, and I'll get you out of there.//*

//Not by yourself, you won't, and first things first, anyway. How's Sela?//

//She hit her head pretty hard, but she's awake and coherent even if she does have a hellish headache. She'll be all right.//

//Is Carago planning on moving on?//

//I don't know. Right now, he's talking to your German friend, Johann. Apparently, the police let him go.//

Tobyn thought quickly, knowing that Araminah would 'see' every step of the convoluted path. If they had already released Johann, either they could find no crime to blame him for, which was unlikely, or they simply weren't interested in him. If that were the case, then the constable only wanted Tobyn, which, while flattering in a twisted way, was also difficult to imagine. But the bet over the *kris* knife had been so intricately staged, so carefully played, and the theft so easy...he should have guessed it to be a trap.

//You did,// Ara told him. *//That's why doing it seemed so appealing. I know the way you are about a challenge.//*

//Hush and let me think.//

Why had the constable gone trolling for Tobyn? Why present him with so desirable a target, and so openly? Why Tobyn in particular and not Stefan Dreillo, for example, another Rom who had invaded the village to sharpen blades for coins? How much money had passed between Antonio and Beurling, and who had paid whom?

//I'll kill him,// Ara growled.

//Antonio? Do it and I'll never forgive you. He's mine.//

There was a heavy pause. *//Are you all right?//*

//Fine.//

//You sounded...strange.//

//Don't worry about it,// Tobyn advised. *//Just get me out of this damned cage before Carago moves out.//*

//I'll get you even if it kills Nikolas.//

He smiled, laughing quietly. *//Especially if it kills the Lump.//* The guards approached his door, opening it to drag him back out for another go-round with Beurling, who was flexing his wrists and snapping a leather strap against his thigh. Tobyn closed their conversation with an urgent, *//Hurry.//*

~✑✐✒~

Araminah was waiting for Johann when he left the Carago *vardo*, his blue eyes glinting with anger at his summary dismissal. She grabbed his arm and pulled him aside. With the authoritative air only a *chovihani* could really pull off, she spoke before he could react.

"I'm Tobyn's sister," she told him. "Help me get him out of that jail before morning."

The German blinked once, then replied, "That won't be easy..."

"I don't give a damn about easy! I want my brother back where he belongs." She put her hands on her hips. "You know this village, the way it works. That's why I've asked you. But don't fool yourself—it will be done with or without you."

Johann held up his hands in a placating gesture. "I never said I wouldn't help. I just said it wouldn't be easy." He waited while Ara reeled in her anger and locked it down once more. "The best time to do it is after dark, probably a little after midnight. The guards will be sleepy and careless and easily distracted."

She could see what he was thinking. "I'll do anything I have to do to get him free."

Johann studied her face, acknowledging her beauty's potential when applied in just the right way. He nodded.

"Good. You may have to."

"Midnight," Araminah mused. "That's a long while from now. Is there anything at all that we can do before then? I'm afraid of what they'll do to him."

"If we try to break him out during daylight like this, the attempt is bound to fail. They may even penalize Tobyn for our failure." Johann shook his head in disgust. "All over a knife. I promise you this: if they injure your brother in any way, I will make them pay for it."

Ara's green eyes scanned his expression for a moment, and she seemed to be reading his soul. Finally, she said, "I believe you. Please, come stay by my *vardo* until it's time to get him. You're welcome to eat with us, and I'd like to speak with you more."

A bit surprised by her sudden hospitality, the German hesitated before saying, "Thank you. I would be honored."

"Good." She grinned up at him. "It's over here. You can talk with my husband while I check in on Sela."

Johann walked beside her to her home, trying to ignore the petulant glares from other Rom that Ara seemed to enjoy. "Is Sela all right?"

"She'll be fine. I'm far more concerned about my brother."

He nodded and mumbled, "Me, too."

Johann had not intended to be heard, but the woman at his side smiled widely at him, a strange gleam of fascinated curiosity in her eyes. "We have a lot to talk about," she told him as she started into Tobyn and Sela's *vardo*. Laughing to herself, she left him alone with his bewilderment.

Sela looked up at her as she sat by her side. Ara took her hand and swept a gentle touch over the other woman's fever-warm brow. The bump on the side of her head was slowly shrinking, and the dazed look had faded from her eyes. Casually, Araminah said, "I think you'll live."

Her friend closed her eyes with a wan smile. "It certainly doesn't feel like it." She glanced up once more. "Where is Tobyn?"

"He's in the jail in the village." Her tone was gentle and easy even if her words were not.

Sela tried to rise up, wincing, but her sister-in-law pushed her back down. "Is he hurt? Please, Ara. I have to know. I know that you can see what happens to him, that there's some strange connection between you. I know all about the two of you."

Ara hesitated for a moment, breathless guilt and shock taking her before she could control them. She licked her lips and decided to tell the truth. "He's hurt. They've been beating him." When Sela dissolved into silent tears, she quickly added, "We'll get him back, I swear it. Johann and I will get him tonight, and we'll bring him back here to you."

Sela squeezed her hand. "I trust you. Be careful, Ara—the police aren't as dumb as you might think, and they might have friends here with us. I don't want you to join Tobyn in that cell."

"We'll be careful," the healer promised.

A strange pleading covered her friend's face as she said, "Be careful once you're back, too. I meant it when I said I knew all about the two of you. Papa would not look kindly on incest."

Araminah blanched and stammered, "S-Sela—"

"It's all right," she said with a weary wave of her hand. "I don't understand and I don't approve, but he needs you somehow." Sela shrugged and tried to laugh it off. "*Chovihano*. I don't know why it is, but I know that he would die if he couldn't have you. I won't try to stop it, because that would only hurt him and make him hate me. Just remember that I'm his wife."

"I could hardly forget." She whispered, "You're angry."

Sela sighed. "I was, and hurt. But I've always known that he's never loved me as much as he should, or as much as he could have. There's a part of him that's always tucked away from me, and I know that it's that part that belongs to you. I can't say it didn't upset me at first, but after a while, a woman gets used to certain things. Tobyn is very good to me in every other way, and he never goes to anyone but you, except to flirt. Maybe it's because you're twins. I don't know." She smiled again, this time with a bit more spunk. "Besides, I'd worry about any woman who tells him no. He's very persuasive."

Ara returned the friendly expression with relief. "And very good at what he does."

"Oh, yes. Tell me...does he say he loves you?"

She faltered. "Yes."

Sela nodded. "I thought so. He never says it to me."

"He does love you. I can tell." Araminah looked at her, feeling guilty and wrong for the first time. "You have to believe that."

She glanced up, then laughed softly. "We'll see. I'm very tired now, so..."

"If it bothers you," Ara said, instantly chiding herself for sounding foolish, "I'll stop. I won't let him—"

"You can't stop it any more than I can. You'd both die without it, I think." She shook her head. "*Chovihane*. All I ask is that you're careful. Don't make stupid mistakes, all right? And please—don't make me watch. Not unless I can join in, of course," she teased.

"You're taking this very well."

"I've had time to adjust. Besides, he's still in my bed more often than yours. If that changes, there might be trouble, but for now I can manage."

Araminah considered asking her where she got her information, but decided that she really didn't want to know. Patting Sela's shoulder, at a loss for how to continue the conversation, she let the subject drop. "You'll be fine soon. I can give you something for the headache tomorrow morning if you like."

"I'd like that very much." She watched as her friend prepared to go, then said, "Don't feel badly, Ara. If it had hurt that much, I would have called you on it long ago."

"Why did you mention it now?"

"I wanted you to know where I stood. If you weren't *chovihane*, and if you weren't linked the way you are, it would bother me more. This way, it all just seems...inevitable. Just don't get caught. Others wouldn't be as understanding as I am."

Ara smiled back over her shoulder. "I'm surprised that you are."

"I'm not an everyday sort of person. That's how I can stand to be married to Tobyn." She shifted position slightly. "Get him back here, Ara, and the three of us will have a nice, long talk."

"I'll do that," her sister-in-law vowed. "You should rest and stop talking so much. I'll check in on you again in a few minutes."

"All right."

Ara left the *vardo*, her head swimming madly with conflicting thoughts and emotions. It had been a very odd day, indeed. First the arrest, then this...she only hoped that Sela wasn't lying about not being bothered.

Back in the quiet darkness, Sela was lying awake, hoping that she wasn't lying, too.

⊱⊰⊱⊰

It was nearly nightfall when Nikolas pulled his wife aside and gestured toward the German sitting quietly beside the fire. In a hushed voice, he said, "You don't know about that *gadjo*, do you?"

Ara looked at Johann, then at Nikolas. "I know he's Tobyn's friend."

Moreno spat on the ground between his feet. "Friend. Hah. I think you ought to worry about your brother. That *gadjo* is a pervert."

She raised an eyebrow above a shatteringly bored stare. "Oh?"

Nikolas sounded scandalized as he hissed, "He fucks boys."

"So what if he does?"

"It's disgusting! Why do you think he's so willing to help you get your brother out of jail? He wants to dishonor him, you mark my words. Your brother is better off where he is, where that *gadjo* can't touch him."

"My brother has a name, Nikolas," she said coolly, freeing her arm from his ham-fisted grasp. "You can use it. He isn't dead, and hearing his name won't bring him back as a vampire."

She wanted to kick herself for saying that, but she was distracted as her husband's face darkened in anger. "Do you want to let that man use Tobyn? Do you want to see him unman your brother?"

"Tobyn can take care of himself. If he doesn't want to do something, it isn't done. Johann isn't the sort to force him."

"So you think Tobyn might be a pervert, too? Is that what you're saying?"

She wanted to slap the look of utter distaste from Nikolas' face. Anger flashed in her eyes as she growled, "You're raving, and I'm not going to listen to you anymore."

"I won't have that...*gadjo*...near my *vardo*," he sneered, issuing an order for the first time in their marriage.

Araminah glared more fiercely. "You'll just have to learn to live with it."

"Don't you dare defy me, woman!"

She stood her ground as he advanced threateningly. She could smell alcohol on his breath. "What are you going to do, Nikolas? Hit me? Will that make you feel like a man?"

Moreno took another step forward, unbuckling his belt. "Antonio is right. It's time you learned to obey me."

She laughed harshly, tossing her head. "Big man, Nikolas. Beating your wife, now? Do you really think it's wise to hit a *chovihani*?" When he paused, she drove her point home. "I know a million ways to kill you in your sleep. Don't forget that."

His hand sagged, the belt dragging the ground, his cowardice and self-preservation instinct rendering his threats impotent. "I will not be defied by a woman," he sputtered. "Romany men are always in control of their wives!"

Araminah's eyes narrowed. "You're drunk," she bit, "and you're pathetic. Johann is more of a man than you'll ever be."

She turned on her heel and marched away, leaving Nikolas to stammer promises of taming as she left him in the darkness.

"I'll teach you your place, Araminah!" he growled, slapping the dirt with the strap. "Just see if I don't."

~~~⚬~~~

Tobyn awoke quite some time after the Germans had thrown him back into his cell. Silent out of disrespect for his captors, he probed at the bruises on his face and at the swollen lump that should have been his left eye.

//Hey, Ara,// he called, opening the line tentatively. *//I look like your husband.//*

//We're coming for you tonight.//

He smiled at her crisp, almost military tone. *//Who is 'we?'//*
//Johann and me. After midnight, we'll get you out.//
//Don't be late.//

～✴✦✴～

Johann looked up at Araminah as she paced, her arms crossed
beneath her breasts, her jaw set in impatience. It seemed that she was
always angry about something. He thought it was strange, considering
how calm her brother seemed to be.

She sank down to sit beside him, sighing heavily. When he chuckled,
she defensively said, "I don't like waiting."

"Only an hour more. We can start walking soon. Going into the
village from behind will take a bit more time."

"Not that much more." Ara poked at a twig with her foot. "Tell me,
why do you care so much about what happens to my brother?"

He hesitated. "I like him."

"The way you liked that Rom boy everybody keeps talking about?"
She nodded into his stunned look. "You're well-known, it seems." Breaking
into a wicked grin, she asked, "So, you like sex with other men. How does
that work? Where do the parts go?"

He colored so dark and so fast that she was afraid his head would
burst. "I—uh..."

Taking pity of a sort, she went on. "Do you fancy my brother?"

He licked his lips nervously. "He's very nice—"

"—To look at," Ara finished impishly.

Johann blushed again. "Well, yes, I suppose so."

"No repeating what happened before, all right?" She met his gaze
with complete sincerity. "Don't get my brother into trouble."

"I swear, that's the last thing in the world I want."

"Do you want Tobyn?"

He could see that she would not let him evade the question this
time. Bewildered, completely unable to determine her motivations, he
stammered, "W-well, yes."

Ara's joking veneer slid away. "That's all very well and good, I
suppose, but remember one thing: if you ever hurt my brother in any way,
if you do one thing that's not his idea, too, you'll have to answer to me.
And I don't think you really want to do that."

"I'm not going to rape him, if that's what concerns you."

"Good. That's one thing he doesn't need."

"It's something that I would never do."

She grinned into his indignation. "Good, again. I'm glad we
understand one another."

Johann shook his head. "I wish I could say the same, but I don't understand you at all."

"You aren't meant to." Ara rose and straightened out her skirt, catching a glimpse of—and ignoring—Nikolas skulking in the shadows on the outer edge of the firelight. She didn't have time for him now. Nodding briskly to Johann, she said, "Let's go."

⚇⚇⚇

Carago watched his healer and her German friend heading off toward the village, and he knew what they were planning. It didn't take a genius to figure out that Ara would want to get her twin out of jail as soon as possible. No gypsy ever did well in confinement, and the really unusual ones, like the twins, took it worse than most.

He wished them luck.

He left his *vardo*, walked a circuit of the encampment, and thought. He thought about how his daughter loved her husband so much that she would not allow her father to ask questions. He thought about how quiet his *kumpania* had been before they'd taken in the riotous Reyes and Moreno group, and how chaotic it was now.

He thought about Antonio, who was currently saddling up a black stallion, one of the prize studs that Tobyn had obtained—stolen was such an ugly word—in Bavaria not long ago. The elder Reyes had his eyes on the village, too, and a long, wicked-looking knife in his belt. Again, it didn't take a genius to see what was going on, and while Carago had no proof, and he could only interpret Antonio's intentions, he knew that the man would only interfere with the rescue attempt.

Clearing his throat, he decided to call an emergency *kris* meeting to discuss the arrest. Antonio would have to stay in camp for that.

Fourteen

Dumas looked up in mild surprise as the door to his study opened with a click. He raised one brushstroke brow, his cool gray eyes appraising his wind-blown visitor.

"Well, Elisa," he greeted. "This is an unexpected pleasure."

Dieter passed a hand over her blonde hair, smoothing it back into place. "Are you still hunting your gypsy, Dumas?"

The French vampire put his quill pen aside, meeting her gaze eagerly. "You've found him?"

She smirked. "You are so hopeless, Michel. Such trouble over a mortal! Was he worth alienating me? Was his taste that good?" Elisa drew nearer, studying him with narrow eyes. "You humiliated Roger and you humiliated me, all for this little pet."

Dumas sighed theatrically. "Have you come to demand atonement?" He picked up his pen and dipped it into the ink well meticulously placed at the corner of the page. "You may be disappointed."

"As may you. How badly do you want your Tobyn Reyes?"

That won his attention. "You know his name."

"And his location," she nodded, wearing a dangerous smile. "What does it mean to you to know these things?" She sidled closer still, her voice dropping to a whisper. "What would you give to get him back?"

He weighed his dislike for blackmail against his desperation to regain what he had lost. "What do you want?"

"A full apology at the next Congress of the Prime," she cooed, sitting on the edge of his writing desk, "and a full membership in the Triad." She smiled down triumphantly into his affronted expression. "Make me Secondary Prime, and I will make you the proud owner of a pretty mortal."

Dumas scowled and pushed away from his seat, pacing over to stare into the hearth. Stalling for time, knowing that Elisa would wait, he poured a wineglass full of watered-down blood from a crystal decanter, then returned to warm it by the fire. The taste was cold and gray; blood lost something when it was not fresh.

"You are an ambitious woman, *Fraulein*. It must be that quality that brought immortality to a common Berlin whore."

"Nuremburg," she corrected, "and my mortal years do not concern you. What is your answer, Dumas? Do you agree to my terms, or do I murder your gypsy in his sleep?"

He acknowledged the promise behind her threat even while he refused to react to it. He drained the glass and turned to face her with fire in his eyes. "It is done. Now tell me where he is."

"He is currently languishing in a jail in a village called Neufstadt. I can take you to him, for a price."

"Once a whore, always a whore. Haven't I already paid you, Elisa?"

She straightened, her lips pursed into a belligerent line. "I want command over Germany, with permission to eradicate the Brethren."

He put his empty glass aside. "You would start a war?"

"Yes," Dieter answered primly. "I would." She saw him vacillate on the point. "Come now, Dumas. Don't tell me that you harbor any sort of love for those people." She sneered. "I didn't think zealots were your type. Isn't your Tobyn worth at least that much to you?"

"He is everything to me," he whispered, more to himself than to her. Wearily, he nodded and waved a hand. "Fine. Have your wish, start your war. Just show me where he is to be found."

Elisa's face nearly split with the ferocity of her grin. "Just follow me."

"I warn you, do not attempt to deceive me or lead me off-course. Interference will be dealt with most harshly."

The German vampire laughed. "Really, Dumas. I have far more to gain from our arrangement than do you. I'll take you to your little obsession, never fear."

Swallowing both his suspicions and his pride, he followed her out of the chateau and into the dark sky, flying east toward Neufstadt, vowing that he would have Tobyn again that night.

～✺ॐक़✺～

The guards on Tobyn's cell were awake only through pure stubbornness. They spoke in low, gravelly voices over their card game and their ale, casting occasional wary, hostile looks at the gypsy who crouched in the corner. The larger of the two Germans eyed Tobyn, muttering to his companion; he looked away in irritation as Reyes waved to him with a cheeky smile, marred only by the bruises on his face.

The door to the constabulary opened, admitting a gust of cool air and Araminah, who reeled into view with disheveled clothing and a bottle of wine clutched in her hand. Giggling, she swept up to the biggest guard, babbling in slurred pidgin-German.

"You palm, *mein Herr*. I read for you. Yes?"

The other guard laughed harshly and clutched his genitals. "Read this."

Ara's eyes widened, and she took a swig of wine. "But it's so big!"

//You're enjoying this, aren't you?// Tobyn asked her.

//Hush.//

"I'll bet you can make it bigger," the guard leered.

"Mm, good," Ara sighed, sitting in his lap. "Ooh! There it goes already. Gypsy men are all so small..."

//Watch it!//

The big guard rose from his chair. "I'll close the door," he told his companion, "and then we can have a little fun."

Ara wrapped her arms around the first guard's neck and straddled his hips, cooing a nonsensical stream of babytalk while he got friendly with her neckline. At the door, the big guard watched her, fumbling for the latch. His outstretched arm was suddenly wrenched up behind his back, and his mouth was firmly covered by Johann's hand. The guard shuffled forward on his assailant's hissed command, obediently clearing the way for the door to be closed. Ara plucked a knife from her skirt and held it to her mark's throat.

"Get me the keys to that cell," she ordered flatly, utterly sober and clearly in no mood to negotiate. "Now!"

Wisely, the guard fished his key ring out of his belt pouch and handed it to her while Johann borrowed the wall long enough to try denting it with the other man's skull. Ara smashed her guard in the temple with the hilt of her knife, stunning him into compliance. A second blow sent him spinning off into dreamland.

Tobyn met her at the door to his cell, watching her sort through the keys. "It's that one," he supplied helpfully. "Good show. Do you handle the Lump the same way?"

"Pretty much." She opened the lock and cast a concerned glance at his abused features. "You look terrible."

"Thanks. I guess they didn't like my sense of humor."

Johann finished binding the guards. "Come on, before Beurling wakes up."

Tobyn briefly considered giving his captors a parting kick or two, just for old times' sake, but the urgent way Ara tugged at his arm convinced him to leave well enough alone. Under cover of the night, as silently as they could, they returned to the *kumpania*.

~✷~

Sela stirred at Tobyn's touch, drifting back into consciousness as he settled down beside her. She opened her eyes and frowned in concern when she saw the marks on his face. He smiled for her and planted a gentle kiss on her forehead.

"How do you feel?" he asked her softly, his hand petting her long black hair.

"Better, now that you're here." She touched his cheek, carefully avoiding the worst of the damage. "They hurt you..."

He shook his head and took her hand. "It's nothing. Ara's coming in soon with some compress or other for my eye, so I'll be fine in a little while."

Sela blinked away tears. "I was so afraid I'd lost you..."

"Never." Tobyn gathered her up into a tight hug, whispering in her ear, "You'll never lose me."

Ara and Carago let themselves into the *vardo*, and the couple relinquished their embrace. The old man sat at his daughter's side while Ara saw to Tobyn's injuries.

"The *gadjo* who helped you," Carago began. "He wants to stay with us."

"Let him," Tobyn shrugged. Ara pressed a cloth to his eye, and he flinched away. "Ouch! Be careful."

"I am. Quit complaining."

He returned to his conversation with his father-in-law. "He can't stay at this village now, obviously, and I don't see what the trouble is if he wants to join us."

Carago glanced at Sela's hand, entwined with her husband's. Frowning, he said, "But he's unclean. He's—"

"I know what he is," Tobyn cut in, pulling away from Ara's herbal salve. She grabbed his head and held him still. "If you like, I'll make myself responsible for his behavior. I owe him that much."

"Where will he stay?"

"With us." Sela squeezed his hand in support of his words, and he weathered Carago's strange stare. "Don't look at me like that. I won't do anything to embarrass you."

"You're very set in your decisions."

"Absolutely."

He looked at Sela, then said, "And you aren't...tempted...by him, Tobyn? He hasn't turned you?"

"He doesn't have a disease, Carago. Besides," he added, holding out his arms, "everything I need is here in this *vardo*."

Ara snorted quietly and dabbed at the corner of his mouth. *//Very clever.//*

//Thank you.//

The old man did not seem convinced, but he gave in, muttering, "*Chovihano.*" Shaking his grizzled head, he sighed. "Fine. Your friend can stay, but only for a short while. The *kris* will not be pleased."

"Screw the *kris*." His comment earned him a harsh glare from Carago and a slap in the stomach from his wife. Ara held her silence, probably because she shared his opinion of the council.

"Don't let yourself fall into any *gadjo* traps," Carago warned as he rose to take his leave. "Sela, rest yourself and take care of your husband." Father and daughter exchanged a long, silent glance, then he was gone.

//Papa just appointed a spy,// Ara observed.

//She wouldn't do anything like that.//

//We'll see. She's not above a little sneaking around to get what she wants.// She put her medicinal supplies aside and sat back. "I think you'll live," she announced casually. "Just keep a cold compress on your eye for a while so the swelling can go down."

"Yes, mother," he teased. "Where is Johann now?"

"Probably skulking around outside," Ara shrugged. "Do you want me to go get him?"

"At least tell him where he'll be staying."

She nodded and rose, gathering up her things. "Fine. Just get a little rest."

"All right," Sela agreed, still clutching Tobyn's hand. "Thank you, Ara."

"It's what I'm here for."

//Among other things.//

Ara paused, then sent back, *//Tomorrow, when you've slept, we need to talk about that.//*

The gravity in her tone forestalled any teasing remarks he might have made. *//Is there something wrong?//*

//Ask your wife.//

//What?//

"I'll be going," Ara told Sela with a smile. "Keep an eye on this one."

"I will. Thank you."

As his sister left the *vardo*, Tobyn pulled his lady closer, feeling the warmth of her body everywhere they touched. He interlaced his fingers over her stomach and curled around her back, listening to her breathing and the throb of her pulse. She pillowed her head against his shoulder, and he kissed her hair, liking the silkiness of it.

When Sela spoke, her words surprised him. "You aren't...interested in Johann, are you?"

He looked down at her in amazement. "Of course not! Why do you ask such a thing?"

"Curiosity." She snuggled closer, drifting farther into sleep. "There's no telling what a *chovihano* will do."

"Well, that's not one of my plans."

"Good. I can handle you sleeping with Ara. Sleeping with a man might be harder to take."

He straightened abruptly, staring into her relaxed face. "What did you say about Ara?" he rasped.

"It's all right, Tobyn. I don't care." She turned over onto her back. "Let's talk about it tomorrow, please."

"No, we'll talk about it now. How long have you known?"

Sela sighed, trying to think back. "Since December."

"How did you find out?"

The stricken look on his face made her smile in spite of herself. "I followed you when you left the *vardo* in the middle of the night. I saw the two of you making love on the beach."

"Italy?"

She shook her head. "Spain."

"You've known for almost two years?"

"It's a long time to keep a secret, isn't it?" she asked, giggling into his stare. "Bet you didn't think I could do that."

"You never said anything..."

"No, I didn't, not even to Papa. And I won't tell."

He looked away from her. "Christ...I never wanted you to—"

"It doesn't matter. I don't think it's right, and I was very angry and hurt at the time, but I've gotten used to the idea." She shrugged. "I don't think I could make you stop, anyway." Taking his face in her hands, she made him look at her. "I don't care, not anymore. I'd rather you did this, when I know who the other woman is and when you still spend more time with me than with her, than having you running around behind my back with every *gadja* you meet. I won't betray you to my father."

He sighed. "I don't understand why you're doing this."

"I love you. And I need you the way you need her. But you listen close, now: nobody else. You can't be with anybody but me or Araminah from now until the day you die of rotten old age. I can stand a little stepping out, but don't press your luck."

"Sela—"

"Shh." She covered his mouth with her hand. "I'm not finished yet. One thing that I will never stand for is if you take it into your head to sleep with Johann. You're my husband, and I love you, but that's just too much."

He regarded her for a long moment. "What will you do?"

"If I catch you with the *gadjo*? I'll scream for Papa." She shook her head. "It's not that much to ask, is it?"

"No, not at all," he admitted, feeling strangely caught and possessed, and finding that he rather liked it. "So...those are the rules."

"Those are the rules," she echoed with a nod. "No men, no other women, you're careful with Ara, and you're available to me and your bed is empty when I want it that way. Understood?"

"Perfectly, Rawnie," he said with a wry smile, applying a Romany honorific. "Should I put myself on a leash for you?"

"No, that won't be necessary," she yawned. "Just make sure you put yourself on me."

～✺✺✺～

The night was threatening to give way to morning when Elisa led Dumas to the sleeping *kumpania*. The German vampire drew her cloak tighter about her shoulders and pointed out a richly-appointed wagon.

"That's the leader's," she said. "I'll keep him occupied for you while you fetch your toy. Tobyn's wagon is over there, the blue one with the red door."

He nodded. "Thank you, Elisa. The conditions of our agreement shall not be forgotten."

"I hope not, Dumas," the woman smiled, malice implicit in her voice. "Happy hunting."

The Frenchman went to the wagon where he could sense his mortal lover sleeping. It was a simple exercise of his night-born abilities to convince the other sleepers with Tobyn to lock themselves in dreams too deep to be escaped. Loosing the catch quietly, he stole into the interior to see his gypsy.

In the darkness, he could see the young man nestled close beside a lovely young woman, his arm protectively about her waist. Another youth, far less interesting than Tobyn, slept not far away. Dumas winced in distaste and even a modicum of sympathy when he saw the marks on Tobyn's handsome face. He could not bring himself to claim the gypsy while he was damaged. Still, he would not be denied the pleasure of seeing Reyes react to his presence.

"Tobyn."

The sound of his name tickled his mind, and he stirred restlessly, extricating himself from Sela. The voice he heard appeared in his dream, carrying the memory of a face that twisted him into nightmares.

"Tobyn."

He opened his eyes slowly, then recoiled in terror at the sight of the vampire crouching at his side. He lunged for his knife, but Dumas grabbed his wrists and pulled him closer despite his struggles.

"No!" Tobyn gasped, trembling in the Frenchman's grip. "Dear Christ, please—"

"Be quiet," Dumas hissed. "If these others awake, I will kill them."

Reyes swallowed hard and stopped fighting. He stared into Dumas' eyes, trying to read his intentions, and the connection of that gaze was too much for the vampire to resist. He pulled Tobyn to him, seizing his mouth in a fierce kiss that left the gypsy gasping. The Frenchman pulled away, letting his tongue trail over Tobyn's lips for a fraction of time before he relinquished the embrace. Tobyn trembled in his hands.

"Don't hurt them," he finally said, quieter than before but in a genuine state of panic. "I'll do anything you ask."

Dumas laughed softly, mockingly. "Anything? It's a pity I don't have Matthieu with me."

Tobyn's cheeks burned in shame, but he did not look away. "What do you want from me?"

"Your life," he answered simply. "Your mortality." He glanced at Sela as she moaned in her sleep. "Who is this, then? It's been a long time. Can it be that you have taken a bride?"

Reyes found resolve at his words. "Don't you dare touch her, Dumas! So help me God, I'll tie you out to wait for sunrise!"

"Such promises, little one. Is that any way to treat a faithful lover?"

The mortal spit squarely in his face. Dumas pushed him away with a snarl and wiped his cheek with one hand. Tobyn scrabbled for his knife again, and Dumas lunged for him. Across the camp, a loud cry of "*Mullo!*" ripped the night, and Tobyn joined the shouting. The French vampire silenced him with a slap, then seized his throat, his fangs bared for the assault. The door to the *vardo* flew open as Dumas was halted abruptly by a knife between his shoulder blades; he rounded on a wide-eyed Johann as a trio of Romany men approached. The vampire threw Tobyn at them and created a new exit in the ceiling of the wagon, joining Elisa in the air. The German's lips glistened with gore as she laughed at his futile attempts to remove the steel in his flesh.

"You were unlucky again," she mocked, hauling him after her to Nuremberg.

Inside the damaged *vardo*, Sela and Johann unraveled the confused, knotted pile of men. Tobyn grasped his wife's hand with fear-cold fingers while one of the rescuers, David Dera, checked him for wounds. To the vast relief of the assembled Rom, he announced, "He is unharmed."

"Get the *chovihani* for Perita Carago," someone called.

"No, it's too late for that." Antonio shoved his way into the center of attention, flanked by *kris* members. He ordered, "Set up watchers until daylight, and have the *chovihani* work up protections."

Johann knelt beside his shaken friend, helping Tobyn sit up. "Are you all right?"

Pale as moonlight, the young man lied. "Yes. Sela—"

Her tear-flooded brown eyes turned to him. "Mother," she whispered bitterly.

"Go to her," he told her. "Do what you need to do."

"No." She leaned against him, her face pressed into his shirt. "I won't leave you."

Antonio interfered. "Go now, girl. Do what your husband tells you." Ignoring the fact that Sela was staying put, he sneered at his nephew, "Strange that the *mullo* should pick you, Tobyn."

Both unwilling and unable to respond, the younger Reyes turned away to stare at the hole in his roof. He had been a fool to think the night was safe.

In the welcome morning sunlight, precautions were taken to ensure that the murdered Perita Carago would not rise from the dead. Tobyn held Sela as she wept throughout the gruesome process of dismemberment and conflagration, shielding her from seeing the display. Ara joined them when it was over, giving her sister-in-law a potion to calm her tremors and telling her softly that she was brave. When he was certain that his wife was in good hands, Tobyn went to where the other members of the *kris* clustered to console Carago.

"We should leave, now," David Dera was saying.

"Of course we're moving," the *kumpania* leader snapped. "Don't be stupid."

Tobyn spoke quietly but intensely, attracting their undivided attention. "As soon as we reach our next camp, I want to discuss a matter of betrayal with you all. The *mulle* are not our only problems."

"What are you nattering about now?" Antonio asked sullenly.

Tito spoke in echo of his brother's stance. "Your petty politics can wait. This is more important. Don't you care about *mulle*?"

"Maybe he knows them too well," Antonio suggested archly.

Tobyn shook his head in irritation. "Of course I care! But standing around and worrying about them won't do a damned thing to help. Trust me, if *mulle* want something, we can't stop them." He bit back on his emotionally-charged words, realizing that the *kris* were beginning to stare.

"Such an expert," his eldest uncle cooed. "Is there something you want to tell us?"

He stood tall and delivered his own shot. "I'm *chovihano*. I don't have to tell you anything." Silence held the group in the wake of his words, and he gently told Carago, "The precautions were enough. She is at rest."

The old man, looking decades older, nodded his gray head. "Thank you."

Tobyn embraced his father-in-law as Carago had embraced him in his own grief; while Carago wept silently on his shoulder, Reyes caught Antonio's eyes with a pointed gaze. *Remember this, Antonio*, he thought. *Who is stronger between us, now?*

His uncle may have heard his thoughts or read them in his look. His face soured, and he glared at Tobyn, not caring who saw. He knew as well as his nephew what the betrayal in question would be shown to be; he accepted the implied challenge and vowed to slap Tobyn with it at his first opportunity. He was determined not to allow the younger man dominion over him.

Tobyn stared at him over Carago's bowed head, shining in his status as *chovihano* and heir to the caravan. Antonio hated him, hated to see him in so favorable a position. The younger man locked his gaze with his uncle's and coldly, with infinite malice, smiled.

Fifteen

Nearly two months of constant moving passed after Dumas' attack, and the *kumpania* seemed as though it would never stop running. The travel was hard, and because they rarely put down roots anywhere, supplies and food ran short; Araminah prayed that it was hunger that kept her body from its monthly flow. Even as she hoped, though, she knew the difference inside of her, as she could see the lack of a difference in Sela. She knew pregnancy when she felt it. She counted days in her memory, hoping that she was wrong, but the conclusion that logic and knowledge of her own body forced her to was cold.

She had given the wrong potion to Sela, and that was why her sister-in-law was still without children, and why she was now carrying a baby that could be either Nikolas' or Tobyn's. She had heard horrible tales about children born of siblings; in twins, such a child would be so much worse. With panic in her heart, she remixed the potions, getting it right this time, hoping against hope that the contraceptive drug she was drinking would poison the fetus within her.

So she drank the potion, worked herself to exhaustion, and prayed for a miscarriage. This child could not be born. And all the time she prayed, she felt guilty and wrong. Many nights she cried herself to sleep after Nikolas had finished his husbandly demands. It was hard to turn from healing to harming.

The *kumpania* finally stopped moving at the end of the summer, nestled in a craggy valley in northern Italy. Despite Tobyn's repeated requests, the *kris* had not convened to hear his accusations, and he was frustrated to the point of fury. Every day that passed without a council meeting meant Antonio's life was one day longer, and the insult to Chavo Reyes that much graver. Tobyn wanted to see his uncle bleed for what he'd done.

The sun was very hot on his back as he worked to finish the repairs to the hole in the roof of his *vardo*. He had finally gotten hold of some good supplies, and he intended to make his patchwork repair a permanent fixture. Beside him, lending an appreciated hand, Johann had discarded his shirt to ease the heat. Tobyn joined him, tossing his clothing down to where Sela was mending a pair of his trousers and talking with Ara. She waved up to her husband as he discarded the garment, muttering to her friend, "I hope the *gadjo* enjoys the view."

Araminah chuckled. "Don't worry so much, Sela. They'd be crazy to do anything up there."

"I hope you're right."

Up on top of the wagon, Tobyn watched Antonio chattering with David Dera and Miguelito Tcherbo, two of the *kris*'s staunchest members. Frowning, he rested his hands on his thighs and mumbled, "Strange."

"What is?"

Tobyn blinked at Johann as if for a moment he'd forgotten that the German was there. "My uncle has so many friends in the *kris* these days."

"He's probably getting them to ignore you."

Reyes picked up his tools with a sneer. "Buying them with blood money, you mean." He shifted the *kris* knife that was tucked into his belt and resumed his work. "His money won't protect him forever."

Johann fitted a board into place and held it steady while Tobyn nailed it down. "Can I ask you a question?"

"Go ahead."

"Will you answer it?"

The Rom grinned into his companion's knowing eyes. "If I want to."

The German laughed. "I suppose that's all I can expect from you."

"That's right." He pounded in another nail. "What's your question?"

"The vampire that came after you...he seemed to know you." He looked at Tobyn with concern and open curiosity. "Does he know you? Was the attack personal?"

Reyes sat back and stared at Johann for a heartbeat, then rasped, "I don't want to answer that."

"If it was particular," the blond said quickly, "I was going to say that I...I won't let him hurt you. I'll watch your back."

He smiled darkly. "I appreciate the offer, but I don't think it will help."

"I just wanted you to know."

Their eyes met and held for a moment, then Tobyn smirked and nodded. "I know. *Trabajamos, hombre.* Back to it."

Johann smiled. "No fair. You know I don't speak Spanish."

"We all have our imperfections."

"Even you?"

"Even me." His blue eyes flickered when another *kris* member joined Antonio's little group. "But especially my uncles."

"Both of them? What is Tito guilty of?"

Tobyn spoke his reply while putting his hammer to work on another board. "Complicity."

Johann considered asking for an explanation, but he could see on Tobyn's face that his friend had spun off into another of his black rages, and he thought better of it. The explanations could wait, at least until the Rom was no longer holding tools in his hands.

ᘏᕲᣟᣞᕲᘌ

Ara tied off her thread and severed the line with her teeth, listening while Sela talked quietly about Tobyn. "He's been so moody lately, angry at nothing one minute and sweet as can be the next," the young woman whispered. "Sometimes he frightens me. And every night, he gets so...I don't even know how to say it. He wants to make love every night, and he's so involved, wrapped up in it. But it never seems to be enough."

"It's like a lifeline for him," Ara agreed. "I've noticed that. And he's getting careless. He was trying to convince me to go into the woods with him, and Nikolas almost caught us."

Sela put her work into her lap and looked worriedly at the other woman. "Does he suspect?"

"I don't know. All I know is that he and dear uncle Antonio are the best of friends lately."

"Oh! Don't tell Tobyn."

"I don't plan to." Ara glanced up at the roof of the *vardo*, where she could see the two men in the bright sunlight, then turned to her friend. "I still haven't talked with him about us."

"I think you'd better. All three of us need to discuss it. I don't like the way he's being so reckless." She shook her head and raked a hand through her hair. "I don't know what's wrong with him."

Ara abruptly altered her posture and said in a louder voice, "Anyway, I told Ana that she was imagining things."

Sela frowned in consternation. "What?" Her friend gestured subtly with her needle, pointing to where Nikolas was fast approaching with anger in his eyes and a glass vial in his hand. Antonio was at his side, full of eager encouragement. Chilled, Sela sat back.

"Ara..."

Nikolas strode up to them while Antonio waited a few paces behind. Glaring haughtily down at his wife, Moreno ordered, "Get up, woman."

Araminah refused to grace him with so much as a glance. "Are you talking to me?"

In answer, he slapped her as hard as he could, knocking her from her seat. She gasped and covered her reddened cheek, staring up at him. Tobyn appeared at the edge of the roof as Nikolas held out the vial. "What is this, Araminah? It was in your clothes."

"You were looking through my things?" she demanded indignantly, anger making her foolishly bold. "How dare you!"

He raised his hand to strike her again, and Sela grabbed his wrist. He whirled on her, and the alcohol on his breath almost made her choke. Trying to calm him, she smilingly said, "*Chovihani* herbs, that's all."

Nikolas threw her to the ground. "Don't lie to me!"

Tobyn leaped from the roof and onto Nikolas, sending him sprawling in the dirt. The smaller man rolled him over and pressed one knee into Moreno's chest even as he pointed his knife blade at his throat, fire dancing in his eyes. Nikolas squirmed and was rewarded by a sharp knee blow to his sternum.

"Never," Reyes hissed, "raise a hand to these women again."

A crowd of Rom was quickly gathering around them, eager to watch a good fight. Nikolas gagged out, "Araminah is my wife!"

"And my sister. And Sela is mine." He smiled coldly, the point of his knife digging a little deeper. "I hope that's clear enough for you."

"I can treat my wife—"

"If you ever hurt her, I'll kill you," Tobyn promised. "It's that easy."

Nikolas' eyes took on a tint of desperation as his brother-in-law's blade drew a trickle of blood. "Tobyn!"

Tobyn didn't hear him; his blue eyes seemed to change color, shifting into an alien silver. His gaze was riveted by the scarlet droplet that ran slowly down Moreno's skin. He could smell it. It was sweet, so very sweet...he bent a little closer...

Carago and Antonio were on them then, pulling them away from their hateful tangle. The old man chided, "What are you doing, Tobyn? This isn't some *gadjo!*"

Nikolas staggered to his feet, his hand held to the wound on his neck. Wide-eyed, he exclaimed, "He's mad!"

Tobyn lunged at him again, but two on-lookers held him back while Moreno took cover behind Manuo and Tito. Carago hissed at his son-in-law, "Control yourself!"

Reyes freed himself from his keepers' grasp and shook himself into line. His animated features settled back into a semblance of the look they usually wore, and his eyes, although hot with anger, were themselves again. Stepping back, he helped Sela to her feet while Johann stood by the enraged Araminah.

"Are you all right, Rawnie?" Tobyn asked his wife tightly.

She smiled and nodded, albeit shakily. "Fine."

//Ara?//

//I am furious, but I'm fine.//

//If he ever hurts you—//

//You'll be the first to know.//

Nikolas grabbed her hand and pulled her after him to their *vardo*, somewhat chastened and definitely scared, but his mind in no means changed. Sela stroked Tobyn's arm to calm him, her hand warmed by the heat of his sweaty skin.

"Are you ill?" she asked, concerned.

"No."

Carago turned an irate glare onto the young man. "How many times do I have to tell you, Tobyn? I hate fights within families. It is unseemly and I won't have it. You've been burning to attack the people of this *kumpania* for days, and it ends now. I won't listen to your accusations and

I won't ignore the way you're acting. And if you take one step toward Nikolas' *vardo* without my permission, I will personally expel you from this group!"

"I defended my wife, old man," Tobyn rumbled dangerously. "I defended your daughter. I was within my rights."

"By what right did you injure Nikolas Moreno?" Tito demanded.

"Keep quiet or I'll teach you."

Carago turned to disperse the crowd, then jabbed a finger at the younger Reyes. "You are losing control, *chovihano*. Don't make me help you get it back."

He lifted his chin in aristocratic arrogance. "What would you do?"

The disdain in his voice set Carago's nerves on edge. "Do not forget that I am still the leader of this *kumpania*, boy. Punishments are done by my order."

"You overestimate yourself."

Sela gripped his hand tightly. "Tobyn!" In a low voice, she urged, "Go along with it."

Carago glared at his son-in-law for a moment before he bit out, "The sun has confused your brain. Sela, take him inside and keep him there until I can stand the sight of him again."

"Yes, Papa. Tobyn, come in."

Her husband had one last shot to take. "If he hurts Ara, it's on your head, Carago. How well can you do with no help from *chovihane?*"

The remaining gawkers muttered nervously among themselves as Sela tugged on Tobyn's arm, urging him into the quiet of their home. He realized that he still clutched his knife, and he slowly inspected the ruby stain on the tip as his wife pulled their door shut with a click. Sela sat beside him, concern etched on her face, and silently watched him lick the blade clean.

⁓⧉⁓

Nikolas pushed Ara into the privacy of their *vardo* with an ominous snarl. She caught herself and backed warily away from him as he stalked her, the vial once again in his hand.

"What is this?" he demanded. "Antonio told me about ways women have to poison the children inside them. Is that what this is?"

"Nikki, I'd never do that," she lied as convincingly as she could. Violence was coiling inside him, and the sight of it frightened her.

"Then it's to keep from getting a child. I know that's what you're doing. Isn't it?" He grabbed her hair and wrenched her to her knees, pulling her neck painfully. "Answer me!"

She could only gasp out, "Nikki, please—"

"Lying bitch!" As he shouted at her, he smashed the vial against her face. The shattering glass cut angry gashes into her skin. She cried out, and he kicked her. "Quiet! I'll have no more of these lies, Ara! By God, you'll give me a child if I have to kill you to do it!"

Over her pain-filled whimpers, he dragged her, bleeding, to their bed. With a snarled curse, he threw her onto the blankets and shredded her clothing away, punctuating his destruction with punches and slaps. She lay, dazed and crying, as he rid himself of his own garments and bound her wrists with the remnants of her skirt just the way Antonio had coached him. He felt strong; he felt virile. For the first time in months, he felt like a man.

"Nikki, please, don't..." she begged, sobbing.

"Shut up," he snapped. "Lying woman! Slut!"

Ara closed her eyes and tried not to scream as the beating progressed and the rape began.

~❦~

Tobyn was waiting outside his own *vardo* when Nikolas finally emerged hours later. The pure hatred in Reyes' eyes gave the other man a bad start, but Tobyn only pushed past him to Carago with a case of medicines in his hand. The *kumpania* leader nodded his permission, and the male healer went to this sister's aid. Nikolas had barely sighed in relief when Carago marched to him and issued an order.

"You will speak with me, now."

Remembering too late his vow to treat Ara well, Moreno gulped and stammered, "Y-yes, sir."

~❦~

She was motionless on the bed, covered only by a blanket thrown carelessly over her. Livid bruises stood out against the pallor of her skin, and blood seeped from the dozens of cuts on her face. She was covered in a sheen of unhealthy sweat and curled on her side in a fetal position, clutching her abdomen. Tobyn knelt beside her, eyes tearing as he saw his twin's wounds for the first time after feeling them through their link.

He gently rolled her onto her back and saw that her stomach and abdomen were purple and swollen, with one very distinct footprint standing out against the mottled background. She shook beneath his hands, and he could see a slick of blood over her thighs. She was miscarrying, and he hadn't even known that she was pregnant.

As he prepared the only salves and compresses that he knew, he gently touched her mind. *//I'm here, Ara. I'll take care of you, I swear.//*

Her green eyes opened, unfocussed. "Tobyn—"

"Here, love." He leaned closer to wash the blood away, seeing the glass still embedded in her cuts. "This is going to hurt."

//It already does.//

He grieved to hear her sound so weak. *//I know.//*

The young man treated her as best he could with the medicines he could put together, then washed her wounds. He carefully cleaned her cuts of glass and dirt, softly whispering soothing words to her. She stayed perfectly still, her tear-damp eyes open wide, bravely holding her silence. Tobyn collected the glass pieces in a handkerchief and secreted the shards in his pocket before he moved on to her other hurts.

He administered to all of the visible wounds and did what he could for the ones he couldn't see, but he had seen and felt enough to know that there were others so deep that he could never help them. He stroked her hair from her forehead and held her hand, his eyes searching her face as the pain of her miscarriage wracked her.

She husked, "He'll do it again."

"Not if he doesn't get the chance." He shifted to sit closer to her. "Carago is lecturing and threatening him right now, and I can make sure that he stays away from you until you've healed."

"After that," she said, shaking her head. "He'll come after me..."

"Not if he isn't here anymore."

Their eyes met, and she stated in a very quiet voice, "You're going to kill him."

Tobyn kissed her temple and whispered, "I love you. I won't let this happen again."

She blinked a tear free of her lashes and weathered another round of cramps. When the agonizing grip of them released her, she gasped, "Don't get caught."

"Never." He squeezed her hand lightly. "I'll be right here if you need me."

"You're going to kill him," she repeated wearily, her eyes drifting closed. "I'm glad."

～✴～

"Marriage to a *chovihani* is a special thing, a privilege you have abused. Araminah is too important to us for that kind of treatment," Carago was rumbling. "You might have killed her, Nikolas! And for what? Suspicions put in your head by a venal man!"

Moreno raised his chin and looked the *kumpania* leader in the face for the first time since the lecture began. "Antonio Reyes is a wise man, a traditional man. He—"

"He's no wiser than a donkey," Carago spat. "Jealous and hateful...is that the way you want to be?"

"No."

"Or a drunk? Or a man who can have his wife only when he forces her?" His voice fairly dripped sarcasm. "Or a 'traditional' Rom with no respect for the *chovihane?*"

"No!"

"Then why is that what you have become?" When Nikolas remained silent, the old man snorted. "You are a miserable man. Be grateful that Tobyn was here to see to the wounds that you inflicted. Not every *kumpania* is lucky enough to have two healers, and the last man with the gift died hundreds of years ago. Those twins are precious to our group!"

Nikolas peered at him. "Whose side are you on?"

"My own. And my interests are best served by a healthy *chovihani*, a controlled *chovihano*, and peace between my people. As of today, I have none of these." The leader shook his head in disgust. "Get out of my sight, Nikolas. Wash the stink off of you, and sleep in your father's *vardo* tonight like the spoiled child you seem. Stay clear of Araminah. And if you ever raise a hand to her or her brother or my daughter again, I promise you I'll cut that hand off at the wrist."

Moreno glowered but obeyed, stomping away from Carago's wagon. Carago watched as Manuo and Cristina cooingly claimed their son, treating him as if he were the injured party in this episode. It made the old man sick inside to see a violent and wrong-headed youth so coddled by his parents. With young people like Nikolas and Tobyn, he feared for the future of his race.

Tobyn. Now there was a cipher. Carago should not have treated him so harshly, perhaps; as Reyes had said, what he'd done had been within his right. Defense of his wife only went so far, however, and Carago knew that Tobyn had intended to murder Nikolas. There was a hatred in his chosen heir that poisoned him and made him see the world with a jaundiced eye. For so long as Tobyn was so fouled, his actions would never be accepted by the *kris*, most if not all of whom were slowly going over to the side of Antonio Reyes.

Carago did not doubt the veracity of Tobyn's claims against his uncle, but he also knew that those claims could not be proven. The *kris* would never listen to Tobyn; they were too offended by his youth, his temper, and by his *gadjo* friend, just as they were frightened of his strangeness. A male healer was always a difficult creature to control, and Tobyn Reyes was worse than most. It may have been that his internal power was too much for him, making him mad.

Carago didn't know. He only knew that he still somehow trusted Tobyn, that he wanted to trust him, and that he loved him dearly. Tobyn was his son-in-law, his heir, and his biggest problem. For as long as the *chovihano* was out of Carago's control, the *kris* would listen harder to the fevered whisperings of men like Antonio. The more they listened, the less they would obey. Carago had to convince Tobyn to at least put on an appearance of normalcy.

But how could he shout down the wind?

～⌘～

Sela stirred the thin soup she was making over the cookfire, acutely aware of the way Antonio was staring from his perch on his own *vardo*'s step. He watched her the way a wolf watched a fawn, and it made her extremely nervous. He saw her glance at him and smiled a slow, lecherous grin, then tipped his hat to her like a *gadjo* gentleman.

That was too much. Leaving her cooking behind in Ana Paolito's care, she joined Tobyn's vigil at Ara's side. She helped him put fresh cloths over the cuts as the bleeding slowed and stopped. She might have wished that her husband would notice her agitation, but his concerns over Ara occupied his mind completely, and Sela supposed that she could understand.

The miscarriage was over, and Ara was sleeping quietly. Her fever was still high, and Sela had received enough midwifery training from her husband and sister-in-law to fear an infection from some unhealthy vapor. She helped Tobyn put clean bedclothes beneath the unconscious woman, bearing the blood-soaked blankets out of the *vardo* to be cleaned and purified.

The two of them took up vigilant positions on either side of Ara's bed. Neither of them spoke, both out of consideration for their sleeping companion and lack of things to say. As Sela occupied herself with the mending the fight had interrupted and with enjoying the safety from Antonio's leer, Tobyn settled down with his back to her, head full of plans and schemes.

Quietly, intently, using the handle of his knife, he ground the glass in his handkerchief to powder.

～⌘～

Nightfall found Ara sleeping peacefully, her body's rest allowing the cures her brother had applied to take effect. Beside the bed, Sela dozed, her hands with their embroidery still upon her lap. Tobyn listened to his sister's easy breathing, his eyes on his wife's beautiful face. The glass in his pocket waited. His plan was complete. He should have felt satisfaction, or anticipation; why, then, was he so full of phantom urgency? At the base of his spine, deep within him, tiny teeth were gnawing at his self-control. A terrible want, a need he could not define, distracted him night and day.

He had tried to fill the void with food, with Ara, with Sela; food was unpalatable, and while his dalliances with the women he loved soothed, they did not satisfy. Nothing seemed to help.

But, no, that was a lie. Violence filled the void. The ache, the need, had been stilled after the fight with Nikolas. The welcome solace had been only temporary, though; when Ara's wounds were dressed and Tobyn's temper cooled, and when the whole *vardo* smelled of the blood she had shed, the feeling had returned with double strength. On some level, he could sense the answer to his problem within his slumbering companions. Sex was close, but not the answer, and he would sooner die than hurt either Sela or Araminah. And yet...the more he watched them, the more his need howled inside his heart. If he waited a moment more, he would know the truth behind this want.

He began to creep toward his twin, his eyes fastened on her abused face. Ara held the answer, somehow. She *was* the answer. His left hand, trembling, touched the bandage on her temple. His right sought and found the hilt of his *kris* knife. Drawing the weapon, he inched closer; his breath stirred the black curls on her forehead. Slowly, the tip of the knife reached toward the bandage.

Reality slapped him, hard. Cursing beneath his breath, he flung himself way from her. He banged his way free of the *vardo*, noisy in his drive to escape himself. Tobyn did not wait to see if Sela and Ara awoke. Staring straight ahead, teeth clenched, he marched away from the *kumpania*'s camp, vowing to find a little self-control before he returned.

Outside of Tobyn's own *vardo*, Johann saw his departure. The fury on the gypsy's face alarmed him, and he put his book aside to follow. Reyes led the way to a craggy outcropping that stood as a junior partner to the mountains the caravan had traversed to reach Italy. In the broad moonlight, Johann could see Tobyn climb to the highest point and sit, face upturned, arms locked around his knees. Gathering his conviction, the German clambered up to join him.

Tobyn listened to the wind, his eyes squeezed shut to trap the sound. The mountains were in mourning. He wished that he could join their song. He could hear the clumsy scrabbling of another human on the rocks, and he had no intention of admitting his madness, if such it was, to any visitor. Clasping his hands more tightly to mask their trembling, he waited for Johann to find a place to sit. The *gadjo* plopped down beside him, their shoulders touching. He did not speak.

Tobyn broke the silence. "Go away, Johann."

"Why? Perhaps I can help you."

The Rom snorted softly. "I only wish you could, my friend. This goes considerably beyond anything you can do."

"You don't know that." Johann licked his lips nervously, studying Tobyn's clean profile; the moonlight and his companion's beauty were making him brave. "How do you know that I don't have what you need?"

Reyes turned to look at him, and their eyes met and locked. "*I* don't even know what I need. How can you?"

"I have an idea." He smiled gently, encouragingly. "At least let me try to help."

Tobyn sighed and looked away, uncomfortable. Johann's nearness was making his ache start shrieking again. "Ever since you linked up with the *kumpania*, you've been throwing hints and making passes—"

"That you keep sidestepping. Admit it, Tobyn," he pressed. "If it really upset you, if you really didn't like it, you'd have told me to quit instead of dodging me the whole damn time." The German leaned closer, speaking urgently. "Just once, love. If it isn't right, if you don't want me, I'll go away. At least try."

Hesitating, he searched for words. "What about the *kumpania*? They'd kill us both."

"They're acres behind us. Besides, everyone is either busy or asleep." He shrugged. "If you're that concerned, we can hide with these rocks between us and them."

Tobyn stared at him, torn by frightening memories of Matthieu and by the hunger that urged him in quiet screams to take the offer, and quickly. Johann could see the wavering in Reyes' eyes. Taking the initiative, he stole a kiss, gentle and patient but promising more. Tobyn did not respond at first, then made up for the hesitation with near-frenzy.

Johann had his answer. Gazes tied together, they deserted the rocks to feed their desires under cover. Slowly, carefully, Johann showed Tobyn what to do, lovingly erasing Matthieu with the moment's contact.

When it was over and sanity had returned, they lay together in the moonlight, staring up into the sky. Tobyn closed his eyes in fatigue and relief; it had been enough. The void was full, at least for now.

Johann chuckled and nudged his shoulder, jostling him amiably. "You certainly don't take much convincing, do you? Animal." He hugged Tobyn close. "You do get...involved, don't you?"

Cracking one eye, he asked, "What do you mean?"

The blond pointed to a fresh mark on his shoulder, then wiped at the blood that glistened there. "You bit me."

Tobyn blushed. "Sorry. I can make a salve for that so it doesn't fester."

"I'm not concerned."

Abruptly, the sense of calm was shattered by shame that crept like an assassin out of Tobyn's Romany acculturation. Pulling free of Johann's embrace, face burning, he hunted up his clothing. "We should get back. People will wonder."

Johann could have predicted this reaction. "Should we go back separately so you can hide better?" Bitterness stole into his tone despite his best efforts to remain neutral. "God forbid that your lies should be found out."

Tobyn froze. "Johann..."

"You can't tell me you didn't like it. I was there, remember?" He stopped short, reining himself in. "I'm sorry."

The gypsy knelt beside him and gently kissed his brow. "I need time to think, Johann, that's all. You know the way the Rom are, the way that I was taught all of my life. This is...forbidden."

His anger relented. "Yes, I know." He watched as the smaller man dressed, then husked, "I love you, Tobyn. How could they forbid that?"

Reyes stopped in his tracks and turned to stare at him. "Johann, don't say things like that."

"It's true. I can't help it." He shrugged and offered a martyr's smile. "I'm just a slave to pretty gypsy boys, I guess."

"I don't want you to be my slave." He finished dressing, then turned away. "I'll collect more herbs and things for my medicines while you go back. That way we'll be separate, and I can come in from a different direction."

He nodded slowly, stung. "All right."

Tobyn took another look at the blond's face, then left his side to gather plants and to brood on his confusion. Sighing in defeat, Johann gathered up his own clothing and began to dress.

~∞≈≈≪

While he trudged through the underbrush, Tobyn let his mind whirl as it would. He was confused and frightened. He didn't even know himself anymore. First he was set to...well, he didn't know what he was going to do to Ara. Then he and Johann had broken every moral law known to Rom, and in the process had shattered the promise he'd made to Sela. What was it he told her? Something to the effect that getting with the *gadjo* wasn't part of his plan, however enjoyable it happened to have been. And he could not deny that he had enjoyed it more than he had ever thought he would. And while he was not surprised that Johann claimed to love him, he was surprised to find himself beginning to echo that emotion. And that wasn't part of his plan at all.

Plans, he thought with a derisive snort. *Dumas wasn't part of my plan. Matthieu wasn't part of my plan.*

It was enough to make him lose confidence in his schemes. They never seemed to work out, and yet he kept trying to make them. Why did he bother?

As he plucked a handful of herbs to replace those he'd used for Ara's wounds, he remembered why he was bothering. Nikolas could not be allowed to escape punishment for what he'd done. Tobyn took a moment to recall the cuts and the bruises and the pain in his sister's face, feeding his anger, throwing up a smoke screen so he didn't have to think about what was happening to him. He went over every memorized hurt, every wound Ara had sustained, goading himself onward. With one hand, he fingered the handkerchief and its load of crushed glass, reviewing his plan once more.

The void opened inside of him again, but he ignored its pressure as his plot began to alter in his mind. Setting his jaw, he changed the focus of his search, ignoring the cures in favor of the poisons that grew in their shadow. For once in his life, he had a plan that just might work.

Sixteen

The caravan's progress was brought to a halt by a shout from Carago, whose wagon was leading the way through the Italian countryside. Sela glanced at Johann, who was guiding the *vardo* while Tobyn rode Chal at Carago's side. Behind her, Ara parted the curtains and peered out into the daylight, blinking beneath her healing wounds.

"What's going on?"

"I don't know," Sela replied. "It doesn't look good."

Tobyn cantered back to them, his handsome face grim. "We'll have to go around this town and stay to the fields. There's some sort of epidemic in there, and they're dropping like flies. They're blaming gypsies for it."

Ara frowned. "That's preposterous!"

"*Gadje*," her twin shrugged dismissively. He smiled fondly at Johann. "No offense."

"None taken."

"How far do we have to go to skirt around this place?" Sela asked.

"Ask your father. He's planning this. Not too far, though, I don't imagine. Just far enough to stay clear of the disease but still be able to use the roads." He nudged Chal. "I have to spread word. See you soon."

As Tobyn rode away, Araminah mumbled, "I hope the whole region isn't infected. I don't want to go back to France just yet."

They drove silently past the village, trying not to watch as an elderly Italian man shook and vomited in a field. Tobyn rode beside his *vardo*, close enough to touch Sela's hand if she reached for him, studiously avoiding any and all unnecessary contact with Johann. His shame still ran deep.

Johann, for his part, noticed the icy layer of distance that Tobyn wore, just as he knew what lay beneath it. He should have left long ago. Instead, he'd lingered like a puppy for days, waiting for a smile or a touch. He had not lied when he'd said that he loved Tobyn. Perhaps that was his worst mistake.

He looked over at the young gypsy man, who caught his eye and glanced away. Something had to give, one way or another. He could not live in this kind of purgatory, waiting through torture for one second of Tobyn's grace.

Could he?

Beside him, Sela was fretting aloud to her husband. "We needed to get more supplies here. The caravan is low on meat and drinking water." She shook her head. "If the whole area has this sickness..."

"You worry too much," Tobyn scolded her gently. "It might not extend past this village. We'll find food. Don't worry about that."

"Easy for you to say," Ara piped up. "You're not responsible for keeping people fed."

"You're right. Freedom is a wonderful thing."

"I wouldn't know."

In the strained silence that fell behind her words, Tobyn commented, *//You're cranky today. Aren't you feeling well?//*

//No, I'm not. I feel...weird// She sighed. *//Like there's something terrible coming//*

//Is there anything that I can do to help you?//

She edged back into the *vardo*, closing the cloth partition behind her. *//I'll let you know if there is//*

The silence lasted until they reached Carago's chosen stopping place. As the caravan set up camp, Tobyn and Johann saw to the team that drew the Reyes *vardo*. The Rom concentrated all of his attention of the work at hand despite the fact that he'd been caring for horses since he was a boy and could essentially do it blindfolded and sleepwalking.

"You're avoiding me," Johann quietly accused.

Tobyn blinked at him. "Who, me? Why would I? Besides, isn't that a little hard to do while we're living in the same *vardo*?"

"You're doing an exemplary job." The German scratched one of the horses' manes, and the animal snorted in appreciation. "Are you afraid that I'll ravish you in your sleep some night, or that you'll enjoy it too much if I do?"

Tobyn tossed his handful of tack over his shoulder and fixed Johann with a hard look. "I have more on my mind than a casual fuck right now."

Johann considered forcing his companion to talk to him, to explain what he was feeling and why he'd been enforcing this silence, but he thought better of it almost immediately. He already regretted how much he had said, and he knew that coercion would win him nothing.

Making light conversation, he switched the topic and his tone of voice. "How far did that disease spread, do you suppose?"

Tobyn's answer came with a small, secret smile. "Just far enough."

"What?"

Laughing at the confusion on Johann's face, the gypsy clapped him on the shoulder and shocked the German with a sudden kiss. When he pulled away, Johann was gaping like a fish, and Tobyn grinned evilly. He could hardly have asked for a more perfect situation, a better disguise for what he had wanted to do than this Italian plague. As soon as the horses were taken care of and the harnesses put away, he went into the *vardo*.

Sela and Ara watched him while they settled the wagon into order. He took out all of his carefully-gathered herbs and began to mix them, humming to himself as he worked. Ara's eyes took in the forms of the plants he used, and she identified them all to herself in a silent list.

//Tobyn, what are you doing?//

Sela left the *vardo* to start the evening's cookfire, and he cast a wide smile at his twin in her wake. *//I'm taking care of a few problems.//*

//With poison?//

//Absolutely. It's the best way.//

As she watched, he put the toxic potion aside and began to mix a large quantity of what amounted to a placebo. She tried to understand what was being done, tried to get inside his head, but all answers eluded her. Her brother was becoming a mystery to her.

⌐⌐⌐

Sundown brought wakefulness and a momentary peace before his houseguest awoke. Dumas stood on the balcony of his *chateau*, watching the stars rise and enjoying the last few moments he had before Elisa would join him. The German vampire, now fully installed as Secondary Prime, was young; her need for sleep was greater than his own, and it lasted farther past the setting sun. Dumas' age and power let him see at least the glimmer of a few last rays.

At the stroke of the hour, her door would open, and she would descend upon him with her high, scratching voice, shrieking like a demon. Elisa had become his own personal harridan, the bane of his immortal existence. He liked to think of her as his penance for his excesses. At the same time, he was grateful for her presence. However much he hated her, she was still one of his kind, and it was comforting to have another vampire rattling in his life, making immortal noises. He'd been lonely for so long.

He had hoped to have Tobyn fill that gap. To have had the gypsy as his eternal companion would have been the ultimate of all of Dumas' fondest dreams. In mortal life, he had always vastly preferred the company of young men to that of females. His perfect partner in immortality would have been what Tobyn had promised to be: young and beautiful, with spirit and a strong personality, unafraid to oppose him from time to time. It would have been so pretty. Even if, as Isabella had warned, he and Tobyn had come to hate one another, at least it would have been as immortals, together on a single plane. And Dumas had believed that he could make Tobyn love him in time.

Everything had gone wrong. He was still mystified as to why Tobyn had failed to Change, and why Isabella, formerly his dearest vampire friend, had so betrayed him. Since the night he had returned to find Isabella gone and Tobyn stolen, his carefully-constructed world and well-ordered plans had tumbled into confusion. He hurt, as he had not hurt in four hundred years. He only knew that he needed Tobyn back at his side. Whatever was wrong, with the gypsy he could make it right. Whatever was right could become divine.

Elisa appeared beside him, surprising him with her quiet approach and gentle voice as she said, "You're so unhappy, Michel."

He turned to smile blandly at her. "Perhaps."

"Can I do anything to help you?"

"You, Elisa? No, I don't believe you can."

Her blue eyes took on a gleam of inner conspiracy. "We'll see."

Tobyn circulated through the *kumpania*, meting out the drugs he had concocted. As he explained to his fellow Rom, the herbs he added to their evening meal were medicines to prevent the Italian epidemic from touching the caravan. Almost all of the "patients" received a harmless and completely ineffective dose of grass shreds and mints that altered their dinners' taste enough to seem to be working.

Not every dosage was so innocuous, however. Antonio, Tito, and their assorted *kris* allies received his poison in variant strengths. None of them would die, or at least Tobyn did not expect them to. Rather, they would become ill, vomiting like the Italian man they had passed. As a smoke screen, innocent Rom who were not among his enemies received a tiny dose, and he doctored his own food with the toxin. There would be no incriminating patterns to the *kumpania*'s epidemic, and though he would suffer, he would enjoy the knowledge that his enemies were suffering more.

Of course, no proper plague ever visited a group without causing the occasional fatality. Along with the poison, Nikolas, Manuo and Cristina Moreno received equal parts of crushed glass.

Once his medicines ran out, Tobyn joined his family at Carago's *vardo*, sitting between Sela and Araminah to eat his poisoned stew while Johann attempted to chat with the group leader.

Sela turned to him. "Do you think this will hold the disease off well enough?"

He shrugged and forced himself to swallow. "It's hard to say. I've done my best, but it's a strange sort of illness. It might be too strong for my mixes."

She snuggled closer to him as Ara poked doubtfully at her plate. "Just as long as you don't get sick, I'll be happy."

"It works both ways, Rawnie."

Ara glanced at her brother as Sela kissed his cheek and sat back with a secret smile, her hands folded over her belly. Ara wondered briefly when Sela would tell about the wonders her potion had wrought, then shook her head. She didn't want to think about babies right now. *//What did you take, yourself?//* she 'sent' to her twin. He did not reply, simply turning back to choke down the last scrap of his meal. *//Tobyn.//* She frowned and put more strength behind her mental transmission. *//Tobyn! Answer me!//*

Again, he did not react. She realized that he was not ignoring her. She had all but shouted his name at him, and as he talked vacuously with Carago, it was all very clear. He simply hadn't heard.

At morning's first light, Ara found that as the *kumpania's* only functional healer, she had her hands full to overflowing. Her brother's mischief had taken hold, and no less than thirteen individuals, including Tobyn, were violently ill. Fear followed the sickness through the camp, compounding her chore.

Clenching her teeth against the aches in her still-healing body, Araminah went from *vardo* to *vardo*, prescribing cool water compresses and rest for the poisoned. She kept the cause of the caravan's affliction to herself, although she did brew an antidotal tea for the worst hit. She had seen enough of Tobyn's collection of plants to know how to counteract their effects.

Tobyn was her last patient before she braved the Moreno wagon. The *chovihano* lay, gasping, on the cool soil beneath the wagon. He was curled on his side and clutching his stomach, deathly pale and wracked with dry heaves. Sela sat with him, anxiety on her face, swabbing his clammy brow with cool water.

"Have him drink this," Ara told her friend, ladling out a cup of the curing tea.

"What if he can't keep it down?"

"We'll keep giving it to him until he can."

Sela accepted the cup, her eyes fixed on Ara's face. She knew where her sister-in-law had to go next. "I'll go there if you want. You don't have to go near him."

Araminah set her jaw. "Yes, I do." She felt certain that what awaited her in her husband's *vardo* would be extremely unpleasant. Sela didn't need to see the ugliness. "I'm the *chovihani*," she added carefully. "It's my job. Stay here with my shitwit brother."

The word choice and the tone brought questions to Sela's eyes but none to her lips. Ara left her to attempt to dose Tobyn.

The Moreno *vardo* was deceptively still. While there was no movement to be seen, Ara could all but smell the wrongness that surrounded the thing. As she drew closer, she could hear the soft, pained moaning of a soul not completely dead but already seeing the fires of hell. *What did you do, Tobyn?* she thought, not caring to attempt telepathy through their eerily silent twin link. She dimly remembered watching him make preparations for killing Nikolas, but what had he done? It had to do with glass...crushed glass...

Good Lord, he's put glass in their food.

She hurried the last few steps and flung open the door. Inside, all three of the Morenos lay in agony, their clothes and bedding stained with their hemorrhaging. Their cries stung her ears as every cramp, every internal motion made their pain more acute.

She realized that she was staring. Releasing her grip on the door, she went to Cristina's side but could not bring herself to touch the woman. In a flat and startlingly emotionless voice, Ara said, "There's nothing I can do to help you."

Cristina was too far gone to understand that her son's wife was speaking, let alone the meaning of the words; but Nikolas heard, and he grabbed Ara's hand. In a strained voice, he begged, "Forgive me. I never...meant...to hurt you, I—I didn't...please...make it stop..."

She wiped the sweat from his brow, feeling strangely removed from the wifely action. "I wish I could, Nikki."

Manuo groaned once more behind her, then fell silent. She could tell without looking that he was dead, and soon to be followed by his wife and son. Nikolas was sliding into a delirium of anguish, muttering, "I love you, Ara. Love you. Always. I—"

"Hush, Nikolas." She wanted to pull her hand free of his grip; his touch was making her shudder. All she could do was stare at his whitened fingers and consider how much he was bleeding inside. "Hush, now."

"Forgive...me, Ara. Say you...forgive me..."

She looked him in the eye and found that, much to her amazement, it wasn't a total lie. "I forgive you, Nikolas. I forgive you for all of it."

He closed his eyes over a beatific smile of gratitude and relief. "Good," he breathed. He took a shuddering breath. "Oh, good..."

Ara held his hand through Cristina's death, which passed as unnoticed as Manuo's, and through the last of his own great pains. The loss of blood from his internal wounds dragged him into unconsciousness and he mercifully died in his sleep.

As soon as she saw that he was gone, Araminah pulled her hand away from his and backed away. The stink of blood and death made her shudder, and she deserted the unfortunate family with all possible haste. Her pale and shaken expression told the untouched but nervous Rom who stood by in worried vigil that the phantom Italian sickness had claimed its first victims. An old woman named Lirita patted Ara's shoulders to calm her, the abject shock on the young woman's face not boding well at all. Ara took a look around the camp, taking in the sickness and the worry.

//Tobyn!//

Her cry went unanswered; had her brother deserted her just as he had deserted his reason? It was then that the shaking began, and soon she was on her knees, shrieking and sobbing in a total loss of control. Lirita hugged her tightly, shooing away Johann when he sprinted to her side. The old woman was saying something soothing, but the words were lost to Ara. What was wrong with her twin? Why had he murdered all three Morenos so horribly? She didn't understand, she didn't know him any longer.

Lirita led her, unresisting, to Tobyn's *vardo*. Ara sank down beside Sela and her fitfully-sleeping brother, tears still tracing her face. Death frightened and disgusted her. As Lirita took her leave and Sela clasped her hand, she turned her moist eyes onto Tobyn.

Who are you?

After the third day of constant vigil, the Morenos were buried in the rocky northern Italian soil. Ara and Carago walked slowly back from the graves, talking quietly as they returned to the *kumpania*.

"I should send you to live with Antonio," the old man told her. "He is your oldest male relative."

The woman did not reply. Living with Antonio was the last thing in the world that she wanted. At the same time, what she did want was unclear. All she knew was that she needed Tobyn to be himself again, needed their link to be reopened. She felt isolated from her twin, although he was within reach. The silence was a sickness that ate her from the inside out.

Carago spoke again. "How is your brother?"

Ara turned startled eyes to him, almost believing for a moment that he had read her thoughts. She forced herself to relax and replied, "His health is improving, finally. He was able to eat for the first time this morning."

He nodded. "Good. Strange how he and Antonio were so much sicker than the others."

"Yes."

"Makes me wonder about what Tobyn tried to say about betrayals within the group." He clasped his hands behind his back. "Well, we'll set up watches to catch traitors. What do you think, *chovihani?*"

She eyed him strangely, wondering why he would ask her opinion on man's business. "Sounds fine."

Carago stopped walking and faced her frankly. "Tell me, Araminah. Do you want to go with Antonio?"

She could not conceal her shudder. "No."

"I thought not." With a gentle fingertip, he traced a hair-line scar on her face, a legacy from Nikolas. She pulled away without rancor. Nodding to himself, he said, "No, I thought not. Fine. Go to your brother. Heal him, ride with him. Sela will be glad for the company, and you can keep the *gadjo* away from him."

A chill touched her, and she pulled her shawl more tightly around her shoulders. "Thank you," she whispered.

Carago silently patted her back and left her, his head down as he walked and thought. Araminah let him go, then made her way to her brother's wagon.

~〜∂€∽

Darkness was soothing, he thought. When the sun finally hid behind the horizon, the pain and the cramps in his gut receded, and he could throw aside his daytime torpor. Tobyn had come to love the night. Everything seemed so much clearer without daylight's distractions.

He carefully rose from his bed, throwing the blanket aside without waking Sela. The void in his heart, in his soul, had opened up again, and he needed. In the bright shadows, he scanned the three sleeping faces arrayed across his wagon floor. He needed. One of these people could help him. He could smell satisfaction just a heartbeat away, clinging to his companions like mist.

Watching them sleep, seeing their utter vulnerability, excited him. He wanted to touch their faces, but he was afraid that he would find their skin altered beneath his fingers. Sela stirred beside him, and he stared at the way she seemed to glow in the moonlight. She was a beautiful woman.

"I love you, Rawnie," he breathed, his lips close to her ear. He could smell her delicate scent, and it made his mouth water. He needed.

A sound outside the *vardo* caught his attention, and Tobyn let himself out silently. Beside the rear axle, Tito was poking through one of his nephew's supply bags, rummaging in his herbs. He was obviously looking for something, and Tobyn had an inkling of what Tito wanted.

He crept to Tito's side, never making a sound, then grabbed the bag away with a feline hiss. The older man started violently, his face going ashen.

"Good God!"

"What are you looking for, uncle?" Tobyn asked, his blue eyes cold and narrow. "It must have been important if it couldn't wait until morning."

Tito recovered his composure with a heavy dose of bravado. "We know what you did."

Tobyn took a menacing step forward as his uncle echoed the motion in reverse. "We? And who is this 'we'?"

"Me. Antonio. David Dera. Almost the whole *kris*. We're on to you."

He laughed shortly, slowly pursuing the older Reyes around the back of the *vardo*. "Are you, now? What do you suspect?"

Tito stood tall. "You're a murderer, Tobyn Reyes, and we mean to prove it. There are poisons in that bag."

"Are you a *chovihano*, now? How can you tell a poison from a cure?"

He could not be dissuaded by logic. "You killed those three people. It's obvious." He kept backing away from his angry nephew. "But why did you do it? To get Ara back, perhaps? Your interest in her was always more than brotherly."

"Drop this, Tito," Tobyn rumbled. "I'm warning you."

His uncle sensed a chink in the armor the younger man wore. "Too close to the truth?" he pressed, leaning forward, his eyes squinting into Tobyn's face. "Did you want to get under your own sister's skirts?"

Tobyn snarled a curse and backhanded Tito with all of his strength. With a sickening crunch, the older man spun away to land in a lifeless heap at his feet. Tobyn, wide-eyed, knelt beside him, gaining tactile confirmation of what his eyes were telling him. Tito's head lolled unnaturally on a neck broken by the force of the younger man's blow. Ice coated Tobyn's spine. He had to get rid of Tito, and now. Gritting his teeth, he gathered the corpse in his arms and slung it over his shoulder. Taking a belated look in search of witnesses and seeing none, he headed away from the *kumpania* in search of a convenient place to dump the body.

After walking for nearly two hours, Tobyn shoved Tito's body into a crevice between the stony chunks of one of the outcroppings at the foot of the mountains. His hands were shaking as he stacked loose rocks over Tito's face. He needed. The moonlight bathed the makeshift crypt in wan blue as the young man spat at his uncle's cadaver.

"Good riddance," he said. "Your brother will join you soon, I promise you!"

⚬⚬⚬⚬

Dawn was still only a blushing promise on the horizon when he returned to the caravan with his lusts howling in perfect harmony. There was no one to see him make his stealthy way to his *vardo*, no witnesses to the gleam in his eyes. It was a blessing.

He pushed his door open, and his gaze fell on Ara's bare shoulder peeking out around her blanket. Reaching out mentally and physically, he touched her, pulling her out of her dreams. He never even noticed that his telepathic probe missed its mark.

She blinked at him, one hand raking the curls away from her face. "What's wrong?"

In answer, he took her head in his hands and kissed her passionately. Almost reluctantly, she responded, leaning into him as his touch began to wander. She sighed in an uncomfortable mixture of happiness and resignation when he teased open her camisole and ran his fingers over her skin. Johann stirred, and she grabbed Tobyn's wrists, pulling free of his grasp.

"No, Tobyn. Not here, not this way."

He shook his head at her whisper and replied, "Now."

Feeling more than a little trapped, she took a deep breath and grasped his hand. "Come with me, then."

"Outside?"

Sela mumbled, disturbed by their whispers. Ara motioned for her brother to hold his silence, then led the way out of the wagon. Together, they slid onto the ground between the axles, their eyes locked. Something was telling Ara that Tobyn would not be himself this time. The urgency and haste behind his eyes frightened her.

He settled into position above her, his lips nuzzling at her throat; closing her eyes, Ara wrapped her arms around his neck.

"Come on, Tobyn," she urged quietly. "Let's go." *Let's get this over with.*

He heard her soft words, recognized the spirit of surrender that backed them. He took the time to kiss her again, and reminded himself to go slowly, to let her enjoy it, too. But feeling her body pulsing and warm beneath his own did terrible things to his self-control. He needed, and badly. He could feel what he craved just beneath his fingertips. He pulled back and locked his gaze with Ara's, tried to offer a smile, then moved her skirts out of the way with a quick and practiced motion.

Please, he prayed, *let this be enough.*

Sela listened silently to the sounds that rose through the floor boards of the wagon. Beneath her, taking foolish chances, her husband was betraying her in the arms of his own twin sister. No matter how much she claimed nonchalance, no matter how many times she told Tobyn and Araminah that she didn't care about their relationship, every time Tobyn went to his sister instead of his wife, Sela's heart broke. She tried not to be hurt. She tried not to be jealous. But every time this happened, she felt betrayed and inferior, and she endured heated moments of wanting to run to her father and tell. At moments like this, when she listened to her husband making love to another woman, she hated him. She hated Ara. It was all she could do to keep from calling the *kumpania*'s wrath down onto their unclean, sinful heads.

Sela closed her eyes, clenched her fists, and held her silence. She would lose more than she would gain by turning in the lovers. When it was over, Tobyn would return to her side, and perhaps they could pretend that all was well. Perhaps she could preserve her mask of smiles, and maybe even find a little coolness to back it up. Perhaps she could still see Araminah as a friend and sister rather than as her husband's mistress.

Perhaps in time she truly wouldn't mind. But not now. Now, she minded very much.

The sunrise found Tobyn's energies undiminished despite the long hours he had spent with her. Ara, alarmed by the increased light and the activity that began to signify the caravan's awakening, shoved at his shoulders.

"Tobyn, stop," she begged, her voice barely above a whisper. She hated being unable to mind-speak to her twin. "Tobyn."

His only reaction was to push her hands away and move faster. He could sense a tightening within himself, a spring preparing to release. Just a bit more, and it would be over; a little more, and the bone-shattering pressure inside of him would be gone. He moved faster still, and harder, and he gripped Ara's wrists tightly, ignoring her struggles to evade him and likely capture.

Ara did not know the man atop her; she only knew that he was not the Tobyn Reyes she had always known. His harsh touch confused and alarmed her, and Beti's admonition to be careful echoed in her head. She tried to pull free of his grasp, tried to push him away, but to no avail. His preoccupied love making was rapidly degenerating into something hideous.

Antonio's voice suddenly rang out within inches of them. "Tobyn!" Ara twisted her head to see trousered legs beside the *vardo*, almost close enough to touch...if Tobyn hadn't been forcing her hands into the dirt above her head, she could have gripped her uncle's ankle. She was painfully aware of how loud her brother's panting breaths and animal noises were; certainly, others were hearing him, too. Antonio's voice held suspicion as he took a step closer to the side of the wagon. "Tobyn?"

Sela clattered out of the *vardo* and lied, "He went out early this morning to collect herbs. I don't know when he'll be back. Come and have some coffee."

He would not be led away so easily. Ara closed her eyes and with all her might sent messages to her brother that never got through. Antonio asked, "Who is underneath your *vardo*, Sela?"

"What are you talking about?"

Ara was in tears of frustration, pain, and fear. They would be caught this time, she knew. *For God's sake, Tobyn, stop!*

"Under the wagon. Listen."

There was a pause. "I don't hear anything. Come over—Antonio!"

The elder Reyes dropped to his knees beside the wagon while Tobyn vociferously hit flashpoint. Ara burst into sobs as Antonio hauled his nephew out into the open. His rough hands flung Tobyn, gasping and barely sane, to the ground as their uncle hissed curses at him. The other Rom were gathering quickly as he pulled Ara bodily from the ground beneath the *vardo* and pushed her down, as well.

"Filth! Disgusting filth!" he spat, a foot lashing out to kick his nephew in the groin.

Moaning and shaking with sobs, Ara curled protectively and covered her head with her arms. She could sense Antonio's approach in the air and in the offended yammering of the assembled gawkers. A man called out, "Don't beat her, you fool! Can't you see that it was rape?"

Sela's voice reached her panicked ears weakly. She was choking on tears of her own. "Tobyn..."

Carago arrived with David Dera in tow. He took in the sight of his *chovihane*, clothes askew in tell-tale fashion, and demanded, "What is happening here?"

Antonio was only too happy to time his reply with another kick in his coughing nephew's solar plexus. "Incest!"

"Rape!" a woman cried. "He was doing it to his own sister!"

Silence was heavy, broken only by Tobyn's rapid breaths. Ara wanted to look at Carago but was afraid to risk the motion. Keeping her head down, she wept and waited. Finally, the old man ordered, "Sela, care for her. Dera, Reyes—bring him."

Wordlessly, Sela helped Ara to her feet and pulled her into the silence of the wagon while Johann attempted to follow Tobyn. Once the door was closed on the outraged curiosity of the crowd, Carago's daughter set about packing her husband's belongings into a deep brown sack.

"Sela, I'm so sorry," Ara sobbed. "I tried to stop him, I—"

"Save it," the other woman said flatly, hunting up Tobyn's *kris* knife and shoving it into the bag.

"You don't believe me."

"It doesn't matter now." She folded one of his shirts and added it to the collection. "You know what's going to happen to him now. They'll hurt him and they'll leave him behind. He'll be ejected from the *kumpania*."

The overly-calm tone of Sela's voice made Ara anxious over the storm that was soon to break. Holding her silence, she rearranged her clothing and waited meekly for her sister-in-law to continue.

After packing more clothes and a tin of her hard-won coffee, Sela turned intense dark eyes onto her companion's face. "I want you to go with him. He'll need you to heal him after the...the punishment, and he'll need a woman to take care of him."

"Come with us," Ara urged. "He loves you."

The other woman's response was a mirthless half-smile. "But less than he loves you."

"He's your husband."

"No, not anymore. He is dead to me, now." She pushed the bag into Ara's hands. "Take Chal. You'll need him after they burn the wagon."

She sat back, wide-eyed. "Sela—"

"My father needs me." Tears appeared on her lashes, and she rose quickly. At the door, she choked, "Take care of him."

In the wake of Sela's departure, Ara began to pack some things of her own.

Seventeen

It was difficult for Tobyn to pay attention to what was happening around him. While he dressed and waited for the *kris* to assemble, he was torn between absolute emotional distance and the increased raging of the fire within him that refused to be quenched. He was aware of his crime, and he knew what his judges would command for his punishment. Apart from a vague relief that Ara was being perceived as a victim and therefore not subject to official wrath, he could not bring himself to care one iota about anything that was going on. The men clamored and shouted on all sides of him, and he could hear their anger. He was simply too busy listening to the throb of a dozen hearts to respond.

Carago could not make himself look at Tobyn. Instead, he kept his eyes focused on David Dera's vest while Antonio noisily banished the German *gadjo* from the proceedings. Johann struggled against the older man, and he looked into Tobyn's face with a fear and a longing that made their relationship clear to the watching men. Tobyn stood impassively, staring back at Johann as he was expelled. The old man could not bear to see the unnatural calm around his son-in-law's madness-glazed eyes.

The council assembled rapidly, and Antonio Reyes called it to order, playing and enjoying his role of moral outrage. The noise within the *vardo* fell still, and the *kumpania* leader, feeling a century old, spoke.

"Tobyn Carlos Reyes, how do you answer to this charge of incestuous rape your uncle brings against you?"

The young man's tenor voice was unnervingly smooth in the hush, and he sounded like he was singing. "I am guilty."

Carago noted the far-away tone with concern, then instantly chided himself. He had no business caring for a criminal. "Men of the *kris*, how do you decide?"

One by one, every member in his turn replied, "Guilty." Antonio in particular spoke the word with an unpleasant gleam of pride. Carago felt betrayed by the entire Reyes family.

In a slow, reluctant voice, the old man passed sentence. "Tobyn Carlos Reyes, you will be stripped and beaten in the center of the camp. You are no longer a member of this or any other Romany *kumpania* or clan. You have no wife, you have no family, and you have no friends here." As satisfaction spread throughout the *kris*, he ordered, "Tcherbo, spread the news. Golobao, set up the whipping post."

The councilmen sprang into action, eager to punish this virulent transgression of their cultural morality, doubly pleased to finally get at the man they'd been so richly paid to hate. As they left the *vardo*, Carago forced himself to look at the recipient of his justice.

Quietly, at some private inner joke, Tobyn was laughing.

~✥~

David Dera stopped Antonio outside Carago's wagon. His weather-beaten face was creased in confusion as he said, "Reyes, you never raised your other charges."

Antonio nodded. "What good does it do now to prove that he is a murderer?"

"He could pay the price."

"Yes, by dying." The taller man's mouth curved in an unpleasant smile. "Death is far too quick and easy a fate for my brother's son. It's better that he should be left this way, humiliated and alone for all time. Besides," he shrugged, "if the beating goes well, he'll either have enough scars on that pretty face to punish him forever or he'll never leave this valley." He pressed a gold coin into Dera's hand. "It's your choice."

∼⊱≼≽⊰∼

Johann followed Araminah as she was saddling Chal, the bulging bag slung over the animal's back. The German's face was grim.

"Well?" she asked, seeing that he had news for her.

"They wouldn't let me listen to the voting, but Tcherbo announced that Tobyn is being driven out of the caravan."

She nodded solemnly. "I expected that." Her eyes were snagged by the sight of a trio of men erecting a tall wooden post. She shuddered as the leader of the little group attached shackles to the pole. "Jesus..."

Johann frowned, his suspicions bearing fruit. "It wasn't rape, was it?"

Ara turned her back to him and secured the saddle. She had no intention of answering him, even if she'd known what her answer would be.

He continued to speak, undaunted by her uncooperative ways. "I'm staying with him. I won't leave him."

She heard something in his voice and looked up at him, her eyes guarded. "You love him."

"Yes."

"Have you...have you been with him?"

He saw no harm in the truth; as he perceived things, he could hardly make Tobyn's situation any worse. "Yes."

"How many times?"

He thought back, counted the maddening nights when Tobyn's running stopped just long enough for a quick tumble, then picked up again at twice the speed. "Three or four times."

Ara looked away, deeply disturbed and unable to say exactly why. Lamely, she muttered, "Just don't tell Sela."

∼⊱≼≽⊰∼

Tobyn scarcely reacted when his wife entered the *vardo* where he waited for his punishment. She stood and watched him in awkward silence as he rocked slowly to and fro, his eyes cast upon images that only he could see. She crossed her hands over her stomach and took a slow, careful step away from him.

"He is mad," Carago told her wearily. "Come away, Sela."

"Give me a moment with him, Papa. Alone."

The old man hesitated, looking from his daughter to her husband and back again. "All right. But remember that there isn't much time."

The click of the door behind Carago penetrated the fog that choked Tobyn's brain, giving him a respite from the vertiginous spinning of his thoughts. The pressure inside his head was incredible; it seeped into his muscles and made him quiver, tense and waiting. He became vaguely aware of his wife staring at him, and he smiled at her. Why was she shimmering like that?

The smile he gave her looked unbalanced at best, and Sela hesitated nervously before she knelt beside him. "Tobyn." She took his hands and looked into his eyes, wondering why he wore such a rapt expression. "Tobyn, I want you to know that I will make Antonio pay somehow for doing this to us. I'll find a way to make him sorry."

He stroked her face gently, and for a moment he looked like the man she had so carefully hunted into marriage. "You're so beautiful," he breathed. "I've never seen you this way before."

Tears destroyed her control, and she held him tightly. "I'll miss you," she rasped as he returned her embrace. "God, Tobyn, I love you so much!"

The door opened abruptly, and Daniel Oras sternly announced, "It's time."

They separated, and Sela dried her eyes. Tobyn touched her hair once more. "Remember me."

"Always."

Oras escorted him to the whipping post, leading the unresisting *chovihano* through the circle of Rom to the sun-drenched clearing in the middle of the camp. Tobyn allowed his hands to be bound without complaint; his stoic and uncharacteristic acceptance of the *kris* ruling was unsettling to the onlookers.

Inside Tobyn, the coil tightened another notch.

He squinted into the almost painfully bright light as his clothes were cut and ripped away from his body, removing the slender protection they could have given against the blows to come. Antonio appeared before him, grinning evilly into his nephew's eyes. Without a word, he spat squarely into Tobyn's face, then marched away, symbolically severing the terminally loose Reyes family ties.

The bound man grinned. *"Adios,* Tio Antonio."

Behind him, Tobyn could hear the whips from the horse trade being passed around among the men. Every adult male in the *kumpania* would have a turn at him, some distant part of Tobyn knew. Gritting his teeth and closing his eyes, he vowed not to give them the satisfaction of his screams.

Sela and Ara stood at Carago's side, present because they were required to be. Matching expressions of dread covered their faces as Antonio took up position behind Tobyn's naked back.

"Father, don't make me watch," Sela begged in a whisper. "Please."

"Hush, child." Carago sounded weary of the whole business. "It will be over soon."

Antonio smiled and limbered up his right arm. This was fine sport! He'd wanted to beat his nephew bloody for a very long time. How wonderful to finally have an officially-sanctioned opportunity. He gripped the braided leather handle of the whip and took pleasure in the mental images of the lash wound he would give his nephew's skin. His just reward for losing out on a beautiful Irish girl, his vengeance against Chavo was nearly complete.

That's what happened to men who took women away from him.

"Are you ready, Tobyn?" he mocked, scorn heavy in his voice.

"Ready, uncle."

The whip cracked; the blow landed on his shoulders like white flame. He gasped but held his tongue. Ara, unlike Sela, was unable to avert her eyes. Frozen with horror, she stared at the spectacle at the post. She tried instinctively to send her brother support, strength, or just to siphon away some of the pain. Their link was still utterly inactive.

"Tobyn," she breathed.

Antonio added two more lashes to the first, opening long splits in the prisoner's back. He was beginning to enjoy himself. With the fourth and fifth strikes, he got creative, circling the younger man in search of better angles from which to attack more sensitive areas. His shot to Tobyn's face was right on target, scoring his cheek and cutting the skin at the corner of his clenched eye. The fifth, aimed for the genitalia, lanced over his hip instead.

Ara saw Antonio raise his arm for another blow. "Stop him," she said huskily, gripping Carago's arm. "He'll kill him."

Mikal Torres apparently shared that view. He stepped forward and grabbed Antonio's hand, stilling the motion. "Let others have a chance."

Reyes glared at the other man but backed away, kicking dirt at Tobyn. Torres took up Antonio's spot and nervously kept his part of dealing the *kumpania*'s justice to one blow. He stepped aside and rejoined his family, glad to be done with the thing, eager to leave the imprisoned and laughing *chovihano* behind.

Tobyn leaned his head against his upraised arm, eyes closed and watering. He would not cry out, he would not. The pain raged around him like a bonfire, burning within and without, and he covered the urge to whimper with laughter. He would do anything to ruin his enemies' game.

More men came, and more wounds tore into his flesh; his body trembled with agony, his promise to himself fading away. Another lash brought a ragged cry, and he sagged in his chains. The coil inside of him twisted tighter still, and he felt as if parts of his insides were being ripped away. Tears streaked his face as more whip scars were added to his increasingly impressive collection. Blood was flowing down his skin. He could smell it.

The coil tightened. He needed.

David Dera brought his whip to Carago and wiped the sweat of exertion from his brow. His glittering eyes were full of challenge as he extended the evil thing to the *kumpania* leader. "It's your turn, Carago. Just one, for the offense to your daughter?"

Numbly, Carago accepted the whip and walked to Tobyn's side. Ara glared viciously at him, too afraid of the size and anger of the crowd to act. The old man looked back at his pale daughter and the *chovihani*, seeing accusations of betrayal on their faces. He had lost much today.

Carago looked into Tobyn's abused, contorted face for a long moment, trying to understand. Tobyn clenched his jaws and held his eyes tightly closed; his tremors were worsening, and his breath came only in gasps. He no longer stood on his own, the chains at his wrists now holding him from the ground. Carago worried.

Resolve returned with Antonio's voice. "What are you waiting for, old man? Are you too weak? Punish the rapist or step aside to let someone else at him!"

Johann appeared at Ara's side, and she clutched his hand tightly. The German glared at Antonio, wishing that looks really could kill. Carago raised the whip.

Tobyn only dimly heard his uncle's shout. The fire surrounded and consumed him, eating him alive from the inside out. His world was edged with pain; it was his focus, his detail, his soul. There was nothing but the double agony of internal fire and the *kumpania*'s whips, and the coiled spring that trembled deep in his gut, ready to release. His ears throbbed and pounded, and his nose filled with a sweet smell that set his need to screaming.

The lash wounded him again, but he felt only the torturous snapping of the dreadful inner coil. Tobyn threw his head back as his body jerked, shrieking like a demon caught on holy ground. Convulsions seized him, gave him strength to pull the whipping post from the ground. The crowd edged away from him, frightened by his cries and spasms. He never noticed them.

Tobyn fell to his knees, unable to control his limbs as they danced wildly in some possessed gavotte. He was dying, his body was destroying him from the inside out. He was in the agony of the damned.

He was Changing.

His mind was suddenly free, snapped away from the twitching of its corporeal container, and it was all so clear to him. The fire was the sun. The entrancing scent that sparked his need had been that of his own blood. His eyes flew open with the realization, and the light stabbed them viciously, calling up an anguished moan.

Ara stepped toward him, her eyes filled with horror as she, too, saw what was wrong. Memories of what her brother had endured in the *mullo*'s house returned to her, and she knew with terrible certainty the cause of his current pain.

"Oh, my God...Tobyn..."

Tobyn lurched to his feet with a snarl, protecting his eyes with still-shackled hands. Carago, who until now had been paralyzed in fear, backed away a step, his gaze riveted on the feral teeth that extended even as he watched.

"*Mullo!*" a woman screamed, and suddenly the camp was a mass of confusion. Men scrambled for their weapons as their wives and children ran for safety. Sela was bodily seized and dragged into a *vardo* by Antonio, who ignored her struggles. Chaos reigned.

Ara rushed to Tobyn's side, trying not to fear him when he rounded on her with wild eyes and vicious, wicked fangs. She threw her shawl around him, covering his face to protect them both. Tobyn snarled and howled with the pain of his continued transformation, jerking beneath her touch. The shackles snapped, freeing his wrists, and he grabbed her. She fought against him, but his strength was incredible. With a soft cry of panic, she closed her eyes and offered her throat.

Hoof beats thundered toward them, and Johann came into view, kicking Chal into a gallop. The horse skidded to a stop beside them, and Johann dropped a thick blanket over Tobyn, who released Ara to fight with the cloth. The succor of sudden darkness penetrated past his involuntary reactions and touched his conscious mind. With a pitiful moan of partial relief, Tobyn fell, shuddering, to the ground.

"Help me get him up there," Ara gasped. Together, she and Johann put Tobyn into the saddle. He no longer fought against them; his quiet cries were piteous in their ears. Johann swung up onto the horse's back, wrapping his arms around the newborn vampire's fevered body. He shushed him tenderly, wishing he could take away the pain.

Ara stepped back. "I'll get one of Antonio's horses. I'll follow you."

Johann spurred Chal past the advancing throng of weapon-wielding gypsies as Ara quickly claimed one of her uncle's favorite beasts. She chose to forego a saddle, taking the more expedient route of riding bareback in Johann's wake. The gypsies were outraged as the horses galloped away.

"Follow them!" Tcherbo cried.

"No!" Carago took back his control of the *kumpania*. "Pack your things. We're heading back to Spain, now!" He looked around himself, shock revealed in the shaky focus of his gaze. "Where is my daughter?"

"With Antonio Reyes," Dera answered promptly. "In his *vardo*."

Scowling, Carago stormed to Sela's rescue.

❧

"Let go of me!" she hissed, kicking at him and scoring a useful hit below the belt. Antonio released her with a startled grunt of pain, but he blocked the exit with his body. Sela glared at him, fire in her eyes. "What the hell do you think you're doing?"

"Getting you...away...from the *mullo*," he said, grinning. He liked her spirit, and he loved it when women fought him. It excited him.

"I don't need your help."

"No? You'll need a new husband."

Sela's jaw dropped in amazement at the man's unmitigated gall. "What? How dare you—"

"The timing is poor, but you'll have to decide. You are too valuable to be lost to spinsterhood."

"And what makes you think I'd choose you?"

"Because it isn't your right to choose," he replied, getting his breathing back under control and taking a menacing step closer. "And once I take this *kumpania* away from your worthless father, you'll have to do what I say. I'll be king here, and I will have you."

"You can't just walk in and take this group," she snorted, tossing her head. "The *kris*—"

"Support me. Your father is weak and old. I am neither. The *kris* will make me their leader. Then I can have what I want. I can either do this nicely, or I can do it so that you'll regret every harsh word you ever said to me. Once I'm in command, nobody can block me from what I want."

She stared at him in shock, suddenly understanding why Tobyn had always hated this man. He was diabolical, and too damned smart for her comfort. Antonio had set things up to suit himself perfectly, and she knew that she was caught. Blood money was speaking loud and clear in the ruling council.

"Don't take this away from my father," she said softly, trying to reason with him, or at least to negotiate. "It's all he has left. And like you said, he's old. Let him keep his position, even if he'll only be a puppet. Let him think that he's still in charge." She shook her head. "It would kill him any other way."

"Maybe that's best," Antonio purred, touching her face. She made herself hold still. "Maybe I want him out of the way." He smiled. "And what do I get if I do this?"

She swallowed her disgust and choked out, "Me. Then you'll be heir to the *kumpania* anyway."

"A tempting offer, little girl. I think I like it."

He stepped toward her, and she ducked under his arm, keeping away from him. "Not yet! I'm not free yet, and I don't want you touching me until I don't have a choice anymore. Talk to my father about this first." He reached out for her, and she batted his hand away. "Don't touch me!"

"You'll want me soon enough, woman," he giggled. "I'll make you."

He tried to block her escape route once again, and she shoved at him. "Get out of my way. My husband needs me."

Sela charged past him and flung open the door, all but decking her father with it as she did. Carago took her hand and pulled her to him, crushing her close in a protective embrace. Against his shoulder, trying to forget the deal with the devil she'd just made, she asked, "Tobyn?"

"Ara and the *gadjo* have taken him into the forest." Carago's own eyes were wet as he pulled away from her. "Forget him, Sela. He is dead to us. We're going back to Spain now. Get ready."

Not knowing how to react to her father's news, knowing only that she wanted to curl up and cry for a week, she did as she was told. All the while, she prayed that Tobyn would somehow, some way, be right again. Tears came when she realized that if he was, she and the baby she carried would probably never know.

⚬⚬⚬

The foothills offered them the shelter of caves, and Johann and Ara occupied the first suitable cavern they found. Johann carried Tobyn into the cool, damp shadows and laid him on the blanket that had protected him from the sun. The German watched as Ara dressed her brother like an oversized doll, tugging clothes onto his bleeding, feverish body.

"What can I do to help?" he asked.

"Stand guard while I get some water. There's a stream just beyond that hill over there. I won't be long." She pulled Tobyn's shirt closed, fumbling with the buttons. "Try to get a little blood from one of the horses. I don't know what he needs, but it might help."

Taking his knife and a tin cup from the bags Sela had packed, Johann managed to drain a little of the ruby liquid from a mildly-protesting Chal. He returned and handed the cup to Ara, feeling vaguely sickened by the whole thought of it, and watched as she put the cup to Tobyn's lips.

He swallowed all of it, not even leaving a drop behind. As if he were controlled by some other mind, Tobyn took all that they offered him, then fell back, gasping, onto the blanket.

Johann's mouth fell open, and he whispered, "His face..."

Ara looked. The whip cut was healing as they watched, the layers of skin reuniting. Within moments, there was no scar to remind them of the day's brutality. She gently checked beneath his shirt and saw that all of his wounds had healed.

"My God," Johann breathed. "How can this be?"

"*Mullo*," she said reluctantly. "He's a vampire now. He isn't...he isn't human anymore."

"I don't understand how this could have happened. The vampire that attacked the caravan never hurt him."

Ara sat back to study Tobyn's lax features as he slept, listening to his unintelligible mumbling. "Not then, no. But two years ago, before I married, Tobyn was caught trying to steal a horse that belonged to the vampire who attacked the *vardo*. He spent a long, horrible time as his prisoner. Tobyn never told me in so many words, but I know that the vampire made him drink blood."

"He was trying to make him into a vampire, too, then?"

"I think so."

"But...why didn't it work at the time? Why did it take two whole years?"

She felt as perplexed as Johann looked. "I don't know. I feel like I should know, but I don't." She sighed and rose. "Keep an eye out for gypsies. They'll probably follow us to try and kill him. I'll be back as soon as I can."

He watched her head for the mouth of the cave. "Be careful."

"I will."

After she was gone, the German sat near Tobyn, close enough to guard him but well out of arm's reach. Tobyn frowned and moaned, trapped in delirium. Johann pitied him, almost as much as he feared him. When Tobyn awoke and knew himself for what he had become, how would he react? Would he be the same person he had been, the one Johann had come to love? Would he be a person at all, or would he be a monster? Johann tried to look into the young man's face, tried to see him as a rampaging demon in an angel's disguise. He could not picture it.

As he watched, it seemed that Tobyn's face was changing. The soaring cheekbones and delicate features were sharper, somehow, lending his beauty a hungry, dangerous edge that only made it more striking. Johann had a momentary fantasy of being struck dumb by a single look the next time Tobyn opened his eyes. The German laughed quietly at himself. What was he thinking?

He understood now how vampires could charm unwary mortals to their graves. Tobyn, newly changed to immortality, wasn't even awake, but already Johann was willing to do anything he asked.

Oh, Johann, he thought to himself. *You're hopeless.*

✧∕∾∾❧

Araminah returned with the water in Tobyn's waterskin, her brow lined in concern. Johann sat at her brother's side, staring with a rapt shine in his eyes and holding Tobyn's hand like the lover he was. The vampire was quiet now, but horrifyingly pale; his white brow was beaded with sweat. Sloshing some water onto a cloth, Ara knelt and swabbed the perspiration away.

"How long will he be like this?" Johann asked.

"Until nightfall, I guess. I don't know. I don't even know what he'll be like when he wakes up." She sat back and sighed, face pensive. "It could be dangerous for us." Abruptly, humorlessly, she laughed. "I never thought I'd be trying to help a vampire."

They were silent for a long while; finally, he said, "It's frightening."

Ara eyed him. "Maybe."

"You aren't concerned?"

"Tobyn would never hurt me, *mullo* or not."

The confidence in her voice almost convinced him. "How can you be sure?"

"I know my twin, Johann."

He turned to watch Tobyn as the vampire moaned once more. "How long will you stay with him?"

"Until I die, whether it's soon or late."

"But—"

She pinned him with a weary gaze. "I've got no place to go. I've never enjoyed being Romany, and now that we've been expelled, I'll never be able to rejoin another *kumpania*, as if I'd ever want to. And I don't know the first thing about being a *gadja*."

He blinked, then straightened. "You're hoping he'll kill you."

Ara smiled at the soft, stunned sound of his voice. "Maybe. My brother is very good at adapting. He'll be able to fit in anywhere, with anyone. Maybe he'll live a while longer if he kills me, and I won't have to worry about belonging in nobody's world."

"That's defeatist and suicidal," he snapped. "Besides, you said yourself that you don't think he'd hurt you."

She chuckled and wiped the cold cloth over Tobyn's forehead once again. "Let's just say that I'm hedging my bets."

Eighteen

Tobyn opened his eyes and was sure the nightmare had not ended.

The pain in his gut was intense, stabbing; his head still spun like a child's toy, unable or unwilling to stop. He groaned and pushed against the ground with his hands, but failed in his attempt to rise. He was simply too weak.

His eyes cleared, and he saw Johann dozing beside him. The *gadjo* hummed like blood, he smelled of it, he shimmered with it. Tobyn's stomach demanded to be filled; the needy void turned into a honed knife, twisting. He tried to move, but again his body disobeyed him. He fell still with a sigh of defeat.

His thirst rose within him like an alien presence and took control. He was nothing but hunger; he was owned and defined by his need. It was the hunger that rose, it was the thirst that crawled to Johann's side. The need put its hand on the German's face, turning his head slowly, baring his throat. It extended its fangs and leaned closer, pressing its inexpert kiss to Johann's pink skin. It was the thirst that lapped up the blood that flowed from the messy incisions, pulled and pulled at the wound until no more red elixir would come.

It was Tobyn, though, who released his lover with a horrified shudder when the German had gone cold; Tobyn who pulled away from the corpse with an aggrieved sob. The void within him was full finally, and he hated it for its smug silence.

With trembling fingers he touched his teeth, feeling the sharp points shrinking painlessly back into the shape they'd held in his mortal days. They were slick with Johann's blood. In desperate, groundless hope, he crawled up to his friend's pale face and tried to find a sign of life. He patted the slack cheeks, and Johann's head lolled grotesquely forward on a broken neck. Tobyn sobbed, distantly remembering the bones snapping beneath the weighty force of his greed. What had he become to kill a friend and lover for his blood?

He was lost. As he cradled Johann to his chest, petting the blond hair, he vowed in a tear-choked voice, "Michel Dumas, I'll make you pay for this."

❦❧

Ara returned from her nightly water-gathering trip to find her brother putting the finishing touches on a shallow grave. Tobyn was pale, but not alarmingly so, and he looked as human as he had before the

Change. His face, sharpened and accentuated by his altered nature, was lined with sorrow and fresh tears.

Monsters don't cry, she thought to herself. Gathering her courage, she stepped forward cautiously.

He heard her all-but-silent tread and turned to face her. His eyes swam with emotions he could not control. "Oh, Ara," he whispered.

She crossed the last few yards separating them and embraced him. He held him close, crying brokenly against her hair, grateful that his sated hunger posed no threat to her now. He could never forgive himself for hurting her.

Ara stroked his back and whispered, "Everything will be all right now, you'll see. We'll get you through."

"I killed him. I just...I..."

He dissolved into sobs, and she shushed him like a mother soothing a wounded child. "It's not your fault. You couldn't help it, Tobyn. You need to survive—"

"Not like this, not at the expense of my friends!" He pulled away from her. "That *is* my fault!"

Ara's strained nerves snapped into anger. "What did you expect? You aren't what you were before." She grabbed his face and forced him to look at her. "Like it or not, brother mine, you are a vampire. Get used to killing. You have to do it to survive."

He took her hands in his own and stared mournfully at Johann's grave. "I'll find a way not to kill, I—How can you bear to look at me?"

Ara squeezed his fingers. "I love you, Tobyn. I always will, no matter what."

He shook his head and warned, "I might kill you next. Can you live with that?"

"It's better than living without you."

Tobyn pulled free of her hands and covered his distracted trembling by stroking Chal's velvety nose. He'd never noticed before how soft a horse's muzzle could be. Speaking quietly, he told his twin, "There's a person who could help me understand what I have to do, what I've become. She's in Spain, I think. I need to talk to her."

Araminah nodded gravely. "Fine. I'm going with you."

"She's a vampire, Ara!" he objected.

"So are you."

"Ara—"

"Listen to me," she commanded. "You've just spent the last two days completely delirious, so your strength is down, and while you're still new to the game, you'll need someone to stand guard for you during the day." She could see him faltering and pursued her point. "You're all that I have left, Tobyn. You have to let me come with you."

His stubborn gaze softened. "I've ruined everything for you, haven't I?" He shook his head and stared at Chal's cheek as he stroked it. "Jesus Christ, what was I doing? I've killed people...my own family..."

"The Morenos weren't family."

"No, but Tito was." He avoided her surprised look. "I hit him the last night with the *kumpania*. I hit him and he died, and I hid his body in the rocks. I killed him, and I killed the Lump and his parents..." He trailed off in mortified disbelief. "And I raped you."

"Tobyn, no. I don't see it that way."

He shook his head. "I only wanted to kill Antonio." He sank down to sit on the grass at her feet. "My God, Ara, I was absolutely insane. It's a miracle that I didn't kill you or Sela." At the mention of his wife's name, Tobyn covered his eyes with his hands and shook in silent tears. *//What have I done?//* When there was no response, he gripped the sides of his head and cried, "You aren't even hearing me anymore!"

She could see where this was going. Setting her jaw, she firmly said, "Stop it, Tobyn. Just stop. If you keep applying old rules to your life now, you really will be insane. You can't live like a...a mortal anymore. So stop feeling sorry for yourself, get up, and let's go find your *mulla* girlfriend. She'll set you on the right path." She took his hands and pulled him to his feet. He obeyed, too shell-shocked to resist. Ara brushed off his pants. "Come on, then. Saddle up that horse of yours and I'll pack up our things. Then we can go to Spain and set things right."

"Ara—"

"Shh. No more arguments."

He caught her arm and pulled her closer, kissing her tenderly. "Thank you."

The young woman patted his hip, the one that had so recently borne the brunt of a whip lash. "We have to take care of each other now."

He watched her as she headed toward their rocky shelter. Just before she passed out of earshot, he said, "Ara...I'm sorry."

She smiled at him, unleashing the gentle side of her personality. "For what?"

"I ruined everything."

"My life could have stood some ruining." She shrugged. "I think I'll like things better this way, anyway."

"I don't think you will," he said. "But I've been wrong before."

"Yes, you have."

They shared a tentative smile, and he drew what little strength of optimism he had from her trust in him.

"I love you."

"I love you, too, Tobyn. We'll get through this somehow."

He took a deep breath. "I hope you're right, Ara. I hope you're right."

᷍᷍᷍

They rode in silence, leaving Johann behind them. The farther he got from the scene of his crime, the more clearly Tobyn was able to think, and he fell into deep contemplation. He accepted what he now was, mostly because he had no other choice. Denial was pointless and it was impossible for him to change his situation. Vampires, from what he knew of them, required human blood to survive. Dumas had killed for blood, Tobyn was certain. It was the nature of the beast that he had become.

But did he necessarily have to be all of the things that Dumas was? He shuddered at the memory of the French vampire's "pantry" and vowed to never leave any mortal, no matter what his or her offenses might have been, in such a hovering state of nothingness. And if he had to take human blood, then he would emulate what he knew of Isabella: he would take it painlessly, and only from those who gave it of their own free will.

He looked at Ara, who napped silently while her horse—Antonio's favorite, he noted with a spark of malicious glee—followed Chal's lead. Ara was still mortal, and Tobyn would do anything to protect her from the pain of the Change. He was grateful that she was still by his side, and he wanted to keep her there forever, or at least until she died. That was where the problems arose. How could she stay with him when he might murder her at any time? And how could he bear to watch her falter, ail, grow old? More relevant to the present, how long could she travel with him at night and keep watch during the day? She needed rest, she needed food, and she needed a reprieve from the danger he now posed. How were they supposed to stay together?

He only hoped that Isabella could have some answers. She was his last, best chance for understanding what it was to be a vampire.

A horrible thought occurred to him. Where could he find Isabella? When he left the *hacienda* two years ago, Serrano had told him that they were running from Dumas, perhaps to Italy, perhaps to England. Tobyn had no desire to go chasing over all of Europe trying to hunt her down while she tried not to be found. Years gave experience, and Isabella was bound to be much better at her chosen task than Tobyn would be in his. He brought Chal to a halt, and Ara's mount stopped as well. Tobyn needed to find the Spanish noblewoman now. He needed answers.

He reached out with his mind, trying a desperate gambit. Hoping that telepathy was the vampire equivalent of a dog whistle, he loudly called, *//Doña Isabella! Tobyn Reyes needs you!//* He repeated the summons several times, then fell still and waited for a reply.

᷍᷍᷍

The manor house was alive with noise and light as the German branch of the Prime celebrated the recent capture of the leader of the Berlin Brethren. Elisa sat in a throne-like chair at the head of the room, holding court in her private domain. Her mind was occupied by the pleasant contemplation of how best to destroy the enemy vampire that languished under lock and key in the courtyard. Sunlight was amusing, but so too was fire...the Brethren, though, deserved something slower, and more painful. Starvation, she decided, and rose to make her proclamation.

It was then that the telepathic call cut through the room, silencing the assembled immortals, almost literally flattening some of the younger members of the throng. Elisa's blue eyes widened.

"Tobyn Reyes," she whispered, a creeping sense of excitement suffusing her body. In answer to his message, she cooed, *//Where are you, Tobyn? I can help you.//*

❧

In his section of Italy, Tobyn recognized the soprano voice that replied to him. While his body ached in sympathy to the memory of Elisa Dieter, he cursed himself for a fool. Of course. Isabella would not be the only one to hear him! Both groups—what had she called them? the Prime and the Brethren, that was it—would have heard him. Dumas would have heard him.

Cursing loudly and at length in every language he could apply, he wheeled Chal around and headed for cover, pulling his sister after him. Ara blinked in the confusion of sudden waking and asked, "Tobyn? What is it?"

"Your brother is an idiot," he growled in reply. "Damn it! How could I have been so stupid?"

She wiped a hand over her eyes and forced herself to be alert. "What are you talking about?"

Tobyn reined Chal to a halt outside a ramshackle, deserted cottage. As he smoothly dismounted, he replied, "I've managed to attract some unwanted attention."

Concerned, she looked around. "The *kumpania?*"

"Worse." He helped her to the ground. "Vampires."

❧

Isabella put her book aside and rose with a rustle of silk. Serrano raised an eyebrow and asked, "Is there trouble coming?"

"Undoubtedly, but not to me." To clarify the mystery, she told him, "I have a novice to rescue. Prepare the guest room."

He had questions, but he knew that his mistress would give answers only in her own time. Nodding a quasi-bow, he moved to obey while Isabella herself went to the balcony of the Italian villa.

//Tobyn, I'm here. I'll find you.//
//Hurry!//

He lacked her ability to close the communication line to anyone but the intended recipient. His reply was loud and unconfined, and she winced. He had much to learn.

Elisa grinned wolfishly to her second-in-command. "There, you have heard him. He is the one Dumas wishes to possess. Get him here, and we will make a present for the Prime."

The celebration transmogrified into a posse, and the blonde vampire indulged herself in a satisfied smile. *What can I convince Dumas to give me now?*

In France, Dumas heard the call and bolted from his library chair as if he'd been hit by lightning. The book he had been reading fell, forgotten, to the floor, and he stared out the wide windows into the darkness of the night beyond. His heart pounded so that he could hear nothing else, and in a soft voice, he whispered the gypsy's name.

He stopped himself before he could move any closer to the siren sound of his lover's voice. Never had any sound touched him so deeply. He ached to find Tobyn, but his pride ached more.

I will not go running after him in the night like an addled school boy, he vowed. *Dignity. Remember, Michel, who you are.*

As he forced himself to sit back down and wait for time and Fate to bring Tobyn back to him—for with him was where the gypsy ultimately belonged—he wondered how long it would take for him to stop feeling both elated and crushed by every near-miss he and Tobyn had.

Isabella focused her attention and the darkness that was inside of her, her vampiric part. Somewhere, Tobyn waited for her. She envisioned his face and his form, remembered his scent and his taste. The immortal force within her leaped forward like a hunting dog, and she pushed it into concentration. *See him,* she told it. *Find him.*

She could feel the wind lift her and bear her toward the northwest. Her mind reached for a point of reference, but she knew how this game was to be played. Thinking would disrupt too much. Carefully clearing her mind of all thoughts, she drifted under the power of the vampire within her. It would take her to Tobyn, she knew. She only needed to ride along in silence.

Hurry, Isabella urged. *Find him first.*

⚜

Tobyn and Ara claimed the tumble-down building, moving their horses inside with them and trying their best to close the door.

"Should we put up a barricade?" Ara asked, trying to see in the dim interior.

"It wouldn't help. They'd only come through the roof."

"What are we supposed to do?"

He disliked the note of panic in his sister's voice. She had never lost control before. He could not afford to have her start now. "Isabella is coming. If she can't find us and help us, then we wait for sunrise. Sunlight destroys vampires."

Her green eyes widened. "What about you, Tobyn? Won't it hurt you? There isn't enough cover from this building. Light will get through."

"I'll figure something out."

"But—"

"Araminah, please!" He sighed and bit back on his frustration, his tone softening. "Keep quiet and hold yourself together. One problem at a time."

The horses huddled together nervously, their ears alert for the sounds outside the cottage. Ara stroked her animal's flank, then looked to Tobyn. His face was tense with listening. She wanted to ask him what he heard, but his warning gesture ordered her to silence and forestalled any questions. The wind rose around their shelter, whistling through the cracks in the walls and howling through the holes in the wood. Ara backed away from the door as a voice called her brother's name.

"Tobyn! Tobyn Reyes!"

The harsh set to his jaw relaxed into a flood of relief. "It's her," he told his sister. He opened the door to allow the Spanish vampire admittance.

Ara studied Isabella as the noblewoman approached Tobyn. Fine silk and lace swirled in tiers around her legs, and her face and figure were things of poets' dreams. Ara looked at her own tattered clothing and clenched her jaws against the irrational and sudden rise of jealousy.

Isabella did not see or acknowledge the scrutiny. Taking Tobyn's hands, she softly said, "You have much to learn, young one. I can teach you, but not here. Come quickly."

He nodded and held out a hand. "Ara..." She stepped forward and took the offered grip, a possessive glint in her eye. He looked to Isabella. "My sister comes with me."

"Fine. But hurry. There is little time. The others are babies, too, but they still can find you here." She pulled the twins out into the moonlight. "I will assume that you haven't yet found your wings."

"No. I've...I haven't tried," he admitted, feeling strangely torn.

Isabella smiled softly. "There will be time for that, my fledgling. I will take the two of you on my own strength, then. Hold your sister, *cariño*, and I will hold on to you."

"Can you carry us both?" he asked, concerned.

"Of course."

Ara felt her brother put his arms around her, and she clung to the feeling. *I refuse to lose you, Tobyn.* She closed her eyes tightly as Isabella's delicate hands stole around his waist to clasp him nearer. There was a sudden lurch, and then they were airborne, streaking over the trees and hills as the wind lashed their faces. Terrified and exhilarated, Ara squeezed her brother's arms. He tightened his hold on her in reassurance.

A wild cry ripped at Ara's ears, and she started in Tobyn's grasp so violently that he almost dropped her. A screaming blonde in red velvet flew through Ara's line of sight, her long arms outstretched, reaching for Tobyn. Isabella hissed and kicked at the other vampire as hard as she could, then added speed and a change of direction to her own flight. Tobyn ached to pull his knife, but he needed to hold Ara safely. Snarling curses, he watched as Elisa was left behind by Isabella's age-strengthened power.

When their feet touched ground again, Ara was trembling from cold and fear. "Who was that woman?"

"The enemy," Isabella replied. She signaled to the servants who came from within the villa. "Be comfortable, Señorita Reyes. You are my guest. No harm will come to you here."

The gypsy shook her head as a maid attempted to lead her away. "I stay with Tobyn."

"You must rest," the other woman insisted, wanting to remove all mortal distractions so that she and Tobyn might talk in privacy.

Ara's jaw set. "I won't leave him."

Tobyn clasped his sister's hand. "She could be useful," he told Isabella. "I'd like her to stay."

The female vampire studied him, then Araminah, who was intimidating in her wild beauty. The mortal woman lifted her chin and moved closer to Tobyn, clearly transmitting her presumed ownership of her brother. The two Reyes seemed to be enjoying a unique relationship; she would have to consider them further. Sighing, she relented.

"All right. Maria, prepare a room for Señorita Reyes."

The servant curtsied and moved off to comply, and Ara felt reasonably triumphant that she'd been allowed to stay.

"Now, then," the Spanish vampire said, "I feel that we have much to discuss. Come into my library and we can begin. *Señorita*, would you perhaps care for a meal? My staff can prepare something for you."

"That would be fine," Ara replied with more than a trace of the old Romany haughtiness.

"Make it two. I'm famished," Tobyn requested.

Isabella stared at him. "Are you sure?"

"Yes. Why wouldn't I be?"

"You may regret this." She shook her head. "Your system has changed, *mi amo*."

"Not that much." He began to feel foolish and self-conscious beneath her gaze, feelings that never failed to put him in a bad humor. "Just ask them, please."

Oñate nodded slowly. "We'll see how it goes. Very well." After dispatching a different maid with the order, she said, "Shall we proceed?"

"By all means."

Isabella led them into the villa, their footsteps echoing quietly off of the tiled floor and unadorned marble hall. The Spanish lady opened a door and ushered the twins into a comfortably-furnished library. Serrano looked up at them with a smile as he stoked the fire. A young man standing at his side, a relative by resemblance, watched them in silent curiosity.

"Leave us, my friends," Isabella requested. "I will call for you if you are needed."

The servant nodded. "Yes, Doña Isabella." To the newcomers, he bobbed his head in polite greeting. "Excuse us."

Tobyn watched the men go, then faced his hostess while Ara made herself comfortable in a plush arm chair, stroking the upholstery with wonder. Isabella was staring at him again, something in her eyes ticking off items on a list. He wondered what she saw, or didn't see, that took so much concentration.

"Tell me, Tobyn," she ventured. "When and from whom did you take the Changing blood?"

"From Dumas, almost exactly two years ago."

"Two years? That was the only time?"

The Spanish woman's eyes widened in open surprise, and Reyes felt that he must have transgressed somehow. One of his hands reached down to clasp his sister's, and he replied, "Yes. How does it usually work?"

"Instantaneously. If Dumas' blood was going to Change you, it should have done so in France." She shook her head. "I don't understand."

"Well, if you don't, I sure as hell never will."

Ara tightened her grip on his fingers in reassurance, then spoke to Isabella. "Can you help him or not?"

"I can." She thought for a moment, then repeated with more confidence, "I can. Together we can determine the laws of your new existence. I do not believe that you are like we are."

"What do you mean? A vampire is a vampire," Tobyn snapped. His patience was not what it should have been, but he thought he had the right to be a little testy.

"There are many different kinds of vampire, Tobyn, almost like different species of butterflies. I believe that you have become a new species of vampire, unique unto yourself."

He smiled unconvincingly, looking more menacing than friendly in his frustration. "I don't find that very comforting."

She shrugged an unspoken apology. "There's little else that I can say."

"You can start by explaining what your laws are," Ara suggested. "Tobyn can use those to figure out how he's different."

They were interrupted by the arrival of the maid bearing two plates of food. Isabella took a discreet step away from the meals, drawing a scented handkerchief up to her nose decorously, but Tobyn and Ara were drawn near. The young vampire had never greeted food so enthusiastically and whole-heartedly. His stomach gnawed like a rat upon his spine, the emptiness inside him twisting and demanding to be placated. He fell upon the plate with such gusto that both Isabella and Araminah stared at him in surprise.

Tobyn faltered and looked up into their dumbfounded gazes. Defensively, he said, "I'm hungry."

"Apparently," Ara returned. "Pig."

"Hush," ordered Isabella. "Go ahead and eat, Tobyn. There is plenty of food."

Around a fresh mouthful, he asked, "I take it that this has some significance to you?"

The Spanish lady smiled. "I'll tell you in an hour."

Araminah hesitated and looked to her brother, waiting for his reaction. He did not disappoint. Putting his knife aside with a snap, Tobyn warned, "Don't play games, Isabella. I'm not—"

She shook her head. "No games. It's just that, for my species of vampire, mortal food is anathema. It causes nausea and horrible cramps, which should have reached you by now, if you were one of my kind."

"Which I don't seem to be."

"Exactly."

He turned back to his meal and was silent for a time, then asked, "What else can't you do?"

"We can drink only blood, and sometimes wine if they are mixed together. We cannot endure the slightest touch of sunlight, or of flame. We cannot make love."

"But we—"

He broke off with a guilty look at Ara, who obliged him by kicking him in the ankle. Isabella suppressed a smile. "No, Tobyn. You. In perfect honesty, although quite enjoyable, the act required little participation from me." When he frowned in confusion, she explained. "That particular restriction applies more to men than to me."

Ara grinned wickedly. "Men have the moving parts."

Tobyn ignored the joke and poked at his plate with his fork, remembering Dumas' use of Matthieu. He had to ask a question. "Have you ever known a...a vampire of my kind before?"

Isabella glanced at Ara, who met her gaze frankly, almost daring the Spanish woman to answer. She possessed either foolish courage, bravado, or hidden strengths, Isabella decided, and probably all three. Turning back to Tobyn, she replied, "No. I haven't. I believe you are the first."

"First and only."

"Yes."

He hesitated, then asked in a husky whisper, "Will there ever be any others like me?" His blue eyes flickered up to meet Isabella's even gaze. "I can't live alone, not forever."

She shook her head. "I cannot say. I don't know what makes you different, or what special circumstances prevailed upon you the night you took Dumas' blood." She spread her hands in a helpless gesture. "I don't know how you could Make another like you if I don't even know how you yourself were Made. I can say nothing about you, Tobyn. You are strange to me."

"I'm strange to myself!" He tried to smile to deprive the strident tone of his voice of some of its power, but the fresh tears that rose to shine in the candlelight subverted the attempt. "I never wanted to be this way. I never wanted to...to hurt, and to kill people, and—I was raised to be a healer! Do you know how it feels for me to murder a man I cared for, just to get at his blood? Do you?"

"*Cariño*—"

"And I know nothing of this life. I don't know what to do or where to go, or even what to do to survive. I'm not even sure if I want to survive!" He shook his head sharply as the tears escaped, and Ara reached out to touch him. He pushed her hand away. "And as for that, I don't even know what will kill me. If I wanted to get out of this hell, I couldn't do it!"

Isabella sighed. "Your instincts will tell you how to survive. They are stronger than you and I and your sister put together. Trust in what your heart tells you, not in the questions your mind creates."

He jumped up from his seat and the chair he'd been occupying scraped loudly on the floor. "It's so easy for you to give advice, isn't it?" he snarled. "You know what you are."

"And given time, patience, and rational thought, we can know what you are, as well." She looked at him sternly, not a bit impressed by his angry display. "Theatrics and emotion will not help you now. This is what you have become, and you must learn to live with it. Adapt. Adjust. Anything else is cowardice."

He glared at her, feeling his teeth shifting behind his lip in response to his fury. "I am not a coward."

"Aren't you?"

Ara rose and stood between the two vampires, interrupting an evil-tempered stare-down that threatened to blossom into violence. "Stop it, both of you. Doña Isabella, I thank you for your hospitality and your help in escaping the others. All the same, I think you should stop badgering my brother until he has recovered his strength. He is tired, and his Change was traumatic. I know. I witnessed it." Switching to the Romany language, she continued firmly, "And you, Tobyn Reyes, if you think for one minute that temper tantrums and threats will get her to help you sooner, you're a bigger fool than I ever thought you were. I realize that it's difficult for you, and that what I told her is true. Tired, yes. Traumatized, yes. But she can help you. Nobody else can. And, so help me God, if you say just one more word about dying to escape, I'll find a way to kill you myself. Is that clear?"

The look he gave her would have sent lesser mortals scrambling for cover. "Yes," he bit out, jaws clenched, eyes shimmering silver behind the blue. "Very clear."

"Good." Undaunted, Ara turned back to Isabella and returned to speaking Spanish. "Now, then. I don't suppose that it ever occurred to you to ask a mere mortal for ideas. I'm not a vampire, but I'm not a block of wood, either." The gypsy woman paused, irritated by the amusement that was creeping over Isabella's face. Raising her chin with pride and attitude, she said, "I can tell you why Tobyn did not become one of your kind. I know exactly what was different."

The Spanish vampire looked ready to laugh. Araminah hated her for that. "And what was different, little one?"

Her face registering all of her displeasure at being patronized, Ara answered with one word. "Beti."

"Who?"

Tobyn watched in sudden pride and realization as Ara nodded and recited the words to their grandmother's old protection charm. "'From now until the end of time, from day into night, they will not become one of these.'"

Isabella shook her head in utter confusion. "But...what is that? Who is Beti?"

"She was our grandmother. *Chovihani*." Tobyn looked back at his sister. "How could I have forgotten?"

"Forgotten what?"

Araminah, amused in her turn by Isabella's frustration, explained, "She put a spell, or charm, on us years ago. It was meant to protect us from *mulle*." She shrugged one shoulder. "I've been thinking that it just didn't work, but I think that answer is in the wording. It did work. It just didn't work the way we thought it would."

"I didn't become one of your kind, like the spell said," Tobyn added, piecing things together out loud. "I became something different."

Isabella nodded slowly. "I understand. Not one of these, but one of those." She tapped her fingertip against her lip. "I only wonder what affect this 'night into day' clause has."

"Possibly, sunlight isn't lethal to him. He Changed in broad daylight and he wasn't destroyed."

Tobyn smirked mirthlessly. "It wasn't fatal, but it wasn't pleasant, either, from what I can remember."

"What do you remember?" the Spanish vampire asked, moving back into a more scientific stance.

The gypsy thought for a moment, then replied with carefully-chosen words. "Pain. I was burning up on the inside, and every muscle was spasming. It felt as if everything inside of me jumped and shifted." He closed his eyes. "And I was so empty inside. It was hunger, but more than hunger." He met Isabella's gaze once more. "Do you understand?"

"Perfectly. It was the thirst that you felt, and your moment of death." She shook her head. "As for the burning, it had to be the sunlight hurting you. Why you weren't destroyed, though, I will never understand. Perhaps it was your grandmother's magic."

Ara said calmly, "I can see no other explanation."

Tobyn sat back at the table and pushed his plate aside. "If the circumstances that made me what I am were so particular, what with Beti's spell and all, then I don't see how I'll ever be able to...to Make another like me."

"Perhaps it will be impossible," Isabella nodded, "but perhaps it won't. The difference lies within you, Tobyn, and if the seed for new immortals is there, you will be able to create others of your kind. I believe that you could be the father of a new vampire race." She leaned closer, her dark eyes locked to his gaze. "You can recreate the world in your own image."

He laughed shortly. "You make me sound like a god. I'm hardly that."

"No, but you're the next best thing. You are immortal. You have the power to decide the fate of the mortals you know, and of those you've yet to meet. You are the very first, Tobyn. You can create your own Adam and Eve in the Garden of Eden."

The gypsy vampire shook his head gently. "You're a dreamer, Isabella."

Ara spoke up quietly. "Tobyn, do you think that you can still heal people?"

He blinked at her. "What?"

"You've changed physically, but what about spiritually? I'm not talking about herbs, now, and you know what I mean, even though you avoid it. All of those things you were able to do before...can you still?"

"You know I can't." Her brother closed his eyes, suddenly looking very weary. He didn't want to talk about psychic powers, not right now, not when some were missing. "You don't even hear me when I speak to you the way we used to."

"Telepathy," Isabella provided. "Is that what you're talking about? Telepathy? Speaking mind to mind?" Ara nodded gravely, and the Spanish noblewoman continued. "Of course you can still do it, Tobyn. You know that. Every vampire in Europe heard you tonight. That's a very strong mind-voice you have."

He half-smiled in irony. "Judging from this evening's reaction, I'd say that I need to tone it down a little."

"Perhaps a touch." She turned her benign smile onto Araminah. "But now I fear that your sister needs to rest. I will call Maria to escort you to your room."

The twins looked into one another's eyes, communicating despite the telepathic silence between them. Tobyn said, "If you don't mind, I would like to go with her. I am very tired, and I don't want to be alone."

Isabella hesitated. "I'm not certain that a mortal would be such a good companion for you tonight."

"I need her."

Sighing, she told him privately, *//You may hurt her. The thirst might—//*

"I'm not thirsty now," he told her aloud, not trusting himself to keep from attracting unwanted immortal visitors with trumpet-loud mind speech. "I'd never hurt my sister."

"Her room is not light-proof. Sunlight may not have killed you once; don't tempt it to try again. Stay with me if you don't want to be alone. My rooms are protected."

He shook his head. "No offense, but I only want my sister tonight." His blue eyes touched her. "Please."

Isabella thought it through for a moment, then relented. Against her better judgment, she nodded and said, "I will have Maria escort you both, then."

❧❦❧

The servant who led them to the guest room was pert and talkative, bursting at the seams with questions. Where had they come from? Was Ara a vampire, too? Had Tobyn lived for very, very long? How many victims? Did he like the taste of blood?

Tobyn was glad for the silence when she finally left them alone. The room they had been given was huge, with three different chambers. In the bedroom, Ara gathered up the white lace bed curtain in her hands and studied the delicate threads, marveling at the luxury of everything around her. She had never seen the inside of a *gadjo* house before, much less the inside of a mansion such as this. With all possible witnesses absent or otherwise occupied, she felt free to gawk.

"Nice," Tobyn commented from the doorway, watching her as she admired the satin comforter on the mattress. "Do you like it?"

"It's beautiful."

"I'll get you one."

She raised a slender brow and fixed him with a teasing glance. "Oh, really. And how do you propose to do that?"

Bitterness crept into his tone. "You heard her. I'm God now, remember? I can do anything I want."

Ara left her explorations and went to his side, her hand gentle on his shoulder. "Tobyn..."

He forced a smile. "No, I'm not thinking about it anymore." He kissed her, his lips soft and sweet. "I'm just tired, that's all. It's the fatigue talking."

"You should sleep." She wrapped her arms around him, pulling him into a comforting embrace. "The bed looks wide enough for both of us. Why don't we try it out? The pillows are probably very soft."

Tobyn returned the embrace, then pulled away. "You've got to be dead tired."

She shrugged. "Why don't you join me?"

"I don't know if I could sleep."

"Try. If you can't then at least hold me for a while." Ara hugged him again, her head on his shoulder. "I don't want to be alone, either. I need you tonight, Tobyn."

His decision was made. "Then I'll be here for you. Anything you want, it's yours."

"I want you," she whispered. "I want you to be happy. I want you to be comfortable. I want—"

"Shh." He kissed her again like a tender lover. "You'll have to take me as I am, tonight. Do you trust me?"

"Of course I do. I always will."

"Even though I've become this?"

"Even though. Underneath it all, you're still Tobyn. That hasn't changed." She stepped back. "Now, come to bed, love. We could both use a little rest."

Praying that the thirst would stay away and that Ara would be safe, he followed her to the beckoning mattress. Rest would be a very good thing. He hoped that he could get some.

Nineteen

Sunlight brushed the curtains of their shared bedroom, poking through the threads in the fabric with slender fingers. Although the cloth that covered the windows was thick, it could not withstand the golden insistence that bathed the room in glowing light.

Tobyn opened his eyes slowly, almost as if he feared what he might see. He stared at his hand where it rested on Ara's shoulder, exposed in the pearly light. He flexed the muscles, watched his fingers as they moved through the filtered sunbeam. There was no pain, no burning; only a tingle of heat upon his skin told him that this sun was not the friend he used to know.

Different, but not so alien or malign that he was dying beneath its touch. He wondered how much light he could withstand, how much of his body could be touched by it before he pulled away from the pain. Looking at the shining window did not hurt his eyes, at least not yet. Curious, he slid from the bed and Ara's sleepy embrace and began to creep closer.

The sunlight beckoned to him, singing its siren song along his nerves, humming hypnotically in his brain. It was seducing him, drawing him near.

He took another step.

Light became more tangible, solid against his skin, the closer he came. Every step was more difficult, like wading through ever deeper water, until pressing forward was an adventure. One hand raised slowly, heavily, and grasped the curtain. Tobyn hesitated, took a deep breath, and briefly debated the wisdom of this experiment. He wanted answers. There was only one way to get them. Bracing himself, he flung the curtains open.

He could withstand the touch of the sun, much to his amazement. He watched the light spread and flow over his hands and arms, tingling and warm. He almost laughed. Throwing back his head, he looked out at the day.

Fire washed through his eyes, bright white pain spreading outward from his miserable core. Gasping, he dove out of the light and into the safety of the shadows in the corner of the room. He flattened himself against the wall, stiff with pain and embattled by cramps and nausea.

"Tobyn?" Ara asked muzzily from the bed. As she came awake, concern crept into her voice. "Tobyn, where are you?"

"Close the curtain," he hissed.

Squinting into the bright morning, his sister hurried to comply. The curtains fell thickly over the window once more, cutting the light into something he could bear. Trembling, he slid down the wall to huddle on the floor as Araminah went to his side.

"Why were they open?" she asked. "I know I closed them last night."

"I opened them," he admitted huskily, clutching onto her comforting embrace.

"What? Have you lost your mind?"

"I was testing." He held up one hand so that she could see the unblemished skin. "No burns. Not fatal."

She held his hand and checked it with her *chovihani* sense. "No burns on the outside, you mean. Oh, Tobyn, you're blistered inside."

He let her lead him back to the bed. "It didn't hurt until I looked at the sun. It was getting the light in my eyes..."

"Now you know how not to do it," she told him, covering him with the soft sheets. "Next time, maybe you'll be all right."

Tobyn caught her hand. "Stay with me, Ara. Please."

She smiled and shook her head. "I'm not going anywhere."

"No, I mean always. Don't leave me alone like this." His blue eyes, blind with sun sickness, misted with tears. "I don't know where to go or what to do anymore. I've lost everything I ever was, everything I ever loved, except for you. And, oh, Ara...what if I lose you, too?"

"Shh." She cuddled him close, kissing his temple. "Don't think about that now."

"But—"

"Hush. Put it out of your mind. I'll be right here, no matter what, until the day I die. I'm young, Tobyn, so there's a lot of time. You won't lose me."

"I'd die if I did," he whispered, hugging her. "I'll find a way to keep you forever."

Ara rocked him like a child until he fell asleep, the shock and weakness he'd inherited from his brush with the sun dragging him down. As his breathing slowed and deepened, she pondered his words. If he could find a way to bring her into his version of immortality, would she take the chance? Did she want to live forever as a parasite upon the mortals of the world, a member of some new and unknown vampire race?

She looked down into Tobyn's face. He looked like an angel when he slept, the innocence of a child settling over his features. She loved him.

If it means staying with you, she thought, *I'd do anything.*

She left him sleeping peacefully and crept downstairs, careful to make no sound, uncertain why she was so nervous about being discovered. The Italian sun was warm upon her skin as she passed the huge windows at the head of the main stairway. She had enjoyed the touch of sunlight, once; now she would never see it the same way again. It did not hurt her, but it hurt her brother. Therefore, forever sunlight would be her enemy, as well.

Araminah found no one stirring on the lower level of the villa, and no trace of her hostess. She had expected none. The foreignness of the thick walls pressed in on her, and she felt an urgent need for fresh air. As she found her way to the veranda, she understood much better the near-madness that her twin had suffered in his French captivity. She could not have endured so much.

The porch, too, was deserted. *Good.* Settling down on the railing between two neo-classical columns, she pulled her skirt up to her knees and idly kicked her feet in a slow swinging rhythm, her green eyes surveying the view from Isabella's home. It seemed that she could see miles of rocks and greenery, little houses and streams and clumps of forest. Araminah smiled, wondering what it would be like to own all that she saw.

Stupid thought from a woman who owns nothing, she commented to herself. Well, not quite nothing. She had the contents of the bags she and Sela had so hurriedly packed before the punishment of the *kumpania*. It wasn't much, but it was something. Some clothes, her herbs, some jewelry, her Tarot deck. A little money in pilfered coins, enough to live on for almost a week.

She sighed and looked down at her bare feet, then laughed cynically. *Not much to show for my life. My Romany life*, she amended. She was in the outside world now, no longer gypsy. But how was she supposed to become a *gadja* overnight? She was woefully ill-equipped for the role, both in materials and information. She supposed that she could have Tobyn ask his noblewoman girlfriend to help his poor confused and ignorant sister, but the idea rankled against Ara's headstrong independence. She would make her own way in this new life, find her own definition and identity even while her brother found his.

No outside help. No charity.

"Daring thing, aren't you?"

She started at the sound of Serrano's voice, gasping and involuntarily raising a hand either to strike or defend, depending on which instinct overrode the other.

The Spaniard laughed and held up his hands. "Easy, Señorita Reyes. I didn't mean to frighten you."

Exasperation won out, and she slapped the column beside her. "Don't ever sneak up behind me like that! God damn it!"

He raised an eyebrow. "Gypsy girls certainly are different. May I sit with you?"

Araminah hesitated, suspicious of his motives, then pulled her skirt down and scooched aside. "Go ahead."

Serrano climbed onto the railing and took his seat with a sigh. "Beautiful day, isn't it? Bright and warm."

"Yes."

"I assume from your attitude that your brother is all right this morning."

She looked at him through the corner of her eye. "He's sick," she answered simply, unwilling to give details. "Too much sun."

"Count your blessings. If he were like Doña Isabella, he'd be dead. If any sunlight touches her at all, she'll die." He snapped his fingers. "Instant. Painful. Her rooms have to have the windows bricked shut, or covered with the heaviest black blankets when we travel. It's not an easy life." He looked at her. "But you'll learn that soon enough if you stay with Tobyn." He gave her the chance to volunteer information; she did not take it. "Are you going to stay with him?"

She straightened, almost offended by the question. "Of course. What else should I do?"

He nodded, satisfied. "Good girl. If you'll be with him, there are things you'll need to know. Being a vampire's mortal traveling companion is a unique situation, with a lot of problems I'll wager you haven't even thought of yet. Come inside and I'll tell you what I can."

Ara hesitated as Serrano regained his feet, then followed him into the villa. He led the way to Isabella's elegant study, waving her to a seat on the divan. She sat quietly, watching him as he opened the liquor cabinet and poured himself a glass of brandy. Serrano, silent, offered her a drink of her own, which she accepted with a nod. Their silence was heavy, pregnant, ready to give birth to trouble. Araminah's instincts coiled in her muscles, and she waited tensely for Serrano to sit.

He took up position beside her on the cushion, not touching her, giving no indication that he would make the attempt. Still, he was a man, and the only man she trusted was Tobyn. She relaxed...marginally.

"Do *gadjo* men always drink with their women?" she asked, only partially teasing.

"No, not like this. But you're not my woman, or even of my race. What we share here, this slice of vampire life, makes us equals, and it's as equals that we have to talk."

She nodded and put her glass aside, untouched. "So talk."

Serrano took a mighty swallow of the alcohol and began. "There are many levels to this world. Never for one instant believe that you know all that exists. The vampire world lies on top of the mortal world, running through it and over it and beneath it, always. It is a world like ours, with politics and nations, clans and wars and constant, never-ending struggles to survive. You know how hard it can be to put together food enough to feed a caravan during its winter travels. You gypsies have to steal enough to survive, yet leave no trace of the theft, no clues on the site or refuse when you leave. So it is with vampires, but the crops they raid don't come from farmers' fields. And the refuse they generate is far different from potato peels and bread crumbs."

"People," she said. "Bodies."

"Exactly. The first thing you must learn as Tobyn's companion is that it falls on you to hide the bodies when he feeds. I don't know what kind of feeding he does; nobody knows that yet. But you can't expect him to always be careful or to clean up after himself. Vampires...many of them lose control when they feed, recklessly slaughtering, leaving the corpses in the open. That attracts attention, needless to say, and it is attention that you least want. Be careful, Araminah, to leave no trail of guilt to lead mortals to Tobyn. The results would be disastrous for you both." He took another nervous gulp, staring out the window at the brightness of the day. "Guard him during his rest. Make certain that no mortal intrudes to find him vulnerable. I don't know if he is like the Doña, but in the day she is paralyzed, helpless. Dead, to all appearances. She needs to be defended in that state. It may be the same for Tobyn."

Ara shook her head. "He doesn't die. He sleeps. But I'll guard him all the same."

"Good."

"You mentioned a war, and clans," she said slowly. "Am I to understand that this means something other than vampire versus mortal?"

He nodded. "Indeed it does."

"Tell me."

"There are two types of vampire: the kind like Doña Isabella, and another. The other...they may be legend. We have encountered none of their kind, but we hear stories, and they've been written about by the Hebrews, who gave them their name. They are called the Watchers, and they are the most dreadful and insidious kind. They are spirit, not flesh, and spirit is what they feed upon. The Watchers are vampires of the soul, Araminah—any soul. They destroy the corporeal vampires as carelessly as the vampires destroy mortals, and as easily. There may be no limit to their power. They are more than a match for the oldest of my lady's kind." Seeing the concern in her eyes, he waved a hand. "But they may not exist. We have no way of knowing. All the best, though, to keep them in the back of your mind, at least to know that they are there.

"Of clans, there are two. Three, actually, if your brother can perpetuate his line. The existing clans that are at war today are the Prime and the Brethren. The Prime are ruled by a triumvirate, the Triad, and Michel Dumas, the vampire who made a nightchild out of your brother, is their leader. The Secondary and Tertiary Primes, Dumas' lieutenants, have recently been replaced. I don't know who holds those positions now.

"The Prime believe that humans are cattle, a commodity to be exploited and used and destroyed at will. They believe themselves superior to humans in all things and in all ways, and they would set themselves as rulers of the world if they could."

He drank again, and Ara prompted, "And what about the Brethren?"

Serrano shook his head. "They are a strange and dangerous lot. Their clan was formed during the Black Death, but they started to expand shortly after Martin Luther made such a ruckus in religious circles. They live in churchyards, crypts, cemeteries; they do not enter churches, because they are among the damned, as they believe. They sleep in coffins, dress in black robes, and call themselves the Angels of Death or Brethren of the Pit, depending on their moods. Not a very cheerful group of people. They believe that they are eternally damned and that they were selected by God to pass out damnation in their turn to the sinners they meet. They 'punish' mortals and members of the Prime this way, feeding on some, putting others to the torch like witches. The Prime they leave in the sunlight, always following the most solemn of trials." He shook his head again. "They are insane, utterly insane."

"I believe you." She picked up her glass and swirled the brandy inside. "Who leads them?"

"A woman named Marita. She helped 'punish' the original leader's sinfulness and won his seat that way. I know nothing about her, nothing at all. But if she's in the Brethren, then it's safe to say that she should be avoided at all costs." He gestured vaguely. "Of course, there are vampires, like the Doña, who exist outside of the rules of these clans. Renegades, they're called, and they are hunted by both sides. Anyone who doesn't 'belong' is instantly fair game."

"That means that Tobyn will be hunted, too," she said, understanding the situation and not at all pleased by it.

"Exactly. He'll be prize and trophy for both clans, mark my words. Dumas already has the Prime out looking for him. Remember the fly-by attack while Doña Isabella was bringing you here? That was the Prime. It's a sure bet that the Brethren are on the trail now, as well."

This time, Araminah did drink. The brandy burned her throat and made her eyes water, but she liked the feeling. She had heard men say that drink gave them courage; she hoped that they were right. "You're in danger now, because of us, aren't you?"

"We were in danger before your brother called," he smiled. "My lady and Dumas had a falling out."

"Over my brother?"

"As it happens, yes, but I think it was inevitable. Doña Isabella is a far too enlightened person to fit with either the Prime or, God forbid, the Brethren." He paused, then asked, "How much influence do you have on your brother?"

"Some," she hedged. "Why?"

"Encourage him to try to form an army of his own, to make others of his clan. He'll need it."

She frowned as Serrano rose from the couch. "My brother isn't going to go off looking for this vampire war."

"No, he probably isn't, but this war is going to come looking for him. Mark my words on that, *señorita*. There is no neutrality in the vampire world." He faced her, his dark eyes full of shadows she could not interpret. "From now on, you and your brother are warriors. Get yourselves good, strong knives and always aim for the heart. And get fast horses, too."

"Tobyn won't run," she told him, proud of her twin's courage and yet annoyed by it. "Not forever."

Serrano nodded. "I thought as much. Then be prepared to fight, Araminah. This war is older than either of us, and it won't stop in our lifetimes." He took a deep breath. "One more word of advice: trust no one, and always watch your back. Don't believe that you are safe, not even for an instant, no matter who you're with."

Silent, Araminah watched him leave the room.

Sun sickness, Tobyn decided, was his least favorite way to spend forty-eight hours. Even after the nausea and blinding headache subsided enough to let him sit up in something approximating his usual posture, the hypersensitivity to light of any kind made even the glow of a single candle utterly unbearable until two more nights had passed. Now, as he was finally up and moving in his brightly-lit, candle-strewn room, he vowed never to be so stupid as to look into the sun again for as long as he lived—and who knew how long that would be?

"It's good to see you up and about," Ara commented from the doorway. He turned to smile at her in her new blue dress, a beautiful thing of gypsy cut that hugged her in all the spots he liked best. Her dark curls hung loose about her face, framing her soft smile. "Do you like?" she asked, knowing what he was thinking even without their telepathy.

"Very much. Ara, you're beautiful."

His sister smiled as he slowly approached, his eyes locked on hers. "I picked this color for you," she told him in a whisper.

"Good choice." He kissed her then, pulling her into his arms with a gentle insistence. He liked the scent and taste of her that his new senses let him know. She was delicious, like fine champagne and roses, like sandalwood and spices from China; she was heady and precious. He wondered why he'd never noticed it before.

Ara's hands clasped behind his neck as she leaned into his embrace, affected as never before by his touch. His fingers traced her spine, and she shivered. His breath stirred the hair at her neck, and slowly, surely, their hearts took up the same beat, the rhythm rocking them both until they were swaying ever so slightly in time with their pulses. Ara wanted him as she had never wanted anyone in her life.

"Oh, Tobyn," she breathed, "make love to me."

He smiled slyly, one corner of his mouth curling up before the other, and an evil twinkle lit his blue eyes. Kissing the tip of her nose, he lifted her in his arms and said, "After dinner."

The spell was broken. Araminah belted him. "You bastard! You enjoyed that, didn't you?"

"Absolutely." Tobyn chuckled. "But I'm very, very hungry, so this will have to wait until after dinner." He looked her in the eye. "And then I promise you that you'll have something to enjoy."

She snorted as he put her back on her feet. "You have a high opinion of your abilities, lover."

"Why shouldn't I? Name a time when I was wrong. Have you ever been—"

"Oh, just be quiet." They walked down the stairs together, and Araminah grumbled, "Maybe I won't be in the mood for it later."

"Maybe not," he conceded, smiling. "But maybe you will."

"I won't."

"We'll see." He watched her walk a few angry steps away, and he considered his newfound powers of persuasion, given their first outing only moments before. Some things vampirism gave him could be very useful.

She would want him again. He could very easily see to that. Somehow, though, he doubted he would have to cheat this time.

❦

The villa's dining hall was lit, the table set, for perhaps the first time since Isabella had claimed it as hers. The Doña rose from her seat at the head of the table when the twins entered the room, a warm smile on her beautiful face. Beside her, a young man with dark hair and Celtic features gained his feet as well.

"Tobyn and Araminah Reyes," the Spanish vampire said, "allow me to introduce a dear friend, Duncan McIntyre. Duncan is from Scotland."

Ara nodded to him while Tobyn clasped his hand. McIntyre was arrogantly handsome, with a twist of wry humor to his sparkling eyes. She liked his looks.

"You're a vampire," Tobyn stated, his tone almost one of problems solved, with a challenge undercutting the solution.

Duncan raised an eyebrow. "So are you. At least, you are a kind of vampire." He dared a smile. "Beyond that, I cannot say what you are."

Tobyn grinned up at the taller man. "I'm rude."

"So I'm told."

Isabella rested a hand on each of their elbows, wearing a smile of her own. "Please, be seated, and the meal can be served. Duncan and I, naturally, will not join you in the food, but company is good without eating." Her guests settled into their chairs, and Isabella signaled to a waiting maidservant.

While the meal was served to Tobyn and Araminah, Isabella poured dark red wine from a crystal decanter into her goblet and Duncan's. The Scotsman tested the scent of his drink, then took a delicate sip before telling their hostess with a smile, "Ah, Isabella, you always find the perfect ratio of blood to wine." He winked at Araminah. "No offense to our lovely mortal companion, of course."

"None taken," she assured him. She felt her cheeks burn with color, and she looked away. Since when did she blush?

There was a silent minute as Duncan sipped his drink and watched the twins eat. Tobyn guiltily accepted a glass of his own, letting the blood in the wine satisfy the other hunger that roared inside him. Isabella sat back, her own glass in hand, waiting for Duncan's reaction to what he saw.

The scrutiny wore on Tobyn's nerves. "I hope this is all very interesting to you, Mr. McIntyre."

"Oh, it is. I confess that I didn't believe Isabella when she told me of the peculiarities of your condition. Now, though, I see that she was right. You are indeed a strange creature, Tobyn Reyes."

"Thank you. It's good to be special." He glanced at his sister, feeling not at all as self-assured as he sounded. He didn't know if he liked this newcomer or not; from the way Araminah reacted to him, he decided that he probably didn't.

"Duncan arrived last night," Isabella told the gypsy vampire. "You were still sleeping off your sun sickness, so I took the liberty of telling him something of your position."

"Oh?" he asked mildly, looking at McIntyre. "And what insights have you had?"

"None, really. I don't believe that any of us can tell you who or what you are." He leaned back in his chair. "That, my friend, is your task."

Tobyn pushed his plate away. "So, Duncan, since you've been told all about me, perhaps you should even up the score."

Again, there was an upward twitch of his eyebrow. "How do you mean?"

"I mean that I should now be told all about you." He turned his smile on Isabella. "Or perhaps you'd like to do the honors."

She smiled icily. "Sun sickness does nothing for your disposition, *amigo*."

"No, I suppose not."

Duncan raised one hand slightly. "It's all right, Isabella. Quite so, fair is fair, and you should know as much about me as I do about you. My name is Duncan Malcolm McIntyre, and I was born in the Highlands. I was Made in 1654 by a woman named Marita who happens to be the leader of the Brethren. I was 25 when she took me from my mortal life. I had a wife and three children, all of whom Marita killed, and since the night of my creation I have been dedicated to destroying her. She knows this, of course, and is less than eager to see me succeed, so I am now the main enemy of the Brethren, after your Michel Dumas, of course."

Tobyn smirked. "Of course," he mocked, picking up on Duncan's redundancy. "So, what brings you to Italy?"

"I was hunting the Brethren in Rome, but somehow the chase was turned and I became the quarry." He smiled at Ara, who had finished eating and was watching him with intense curiosity.

"You're hiding," Tobyn said, nodding sagely.

McIntyre was unoffended, much to Reyes' disappointment. "Yes, exactly."

Tobyn chuckled to himself. "So, here we are in Doña Isabella's home for wayward vampires." His bright eyes cast a smile at their hostess. "How you do collect the strays."

She shrugged, enjoying the levity. "If they're handsome young men, how can I refuse?"

They laughed companionably, then Duncan said, "You should try to be more careful who you take in, Isabella. You've made more enemies than you can easily fight alone." He indicated Tobyn. "Here you have the enmity of the Prime, and I bring you that of the Brethren." He shook his head. "Not wise, lady."

Tobyn spoke up. "If I understand the situation at all, it didn't take you to make the Brethren hate Doña Isabella. They were doing that long before yesterday. And as for the Prime, well...they've been after her and me for over two years, and they haven't caught up with us yet. I'm neither impressed nor frightened."

"Brave words, lad, for a one-of-a-kind type such as yourself," Duncan said gravely.

"My status as the only vampire of my kind is precisely why I need brave words, and true bravery behind them." He looked to Isabella. "Have I read the situation adequately?"

"Astutely," she nodded. "You have a shrewd eye."

"So, you stand alone against both the vampire and mortal worlds?" McIntyre said. It was his turn to mock the gypsy. "Your odds of survival are not high."

"Higher than you think. I'm closer to human than either you or Isabella, if only by virtue of my different nature. I can move virtually unnoticed through the mortal world."

"Except during the day," the Scotsman pointed out.

"No, even then. So long as I keep direct sunlight from my eyes, I believe I'll be fine. Just give me a wide-brimmed hat, and I'll be happy." He smiled at the surprise on Duncan's face. *You weren't expecting that one, were you?* "And as for the vampire world, well, so I'm an outlaw. Being a Romany man, that's sort of what I'm used to. I also quite like it. And I don't believe that I will be alone among vampire kind. Prime and Brethren don't make up all of the vampire population. That would be impossible. Vampires used to be human beings, and most human beings dislike the kind of stupid rules the Prime and the Brethren are made on. There will always be dissent where there is human spirit."

"A pretty speech," Duncan allowed.

"And a true one. So long as you and I are here, *querido*," Isabella told McIntyre, "we cannot contradict him."

Ara spoke up for only the second time that night. Except for her beguiling mortal scent, Isabella would have forgotten that she was there. Duncan and Tobyn, however, were in no danger of overlooking her. She spoke slowly, remembering her talk with Serrano on the veranda. "So the Prime is a clan of sorts, and so is the Brethren. What you're saying is that you'll form a third clan."

"Exactly." Tobyn grinned at her and patted her knee under the table. "I knew there was a reason why I kept you around."

Duncan drained his glass. "A third clan, to use your sister's phrase, would not be well received."

"Of course not. It'll be made up of their criminals and their outcasts. Renegade vampires." He smiled broadly and sat back, visions of his plan filling his head with fabulous images. "Being on the wrong side of the so-called law means that, of course, we'll have to keep moving, at least until we're at a sufficient strength to stand our ground."

"You sound like you're putting together an army," Isabella observed.

"Not an army. A *kumpania*. My intention is not to start a war, but if the Prime or the Brethren come looking for a fight, I intend to give it to them."

Duncan snorted in amusement. "Behold! Alexander the Great."

"Tobyn the Great," the youngest vampire corrected.

Ara rolled her eyes. "Oh, God."

Isabella laughed. "You realize that all of this talk of battles is very premature. Your clan is pathetically small."

"Yes, now. But I have nothing but time to build it up." He smiled at the Spanish lady, his enthusiasm for his sudden dream glowing in his eyes. "Are you with me?"

She returned the infectious expression. "Why not? I've nothing to lose."

"And you, Mr. McIntyre?" Tobyn teased.

Duncan shook his head. "Not I. I have no desire to get involved in warfare, not now, not a century from now. For so long as I keep to my Marita-hunt, the Prime tolerates me. I don't want that to change."

"Are you afraid?" the gypsy vampire goaded.

The Scotsman's answer was a sigh as he shook his head. After a moment, he added words. "You are speaking with the ebullience of youth, my friend, and I can only applaud your audacity. But what you propose will start a war that will never end, not ever. And you are unfortunate enough to be immortal, unable to escape wars by dying the way old soldiers can, and the fighting you must do will be eternal. Every night will bring a new attack, and that will age you more than years alone could ever do. You will never age, but war will make you old all the same."

Tobyn tossed his head slightly, lifting his chin. "You sound like a seer, and a very depressing one."

"I'm not a visionary. I'm just experienced at the sort of fight you're letting yourself in for, and it has made me tired. I don't want to get involved." He shook his own head, slowly. "I can't get involved."

"So this is Scottish bravery, then."

"No, it's Scottish practicality. In time, you will understand what I'm saying here."

Reyes looked him in the eye. "And in time, you'll change your mind."

Duncan held his gaze for a moment, then rose and silently left the room.

~ళ్ళφ~

Midnight found Araminah curled up beside Tobyn, sleeping off the post-lovemaking haze and dreaming gently. He held her while she slept, occasionally kissing her wherever he could reach, enjoying the scent and feel of her, the comfort of her presence. He had never been very good at sleeping alone.

Outside their window, the moon was as bright as the sun, blazing like a signal fire. Nothing could hide from that eager white light; there were no real shadows left. He was glad of that. Too many things might have been looking for a hiding place.

Ara stirred against him, cuddling closer, and he smiled gently at her sleeping face. She was beautiful when she was awake, but asleep and vulnerable, she was devastating.

A night bird fluttered past the window, her wings stirring the air with a soft beating, rhythmic as a woman's heart. The tempo seemed to match Araminah's pulse, and the rhythm drew him in. He held her closer, brushing his lips ever so gently along her skin. In her sleep, she responded, shifting position to leave him an unimpeded path. Tobyn squeezed her tightly, feeling her heart beat as his own, tasting her sweetness on his mouth. His teeth shuddered, then dropped down like a cat's claws being extended, and he felt the points straining against his lip.

Fear and bloodlust gripped him simultaneously, and he battled with both of his selves. He wanted, no, *needed* the blood that waited so tantalizingly close, needed it as a hawk needs open sky. Blood gave him life, it gave him freedom. The watered-down stuff at tonight's dinner could not satisfy him the way that fresh ruby life from Ara could. He felt compelled to take it while he had the chance, before she awoke or pulled away, removing the opportunity for a perfect strike. At the same time, though, he was afraid of giving in, of taking too much, of hurting the person he loved best in all the world. He was not so thirsty that he was controlled by it; that kind of need had been assuaged by a mesmerized mortal brought to him by Serrano during the throes of his sickness. That man had died, drained dry to slake Tobyn's most dangerous thirst. Ara would not suffer the same fate. He thirsted, yes, but sanely, and so long as he could keep his wits about himself, she would live, unharmed.

But he wanted her and the salty sweetness of her blood very badly. Perhaps if he found a way to take it nicely... He could remember, back in France, the difference between the rapture of Isabella's feeding and Elisa Dieter's torture. There was a way to be kind, and even to be generous. Tobyn was grateful. He had not been trained as a healer to come to the point of hurting others for his own satisfaction. Empathy and compassion, healer's traits, would be very useful for a merciful vampire.

He brushed the hair away from her neck, nuzzling her throat and blessing it with tiny kisses. She held him tighter as his hands touched her body lovingly, doing everything she liked the most. Her fingers tangled in his hair and she let out an impassioned sigh.

He held her closer still, his mouth against her throat, teeth not yet released. He waited until his touches distracted her with pleasure before he inflicted the brief, stabbing pain of his penetration into her vein. Ara shuddered and gasped, her grasp flying open then closing again, her eyes wide in ecstasy. He pulled slowly at her, drawing out a taste at a time, feeling his own body react with hers. Energy and life-force rose between them, spiraling to dizzy heights, and still he held on. Ara cried out in her climax, and Tobyn's body followed merrily after while the vampire in his soul drew a little more.

They rode their mad spiral twice more before he released her, dewy-eyed and gasping. To his vast relief, she was alive and well, showing no negative signs at all. She pulled him into a tight embrace, her hands still trembling from the force of the experience, and she wept silently as she held him. He wiped her tears away and questioned her wordlessly, anxious and afraid he'd done something wrong.

"Happy," she told him in a halting whisper. "I'm happy. Tobyn, I love you."

He kissed her and replied telepathically, although he knew she would not hear. *//And I love you. I'll love you forever.//*

～✧✧✧～

Duncan smirked as the sounds from the Reyes chamber faded away. As he stood on the balcony to his own suite, he had listened almost accidentally to the twins' cries of passion. Not that they were particularly loud, or that he was being particularly prurient. There were just some things that couldn't be helped, and vampire hearing was one of them.

Isabella joined him in a whispering of green silk. She, too, had heard, and guessed at the reason for the Scotsman's humor. "They are very much in love."

"Yes, I could tell. But didn't you tell me they were brother and sister?"

Isabella shrugged. "We all have our foibles. You have them, too, if I recall. A certain young mortal named James—"

"It's different for us now and you know it. The way we are, it doesn't matter who we love, male or female or farm animal." He shook his head. "But if I were still mortal, I'd envy your Tobyn's position right now."

She slipped her arm around Duncan's waist and leaned her cheek against his shoulder. "He seems to have found the perfect way to immortality."

"Food, sex, daylight..." McIntyre's voice was heavy with jealousy. "I'd give anything to see one summer day again. I'll wager the little git doesn't even know how lucky he is."

"Oh, I don't know. I think he does." She squeezed him reassuringly. "But there are prices paid, as well."

"Such as?"

"No flight."

He looked into her eyes. "No loss."

"Perhaps. He also doesn't know if he can ever make another of his kind."

"He'll figure it out eventually, and if it does work, that exquisite sister of his will be the first to know." He smiled at Isabella. "Now I understand your proclivity for gypsies."

"Beautiful creatures, aren't they?"

"Hmm. At least these two." They enjoyed the sound of the night for a moment before Duncan spoke again. "What do you think of his idea about clans? You joined him readily enough, but what percentage of that readiness was boredom?"

"You know me too well." She sighed. "Percentages are difficult for me to understand, so I'll just give you the reasons. First of all, yes, I'm bored, especially with Michel and his petty tyranny. I agree with Tobyn that there are many of us who are renegades. If we can unite, we will be stronger against the Brethren and the Prime than by ourselves. There is strength in numbers."

He could tell that she wasn't quite finished yet. "And? There's more."

She glanced up in the general direction of the Reyes suite. "Him. He is magnetic. I think I'd follow him anywhere."

"Because he's different?" Duncan hypothesized, "Or because he's gypsy?"

"Because he's Tobyn." She laughed at herself. "Just listen to me, like a schoolgirl getting all quivery about a good-looking boy!"

"It's good to see you this way. It's been too long since you were really happy, and if Tobyn Reyes makes you that way, then go with him."

"You can come, too."

"No, I can't."

She fell silent for a moment, stargazing and strategizing. "And Araminah. Do you think she's beautiful?"

Duncan smiled. "Yes."

"Then that's why you should come."

"No." He turned from her encircling arm. "That's why I have to stay away."

Twenty

Duncan departed shortly after sunset the next night, wasting no time on good-byes. Tobyn was both pleased and disappointed to see him going. His feelings about the Scots vampire were terminally mixed, torn between respect and a desire to incorporate him into the new clan on one hand and a suspicion of cowardice on the other. Well, Reyes supposed, the man didn't have to fight if he didn't want to. The *kumpania* would not benefit from a weakling.

He watched McIntyre's horse disappear over the rocky horizon and leaned against the balcony railing, his hands loosely clasped. Behind him, in his chambers, Ara slept soundly. He had found that he could take a little blood from her without causing her body undue stress and yet still be able to take enough to quiet his thirst. The edge was gone from that powerful force within him, and while he was less than fully satisfied, he was satisfied enough. He doubted if Ara could hold up to losing blood every day, even the tiny amount he took, without falling ill or weakening. Eventually, he would be forced to look elsewhere for his nightly meal, perhaps among total strangers. The thought did not appeal to him, but he found comfort in the fact that he had no need to kill, conveniently forgetting about the casualty of his illness and Johann on his first night. That, he hoped, had been a fluke of timing. If his Change had not come so recently, he doubted if he would have murdered his lover. At least it sounded good as a theory.

Isabella's voice rose in his mind, the barest whisper of telepathic speech. He did not need to strain to hear her despite her quietness. *//Tobyn, come and sit with me.//*

Half-smiling to himself, he Sent back, *//Where are you?//*

//In the library. Come.//

Pausing just long enough to kiss his sister's temple, Tobyn obeyed the summons of the lady of the house. He found her sitting at the writing desk, her raven hair falling free in light-catching curls. He smiled to her, his head canted to one side as he studied her. "I'm here."

"Shh." She smiled back. *//In your head, Tobyn.//*

"And call the Prime for miles around? I don't think so."

//You must learn some time.//

His jaw set in pugnacious stubbornness. "No." Tobyn leaned against the mantelpiece beneath a huge portrait of his hostess. "I don't want them coming here."

//They're coming anyway. It won't hurt. Just keep it quiet and focused only on me.// She winked at him. *//You remember how to be quiet and sneaky, don't you, gypsy boy?//*

He almost laughed, then replied, *//Very well.//*

//Shh!// Isabella winced. *//There's no need to shout.//*

Confused, he tried to pull in a bit more, replying, *//I was trying to whisper.//*

//You have too much power. Less push.//

Tobyn sat across from her, trying very hard to do it right. *//How do you know that they're coming?//*

//Quiet!//

"I'm trying! If I take any more push away, you'll never hear a damned thing!"

She was unmoved by his anger. "Tobyn Reyes, you are accustomed to speaking this way with mortals. As a rule, mortals are thick as bricks when it comes to telepathy. Vampires are a telepathic race. Where you once needed to shout to be heard, now your barest thought is nearly audible. You do not need to push. Focusing is enough." The set to his jaw had not softened, but neither had Isabella. *//Now. Try again.//*

He sighed. *//Why are you doing this?//*

//Better. I'm doing this because we may soon be separated, and you'll need to know how to call for help without calling your enemies.//

//Separated? Why?//

//Very good! You are a quick learner.// She sat back in her chair. *//Read this. It was delivered this morning by a special courier.//*

From the writing desk, she handed him a tightly-wound parchment scroll wrapped in black ribbon. The smell of death and decay clung to the missive, making Tobyn wrinkle his nose in distaste. *//Who is it from?//*

//The Brethren.//

Raising an eyebrow, he opened the scroll and examined the lines of spidery handwriting. Apparently, reading was not a vampiric skill that automatically came with the Change. Sighing, he handed it back, getting only the psychometric impression of malice.

//I don't know how to read.//

//You shall have to learn.// She took the scroll and put it into her desk. *//In a nutshell, it is a declaration of war. They know where we are, who is here, and that I offered sanctuary to Duncan for two nights. They are going to come and 'punish' us for our sinful excesses and, as an insult to Michel Dumas and all of the Prime, destroy you in the bargain.//*

//How pleasant of them.// He leaned back and crossed his arms. *//They're going to be terribly disappointed.//*

Isabella smiled. *//You are a strong man, mi amo, and I knew you would react this way. But do not underestimate the strength of the Brethren. Many of them are quite old, and age brings power. They are not to be fought lightly.//*

His gaze was level. "I never take any fights lightly."

"Good."

"But why should we separate? We can run together."

Isabella shook her head. "We would be too easy to track as a single group. Separate quarries take longer to hunt."

"I know about that. You don't grow up in a *kumpania* without learning a few things." He sighed. "You think that Ara and I stand a better chance of escaping if we're not with you, don't you?"

//You will make a fine leader.//

//Spare me the compliments and answer the question.//

//Surly tonight, aren't you?// she teased. Turning serious, she told him, *//The power that you have is enormous. The power that I have as a vampire of multiple centuries is equally great. If we were together on the run, the combination of our energies would burn like a beacon to any other nightchild sensitive enough to look. Together, we would never have a moment's peace.//*

//What helped you decide this? Last night you were ready to follow me to the ends of the earth.//

//Less 'what' than 'who,'// she replied.

//McIntyre.//

//He is a persuasive man.//

Tobyn took a deep breath and considered her point. "I can understand why you'd want to be careful, and I agree, your concerns are valid. It wouldn't do to attract hostile attention, not when there's so much of it to go around." He shifted in his seat. "If need be, I can travel with Ara during the day, so long as I'm careful to keep my eyes shaded. You don't have that luxury."

"No, I don't," she agreed, giving up on the telepathy lessons. "You could conceivably melt away into the mortal world for a good long time."

His eyes met hers. "Well. I assume that's what you want me to do, then."

Isabella smiled for him. "Yes, and quickly. The Brethren like to strike between one and three in the morning, and it's nearly midnight now. Wake Araminah, pack your things and leave Italy at once." She opened another drawer and extracted a bagful of coins. "This is the most that I can give you just now. Three thousand in francs. Take it. I don't think I need to explain how you can get more when that runs out."

He smirked. "No, you don't."

"Good." She rose and walked to him, taking his hands in hers and pressing gentle kisses to his knuckles. "Go to France. That is the stronghold of the Prime, and the Brethren will not follow you there." She considered for a moment, then added, "Michel will not think to look for you so close to his home. You will be safe from him for a long time, I think."

"You think." He shook his head. "That's not very reassuring. But where will you go?"

"I'm not certain. I'll need to leave Europe for a few years. Perhaps I will visit Imety in Cairo. Don't worry for me. I've been at this game for too long to lose so easily now."

Impulsively, Tobyn kissed her full mouth, but only for a moment. "Thank you. I'll repay you somehow."

"There's no need."

"Yes, there is. No debts." He grinned. "A man's got to have honor, you know."

"I know." She released his hands. "I'm sorry I wasn't more help for you, but, ultimately, I think you'll need to define your existence for yourself. Good luck, *cariño*. You'd better hurry."

He touched her shoulder. "And good luck to you, as well."

∿➳ଓଓଟ

Ara stirred at her brother's touch, almost waking up but still held in the gentle embrace of her dreams. Tobyn prodded her, and she mumbled into her pillow. Another push received the same less-than-enthusiastic reaction.

He would have found it amusing if the time had not been so short. "Ara. Ara!"

It was the shattering of glass directly below their window that jolted her into wakefulness. Tobyn started violently as his sister gasped and sat bolt upright in the bed, and his hand instantly went to the kris knife he wore at his waist.

"What—" Ara began, her eyes wide.

"Dress and pack. Now!"

The woman moved to obey even while he charged toward the door with fire in his eyes. "Where are you going?" she exclaimed.

"To help Isabella. Just pack, damn it!"

He did not wait for her reply. He was in the corridor and halfway to the stairs when he saw the first of the invaders. The Brethren member he saw climbing the steps three at a time was a pale, cadaverous thing, skeletal beneath its black robes. The face framed by the monk's cowl was twisted and ugly and so inhuman that Tobyn wasn't sure whether he was confronting a man, a woman, both, or neither. The vampire saw him standing at the top of the stairs and howled a banshee cry, propelling itself

forward with a great push of its spindly legs. Tobyn ducked out of the way
of its clawed hands and flashing teeth, drawing his knife as he moved.

The Brother skidded to a halt just shy of the wall and whirled to face
Tobyn with a terrible grin. A high, wheezing laugh that spoke more of
insanity than mirth ripped at his ears, then the thing said, "Tobyn Reyes,
you have sinned!"

He ducked under a sideswipe of a bony arm that splintered the
hardwood panel on the wall, then slashed at the other vampire with his
knife. "So have you."

The creature laughed again. "But you shall be punished."

"Maybe we both will."

The Brother rushed at him, its arms spread wide for a loveless
embrace. Hoping that his aim was good, Tobyn pointed his blade at where
he presumed the other's heart must have been, thrusting the weapon with
as much strength as he could muster. The knife penetrated the vampire's
chest with a dry, raspy pop like the sound of paper tearing, and blood,
thick and black as bile, pulsed out over his hand. The Brother twitched
once, then fell, silent, to the floor. Ara raced out of the room, their meager
possessions bundled up in a pillow case, while Tobyn retrieved his knife
and fought down nausea.

Ara's gaze fell upon the desiccated corpse at her brother's feet.
"What in the hell is that?"

"Dead. Come on; I'll guard you on your way out the door."

She shook her head. "I won't leave you."

"Jesus Christ, woman! You pick the worst times to argue!" A shrill
scream from the servants' quarters punctuated his words. "Just go, damn
it!"

They trotted down the stairs side by side, Tobyn with his weapon at
the ready. Inside the library, they could see flames leaping from the
curtains, touched off by the furniture and books the Brethren had put to
the torch. Isabella was nowhere to be seen.

The door to the drawing room burst open, and Serrano appeared,
carrying on a skillful duel with a sword-wielding woman in Brethren
robes. His face was cut, but he was holding his own. Over his shoulder, he
shouted to the twins, "Go to the stables!"

"TOBYN!"

Ara's warning cry gave him a bare moment of preparation before
another of their robed attackers dropped onto his back like a spider from
the ceiling. One thin arm, surprisingly strong, wrapped around his neck,
and Tobyn could feel the moist, clammy breath of the thing as it bared its
fangs and went for his throat.

Araminah had had enough of the helpless female routine. Plucking
her own knife from a pocket in her skirt, she screamed virulent Romany
curses and fell on the attacker. The Brother, obviously not expecting an

assault from a mortal, was taken by surprise, and Ara's blade slipped between his ribs and pierced his heart in one smooth jab. Tobyn flung the dead weight aside.

"Good work."

"Of course."

Serrrano, caught up in his own fight, was not fortunate enough to have a vigilant sibling nearby. While Ara was busy rescuing Tobyn, the Spaniard was seized from behind and disarmed by a pair of howling vampires. Both stabbed him with their teeth, and he was drained to lifelessness before the twins had finished their skirmish. The Brethren cackled delightedly and one sang part of the Requiem Mass as Serrano's corpse was tossed onto the fire that had consumed much of the library and was lapping at the corridor outside, greedy as a starving demon.

Tobyn grabbed his sister's hand and fervently wished he could fly them over the heads of the grinning Brethren at the foot of the stairs.

Ara nervously sized up their animate obstacle course. "I don't know if we'll make it."

"Don't be stupid. Of course we'll make it."

They hesitated, wondering what they would do, and two of the Brethren climbed a step closer. Ara stared in horrified fascination at the way the firelight glowed on their ghastly, pallid faces, almost as if they themselves were on fire. Inspiration came in the sudden explosion of a kerosene-filled wall lamp, and she whirled to tug at the light nearest her. Tobyn caught on and followed almost instantly, and they splashed the fuel on the approaching vampires.

The foremost of the Brethren threw her head back in arrogant triumph. "Very good, little ones, but you have no flame."

Tobyn took the lighted wall lamp at the head of the stairs and, careful to preserve its little fire, held it ready. "Here it is."

"And here."

Behind the Brethren, dressed in man's clothing, Isabella brandished a burning torch fashioned from a table leg and a scrap of taffeta, her dark eyes cold with rage. When she spoke, Tobyn threw the lamp with all of his might in to the Brethren woman's chest, where glass splintered and flame sprang to lurid life. Isabella stabbed her torch into the nearest enemy, propelling the other vampire into the library blaze that now reeked like a funeral pyre. Ara smashed the last convenient lamp into a Brother's face and scampered to Tobyn's side as her screaming victim wove his flaming path down the stairs. Tobyn and Araminah followed close in his wake, their weapons out and eager for blood, but they went unchallenged as the Brethren broke off their attack and fled from the dangers of the flames.

Isabella led them to the stables. "Take those two horses, there, and ride for all you're worth. Don't stop until daybreak." She grabbed the reins of a third animal, already saddled and waiting, and swung herself into position. "Go, and quickly."

Two frightened grooms shoved the prepared mounts toward the twins, then ran away as Isabella wheeled her horse to look at the burning villa.

"Bastards!" she hissed.

Tobyn and Ara mounted quickly and spurred their animals into a fast canter. Isabella rode beside them, her face furious in the moonlight. At a crossroads north of the villa, they stopped and said brief farewells. Isabella kissed them both.

"Be well and be safe. We will see one another again."

Tobyn squeezed her hand. "I hope so."

Isabella stroked his face once, a short-lived smile on her face before she pulled away. Without another word, she rode east, leaving them to their western road.

Ara brought her horse closer to Tobyn's. "Where are we going?"

He thought a moment. "France."

"Is that wise?"

"Probably not, but that's never stopped me before." He tried to smile, failed, and settled for a noncommittal shrug. "We'll go there anyway." As they headed back overland, he added wearily, "At least we're riding away from the sunrise."

She nodded. "But what will you do when sunlight catches up? How will you keep the light out of your eyes when we're riding into it?"

His answer was as little comfort to her as it was to him.

"I don't know."

❧

They rode with their backs to the light, Tobyn huddling in anxiety. He wrapped himself tighter in his huge black cloak and pulled the wide brim of his hat lower over his eyes. A numbing sleepiness was suffusing him, pulling at him; it was as if he were a hollow doll that someone was filling up with warm water, making him heavy and slow. It was all he could do to both stay awake and keep riding.

Ara kept a careful watch on her brother, and his fatigue did not escape her. Dawn was nearly full now, and soon it would be too hazardous for Tobyn to be out in the daylight. He seemed unhurt so far, but she was unwilling to take a chance on another bout of sun sickness. He needed sleep, and he needed shelter.

There was no good, man-made place to hide him where they were, but Ara was still gypsy enough to remember how to live without such *gadjo* luxuries as houses. She stopped their progress and dismounted, pulling Tobyn down from his own saddle. He slid bonelessly to the ground and landed in a graceless heap. Ara sighed and set to work creating a makeshift tent from her own cloak and a likely stand of bushes. Once she was certain of a constant source of shade, she pulled and pushed her twin undercover. Tobyn did not move or respond; only his slow, shallow breathing and infrequent heartbeat told her that he was not dead.

With Tobyn safely stowed, she saw to the horses and wearily spread a saddle blanket on the ground where she could rest. She was exhausted, and now she understood what Serrano had meant by giving vampires' mortal companions special status. *We're special because we're especially tired*, she thought with wry humor. *No rest for the weary, either, not during night or day.*

The meadow's edge where they had stopped seemed safe enough. There were no human sounds to be heard, no human signs to be seen, only birds flying by overhead. Ara watched them flitting through the sunlit blue, listening to their delicate voices and trying to stay awake and stand guard. The breeze, her exhaustion, and the lullaby of birdsong conspired against her, and as she fell asleep, her last thought was a fervent hope that she could adapt to her new life without too much pain.

～⚬⚬⚬～

Tobyn awoke shortly after noon. He took stock of his situation, curled up inside a clearing made within a clump of bushes and covered by the thick black cloth of Ara's cloak. She had worked hard. He wanted to find his sister, but he was almost too afraid of getting sun sick to move. Shielding his eyes with his hand, he rolled over and found the exit from his safe cocoon.

Do I really want to do this?

Screwing up his courage, keeping his eyes shaded, he left the tent and found that as long as he held his eyes in shadow, to his vast delight, he could function almost completely normally out in the day. He found his sister on the ground not far away, wrapped up in a saddle blanket, and he knelt beside her. Gently, he brushed the hair from her eyes. She murmured in her sleep and turned toward his hand.

Poor lady, he thought, looking into her pale face. *You've been run into the ground. This is hard on you.* Tobyn kissed her temple. *Sleep. It's my turn to take care of you.*

Part Three

Twenty-One

France - 1747

Araminah capped off her dramatic interpretation of the Tarot spread before her with a solemn intonation.

"Thus have the Fates spoken to you. Listen and obey."

Across the table in the tiny room, the middle-aged Parisienne who had asked about her love-life-to-be nodded, her blue eyes huge with awe and wonder. After a moment, she scrabbled together the sous that made up Araminah's daytime fee and shoved the coins toward the gypsy woman.

"Thank you," the matron breathed before she fled from the scene.

Ara picked up her cards as Tobyn emerged, chuckling, from their bedroom. He leaned against the doorjamb, arms crossed over his chest, and said, "So, the Knight of Swords crossing the Queen of Cups means someone is having an illicit fling, eh?"

His sister shrugged, smirking, as she arranged her deck. In her best fortune-teller tone, she said, "I say what the cards do."

"Bullshit. That isn't what that means, and you know it."

She giggled. "No, but she paid anyway, didn't she? They always pay to hear what they want you to say."

"You're an artist," he told her admiringly. "A con artist."

He joined her at the table and smoothed the red silk cloth. Ara pocketed the coins before her light-fingered brother could touch them. He acknowledged her minor financial victory with a brief childish pout, then broke into a sunny smile.

"What are you so happy about?" Ara asked, knowing Tobyn well enough by now to be a bit leery of his good moods.

"While you were busy here, I was out and about on the street, and you'll never guess what's on for this coming month."

"It's obviously got you too delighted to sit still," she observed. "Tell me."

Tobyn leaned on the table, his handsome face alight. "The local nobility are having a summer soirée that's attracting attention for miles around. It'll be a regular festival, with all of the people and foods and colors...just think of it! All those pockets to pick." He caught her eyes. "So many gullible *gadje* who'll want their fortunes told."

Ara laughed, tossing her head. "Sounds perfect. When does this all start?"

"A week from Friday, and it lasts all through July. At the very end of it, there's going to be a huge masquerade ball." Tobyn leaned back and crossed his legs. "I thought it would be fun to go."

She feigned shock. "What? Without an invitation?"

"But of course."

They laughed, then settled into silence. Tobyn caught himself on the verge of speaking through the mind-link they had once shared. The need to speak aloud at all times now sometimes saddened him and made him feel lonely inside his own mind, but he refused to let such things disturb him today.

"So, sister-mine, what say you?"

She slid her cards into their pouch. "I say we stand to make good money."

He grinned. "That's my girl."

They were quiet while Ara finished packing up. After a few moments, she said, "Tobyn, do you think this party will attract the Prime?"

"Of course it will." The topic of his vampire nemeses sobered him. "But I can be sneaky. They won't ever need to know that I'm here, or that I even exist."

"After all this time, I'm sure every vampire on earth knows that you exist," she pointed out. "I'm sure they know your name and description, too. Be grateful that they don't know your address."

"*I* don't know my address," he teased, trying to lighten her mood.

"Liar."

Tobyn responded with a chuckle. The two of them had lived here in their little three-room house on Rue de Gallette for the better part of seven months. The district was a bit rough-and-tumble, which suited the twins, accustomed as they were to the rabble of the caravan. Their neighbors were prostitutes and thieves, but basically good people, who knew Tobyn and Ara as a newly-married gypsy couple who lived by selling fortunes and, less openly, by liberating coinage from over-laden gentry. The neighborhood had become home to the Reyes, or as much of a home as they could find. It was difficult for them to be completely at ease when they were constantly concealing who and what they really were. Somehow, Tobyn thought, vampires wouldn't be quite so welcome as gypsy thieves.

"Will you be going out tonight?" Ara asked as she rose from her chair.

'Going out.' It was a euphemism that they liked to use. It sounded so much nicer than 'going hunting.' "Yes," he said, looking from a safe distance through the filmy curtains at the daylight outside. "I'll be careful, and I won't bring anyone here."

"I know. You never do."

"And I never will."

"I hope not." She removed her heavy gold earrings and hid them in her sash belt. "I was just wondering."

"Why? Did you want to do something?"

"I want to go with you."

He hesitated. "Ara—"

"I don't mean that I want to be there when you take somebody. I just want to go where there's light and noise and music. A pub, I guess. But I don't want to hold you back."

"I don't want you to get hurt," Tobyn objected mildly. "The pubs in this city aren't the safest places for a young woman to be."

"I can take care of myself."

He shook his head. "Not so well as you might think."

Ara set her jaw. "Don't try to protect me so much," she told him. "Let me have a life."

"I want you to be safe," he protested.

"I want to do something besides sit in your pocket!" She shook her head. "You don't understand how frustrating it is to be tied to one place all the time. You get to go out because you have to. I only get to leave this place to get food, and then it's only a quick trip. I'm trapped here."

The urgent unhappiness in her voice took him back to his own captive days in Dumas' *chateau*. He could still recall the feeling of being slowly strangled by too many walls, too many closed doors. Gypsies could not withstand confinement, and here was his sister, a prisoner in their own house. Guilty, he looked away from her.

"Just be careful," he finally said. "I don't know what I'd do if I lost you."

"You won't lose me," she assured him. "I'll be careful, I swear."

Ara came to where he sat and they embraced, his head pillowed against the softness of her breasts. "I love you," he whispered. "Never forget that I love you."

<hr>

They dressed in their best clothes that night, then headed away from their little section of Paris. On the other side of the city, where other shady neighborhoods lay, was Tobyn's hunting ground. It suited all the requirements: populous, noisy, decadent, and far from his home. He always had success when he hunted there. Tonight would be no exception, he was sure, although it would definitely be different. Beside him as they walked, Araminah was humming to herself, her green eyes alight with the pleasure of being out of the house. Her beauty was compelling tonight. He only hoped that it didn't compel any men to take liberties.

She noticed his attention and smiled at him. "Don't worry so much, love. I'll be all right."

"I don't like the idea of leaving you alone in there."

"Oh, it'll only be for a few minutes. I can take care of myself for that long, and longer." She winked at him. "You underestimate me."

"No, not at all," he protested. "I just know French men."

"Hmm, so I've heard."

Tobyn cast her a stern look and, laughing, she trotted ahead of him, excitement making her steps quick and light. Ara led the way to their destination, a dark, out-of-the-way pub called La Biche. It was run by an aging whore named Irene, a woman who had, it was rumored, once run a brothel visited by the highest nobility in France. She herself was said to have been the king's mistress. Tobyn had seen Irene; he very seriously doubted if the stories were true. Kings could afford better.

The atmosphere of La Biche was such that nobody really noticed their arrival until Irene herself saw Tobyn over the bar. The obese woman squealed with delight and scurried over to the corner table the Reyes had claimed. She seized the smiling vampire in an expansive embrace.

"Tobyn! *Ma chère!* It's so good to see you again!" She clucked her tongue. "Naughty boy, where have you been hiding?"

He smirked at his bemused sister. "Oh, there are so many sights to see in Paris, and so many things to do."

"You could do a few of those things with me any time you wanted to," she purred with a wink. "But perhaps you are taken, eh?" Irene smiled amiably at Ara. "Does this wayward boy here belong to you?"

The younger woman laughed, and Tobyn introduced them. "Madame Irene, I present my wife, Araminah."

"Wife?" She scanned their faces. "You look more like his sister."

Tobyn grinned. "She's that, too."

Irene considered this, then chuckled and waved one fleshy hand. "Oh, get away! You can't fool me. Tobyn, you imp!"

Ara took his hand under the table and squeezed it tightly; their eyes met over sparkling smiles. She would like this place. Irene seized Tobyn's face between her plump hands and planted a monstrously wet kiss on his forehead. In response, he poked her in the side, and the pub owner retreated in a cloud of giggles.

Tobyn settled back into his seat as his companion said with a smirk, "Interesting woman."

"I like her. She knows when to stop asking questions." He leaned back in his chair, his blue eyes scanning the crowd. Ara watched him watch the people crowding La Biche, both impressed and unnerved by the way his face sat in a passive expression beneath a gaze of such taut concentration. For the first time, she saw Tobyn as the predator his new nature forced him to be. It was a bit frightening to see, but she would not deny that it was exciting, too.

"Any likely targets?" she asked quietly, uncertain if she should speak to him.

"A few." He broke off staring at the woman he'd selected and smiled at Araminah, for a brief flash looking like himself again. He kissed her on the cheek. "Don't go away. I'll try to make this quick."

"Just do what you need to," she said calmly. "I'll be here."

Tobyn clasped her hand and slid away from the table. He blended in with the mingling bodies that filled the floor space, then seated himself beside the young prostitute he'd noticed from across the room. She looked at him with tired eyes, and Irene handed him a glass of something alcoholic. La Biche was well-known for treating its guests well, both at the bar and in the rooms upstairs.

The prostitute leaned an elbow on the counter top and put her chin in her hand. "Good evening, sir," she told him. The empty sound behind her voice thudded against his empathic senses. "Welcome to La Biche."

"Thank you." He smiled into her bored face. *What would it take to make you interested in this?* "I'm Tomas. Do you have a name?"

"Marielle," she replied.

"A pretty name." He sipped his drink and his tastebuds recoiled. It was heady stuff. "Tell me, what makes you so sad?"

Marielle blinked. "Sad?"

"Yes. Something isn't right with you." He tilted his head to the side and watched the light on her hair and the pulse in her throat. "You're far too pretty not to be smiling."

She was uncertain how to respond. He smiled at her, encouraging her to do him the grace of echoing the expression. Tentatively, she smiled back.

"Much better," he said with a nod of approval. "I saw your face from across the room, and I promised myself that I wouldn't leave tonight until I could make you laugh."

Marielle smirked. "I think you don't know what I'm doing here, *m'sieur*, or exactly who and what I am."

"I know all that." He shook his head. "That doesn't mean that you're not allowed to laugh or smile."

"But it's my job to make you smile."

"So we can make each other happy," Tobyn suggested. "It doesn't have to be all work and no play."

"It's a business, *m'sieur*. After a while, you get a little numb to certain aspects."

"Like pleasure? Are you numb to that?"

Marielle looked him in the eye and fairly challenged him as she said, "Never had it."

"Do you believe that you never will?"

"Sir—"

"No, honestly. Tell me. Because I know you will." He looked deeply into her eyes. "Especially if you give me a chance. I can make you feel it tonight."

Marielle recognized that her challenge had been accepted and met with one of Tobyn's own. "To make me laugh and enjoy my work in the same night? You are ambitious."

"Not ambitious. Just aware of what I can do."

She laughed before she realized that she was doing it. "Not a modest sort, are you?"

"Absolutely not."

"Well, this is something I can't pass up. Do you have gold, *m'sieur?* Nothing is for free these days," she told him with a smirk. "Not even the chance to fail."

"Fail?" He chuckled to himself. "My dear Marielle, you vastly underestimate me."

"You overestimate yourself."

"Ha! We'll see, won't we?" He extracted a gold coin from his pocket. "Here's your gold, Marielle. I've already made you laugh. That's half the battle. I can win the rest."

Somehow, she was beginning to think he could. "Well, let's go find out."

~⚬⚬⚬~

Araminah watched her brother disappear up the stairs with one of Irene's tarts, then sighed as she sipped her wine. She had no idea how long this would take, but, judging from the matching lascivious looks on their faces, Tobyn and his whore would be away for hours.

La Biche was a loud and colorful place. Ara listened to the raucous French babbling all around her, watched the people bustle past, and sipped her drink. Human beings and their interactions were fascinating subjects; she enjoyed watching the men attempt to be manly and impressive for the women who were attempting to be coy. The level of pretense in the pub was fantastic.

"Señorita Reyes?"

She started at the unexpected salutation and turned to look, wide eyed, at the handsome Scotsman who stood near her elbow. Duncan McIntyre smiled slightly, his lips pressed into a wry line of amusement, his eyes dancing.

"May I sit down?"

Ara thought about leaving him standing, but after a moment, she nodded. "All right. Have a seat."

"Thank you." Duncan eased into the chair nearest her and leaned on the table. "What brings you to La Biche, *señorita?*"

"Boredom."

"Yours or Tobyn's? I presume that he's here."

"Mine." She sat back and crossed her legs. "Last time I saw you, you were heading back to England, weren't you?"

He smiled. "I'm afraid that Scottish Catholics are less than popular in Britain these days."

Ara knew little of current British politics and cared even less. "But why are you in La Biche, Señor McIntyre? Are you going hunting?"

"Maybe." He traced a bit of pen knife graffiti with his fingertip. "I assume that you and your unusual brother have heard about the local summer festival." He gave her the chance to confirm or deny; she did not take it. "Well, I'm going to assume that Tobyn is also planning to capitalize on the plethora of foolish mortals who'll be swarming into town. Tell him to be careful. The Prime are aristocracy, too, and they all have embossed invitations."

Ara folded her arms. "Sr. McIntyre, why do you care so much about what happens to my brother? If I recall, you washed your hands of us all quite some time ago in Italy. Why the change of heart?"

"Let's just say that I've become more aware of politics these days," Duncan said vaguely. "You should take more care of it as well. Knowledge of politics could save you a great deal of trouble in your travels, and I don't mean just mortal politics. The Prime is more complex than you know."

"And I'm sure that you'll tell me all about it, hmm?" She raised an eyebrow and said with heavy sarcasm, "Educate the gypsy girl."

"If she needs educating, yes, I will do so. I think you need a good deal more knowledge about many things if you intend to survive both in your world and in ours. There are revolutions coming, in France and in the Prime."

"Maybe I don't care about politics," she said with a quasi-casual shrug. "It's never mattered to me who's in charge. I always get by."

"Perhaps," Duncan allowed, "but the people in charge never knew your name before."

"And they do now?"

"Learn about politics, and you'll know." He rose with an enigmatic smile. "Good evening, Araminah. Give Tobyn my best."

She watched him as he strolled away. *I don't like you, Duncan McIntyre.*

~∽༄ঌৎ৵~

Tobyn stroked Marielle's hair as he pulled away, the taste of her blood mingling with the taste of her body in the afterglow. She sighed contentedly and smiled into his eyes.

"I think I won," he told her quietly. He kissed the tip of her nose. "Thank you."

Marielle hugged him close, oblivious to the feeding he had done during their lovemaking. She kissed him deeply, her hands roaming down his back to cup his buttocks. When their lips parted, she breathed, "Oh, let me feel that again."

Tobyn smiled and kissed the throat that had so recently yielded to him. Feeding was incredibly more satisfying when it went hand-in-hand with sex. Different pleasures, each strong in their own way, joined together and became transcendent, and he doubted if simple feeding would ever really 'hit the spot' again.

"You're an ambitious girl," he teased.

"Mm-hmm." Marielle squirmed closer on the mattress. "Please..."

He smiled. "Never beg, *cariña*. You don't ever have to beg." He kissed her gently, then slid down her body to do as she asked.

━━∽ঌৎ∾━━

La Biche was clearing out, and Tobyn still had not returned from his tryst-cum-meal upstairs. Ara's patience had begun to wear thin when Duncan McIntyre had forced his presence on her and now, a few hours later, it had worn through. She finished off her fifth drink and rose from the table, a bit tipsy but certain that she was steady on her feet.

She nodded to Irene. "I'm going home. If my husband happens to show his face, tell him that waiting for him is a very boring sport. Good night."

Irene chuckled behind her chins. "Good night, dearie. Be careful out there."

"Don't worry about me. I'm very self-sufficient."

Squaring her shoulders, feeling a trifle slighted, she headed out into the night. She knew her way through Paris in the day, and she was sure that she could find her home even in the dark. Stepping bravely, she left La Biche without hesitation.

She took only a few minutes to get hopelessly turned around, and after another minute or two had passed, she began to feel alone. She was steadily working her way into fear when Duncan exercised his vampire's prerogative of appearing out of the shadows like a ghost, startling her badly for the second time that evening. She screeched and lurched away from him, her hand pressed to her pounding heart. Duncan laughed at her reaction, and she converted her fear to anger.

"God damn it! Don't do that to me!" She slapped him, hard, across the face, and her irritation doubled when he only laughed louder. Shouting now, she lit into him with her sharp tongue. "What are you trying to do, scare me to death? You could have killed me! I thought vampires bit people to death, but apparently they just frighten them so they fall over!"

"Ara," he chuckled, "you are amazing. I didn't mean to frighten you so. I simply didn't want you out here on your own."

She was still huffy from her fright. "Well, I don't need your kind of company. If you'll excuse me—"

He caught her arm. "You're drunk, my dear, and you're also lost. There are a number of vampires about, and I'd hate to see you end up as someone's dinner. That would be a waste."

"Why should I trust you? Maybe you're just looking for a little dinner yourself." She pulled her arm free of his grasp. "You can walk your shadow home, Mr. McIntyre. I won't be taken in so easily."

She strode away, and Duncan caught up with her. "I only want to be your chaperone."

"Ha!"

"Do you even know where you're going?"

Alcohol made her imprudent. "The Rue de Gallette," she replied, nodding to her left.

McIntyre smiled. "Well, then, you'd better start turning around, because the Rue de Gallette is that way."

She looked as he pointed to her right. After a moment, she nodded briskly. "All right, fine. Thank you."

He let her take a few steps away, then began to follow. Ara ignored him for as long as she could bear to; then she stopped in her tracks and ground out, "You may as well walk beside me if you insist on following me home."

Duncan smiled. "I thought you'd never ask."

"Well, it was obvious that you were never going to leave, so I may as well give in."

"I love women who give in."

She shot him an evil glance. "Don't press your luck."

The vampire tossed his head and laughed. "You are wonderful, Araminah."

"Maybe. Just stay at arm's length."

Smirking, he took his place at her side. *Oh, I will, little one*, he thought to her. *For now.*

∼✷∼

Tobyn left Marielle asleep in her room and paid Irene at the base of the stairs.

"From the sounds of things, you were pleased, eh, *chèrie?*" the corpulent woman asked.

"We both were." His eyes swept over the empty room and concern filled his gaze. "Where is Ara?"

"Your wife? She left an hour ago." Irene chuckled. "You have an interesting marriage."

He turned his head to face her. "What do you mean?"

"She left with a man."

His heart fell to roughly his mid-shin area while his temper made him hit the roof. "What? What man?"

"I don't know him, but he is very handsome." She hesitated, then pointed to her own teeth. "One of those kind, you know. Like you. He followed her very closely, as I recall."

Tobyn did not wait to hear more. Cursing the mental silence that kept him from his twin, he charged out into the night, determined to find her before some unethical traditional vampire type decided to start teething.

∾𝕯𝖊𝖈✺

Duncan stood, smiling to himself, as Ara let herself into the front room of the house she shared with Tobyn. The tiny fire on the hearth flickered in modest welcome as she bustled in, trailed by the Scottish vampire.

She supposed that she should have been too nervous to turn her back on McIntyre, since at any moment he could drop his friendly demeanor and steal her life away. She simply couldn't muster the proper level of paranoia. Perhaps she'd lived with Tobyn too long, or she was getting her bravery from the bottle tonight, but she had no fear of vampires. She especially had no fear of vampires with handsome faces, deferential manners, and a habit of walking her home. She trusted Duncan not to kill her from behind.

She poked the flame and fed it a handful of kindling while Duncan made himself comfortable at the table. She could sense him looking around the room as she lit a candle in the revivified fire.

"So, you live here with Tobyn, then?"

"Mm-hmm."

"Where does he keep his coffin?"

She smiled and gathered up her long skirt as she sat down. "He doesn't have one."

Duncan looked thunderstruck. "What?"

"It's ghoulish, and he doesn't need one, anyway." She plucked an apple from the bowl on the table and shined it on his sleeve. "Except for certain drinks three or four times a week, he's perfectly normal. Mostly."

"Does he ever drink from you?"

She answered around a bite of fruit. "Sometimes."

He was intrigued. "Does it hurt?"

"No." She crossed her legs. "If it did, he wouldn't do it to me."

He hesitated, but simply had to ask. "Does it feel...good?"

Her only answer was a waggle of her eyebrows as she swung her leg in a slow rhythm, tapping her toe against his calf as she moved. Duncan blushed and looked down at his hands, and Ara decided that she really wasn't afraid of him.

In a quieter voice, he asked shyly, "When does he do it?"

"At night, or else during the day." She fixed him with a frank look. "He does it when he does it, if you understand." She grinned, wondering how McIntyre and his courtly ways would react.

She wasn't disappointed. Duncan flushed furiously and began to rise from his seat. "I—ah—really ought to be going. I'm not certain...that is, I—"

Ara laughed at his discomfort. "If you turn any darker, your face will fall off."

Simply because he couldn't blush any more, Duncan resorted to nervous laughter. "You are a forward creature, aren't you?"

"It's tit for tat. You forced me to let you walk with me, so it's the least you can do to let me do something for you." She smiled at him, her green eyes bright with suggestions that the Scottish vampire had no hope of taking. "Or to you, as the case may be."

"Araminah..."

She reached over, slowly, and rubbed her foot along his leg. Their eyes met, and their hands, as if of their own volition, crept across the table top to intertwine. He smiled in hesitation, the tips of his teeth just peeking out beyond the limits of his lips.

"What are you afraid of?" she asked him. "Haven't you ever kissed a girl before?"

"Of course. I was married once, remember?" Duncan said, grinning. "But...I'm not like Tobyn. Kissing is all I'll be able to do."

Ara shrugged and squeezed his hand. "That's all right. I don't mind. A good kiss is better than bad sex any day."

He laughed softly and shook his head. "You are a wonder."

Her smile was bright as she leaned across the table. "Just wait."

Their kiss had just started to get interesting when Tobyn burst into the little house, his eyes wide with imagined fears for his sister. Ara and Duncan, startled, broke apart and backed away from the table.

"Ara, are you hurt?" the Romany vampire asked, panic in his voice. Without waiting for an answer, he interposed himself between the would-be lovers.

"I'm perfectly healthy," she said, a crisp bite to her tone, "and I will thank you to get out of my way and stay out of my business!"

Duncan wisely held his tongue as Tobyn rounded on his sister, one hand pointing at the other vampire. "You know what he is. How can you be so careless?"

She tossed her head defiantly. "I know that he's handsome, and that I trust him and that I want to spend time with him without my brother getting involved."

"He's a vampire," Tobyn argued. "He might kill you."

"So might you."

Her brother glared back at her, then turned to McIntyre. "Get out of my house," he ordered through clenched teeth. "I don't want you here."

Duncan looked from one twin to the other, uncertain how to respond. He had started this evening more or less in control of the situation, but now he had no idea of where he stood. Ara filled in the gap with a cool, "Duncan, I'll see you tomorrow night after sunset. I'll meet you here, all right?"

Her words set Tobyn to fuming even more, and McIntyre could sense the coming of a tactical retreat. Smiling to his beautiful new friend, he nodded. "All right. Tomorrow night, then." He paused, considering Tobyn's anger, then said, "Good night, Araminah."

Tobyn glared after his sister as she walked the Scotsman to the exit to kiss him goodnight on the front step. He waited for her to close the door. Once that signal was given, the fur began to fly.

"Just what in the hell do you think you were doing?" the vampire demanded, his eyes flashing fire that could not burn brighter than the flares his sister displayed.

"Having fun. It is allowed for people other than you, or have you forgotten?"

He straightened. "Ha! You're jealous!"

"Not at all. I'm bored." She crossed her arms and set her stance. "You have all the time and women in the world, and you expect me to be satisfied with just you, just when you feel like being here." She shook her head. "Unrealistic, to say the least."

"I don't care if you want to spend time with other people, but do you have to bring other men here?" he demanded.

"It's my home, too. And if I have to put up with you fucking somebody new every other night, then you have to put up with me bringing the occasional person here."

"But a vampire?"

"Maybe I just liked Duncan." She was feeling pugnacious and had no intention of making things easy for her brother. "I have the right to spend my time with who I choose, whether you like it or not."

Tobyn growled something beneath his breath and stalked over to the window to glare out at the summer night beyond the glass. The silence between them was heavy and sodden, full of the tension that Tobyn could not express. Ara sighed and let go of her irritation as much as she could, falling into her role of peacemaker.

She came up behind him and wrapped her arms around his waist, her chin propped onto his shoulder. She kissed his ear, then whispered, "What are you so afraid of, hm? Are you thinking that I'll end up somebody's dinner?"

He replied without turning to face her. "It's hardly out of the realms of possibility."

Ara squeezed him closer. "Don't worry so much. I can take care of myself. I may not be a vampire, but I'm still *chovihani*. Those instincts shouldn't be overlooked."

Tobyn reached down to grip her hand, his fear and protectiveness rushing out at the contact. "I just don't want you to be hurt. You don't know how easily things can go bad, or how fast." He shook his head, surprised by his emotions. "You don't know what will happen."

She turned him around and forced him to meet her gaze. In a soft, gentle voice, she said, "Neither do you. And I know that vampires aren't invulnerable. Living with you has taught me that." Ara offered a smile. "You worry too much."

He pulled her into a tight hug. "I just don't want to lose you."

"You won't."

"You sound so sure," he whispered against her hair.

"I am."

Tobyn embraced her more closely, his eyes on the fire that blazed on the hearth. *I wish I was.*

Duncan sighed to himself as he strolled away from the Reyes house, his mind full of Araminah. She was a surprise to him. Even knowing what he was, knowing what he could do to her, she had turned his hunt into her chase. Not that he'd set out this evening to mark the gypsy woman as another of his victims, of course, but he had intended to do something other than kissing if and when he actually wrapped her up inside his arms.

It would have been comfortable to have her there.

From her rooftop perch, Elisa Dieter could watch McIntyre as he slipped away from his disgusting little dalliance with the fortune teller. As Duncan wandered into the night, blissfully unaware, the German vampire considered her options. She could sell him to the Brethren, she supposed, but that would ultimately avail her little. The Brethren were notoriously poor, as bad as priests on vows of poverty, and they could offer a worldly woman like Elisa nothing that she did not already possess. Besides, there was no guarantee that, once they had her, the Brethren would let her escape again. Dieter was the ultimate sinner in their puritanical views, a vampire who drank blood for the pleasure of it and loved gold almost as much as immortality. Her mortal days as a member of the world's oldest profession also worked against her, and Elisa knew that the Brethren had a special stake sharpened just for her. Any attempt to deal with that sect would be foolhardy.

Dumas, then? Could she barter Duncan McIntyre for a better position in the Prime? She had already finagled a great deal from the *vicomte*; perhaps asking for more would push her luck a bit too far.

She would take her chances. The position of Secondary Prime could offer her a number of advantages, not all of them monetary, and she would get that position one way or another. She should have had it once before, if Dumas had claimed his stupid gypsy boy when she'd led him to the caravan. She sometimes wondered if Dumas had refused to steal him then just to frustrate her ambitions. People with power could do that sort of thing. How she wanted to be a person like that! Power was an aphrodisiac for Elisa; it had led her a long time along many long roads. Power and riches made her world go 'round, and she liked to watch it spin. The chance of gaining a little more of what she loved so well was worth the gamble.

Dumas, she knew, had not forgotten his little gypsy toy. Although he'd avoided speaking Tobyn's name for these two years, she could hear it in his mind often enough. She sometimes wondered what had passed between Dumas and Reyes in the privacy of the *chateau* to leave the Prime so enthralled. Certainly mere mortal beauty was not cause enough. Whatever had transpired, she would learn to use it to her advantage. She knew Dumas would give almost anything to have his mortal lover back again.

Well, then, she would have to supply Tobyn in order to receive the "anythings" Dumas would give. Elisa had a strategy, and she was capable of carrying it out. She was ambitious, dangerous, and manipulative in equal measures. All the cards were in place, now. Tobyn was here in Paris, Dumas was on his way, the festival to end all festivals promised throngs of her kind, and Elisa had a foolproof plan. All she needed now was the trump card to be played at the proper moment.

Duncan McIntyre was that card. His friendship with Isabella had put him very much on the Prime's bad side, and his dalliance tonight left him afoul of Prime traditions. He should have killed that mortal girl, that sister of Tobyn's, not kissed her. Elisa smiled. She was older and stronger than the Scotsman, and every inch of her was a huntress tonight. Before her trump card could escape her, Elisa launched herself into the air, a flesh and blood missile aimed at Duncan's unprotected back.

Twenty-Two

Michel Dumas stripped the gray gloves from his hands and cast a bored glance over his gilt-edged accommodations.

"Adequate," he pronounced, passing the gloves, his hat, and his traveling cloak to a waiting servant. The young man bowed over the burden, then scurried away to some hidden part of the mansion called La Madeleine.

"We've prepared the rooms for you according to your desires, my lord," oozed the owner of La Madeleine, a vampire named Gerard duPres. "No expenses were spared, I assure you."

Dumas waved his hand in regal ennui and brushed duPres aside. The other vampire was a venal little man, always trying to impress his superiors with the money he spent on entertainment and gifts. Given a chance, Dumas was certain duPres could produce a ledger as the central topic of an hours-long, hopelessly one-sided conversation.

Gerard scuttled to catch up. Lifting a crystal goblet, he tried to show it to Dumas. "Look—it's gold-edged, with an etched design. I had them monogram it for you." His round face blossomed with a hopeful smile. "It cost me twenty francs for this glass alone."

Dumas stopped and took the glass from duPres, then gave the thing a leisurely examination. When Gerard's beaming grew too unbearable, Dumas let the crystal slip from his fingers and watched dispassionately as it shattered against the intricate ceramic tile mosaic on the floor.

"You have the soul of an accountant," he told duPres in glacial tones, "coupled with the heart of a mouse. Do you think that a goblet could impress me?" Dumas sniffed in disdain and glanced once more around the room. "I thirst, duPres. Can you offer any real hospitality, or can I expect a Brethren welcome?"

Cheeks burning, duPres indicated the sealed double doors that led to the bedchamber. "Your hospitality is waiting in there, *m'sieur*. I selected him myself, knowing where your preferences lay. He is asleep and ready for your pleasure."

Dumas raised an eyebrow but remained silent as he walked to the closed doors. The mortal scent from the room beyond was enticing to his nostrils and set his heart quivering. The coach ride from Milan had been very long, and he'd had little chance to feed. In eager anticipation, he opened the doors and stepped through, bolting the way behind him. This was to be a private meal.

The boy on the bed was young and beautiful, locked into deceptively peaceful slumber. His brown-skinned body was curled tightly around the pillow he embraced, and the white muslin sheet pulled to his waist was his only modesty. With a soft sigh, Dumas sat beside him on the bed, his slender fingers lacing through the sleeper's raven curls.

A gypsy boy, he thought, a wry smile on his lips. *How they all misunderstand.* He pressed the lightest of kisses to the sun-touched temple and came away with knowledge of heady mortal aroma that intensified his hunger but did not touch him. Taking the boy's face in his hands, Dumas contemplated the differences.

The gypsy's youthful features were too square and blockish; Tobyn's face was more delicate, with finer lines and more perfect composition. The hair was a trifle too wiry, too unruly. Dumas missed his gypsy's soft curls that followed where his fingers led them. If they were open, this boy's eyes would have been too dark, too brown, not the beautiful silver-blue that he remembered. The skin, too, was wrong, too weather-beaten and sun-dark to belong to his fair-complected Tobyn, and his scent was not the perfume Dumas had come to know.

"You are lovely, my darling boy," the French vampire whispered, "but you are not my Tobyn." Closing his eyes so that he could pretend, Dumas gently lifted the boy's chin, exposing the tender throat to his attentions.

Thinking of Tobyn, he stole a kiss, then stole the gypsy's life, making love the only way he knew.

~⁂~

Elisa poured more cold water into Duncan's face and waited for Roger to finish slapping him awake. The Scotsman groaned, his eyelids fluttered, and Elisa shifted slightly in her seat on his beleaguered chest.

"Good evening, Duncan, dear," she crooned, her soprano voice sending needles through his ears. "Rise and shine."

Duncan blinked her into focus. "Elisa..."

"Very good. I apologize for the rough handling I gave you earlier, but I didn't think you'd come along with me any other way."

"Come with you?" he asked, still groggy and confused. "Where are we?"

Roger collected the empty bucket and handed Elisa a wicked, long knife as the blonde vampire told her captive, "We are in my private apartments here in Paris. I thought we could come here to discuss a few things."

Duncan's head was clearing, and with his clarity came the knowledge that he was in a great deal of trouble. Fear brushed his spine, but he refused to shame his Highland blood. "Discuss?" he asked, his tone level. "What could we possibly have to discuss?"

Elisa smiled and poked the end of her knife through the links in the chains he had only begun to feel at his wrists and ankles. "Oh, I thought that maybe we could discuss a mutual acquaintance," she said slowly, off-handedly, as the point of her blade started to break his skin. "Shall I give you a name, or can you guess?" Their eyes met, neither gaze giving an iota. "Very well." She leaned closer, all but lying atop him like a monstrous cat. "I thought that perhaps we could discuss Araminah Reyes."

To his credit, Duncan did not react with so much as a blink. "Who?"

"Come, now," Elisa scolded, straightening, her knife threateningly idle in her hand. "I arrived at the Rue de Gallette just in time to see you leaving her house. You even kissed her, if my eyes did not deceive me." She giggled like a broken mirror. "Surely you wouldn't kiss a girl you don't know. Not a fine Catholic boy like you."

"My religious beliefs have nothing to do with it." He tugged at his shackles. "Elisa, this is ridiculous. Let me up."

"No. We aren't done discussing."

Roger piped up from where he was lounging on the other side of the room, enjoying Elisa's tabletop spectacle. "You haven't even started yet."

"Araminah Reyes," Dieter said, lingering on each syllable while her weapon danced through Duncan's hair, "is sister to Tobyn Reyes. And you know how badly Dumas wants to find Tobyn Reyes." She drew the blade down his face, tracing a thin, bleeding line. "I want to find him, too. Maybe you can help me."

McIntyre's eyes flashed. "Maybe you can go to hell."

Elisa's face twisted with violent anger. "Roger, hold his arm steady." Her lackey sprang to comply, and she pressed her knife to the first knuckle of the Scotsman's index finger. "Duncan McIntyre, you know how vampire wounds heal. If I were to cut this joint off right now, it could reattach itself if we hold it on while your blood does the work. Given this ability for severed parts to become whole again, do you know what that means?" She smiled sweetly. "I have an almost limitless ability to hurt you. I can cause you agony, give you horrible wounds, then let them heal up and start all over again five minutes later. That's an infinite number of fingers to cut off, my friend. I can keep you here, torture you here, until you starve to death or until Jesus Christ Himself comes to set you free, whichever comes first."

Duncan did the only manly thing he could think of. Glaring back at her as hideously as he could, he spat in her face.

She readied her knife. "Roger, hold him! One way or another, McIntyre, you'll tell me where to find Tobyn Reyes, and you'll never stop regretting that you didn't tell me here and now!"

～✦～

The servant passed an ivory-handled comb to Isabella, his brow creased in worry. He wished that his father were still alive to fill the difficult position of a vampire's mortal companion, especially in these days of hiding.

"Are you certain?" he asked, anxiety making his young voice turn old.

The Spanish vampire nodded. "I have to go."

"But why France?" the newest Serrano at her side exclaimed. "Every one of your enemies will be there."

"So will every one of my friends." Isabella closed her last bag, then kissed the young man on his pretty mouth. "Besides, Switzerland is boring me."

He followed her to the waiting coach. "You have no taste for safety."

Isabella sighed, then took him in her arms. "This is what I have to do. Stay here, where you are protected. I'll send for you when it is time."

"Be careful."

She graced him with a smile. "I always am."

～✦～

The days of the festival preparations were loud and happy, busy with a steady influx of every sort of person. Tobyn and Ara, their argument forgotten, followed the mob out into the street, chasing after the musicians and picking pockets for recreation.

"I should set up a shop around here," Ara told him, her voice raised to be heard over the chatter of the crowd. "At the very least, I should put up a sign."

"Advertising for fortune telling? Very clever," he nodded, his eyes on a passing streetwalker.

"I need a better name."

"Why? What's wrong with Reyes?"

She put on a mock arrogance and sniffed, "Too common." At his expression, she burst into laughter. "No, it's a joke. What I'd been thinking was that I'd like something...flashier. More supernatural, if you understand."

Tobyn smiled and pondered the question while his light fingers liberated a passing dandy's money purse. "Hmm...something exotic, perhaps?"

"Absolutely."

"Astara."

Ara wrinkled her nose and stuck out her tongue. "Bleh."

He nodded. "I agree."

"Something starry, though," she told him. "That would be good."

"Stars. Planets." He snapped his fingers. "Astrology!"

"What?"

He pointed to the sky overhead. "Up there, look. Constellations. Which one of them do you suppose is like us?"

Ara stood beside him and considered the question as the throng circulated around them. "I haven't the least idea."

"The Twins. Gemini. There's a fellow at La Biche who goes on about the stars all the time. He calls himself an astronomer, but I think he's just insane. He actually believes that someday men will walk on the moon." He twirled a finger near his temple. "More stars in his head than out."

She smiled to herself. "Gemini. Araminah Gemini. I like the sound of it."

"Araminah Gemini, Reader of Tarot," her brother intoned, bowing before her. They laughed, and he wrapped her in a tight embrace. "If you promote yourself shamelessly enough, you'll make quite a bit of money."

"That's the idea." She kissed him. "What say you, Tobyn Gemini?"

"I say we have a lot of things to do tonight." He pulled away and started tugging her down the street toward a colorful performing troupe that was just beginning to set up their stage. "Come on!"

With a game laugh, Ara trotted after him, her eyes full of smiles.

～？◦？～

Gerard scuttled along in his ruler's wake as Dumas strolled through the crowd in the city streets. The Prime spared only the briefest of glances for the noisy merrymakers that he passed, supremely unimpressed, as ever, by the mortal display. The younger vampire shook his head and wondered if Dumas was ever really satisfied by anything.

In an effort to lighten the Prime's mood, Gerard said at his elegantly-clad elbow, "Nearly all of our people have arrived in France now. That party tonight will be the perfect way to kick off the Congress."

Dumas turned tired gray eyes onto his companion. "All you really care about is parties."

"They make life more livable," Gerard shrugged.

"I find them tedious. They are all the same." He shook his head. "All that makes life livable is the taking of other lives. Death dealt by one's own hands is death less powerful. Or at least it serves to break up the monotony of this existence."

The other vampire hesitated, trying to understand the cipher that was Dumas. When that proved impossible, he pointed to a stage being erected by one of the festival's groups of troubadours and actors.

"Maybe that will brighten the night, my lord *vicomte*," he hazarded. "A bit of play might soothe some of your worries."

"Theatricals are only little lies made smaller," Dumas sniffed, "pale imitations of humanity. What is it to be, comedy or tragedy?"

"I think it's a romance."

"Ah! Then it is both."

Gerard considered the props and the set being assembled on the performers' platform. "Yes, I know this story. A man steals away his aloof beloved, locks her away in his castle tower, and compels her to love him in return."

Dumas smirked, his eyes dark. "And does this man succeed?"

"Sometimes. Some versions have the girl being rescued by another lover, some knight in shining armor."

"Knights?" The Prime chuckled in amusement. "I never did have use for them." He smiled at Gerard, who felt both warmed and chilled by the strangeness behind the expression. "Come, then. Let's go and watch the players."

～⤫～

Tobyn and Araminah positioned themselves directly in front of center stage, where they could be within arm's length of the actors. Tobyn wrapped his hands around his sister's waist and leaned forward on her back, playfully hooking his chin on her shoulder.

"Should we be nice, or should we be rude?"

She pondered the question. "Well, we really ought to wait and see how good the actors are. If they're good, we'll be nice."

"And we'll be rude if they're bad."

"Oh, absolutely."

He nodded toward the stage. "Look, idiots wearing metal. You have to be pretty stupid to wear things like that. It would slow you down."

"Can you imagine wearing it all day in the summer?" Ara asked, leaning against him.

"Phew! Don't breathe too deeply around them. Knights in clouds of stink aren't my idea of heroes."

With a sudden blare of a horn and the shiver of a tambourine, the players took the stage. The leader of the troupe, a balding man who was overstuffed, overdressed, and overacting, gave pompous voice to a trite preamble and then scampered offstage as fast as his pudgy legs could go. Several members of the audience sped him along his way with jeers and a handful of pebbles, which did not amuse one of the French vampires in the audience.

"Common rabble," huffed Gerard.

"*Taisez-vous*," Dumas bade. "Let's move closer. I want to smell the actors' sweat."

Uncertain but anxious to please, Gerard held his silence and followed Dumas to the front of the crowd.

The *vicomte* watched as the performers butchered their little play, oblivious to the bad writing and worse acting. When the villain kidnapped his icy love, Dumas did not see French peasants playing dress-up. He saw snow and he saw his home and the room that, in his mind, was still Tobyn's. In the victim's vain attempts to escape, he saw his gypsy, and in the kidnapper's roughness he saw his own sins laid out. He had erred when he'd had Tobyn; he knew that now. But he would change his gypsy's mind when he possessed him once again. This time, he would win Tobyn with kindness, not take him by force.

The knight's rescue mission disgusted him, and he looked away, a sour sneer on his lips. This was not the way the story should have gone. Forsaking the slender entertainment that now held Gerard captivated, he scanned the crowd.

Tobyn's boredom with the play cost him dearly. As he looked up, for the endless span of time between two heartbeats, his eyes locked with the dark gray gaze of Michel Dumas.

//Tobyn—//

"Oh, Christ!" he whispered, backing away. "Oh, Christ!"

Ara looked at him, concerned. "What is it? What's wrong?"

He could only point to where Dumas stood, stunned by the nearness of his Maker. Ara's jaw dropped, and she grabbed her brother's hand. When it became clear that Tobyn lacked either the ability or the will to run, she pulled him after her and plunged into the crowd.

"Tobyn!"

Dumas' anguished cry ripped through the night air and put motion back into the gypsy's feet. Trembling inside with fear and a certain excitement, Tobyn took the lead back from his sister, zigzagging around people and things in his mad flight from his Maker.

Dumas was not to be denied. With the double benefit of supernatural speed and no hindering mortal companion, he raced after his beloved, desperately determined not to be left behind. He gained ground on the weaving twins, his unyielding progress in a straight line winning him few friends but fewer delays.

The crowd slowed both the hunter and the hunted, and in the confusion of the flight, Tobyn and Ara found their grips broken by a bevy of revelers. As his sister's hand slipped out of his own, the gypsy vampire stopped in his tracks, frantically looking for her.

Ara, for once disgusted by her small stature, was borne away by the press of bodies, swallowed by the loud group of party-goers. She caught one last glimpse of her twin before she was picked up from her feet and literally carried away by one man in a gaudy costume. She growled at him as she kicked at his shins.

"Let me go, you stupid ass!"

The man laughed and held her tighter, delighted by the woman's squirming. Ara was in no mood to be fondled by so homely a specimen, and the alchemy of her knee to his groin changed his laughter to a grimace. Wriggling free, Ara pushed back through the crowd to find her brother.

On the other side of the surging group, Tobyn was beside himself. "Ara!" he called, his voice carrying over the noise of the rabble. "Araminah, where are you?"

The crowd parted behind him, and in his distraction, he did not realize what was happening until Dumas seized his shoulders and whirled him around. They froze, eye to eye, staring at each other in ambivalent thrill. Dumas pulled him closer, and Tobyn could not bring himself to resist until they were close enough to kiss.

It was then that Dumas noticed the difference. It was in the scent, perhaps, or in the tint of his eyes, but the French vampire became painfully aware of Tobyn's Change. He stiffened and squeezed his fists tighter on Tobyn's arms.

"What are you?" he hissed. "What are you?!"

The gypsy was captivated by a power he had never understood, a power that transposed his fear to desire. "Michel..." He breathed the lightest of sighs. "Michel Dumas."

The Prime shoved Tobyn away, his eyes wide, his face a mask of revulsion. In a purple, choked voice, he spat, "Abomination!"

The shift in tone snapped Tobyn back into his senses, and he stumbled away from his creator. His anger returned with a blinding rush, and he pulled his *kris* knife from his boot. "You bastard! You did this to me!"

Dumas backed away, his nostrils flaring. "I did nothing of the kind! You...your gypsy magic, perverse..."

"Perverse?" He laughed harshly. "That's a fine thing for you to call me. Have you forgotten Matthieu so soon?"

With a profane snarl, the French vampire spun on his heel and charged off through the crowd. Tobyn launched himself at Dumas' back, the tip of his knife scoring the flesh as the Prime took flight, his motion too fast for human eyes to follow. Tobyn's eyes, though, saw every inch of his escape, and he roared in impotent rage at the blinking sky. The crowd drew away from him, convinced that he was mad.

They were not far wrong. He crouched on the cobblestones, glaring fiercely at the ruby-stained tip of his blade, his trembling fists yearning for a convenient target. Dumas was gone, out of range; his second choice, himself, was no choice at all, his self-preservation overriding even this black temper.

He was muttering to himself when Ara finally wrestled her way back to his side. "Fool," he sputtered. "Weak-willed idiot!"

"Tobyn," she said, putting a calming hand on his hunched shoulder. "Tobyn, come on. Come home with me."

He looked up into her eyes, and for a moment she wondered if he saw her at all. Red laced the silver and blue, and his gnashing teeth betrayed him with their rage-inspired points. She was afraid for a heartbeat, then fixed her mind on the need to get him away from the public, from witnesses and traditional vampires of both clans. More firmly, she repeated herself.

"Come home with me."

He hesitated, then pushed his knife back into his boot. Nodding once, sharply, he rose and followed her from the square, silently fuming and stewing in his anger, both at himself and at Dumas, the demon of his waking nightmare.

From now on, this is war.

❧❦❧

Dumas soared through the highest winds, shrieking into the blast that stole the sound away, all but ripping it from his throat without his participation. He was screaming inside, as well, convulsed by the shuddering collapse of his illusions. His perfect lover, the sainted gypsy idol he had created in his mind, had proved to be more clay than stone. The dream he'd hoped to live was vanishing with every anguished heartbeat.

Betrayal. Hatred. Anger. His soul rotted with it. Every iota of love he'd ever felt for Tobyn, every jot of soft feeling, was transmuting into darkness, dying and decaying and lurching into hideous undeath. He hated Tobyn now, wanted his death as much as he had once yearned for his everlasting life. There was no place in Dumas' vision of the world for what the gypsy had become.

And what had he become? The Prime could not identify the creature Tobyn was. He was no longer human, certainly. It was undeniable that he was a vampire. But what kind of vampire? If he was not Prime or Brethren, then he was not acceptable. And what was unacceptable could not be allowed to live.

Tears of rage and pain coursed down Dumas' face as he dove toward Gerard's mansion, screaming as he went.

"God damn you, Tobyn Reyes! Damn you to hell!"

Elisa and Roger dragged the wasted husk that had been Duncan McIntyre into the ballroom, crashing Gerard's soiree in grand style. Silence fell over the Congress of the Prime as the German led her companion and their burden to the front of the room. Behind her mask, Isabella skulked closer, wondering what the unreformed Nuremberg whore had up her sleeve this time.

Dieter faced the party, a self-satisfied smirk on her waspish lips. "I have information for the Prime."

A murmur, low and indistinct, greeted her announcement. Isabella stared in morbid horror at Duncan. She had not known that vampires could scar. She wanted to steal him away, but in the present situation such an act would be sheer lunacy.

Duncan, Duncan, what have they done to you?

Elisa shoved McIntyre to his knees and Roger held him there. The Scotsman could not resist; he knelt there, head hanging, his eyes unfocussed and leaking tears.

"I have information for the Prime!"

Dumas crashed through the main doors, his face livid. "What information? Speak it out, Dieter, and stop your damnable displays!"

The uncharacteristic loss of composure struck the Congress, and utter silence took the room once more. Dumas strode forward, barely even looking at the vampire kneeling on the floor. Elisa simpered in delight.

"I know where you can find your Tobyn Reyes." She enjoyed the reaction of the onlookers, then said, "Now you can claim your gypsy consort."

"I want no damned consort!" Elisa jerked in open surprise, and he stepped closer still. "Tell me what you know."

The German woman hesitated, then said, "This man here has told me that your Tobyn—"

"Not *my* Tobyn."

"—that Tobyn lives with his sister, Araminah, in a house on the Rue de Gallette. The woman tells fortunes for money, and Tobyn lives from her earnings."

Dumas glared into Dieter's eyes; she did not shrink, which testified either to bravery or mania. "Where on the Rue de Gallette?"

"Number thirteen."

The Prime turned to face his Congress. "I will find this Tobyn Reyes and destroy him. The thing he has become cannot be allowed to exist." He silenced the muttering of the crowd with a slashing gesture. "I will destroy it!"

Elisa smiled at Dumas. "Am I to be rewarded for my work, *monsieur?*"

The Frenchman narrowed his eyes. "No. Not until I have gained what I desire."

Anger brought a flush of red to her cheeks. "And what do you desire, Oh Prime?"

He smiled thinly, his hatred palpable. "The death of Tobyn Reyes."

~⤙∂℃⤚~

Tobyn paced the darkened house after Araminah had gone to bed, his night vision correcting for the utter lack of light. He twirled his *kris* knife in his hands, his eyes staring straight ahead as he pondered his situation.

He had been discovered by an enemy with an army at his command. Tobyn had never felt so vulnerable and exposed. If Dumas was to come for him with the power of the Prime behind him, then Tobyn stood a snowball's chance in hell of surviving. Worse, his sister would be in danger as well, and all because of him. He had to run. There had to be a way for him to escape this threat and yet not forsake his sister or the pleasures of European civilization.

On the bed, Ara stirred restlessly in her sleep, moaning softly in some dream he could not see. He stopped and watched her, his eyes burning. It was so unfair; he had never asked for this Change in his life, and Araminah had never asked to be included on the Prime assassination list. And now they were facing the wrath of the entire clan, the two of them against virtually the entire vampire world. How could they hope to stand against that?

They had to leave. They simply had to get away from France before it was too late. He would arrange passage to England, or to America, even if Ara resisted, and he suspected that she might. He would arrange their getaway. As soon as possible, they would leave Paris and leave France and never look back.

But this business of booking passage would take time, and time was something that Tobyn could ill afford to spend. Until they actually left the threat behind them, Tobyn and Ara would be in danger. Danger to himself he could accept; danger to Ara made him sick.

I will protect you, he promised the woman on the bed. *So long as I am here, you will be safe.*

He hoped that his words weren't empty air. He hoped that the Prime wouldn't force him to keep his pledge. He hoped that everything would be well.

He knew that his hopes were waiting to be dashed.

Twenty-Three

Elisa stormed her way into her apartments, Roger in her wake. Before them they kicked the helpless McIntyre, too drained and wounded to resist or even to protest the brutality.

"That man," the German snarled in her fury. "That man!"

Huntingdon dealt Duncan another vicious kick, snapping bones they'd somehow missed before, and added fuel to Elisa's fire. "Dumas made you look foolish."

"I know that, God damn it!" she spat, her brittle voice raising to an ear-shattering pitch. "He has insulted and humiliated me for the last time. Who does he think he is? He's not omnipotent, no matter how old he is! He can be killed the same as anybody else." Her eyes narrowed to glittering slits. "He'll learn that, soon enough. Oh, he will regret the day he failed to show me proper respect!"

Roger eyed her from a safe distance. "What are you planning to do?"

"Oh, I have so many plans..." She stopped pacing beside the Scots vampire's weakly-stirring form. "If the Prime won't pay for my prisoner and my information, then maybe the Brethren will."

"The Brethren? Are you mad?" Roger scoffed. "You're exactly the kind of sinner they would kill on sight."

"They may be fanatical, but they're practical. They won't kill me when I can offer them something they can use." She smiled and knelt beside Duncan. "Our friend here is very valuable to their leader, and I think they might put more value on killing Dumas than on eliminating one more sinner."

The Englishman's roaring laughter marked his agreement.

<hr />

After sunrise took its three hours' mandatory death-like sleep out of Tobyn's day, he rose and swathed himself in a cloak and low-brimmed hat. The torpor that so irresistibly stole him in the mornings was slow to leave him today, and the light from the open window stung him. Cursing the sun, he closed the wooden shutters with a snap.

Ara looked up from her cards. "Where do you think you're going?"

"I'm going to arrange passage for us to England."

"England?" The disbelief in her voice waltzed briefly with a laugh. "We have no business going to England."

"Business or not, we're going."

His voice was firm, but Ara felt compelled to argue anyway. "Tobyn—"

"This is not open to debate!" he snapped, for the first time in years sounding like a typical domineering Romany male. "I said we're going to England, and we're going as soon as possible, and there will be no complaints from you!"

She lifted her chin and tossed her head. "You're running away," she accused. "We just got settled here, and now you want to leave."

He rounded on her, anger in his eyes. "Yes, I'm running. Think about it. Dumas found us. He has hundreds of vampires at his command. How am I supposed to fight that? How am I supposed to protect you, one against an army?" He shook his head. "I have never been a coward, sister dear, but even I can see that it's a fool's risk to stay!" He wrapped his cloak about himself. "Grumble all you want, but we're going. And as for being settled—you and I are gypsies. Being settled means nothing to us."

Her eyes filled with tears as she felt helplessness overwhelm her again. When would she control her own life? In a throaty voice, she whispered, "It means nothing to you."

Tobyn would never understand women, and he didn't have the time to try to unsnarl the latest puzzle. Growling a Rom expletive, he left the house, slamming the door behind him.

Ara watched him go, her hands clenched in fists on the table. Before her, the Tarot deck stared up impassively, saying nothing. She was acutely aware suddenly of the walls of her house, of her trap, and while her mind knew that Tobyn was right, her spirit rebelled. Here was another man making decisions for her, setting his rules and limits to confine her life. She had thought Tobyn was different, but at the heart, he was only a gypsy man with infuriating gypsy ways.

She hated gypsy men. They locked women up in tight rules, considered them evil, treated them like slaves. Beat them, raped them, forbade them to fight back, forbade them to speak out of turn. Controlled them, owned them, coerced them—

With a scream of rage contained too long, she swept the table clean with one arm, kicking her chair over as she rose. Cards scattered across the floor as she pulled the curtains from the windows and knocked the pots from their hooks above the hearth. Like a cyclone, she turned the neat little house into chaos until finally, strength spent, she collapsed in a sobbing heap in the middle of the wreckage.

What made her think that *gadjo* men were any different? She had seen plenty of *gadjas* wearing the same glazed look as gypsy women, showing souls with the fires beaten out by too little understanding and too many children. She was endlessly grateful that she had never borne a child. She would not be responsible for adding more men to this world, or more women to be destroyed.

Tobyn was different, but not enough. He had never been anything but gentle and kind to her, but he still made choices for them both, as if she had no mind of her own. Even Duncan McIntyre, whom she recalled fondly, had been patronizing and oh-so-male. No man was different from Romany men, and the knowledge depressed her. She would escape the gypsy life she had always abhorred and felt separate from, and she might escape Dumas and his kind, but she would never escape the tyranny of men.

Hugging her knees, she allowed herself the time to weep before she had to acquiesce once more.

The coach took him to the proper office, where he fought with the portly clerk over politics, fares, and papers. There was more to legitimate travel than Tobyn had ever considered, and he did not appreciate the hassles.

As the round little man went to make yet another document, Tobyn sighed and glanced at the open window. His skill at keeping his eyes out of sunlight was sparing him sickness even though the day had been bright. The clerk's stalling inefficiency had kept him long enough that now the sun had cooled and was dipping toward the horizon. The cool feeling of approaching night marginally soothed his jangled nerves until he realized that the darkness would bring out the Prime.

Hurry up, you old jackass, he thought at the clerk. *I have to get to Ara before nightfall.*

Darkness put will and motion back into Isabella, and she crept from her hiding place in the basement of du Pres' mansion. Gerard was her ally, and despite his habit of sniveling before the Prime, he had granted her his protection from Michel Dumas. Isabella did not expect the French vampire to be overly concerned with her; he was undoubtedly quite preoccupied with his new-born enmity for Tobyn.

So Michel has seen what Tobyn has become and is displeased, she thought. *Hate that comes from love is the strongest. They will be enemies forever, now.*

She found Elisa's door locked from the inside. She was certain that the German and her friend Roger were within, standing cruel guard over Duncan McIntyre. Surely they could find no further use for him. Why were they still holding him hostage? Isabella knew Elisa well enough to know that if she felt vindictive about Dumas' lack of civility at the ball, then Duncan would bear the brunt of her anger. And from the look of the Scotsman, he'd borne enough of that already.

//Duncan,// she called to him, gently nudging his mind. *//Duncan, can you hear me?//*

There was a moment of pain-hazed confusion, then he weakly replied, *//Yes.//*

//Can you move?//

Duncan paused, taking stock. *//Barely. I'm unbound, at least. 'Bella...the pain, and the thirst...//*

//Shh. Where are Elisa and Roger?//

//She is out, I think, and he is sleeping by the door. He gorged himself last night and now he can't wake up.//

Isabella gathered her courage and her strength, then kicked the door open. As it swung aside, propelled by her attack, it slammed against the wall with a bang that jolted Roger to his sluggish feet. Isabella shoved him aside, knocking him to the floor, then rushed to gather up Duncan. His ordeal and his thirst made him hollow-light in her arms, and she had no trouble picking him up and carrying him to the window through which Elisa had made her own departure the night before. Before she could look back at the hollering Englishman on the carpet, Isabella launched herself into the air, bearing Duncan away to safety.

Elisa would not be pleased.

⌐⌐⌐

Ara spent the day cleaning up the debris from her temper tantrum, picking up the pieces and making the house look as if nothing had ever happened. As dusk began to fall and the festival-goers started to wander past the windows, she set up shop, putting out her sign and spreading her cards on the table. She smiled to herself and considered the new name Tobyn had selected for them: Gemini. The Twins. She would have to change her sign as soon as they got to England and learned how to speak the language there.

She was clearing away a practice spread when a soft knock sounded on the door. A honey-smooth voice asked, "Is the fortune-teller in?"

"I am," she told the man. "Enter and seek answers."

A tall figure, robed and dark in many ways, stepped into the house and closed the door behind himself. Ara watched him approach the questioner's chair, his motions graceful as a dancer's. She caught a glint in his cool gray eyes and thought of birds of prey. She began to shuffle her cards nervously.

"You have a particular question in mind, perhaps?" she asked, her gaze pinned to the shadows hiding his face. Why did this man make her feel so uneasy?

There was a smile in his voice. "Just read for me, *bohemienne*."

Reluctantly, she nodded, her heavy gold hoop earrings bouncing against the corner of her jaw. "My price is simple. Truth is golden, and only gold coin can buy it."

Three gold coins rolled onto the table from his elegant hand, which quickly retreated back into the folds of his robe. "I buy your truth, then."

Ara tested the coins, then slid them into her sash. Her fingertips on the cards were tingling, something they'd never done before in a hired reading. Swallowing the mysterious lump in her throat, she laid out the cards.

The Significator was the Devil, and she saw a human face on the painted goat's head. She blinked, saw the real paper picture for a heartbeat, and then the human face returned. It was familiar but indistinct at the same time, and something in her mind screamed caution. Crossing the Devil came the Emperor, and she could see only a reaffirmation of the first card.

Her voice was thick and her throat inexplicably dry. "You are a man of great power, *monsieur*, but it is dark power."

His whisper unsettled her. Calmly smug, he replied, "I know."

The cards continued to fall. Three of Swords, five of Cups, the Moon—darkness and hidden things. Traps, danger, and ill feeling. Ten of Swords, nine of Swords—the blood on the card was wet, glistening, until she touched the painted image. Her finger on the surface of the card burned, a shock traveling like lightning up her arm to dance along her spine. She gasped and pulled away.

"Evil," she breathed, unable to stop herself. "*Monsieur*, I cannot read for you."

He chuckled, and there was malice in the sound. Ara backed away from the table and the man who sat at it, her back to the solid wall behind her, one hand unconsciously groping for something she could use as a weapon.

"What did you see, little gypsy bitch? Death, perhaps? Threat?" He rose and stepped slowly around the table, neatly putting himself between her and the door. "A threat to you, or perhaps to your brother?"

Her small hand closed around the grip of the hearth-hook, removed along with the cooking pot for cleaning. Her eyes narrowed. "Who are you?"

Again, he laughed, hovering between malice and insanity. "Don't your mystic senses tell you, Mademoiselle Reyes?" He pulled his hood away from his face. "Maybe this will help."

Fear and anger flooded her. "Dumas!"

"Where is Tobyn?"

"Out."

"I can see that, silly wench." He stepped nearer. "Where?"

Her reply was to swing the hook at him with all of her strength. Hissing, he caught her wrist in a punishing grip, squeezing ruthlessly until she dropped her weapon with a cry. Not yet satisfied, he forced her to her knees, his eyes blazing with cold fire.

"Tiresome, loathsome creature! Detestable woman! Tell me where to find your brother or, I warn you, the penalty will be severe!"

She tried to pull free and succeeded only in wrenching her shoulder painfully. "What do you want with him?"

"I want to kill him."

"Go to hell!"

He pulled her to him, one hand tight around her throat while the other still mastered her arm. "Foolish woman! Don't you see that you gain nothing by fighting me? Help me or do not! Either way, you will die. But if you do not help me, then I promise you that you will die slowly."

Her green eyes were venomous as she spat, "Better to die in pain than to die in disgrace!"

"Then so be it!"

Dumas seized her roughly, one hand yanking on her hair to pull her head back, laying her throat bare. He twisted her arm up behind her with his other hand, dislocating her already-sore shoulder and making her yelp. The sound of her pain encouraged him, and he bared his teeth for an instant before shoving them into her. She screamed and struggled against him, but he easily overpowered her; her efforts only resulted in jagged tears in her tender skin.

He reveled in the blood that pulsed against his tongue, springing forth unpulled. Ara was whimpering her pain and terror in his ears, and he smiled to hear it.

Tears streamed down her face as she suffered the worst agony she'd ever known. Her senses vibrated with it, her nerves trembled, and she called out desperately to her twin.

//Tobyn! Help me! Oh, God...//

Somehow, somewhere, she hoped that he would hear.

Somewhere, somehow, he did.

*Ara...*He bolted from the carriage and left the protesting, unpaid driver far behind him. He took to the alleys and backstreets, trusting his vampire's running speed to take him home faster than a coach in a congested street. He was out of breath, his heart pounding, when he reached his door and flung it open.

Dumas dropped his victim as Tobyn burst into the house. Ara fell to the floor and lay, motionless, deathly pale, her throat cruelly wounded.

The Frenchman's lips were scarlet with stolen blood as he whirled to greet his nightchild with a horrid grin.

"*Bastaris!*" Tobyn growled, seizing his knife from his belt.

Dumas tossed his head and spread his arms. "Come to me, Tobyn."

The younger vampire lunged, his *kris* knife digging at the Frenchman. Dumas, overconfident in his supremacy, underestimated Tobyn's speed, and the gypsy's blade buried itself in the middle of his chest. With a tremendous effort, the Prime avoided letting his heart be wounded, but the pain still left him flash-blind. Tobyn hauled on the grip and cut Dumas deeply from chest to waist. The older vampire howled and pushed Tobyn away. The gypsy would not relinquish his hold on the knife still buried in Dumas' body, and the two of them fell, rolling across the floor, smashing Ara's chair.

"Abomination!" the Prime abjured, his fangs gnashing in their lust for the young one's throat.

Tobyn tried to stab Dumas again, but they wrestled for the knife, and neither could secure the upper hand. The older vampire gave a shout and threw Tobyn away from him. Surprised by sudden flight, Reyes scrambled to land on his feet but met the ground on his back instead. Dumas rose unsteadily but quickly took advantage of Tobyn's dazed state. Picking up the gypsy vampire, the Prime hurled him at the fire that roared on the hearth. His strength was sapped by his wounds, and his intended burnt offering escaped with only his right hand sacrificed to the flame.

Tobyn jerked out of the fire and extinguished the torture in his hand by rubbing the blackened fingers in the ashes on the hearth. Dumas, dizzy and badly hurt, staggered out of the house and into the night, deserting revenge in favor of safety.

Teary-eyed, Tobyn crawled to Ara's side. He pressed his good fingers to her wrist and listened with an ear pressed to her chest. He heard a beat, barely, and wept in relief. His mind searched for a way to help her, but every thought returned to blood, his and hers.

If vampires could heal themselves in the blink of an eye, perhaps they could also heal others. Ara needed blood; she needed strength. He believed that he had both. Without a second thought, he slashed his wrist with his scorched knife and let the scarlet potion wash over her gaping wound. The tears obscured his vision, so he could not see the healing that his blood brought. Her skin and the flesh beneath it grew together, folded and became whole until no mark remained.

"Ara?" he whispered, touching her pale, lax face. There was no response. "Ara?!"

Sobbing now, afraid of losing her and aware of only one impulse to prevent that, he reopened his self-inflicted wound and pressed his bloody wrist to her parted lips. She did not react as the fluid filled her mouth, and he stroked her neck to make her swallow. She choked on the first drops but recovered swiftly, and soon she was freely taking what he offered.

"Drink," he whispered. "Oh, Christ, Ara, keep drinking!"

His voice penetrated the fog, and she obeyed, taking his blood in a delirious ritual of lips and tongue. He pressed his Gift on her, feeling her accept it wholeheartedly until he began to falter. She was greedy. He pushed her away with some difficulty, and she lay gasping in the ecstasy of feeding.

Tobyn could see the pulse in her throat, could hear the deep thrum of her heart. She seemed to glow with life and blood, and he could feel his own fangs descending, stretching into place in answer to his shrieking thirst. His last conscious act was to hurl himself out of the house to do his hunting away from his vulnerable sister.

Instinct owned him now. Scenting blood on the wind, hissing at shadows like a giant cat, he belonged to the thirst, to the Other that was his vampire half. In less than a minute, he killed a neighbor's wife. Another minute, and he killed again. Sanity did not return until he let fall the body of his third victim. Moaning in horror at himself, he backed away, his wide eyes seeing nothing but the husk-like corpse before him.

"*Ay, Dios*," he cried. "*¿Que soy?*"

Isabella stepped gingerly over the threshold of 13 Rue de Gallette. She could smell blood, burnt flesh, and the fear and anger of a fight. In the corner, locked in deep unconsciousness, was Araminah, lying in a stained heap. The Spanish vampire gathered the gypsy woman into her arms and carried her to the bed.

//What's happened here?// asked her companion from the doorway, his blue eyes full of concern.

//I don't know. Something calamitous.// Isabella arranged Ara comfortably on the pillow. *//There is a sweetness to this girl's breath.//*

//Where is the brother?//

//I'll find him.// She patted his broad shoulder. *//Stay with her, Tristan.//*

She found Tobyn crouched in an alley beside his kill, sobbing and cradling his hand. It was outwardly whole, but vampire burns went deep, and the pain still roared. He heard her coming and knew her for another vampire, but in his despondent state he did not care if he lived or died. He watched her turn the corner, then his eyes were drawn inexorably down to the morbid scene beside him and his crying continued in earnest.

"Oh, *cariño*," she sighed, kneeling beside him. He did not move when she put her hand on his forearm. "Tobyn."

He turned miserable eyes to her, then leaned into her embrace. Against her chest, he moaned, "Oh, terrible..."

She held him and stroked his back in comfort. "Shh, *cariño*, *mi amo*, hush." He sobbed into her arms, and she pulled him tighter until he regained a little control. He trembled and still wept quietly, but his wracking sobs subsided. Their eyes met, and she told him, "Come with me, Tobyn, and I'll take care of you. Come with me to a place where you'll be safe."

Unable to think of anything but his weariness and appalling guilt, he bowed to what seemed superior logic and followed where she led.

Twenty-Four

Ara hovered in fever for weeks while Tobyn sat silent guard at her side. The infusion of her brother's vampire blood had healed her wounds and kept her alive, but she had been so weakened by Dumas' attack that recovery was slow. There were times when delirium took her, and she would cry out in the grip of some violent nightmare, but mostly she was still, silent, and so very pale that Tobyn feared he still might lose her.

While he worried, he had recovering of his own to do. Although his hand bore no scars from the terrible burns it had received, it still pained him in the night and doubly so when struck by the light of the sun. He wore gloves now constantly, guarding his hand against sunshine as jealously as he guarded his eyes. He had no desire to be sun sick, or to weaken to the point where the thing within him could gain control again.

Tobyn suffered his share of troubled sleep during the dark days of Ara's convalescence. He would dream-remember what it had been like to steal life in liquid form until the soul attached to the blood snapped with a shrill scream. In his dreams, he was once more the rampaging monster, controlled by the thirst within, unable to stop or mitigate the damage done by his primal need. He seized victims, drained them, felt their hearts shudder and break, and every one of them wore Ara's face when he finally let them fall. He would awaken, shaking, from his nightmare and hurry to his sister's bedside, anxious for a sign that she still lived. Only when he saw her breathing and heard her pulse would he relax, return to his own bed, and be caught up in nightmares once more.

The worst dark visions were the ones that came during his compulsory rest at daybreak. For those three hours when he was as helpless as a moth in a cocoon, unable to move or wake, he could find no respite from his dreams. They would pursue him through the dark tunnels in his mind until finally sleep released him and he could escape with a desperate cry.

Isabella watched over them all the time, guarding their weakness and trying to pull Tobyn out of his sullen silence. She sat with him at Ara's bedside and talked with him from dusk to dawn, taking only the briefest pause to feed in the town outside the manor walls. Tobyn fed as well, but sparingly, accepting the 'donations' made by the staff of the old house where they stayed. He had to keep the monster within him mollified, keep it under control. He would not allow it to gain the upper hand again.

The donors and the house in Nice belonged to Isabella's friend, the companion who had helped her take in the twins as he had helped her with Duncan McIntyre. His name was Tristan of Carmaugh, and he was very old. He glowed with power when Tobyn looked at him, and that halo made him almost painfully beautiful to look upon, almost like an angel from a cathedral window. Isabella claimed that Tristan had been born to a Roman father and a Celtic mother, and that he had seen the Saxons take Great Britain for their own. Tobyn had no idea who Saxons were, but Isabella seemed impressed, so he showed Tristan the utmost respect.

August's sultry heat was beginning to give way to September when Ara finally opened her eyes in the cool velvet of early evening and actually saw her brother at her side. She tried to speak, but her throat and tongue were thick and dry. Isabella appeared in her line of vision, holding a crystal goblet full of water.

"Drink this," she urged quietly, holding the glass for the weak mortal woman in the bed. She encouraged Ara to take several swallows before she sat back, disappearing from her patient's sight once more.

"Tobyn," Ara whispered, her voice rusty with disuse.

He took her hand in his and kissed her pale fingers. "I'm here."

"Are you hurt? Dumas—"

"Shh. I'm all right." He squeezed her hand. "We're both safe. Dumas got his nose slapped, and now we're with Isabella and her friend Tristan."

"Tristan." She licked her cracked lips. "I don't know the name."

"He's a good man," he said, glancing at his Spanish friend. "I trust him. Besides, I've got Isabella to watch my back. Now hush, darling. You're still very weak and you should sleep."

She sighed. "I've slept so much..."

"Sleep." The timbre of his voice changed, became more soothing, and he silently pulsed with energy that enticed her heart to follow its slower rhythm. He massaged her forehead and temples. "Sleep."

She didn't need much convincing. Within moments, Ara was oblivious to the world at large. Tobyn gently kissed her brow, then slipped from the room in Isabella's wake.

"She'll be just fine," the noblewoman said. "The brush with Dumas frightened her, but she'll recover perfectly."

"And then what?" he asked, the silence of his bedside vigil broken. "She took blood from me. What will happen if she starts to Change?"

"Then she Changes, and there are two of your kind in the world."

"What if she's something different, too? What if she ends up being one-of-a-kind, not like me, and not like the rest of you?"

She sighed. "Tobyn, I can't say what will happen in the future. Like all the rest of us, you can only wait and see. You are a special case, and wholly unknown. Who can say what will happen with her? Perhaps your sister won't Change at all. You don't know. I don't know." She shook her head. "No one will know until it happens, whatever it is. Now, come. Let's tell Tristan that his guest will live."

They found him on the lawn, throwing sticks for his dogs, bouncy and excited creatures who never failed to get on Tobyn's nerves. The old vampire, tall and blond and handsome, turned to face them, his sad-looking blue eyes full of questions.

"Araminah woke," Isabella announced, "and she seems to be doing well."

"Then she will recover," he said, satisfied. "I'm very pleased. And how are you tonight, Tobyn?"

"Well."

The gypsy's flat tone amused Tristan. "And worried sick, too, eh?" He shook his head. "Don't be so nervous, my friend. Everything will work out, because it always does."

Isabella looked up from patting one of the dogs. "How is Duncan?"

"Much improved, I am happy to say. He's out hunting even now. When his strength is up, he'll be traveling to the New World. I argued against so long a journey, but he would hear none of it. My grandson is a very stubborn vampire, 'Bella, and he won't be kept down for long."

"'Grandson?'" Tobyn echoed, puzzled.

"In a non-literal sense, yes. Or I suppose it's literal, too, in a manner of thinking. I created Marita, who created Duncan."

Isabella smirked. "We all have lapses of taste."

"Well," the blond shrugged, "I guess we do, at that. I'm told that your tastes will soon be fascinated."

The Spanish woman laughed. "Oh?"

"Yes. My house matron informs me that a band of Spanish gypsies is traveling this way from the coast."

Tobyn poked at a rock in the ground, listening but not overly interested in what he heard. Spanish gypsies were plentiful, and he'd been away for a long time. Still, he wondered sometimes about the people he'd left behind, and he'd not forgotten Antonio's treachery. He was just so far from them now, and not just in distance. It made him almost homesick, and he suddenly wanted very much to spy on some Rom and vicariously relive his golden days.

"I don't suppose this house matron of yours said which band it was," Tobyn said at last, scarcely daring to hope.

Tristan chuckled. "To Marie, all gypsy bands are the same. She did say that it was one of several heading through this part of France. They're following festivals."

"I'll have to take a look," Isabella said. "I love to watch the Romany. They're such interesting people. Tobyn, would you like to come along with me?"

"I don't think so." He offered her a smile. "You go ahead. I've seen *kumpania* before."

She did not believe him, clearly, but whether she doubted his indifference or his reasons for it he didn't know. She only nodded once and Sent to him, *//We'll see.//*

"Isabella tells me that you want to go to England," Tristan said, tossing another stick for his pets to chase.

"That's right. I had booked transport on the night Dumas attacked, but the ship we were to be on has already left Calais."

"Why England?"

Tobyn shrugged. "It's away from the Continent, and I thought it would be relatively safe from the Prime. That's vital, especially now that Ara has been hurt."

"I understand completely," the taller man nodded. "No doubt England would be safer than France, but you must remember that it's not completely isolated. Roger of Huntingdon is English, don't forget."

"Let's just say that I've run out of hiding places in France," Reyes said testily.

"If it's hiding places you want, I know just the spot." He flung the dogs' toy once again. "In fact, I'll give it to you. I have a home in County Kerry, Ireland, that could be comfortable for you. You could take Araminah there and wait out the storm. If she does Change, Ireland would offer her a peaceful place to do it." He threw another stick, and another pet scampered after it. "The house is large but unstaffed. I could leave you the necessary coin to hire a dependable staff and keep the place running, if you like."

Tobyn considered the offer through narrowed eyes. "Why are you doing this?"

"Because I like you."

His *chovihano* senses clattered. "Liar."

Carmaugh smiled and sighed, a strange bittersweet combination. "All right, then, obligation. I take care of my family."

"How am I your family?"

"You are every bit as much my grandson as Duncan McIntyre. I created Michel Dumas. He was my nightchild many years ago."

Tobyn snorted. "Another of your little lapses in taste?"

"You could say that."

"And now you feel duty-bound to look after the ones your—what was it? Nightchild?—leaves behind." He crossed his arms. "Or maybe it's guilt that drives you. Which is it, 'grandfather?'"

"In all truthfulness, it may be both." He turned away. "I hold myself responsible for the abuses my children make of their powers, and that includes making restitution when necessary. Isabella has told me the circumstances surrounding your creation, and I know that my son has done you a great injustice. It was an act made possible only by the abilities that I gave to him. In an extended view, the damage done to you was started by my own hand." He met Tobyn's frank gaze. "That is why I've made you this offer. Duty and guilt, perhaps. Moral obligation, most definitely."

Tobyn smirked. "Ethical for a monster, aren't you?"

"Perhaps. And I do not consider myself a monster." He smiled sweetly. "What do you say, my friend?"

"I say that ethics are overrated, but I accept your offer of the house anyway. After all, who am I to refuse a gift?"

The reply seemed to gratify him. Carmaugh took a deep breath, then let it out in a rush. "Thank you, Tobyn. I'll arrange passage for you and Araminah to Ireland as soon as she is strong enough to travel."

"Good. I don't know when that will be, but I do know that a wait will only help. I'll gamble with many things, but her life is not one of them."

"Quite understandable. Let me know when you think she'll be ready." He thumped one of his dogs amiably, and the animal responded with wild tail-wagging. "Until that time, please consider my home to be yours. No one will dare to assault you under my roof. Not even Michel Dumas."

～⚞⚟～

Tobyn returned to the house after a long silence, leaving Tristan and Isabella to their casual conversation. His feet were leaden as he walked down the entrance hall, listening to the distant scraping of his footsteps echoing minutely from the tiles. He was so tired. By rights, he was only twenty-four years old, but already he felt as though he'd walked the world for centuries. An unaccustomed sadness was creeping over him now, and it oppressed him. He did not like having innocent blood on his hands. The weight of his victims hung around his neck like a stone, and he could think of no way to rid himself of the terrible knowledge of his crimes. How could he atone for what he'd done?

Thirst prodded him blankly like an afterthought. Ordinarily, he would ignore it, but he was so afraid of losing his grip on reality...with heavy steps and a heavier heart, he went to where Tristan's donors kept their rooms.

He knocked on the door of one Madame le Brey, a matron and mother who had provided for him twice before. There was a hesitation, then the door was opened by her teenaged son, Philipe. The boy stepped aside to give Tobyn access to the room, his brown eyes full of knowledge of what the visitor wanted and yet utterly devoid of fear.

"Where is Madame le Brey?" the vampire asked quietly, his French suffering beneath his Spanish Rom accent.

"She's gone to see the gypsies and have her fortunes told. She won't be back until tomorrow." Philipe raised his chin. "None of the woman donors are here, Monsieur Gemini."

Tobyn had to smile at the name the youth had used. He'd introduced himself as Tobyn Gemini just to get used to the new tag, but it still felt strange. In his heart, he supposed that he would always be a Reyes. Sighing, he said, "Well, then, I suppose there's no reason for me to stay."

Philipe held up a hand to stop him. "*Monsieur*, I can help you. I'm strong and healthy, and I'm not afraid."

Tobyn considered the young man before him. With time, he would grow into a truly handsome man, dark and well-muscled. Already, his body was athletic and his scent ached with life. "How old are you, Philipe?"

"Old enough."

"How old?"

"Sixteen."

Almost a man, but not quite. What would Madame le Brey think about her only son offering himself as a snack for a vampire? Thirst touched him again, this time with the threat of growth, canceling all moral considerations. While he healed, his body demanded more blood than it would ordinarily need. He shuddered. Better to take the boy gently now than to murder him later.

With a husky whisper, Tobyn extended his hand. "Come here."

Philipe came willingly, sedately, neither rushing nor hesitating at the last moment. Tobyn squeezed his hand, his fingers interlacing with the boy's, and pulled him into a tight embrace. He guided them to the bed and pushed Philipe back, stretching out along the length of the young body. LeBrey wrapped his arms around Tobyn and closed his eyes, waiting.

The vampire touched the long lashes on Philipe's cheek with a trembling fingertip. *I won't hurt you...* "Have you done this before?" he breathed into the nearest ear.

"Yes." The word was a sigh, full of pleasures both remembered and anticipated. "Twice."

Tobyn petted Philipe's soft, dark hair. "Three is the charm."

He kissed the boy's soft lips once, tenderly, before he shifted his attention to the vibrant pulse point in his throat. Desire overwhelmed Tobyn, and Philipe did not protest; he clung to him instead, crying out softly as he was taken. It was not a cry of pain, for which Tobyn was endlessly grateful. Drinking the heady wine of the young, passion-filled blood, he quieted the nagging voice that had brought him here. The pleasure he felt was shared by his donor, echoed wave for wave, which was as Tobyn wanted it to be.

When it was over, Philipe kissed his hand. "I could never fear your kind, Monsieur Gemini. No one can convince me that vampires are horrible things."

Tobyn touched his donor's cheek. "Don't be so certain, *querido*. At the heart, we are all monsters, and we are all dangerous."

"Not you."

"All of us. Never trust one of us, Philipe. Not completely."

Without another word, he slipped from the room.

~~⚬~~

Isabella rejoined him at Ara's bedside a scant few hours from sunrise. She pulled up her customary chair and sat quietly for a long moment.

//I presume you went to see the gypsies,// he said to her, his command of this brand of telepathy now absolute.

//Yes. The dancing was exultant.//

//And?//

She knew what he wanted to hear. *//They were the Sevilliano band.//*

He sighed, not knowing whether he was disappointed or relieved. *//Any news of the Carago band?//*

//They will be here by week's end. Your Sela has remarried.//

The news stung, and he strove to hide it. *//No surprise. It's been two years, almost.//* He brushed a stray curl from Ara's eyes. *//Who was it?//*

Isabella considered the wisdom of telling the truth, but she'd always been a terrible liar, even when she wasn't being betrayed by speaking mind to mind. *//Your uncle Antonio.//*

Rage exploded within him and it was all he could do to remain silent. Antonio! Surely this wasn't Sela's idea. She'd hated the man almost as much as Tobyn had. How many Rom had Antonio had to sell out to buy Carago's daughter? But perhaps it was Carago's integrity that had been bought and sold.

//Tobyn? Are you all right?//

He faced her, anger glowing in his eyes. *//That all depends on what I see when the Carago band gets here.//*

⌒᷒᷒᷒

By the end of the week, Ara was sleeping only her usual hours, eating well, and gaining strength. She was still pale and tired easily, but she was no longer really frail, and during the day she walked through the house with Tobyn as her guide. There was only so much to see within a house, though, however palatial it may be; finally, she turned to Tobyn over her lunch.

"Let's go outside today. I need some fresh air."

His brow puckered in concern. "Are you sure you're ready for that? It's an awful lot of exertion..."

"I'm up to it, and if I get tired, I'll stop to rest." She pushed her bowl aside. "Please, Tobyn. I need to feel the air around me again."

He looked into her green eyes and relented. Taking her hand in his, he brought her fingers to his lips and pressed a kiss on her knuckles. "All right. Give me a chance to get ready and we'll go."

While Tobyn collected his low-brimmed hat and his cloak, Marie, Tristan's house matron, helped Ara comb and pin her hair. "If you like, I can call the coach for you. It's a long walk, and not very safe, especially with the gypsies in town, and..."

Ara froze, staring into the eyes that were shown her by the mirror. "Gypsies?"

"Yes, wild and colorful things from Spain. They're dangerous, thronging in the marketplace, but still it's better than any bazaar I've ever seen." She coiled Ara's dark curls into a neat twist at the back of her head. "You can enjoy yourself there, if you're careful."

Slowly, she asked, "Does Tobyn know?"

Marie paused, her hands on Ara's shoulders. "Yes, I believe Tristan told him a few days ago."

"I see." She tapped her fingertip on the vanity table. "Thank you, Marie."

"Oh, any time," she said, not completely understanding. "I'd give anything to have curls like yours."

Tobyn appeared in the doorway as Marie left. His hat was pulled down to shade his vulnerable eyes, and his gloves were tight over his hands. "Are you ready? We can walk down through the garden."

"I want to go to town." She rose to face him. "Marie is sending the coach for us."

Their eyes met, and automatically, Tobyn Sent, *//What are you up to?//*

For the first time since his Change, Ara heard him. Her eyes widened, and she stared at him before tentatively Sending back, *//What did you say?//*

He smiled uncertainly. *//My God...I'm actually getting through...Ara, something's different.//*

She nodded. *//Do you think this means I might be Changing, too?//*

//I don't know.//

Aloud, she said, "There's no other explanation." They looked at each other silently. "Are you happy?"

"I don't know," he answered honestly. "I'm afraid for you."

"Then that means we're still two of a kind." She took a deep breath. "We'll see what we see, I suppose. There's no way to reverse it. Even if there were, I'm not sure I'd want to."

Marie came into the room, her face alight with a brilliant smile. "The coach is ready, dears. Have a good time in town."

Tobyn slipped on his smile like a mask. "Well, I think I'd better get a bit more spending money."

~⚏⚏⚏~

The marketplace was loud and vivid with the riotous mix of French merchants and Romany visitors. Tobyn led Ara through the crowd, her arm in his hand as he gently guided and guarded her amid the press of people. The babble of their native tongue was both soothing and aggravating, and they simultaneously tried to watch for familiar faces and yet remain unseen.

Ara, already tiring but trying not to show it, went to look at fabric in a laden booth while Tobyn scanned the crowd. He saw a few of the Carago band's peripheral members near one of the winestands, picking pockets and throwing dice, and the knowledge that their former *kumpania* was in town did not please him despite his recent bouts with nostalgia. His last memories of the Carago group were less than cheery.

His sister led him from booth to booth, her slender energies focused on spending his money. Trying to call Tobyn's attention back to her and away from the watchful Carago Rom, she held up a swath of midnight-blue fabric.

"What do you think of this?"

"It's nice," he said noncommittally. He stared at the winestand and the fragile-looking gypsy woman selling fortunes there. *It couldn't possibly be her.*

"Tobyn?"

"Look over there," he said, nodding in the woman's direction. "Is that Sela?"

Ara glanced over. "No, it couldn't be. Too thin, too pale."

"Look again. Are you sure? I could swear..."

To humor him, she looked. What she saw greatly disturbed her. "My God...what's happened to her? She never used to be like that." She shook her head. "I can't believe it. All her fire's gone."

Tobyn sighed deeply, looking at his wife's gaunt and shadowed face. She looked emaciated, and the fearful gleam in her eyes reminded him of a dog that had received a few too many kicks. The slender arms that flashed in the sun as she spread out her tarot cards bore scars that he could not remember.

He forced himself to turn away from the ruin that Sela had become. "If you want that cloth, then buy it. It would look wonderful on you." He handed her the money with a smile they both knew was false. "Keep looking, too. See if there's anything else you want. I'll be right back."

She didn't need to be *chovihani* to predict what he was going to do. "Tobyn, don't go over there. You'll only make matters worse."

"I have to talk to her."

"Leave her." She shook her head. "Don't flaunt yourself in front of her when she's got no way to get out of the *kumpania*. You'll hurt her." She reached out for him. "Leave her some self-respect."

"What makes you think she has any left?" He pulled away. "I have to talk to her."

"Tobyn..."

The gypsy vampire walked away from his twin's objections. Careful to keep his face in shadow, he approached Sela's seat. She barely spared him a glance when one of the men who stood around her, undoubtedly part of a guard battalion sent to keep Antonio's property chaste, nudged her shoulder and muttered in her ear.

"Fortune, *m'sieur*?" She offered him a glimpse of her cards. "Learn your fate?"

He settled into the chair that stood opposite her. Did she really not recognize him? Did fine French clothes make so much difference? Barely able to make a sound, he whispered, "*Oui, madame.*"

Sela spread the cards with quick motions of her bony wrists, the thin white lines of scars on her skin gleaming in the daylight. He wanted to weep.

"You are a man of power, *m'sieur*, deep power, and not of a worldly kind. Are you a soldier? I see war and fighting in your future—" Something in the cards, perhaps a true resonance that she hadn't expected to find in a sold reading, made her look up at him then, and in her dark eyes there danced a spark of recognition. Sela, breathless for a moment, gaped, then struggled to continue. "But you will be victorious, I think, in whatever fighting you might do."

He eased a gold coin to her, and their fingers touched. It was all he could do not to grasp her hand and pull her to him. She glanced up at her escorts, then retracted her hand. Tobyn slipped her another coin.

"No," she barked, her voice rough with tears as she tried to hold her head high. "No more money. No more reading." Over the objections of her keepers, she rose and packed the cards away. "No more today."

Before he could say a word, she and her entourage had swept away. He followed her departure with his eyes, only stopping when his gaze fell onto Ara's knowing expression.

They returned to Tristan's house not long after Sela had brusquely ended the fortune-telling session. Tobyn was silent for most of the ride, staring at the seams on his gloves. Ara let him brood, understanding her twin. She knew that Tobyn loved Sela very much, which was as it should be. While Ara was Tobyn's lover and often jealously possessive, she was his sister first of all. There would be other lovers for them both, which was how she wanted it to be, for other loves would never come between the twin-link they shared, even loves as deep and as currently painful as Tobyn's was for Sela.

Their link was alive now with the echoes of her brother's distress. Ara wanted to help him, but she didn't know what to do except leave him alone and let him come to her when he was ready.

She hoped it would be enough.

The next afternoon found Tobyn back in the marketplace, hunting through the pockets of gypsies until he found the little kiosk where Sela had set up shop for the day. She blanched when she saw him coming, but this time she did not run away. Her nervous hands rapidly shuffled the cards as he approached.

One of the burly Hidalgo men stopped him, and Tobyn palmed a coin to him, buying passage to the fortune teller whose shadowed eyes were made darker by new bruises. He seated himself across from her.

"Tell me my fortune," he said. "I want to know about romance."

She hesitated, but threw the reading to the cloth-covered box before her. "There are two women in your life, both of whom you love." She took a deep breath and examined the cards. "One is very beautiful, very strong. She is your sister. You are with her?"

He smiled faintly. "Not today, but yes."

"You are...very close."

"Sometimes."

Sela pursed her lips. "The other woman is your wife." She waved a hand at the card with its picture of a woman in rags begging at an opulent window. "You can see how she is."

"I'm sorry for that," he said sincerely. Hidalgo peered at him, suddenly interested in the course of this reading.

"It's not your doing, exactly," she said, laying meaningless cards. "What has become of her is your fault only indirectly."

"But it remains my fault."

"And hers. She made...bad choices."

He crossed his arms and crushed his fingernails into his palms in an effort to keep from touching her. "And what does my wife think of me?"

Sela's cards answered with The Lovers. She looked up at him, meeting his eyes rather too boldly for their present company. "She loves you very much."

⁓෨෴ල෴

Tobyn waited until Ara was asleep that night before he sought out Isabella among the roses in the garden. The Spanish lady watched him coming, her face open with expectation. When he reached her side, he said without preamble, "I need to go to where the Carago band is camped."

She nodded, not in the least surprised by his request. "Shall I call the coach, or would you like me to take you there?"

"I want to fly."

Opening her arms, she nodded. "Hold on to me, then."

He wrapped his arms around her waist, and then they were airborne, streaking silently over the mansion and the town below. The camp appeared beneath them quicker than Tobyn would have thought, and they could see the gypsies milling about by their fires. There was music and dancing, and even from their great height Tobyn could hear the guitars and smell the liquor.

He picked out his uncle's *vardo* by the protection symbol painted on the roof. *//There,//* he told Isabella, flashing her the mental image of Antonio's home. *//Quietly.//*

//Is there any other way?//

She dropped him, feather light, on the shadowed side of the wagon. He thanked her silently, and she retreated, ready to come to him in a heartbeat if he should need her. Tobyn crept to the end of the *vardo* and peered around the corner. Antonio was dancing by the fire, his attention away from his wagon, and Tobyn took advantage of his distraction. He bolted into the *vardo*, his vampire steps falling without a sound.

Inside the wagon, Sela was sleeping, her face stained with old tears. Her slender hands were wrapped around a scrap of fabric, almost desperate in their grip as she curled on her side, her dark hair spilling over her shoulders. Tobyn closed the door and locked it, then went over to kneel by her side.

He touched her arm with gentle fingers and whispered, "Sela?"

She jerked awake, flinching as though she expected to be struck at any moment. He grabbed her hands and shushed her. "It's all right! Sela, shh!" She calmed somewhat; at least her breathing slowed to something less than a pant.

"Tobyn..." Her eyes filled with tears, and she touched his face. "Is it really you?"

"It's really me." He gathered her into his arms and she was skeletal beneath his hands. "My God, Sela, what has he done to you?"

She tried to answer, but could only weep onto his shoulder, her hands stroking his hair. "Oh, Tobyn, Tobyn...I've missed you so much!" She pulled herself together a little more, then sobbed, "I thought I'd never see you again. Oh, it's been horrible!"

He held her tight, adding his own tears to hers. "I thought you wouldn't want me."

"Not want you? Tobyn, I would die for you."

He gripped her hands. "Where is your father, that he let this happen to you?"

"Antonio," she said simply. "He sold him to the burgermeister in Hamburg for a murder that another man committed. He was hanged in the middle of the town, and buried at a crossroads. My husband leads this *kumpania* now."

"For God's sake, Sela, why did you marry him?"

Anger crept into her eyes. "Who else would have me? I was dishonored by what you and Ara did. I was untouchable because I had been married to a *mullo*. For months, women would hide their children from me." Her voice caught in her throat. "And he threatened my father...as if I saved him!" She looked away, bitter and torn. Her hands pulled at the cloth she still held. "And I...I was...pregnant."

He sank back, his eyes cloudy. "Pregnant?"

"Your daughter," she said, gasping around her tears. She displayed the tiny shirt that she had been gripping. "She was conceived just before you left, and she was born in Madrid."

"Daughter," he echoed, stunned. He could barely hear what Sela was telling him around his shock.

"She was beautiful," she sighed. "Black hair, great dark eyes...just beautiful. But because she was born with a caul, and because she was born with two teeth, and because she was born of you, the *kumpania* wanted to kill her. Antonio wanted to dash her brains out the instant she was placed in my arms." She shook with remembered rage. "I wouldn't let them touch my baby. I wouldn't let him kill her."

"Where is she?" Tobyn asked, his voice barely above a whisper. "Where is she now?"

"I gave her to the priest in Madrid. He promised to give her to a well-off woman, a barren woman, to raise as her own. I...I handed her over late in the night, and then I came back to the *kumpania*, and I never saw little Alicia again." She broke into sobs once more. "She was only hours old when I had to give her up!"

Tobyn clutched her, letting her cry. His head was swimming. *What priest in Madrid? What church?* Surely, there must be a way for him to find his child. He rocked Sela as she continued to talk.

"Antonio was waiting for me," she sobbed against his shoulder. "He wanted to know where the baby had gone, and that he wanted to send her back to hell. I told him to go there himself. That's when the beatings started."

"Sela...my poor Sela," he whispered, clutching her. "I didn't know."

"I wanted to die, but I was afraid that if I did, then you would come for me, and I would miss it. I've waited for you for so long." She drew a ragged breath. "I've been through so much."

"I'm so sorry..."

"But now you're here. Oh, Tobyn, I've missed you."

"I've missed you, too." He held her face in his hands, then kissed her gently. "I love you."

Sela sighed, tears sparkling on her lashes. "No one's been so sweet to me since you left. Antonio doesn't know how to kiss."

Taking her hand, he rose to his feet. "Come on. It's time I took you from this."

She gladly dressed to follow him outside. As she tied back her hair, Tobyn called for Isabella. *//We need to go back now.//*

Her voice returned teasingly. *//"We?"//*

//Just come here!//

Sela tied a scarf over her head, then turned to him. "I'm ready."

Antonio's voice rose from outside the *vardo*. "Open the door, woman! It's time to be a wife tonight!"

Under cover of the masculine laughter outside, Tobyn moved to stand against the *vardo* wall beside the door. He nodded to Sela, who quickly tossed aside her scarf and opened the door for her new husband. Antonio reeled in, reeking of wine, and slammed the door behind himself to the cheering of his retreating friends. His bleary gaze was fixed on Sela so narrowly that he never saw Tobyn in the darkness.

"Come here, bitch," Antonio growled. "Bend over and let me take you like the dog you are."

Tobyn drew his knife and sprang upon his uncle's back. One arm was tight around Antonio's throat, and he pressed the point into the older man's side as he hissed, "Remember me, uncle? I think we have a score or two to settle."

Even through his haze, he knew the voice. Suddenly frozen in fear, he husked, "Tobyn?"

His nephew pushed harder with the knife, slowly penetrating Antonio's skin. "That's right. You do remember. I'm honored." His anger called his fangs down, and he let them come. "You are the worst sort of animal, Antonio. Worse than a criminal, you are a traitor to your family and to your kind! Sell out other Rom, will you? Murder my father? Try to kill my child? Rape and beat my wife?"

His uncle whimpered drunkenly. "Mercy, please...I beg you—"

"You beg me for mercy? What mercy have you ever shown anyone?" He pushed the knife further in, enraged beyond recall. Antonio groaned in pain. "I should kill you slowly like you deserve. I should take your blood in as much agony as I can cause you."

"Tobyn, please!"

"But I don't want to touch you for that long. You sicken me." With a wrench, he snapped Antonio's neck and dropped him to the floor. He pulled his *kris* knife free and wiped its curved edges clean on his dying uncle's shirt, then held out his hand to Sela, who watched him, pale and shaken. "Come on, Sela. We're going."

Frightened by the fangs and the silver in his eyes, shocked by the murder she had seen him commit, Sela obeyed with a silent flinch. Tobyn took her hand and pulled her out of the *vardo* as Isabella arrived. She glanced between Tobyn's revealed vampire nature and the frightened woman at his side, then opened her arms to them without question or comment.

"Let's go."

⟨≈⟩

Sela slept deeply in the bed next to Ara while Tobyn kept silent watch over the room, pacing from door to window and back again like a sentry. He had much to think about.

A daughter. Somehow it seemed unreal; he'd never even considered that he might have fathered a child somewhere. To know that he had, to know her name but nothing else, filled him with bittersweet sadness, pride laced with regret. He would have liked to have seen his child born.

But what manner of child would this Alicia be? He had been almost completely Changed when she was conceived. How much of his new vampire nature had been passed along? He had learned that vampirism was a mutable condition. If he had become some new breed of immortal, then couldn't the same have happened to his daughter? Or perhaps she was caught between the two natures, not vampire but not exactly human, suspended in an eternal half-life. What if she was something entirely different, neither human nor vampire, something painful? And as the Change had worked on his mind to make him homicidal, had the Changed elements from him created an unbalanced child?

He wanted to weep. Madrid was too far away for him to visit before Tristan's ship left for Ireland, and he and his two female companions had to be on board. He had no wish to weather another attack by the Brethren, or to stay too long in one place and risk discovery by Dumas. He could send a letter to the Spanish priest who had taken Alicia, if only he knew the man's name...and how to write it. Almost absently, he made a mental note to do something about his illiteracy. It was becoming a handicap, and Tobyn disliked being at a disadvantage.

And if he did find his child, what then? Could he really countenance taking her away from the parents who had been raising her, ostensibly rich ones, if the priest was to be believed? Tobyn was not a devout man, but he believed in the integrity of men of the cloth. Priests, he thought, did not lie. Somewhere, Alicia was being raised in privilege. Could he take her from that, from a safe place, and put her in the middle of a brewing vampire war? He didn't even want Ara or Sela involved in this fight, but they were far more able to take care of themselves than an infant would be. If he claimed Alicia now, he would do her nothing but disservice.

There was nothing to be done about it tonight. But before he could lose track of her forever, he would return to Madrid and find her, if only to see her one time. First, though, he had escape to Ireland to think about, Ara to see through her Change, and Sela to heal. It was more than enough to keep his mind occupied without worrying about Alicia.

He stopped pacing before the window and watched the eastern sky lighten. Sunrise was coming with weights upon his limbs, and he could feel himself sliding into the inevitable, helpless, but exact three hours of death-like sleep that he could not fight. His thoughts slowed, and all pondering and questioning faded in the coming daylight. It was time for him to sleep. He felt that he had somehow earned it.

Tobyn knew nothing about ships.

As he peered at their waiting transport from the shadow of his hatbrim, he couldn't decide whether he was excited, pleased, appalled, or disappointed. The little vessel bobbed at her moorings, her single mast poking at the sky while her crew of five scurried about and made ready for the voyage.

Beside him, Sela, much improved by long rest, regular meals, and tenderness, shook her head. "Will there be food? What are we going to do about cooking fires?"

Ara added her own question. "How long is this going to take?"

"The answer to all of your questions is: I don't know."

"Some help you are," his twin teased.

"Do I look like a sailor to you? Spare me." He sighed and picked up the heaviest of their traveling cases. "Well, let's get this over with."

The first mate of the *Kerry Belle* helped them aboard, then solemnly welcomed them in formal tones before dispatching the cabin boy to prepare their rooms below.

"Tristan said to put you all together in the captain's cabin for this trip," the man explained, his French heavily accented with brogue and difficult for Tobyn to understand.

"Thank you," he offered, sounding and feeling at a loss.

"Garridan here will show you the way. The captain will see you after we're away."

He had few words with which to reply, it seemed. "Thank you."

Garridan, the cabin boy, smiled and led the way, his steps light. He kept up a constant stream of chatter in English, most of which went completely over Tobyn's head, and flirted shamelessly with the two women, neither of whom understood a word he said. Once he had led them to their door, he left them with a big smile and a jaunty salute.

Sela watched him go. "Talks a lot, doesn't he?"

"I wonder what he was saying."

"Well, don't ask me," Tobyn said crossly. "It was just noise to my ears. Hopefully, the captain speaks a civilized tongue. Let's just try to get comfortable."

The cabin had one room that smelled of whisky and tobacco. A table with four chairs, liberally strewn with maps and charts, stood beneath the single oil lamp that hung from the ceiling by a peg. The bed was large and soft, its down-filled mattress inviting, and it was blessedly free from stains or vermin. A few interesting knickknacks were scattered around the room, but for the most part it was bare.

"I suppose it'll do," Sela pronounced. "At least it doesn't smell like sweat and dead fish."

"That's how it'll smell in a week," Tobyn promised.

Sela's dark eyes widened. "We're going to be in this tiny room for a week? All locked up like this?"

"It could be worse. Just relax," she was assured by her sister-in-law. "You never know. This could be fun. Where's your spirit of adventure?"

"I exorcised it."

"You're so boring."

Tobyn went to the single porthole and looked out at the other ships bouncing against the backdrop of stationary land. His head and stomach instantly decried the view, and he sat down with a miserable groan.

"I'm going to hate this."

Twenty-Five

Their first twelve hours at sea were a nauseating constant roll on the turbulent, wind-churned waters of the North Atlantic. Tobyn clung to the chair he was trying to sit in as the *Kerry Belle* pitched in the night, every lurch sending his stomach careening into his throat. He kept a nervous eye on the swaying oil lamp, too afraid of a sudden fire to be comfortable, but far too aware of the pressing dankness of the cabin walls to put it out.

On the bed, curling up together like sisters, Ara and Sela slept, virtually unaffected by the waves. They had dined well, enjoying the talents of the *Belle*'s masterful ship's cook, but Tobyn had been unable to touch a morsel without running to the bucket that now stood, empty and waiting, in the farthest corner of the room. The merest thought of food made him shudder, and for the hundredth time that night, he wished the trip was over.

It was well past midnight in his miserable vigil when the door shuddered beneath a solid pair of thumps. Uncertain whether those thumps had been knocks or merely the ship falling apart, Tobyn rose and staggered closer. When the sounds were repeated, he opened the door.

A tall and burly man, squarely built and dewed with sea spray, stood at the threshold, his bulk nearly obliterating the view of the corridor outside. He removed his cap and swept a meaty hand through his curly black hair, his blue eyes studying Tobyn with mild curiosity. When he smiled, he showed the long teeth of the Prime.

"Welcome aboard the *Kerry Belle*," the other vampire greeted, offering a hand with his Spanish. "I'm the captain whose room you've occupied."

Tobyn backed away and crossed his arms, trying not to look as sick as he knew he was. "I am Tobyn Gemini, and these are my companions, Araminah and Sela."

"Both Gemini?" the captain asked, his eyes lively. "Your harem, sir?"

"Hardly that, but yes, Gemini." He sat heavily on the edge of a nearby trunk. "And your name, if I might impose enough to ask?"

"Cain O'Herlighy. Come with me, if you're really what Tristan says you are." He motioned to the corridor. "I keep a supply in the hold, if you understand."

"I can't even eat real food. How am I supposed to keep blood down?" the gypsy asked, surly.

"You'll do it, because you'll have to. I don't really know about your kind, but for me, this vampire half has its own agenda, and it's very self-preserving." He put his cap back on his head. "It's not the most appetizing in the world, cold and all, but it's better than nothing, and I won't be having anyone, you or me or one of the ladies there drinking from my crew."

"The ladies aren't of my kind, or yours."

Cain studied the women on the bed, then grunted. "Hmph. Not yet, no. But I don't suppose that will last, will it? At least not for one of them. She's already a little...different, isn't she?"

Tobyn held himself impassively. "I hadn't noticed."

"Well, that's neither here nor there. They're welcome to a little nip from my bottles whenever they get the need, but if they don't, then that's all the more for us."

He moved off down the corridor, and Tobyn followed him reluctantly. The captain tugged open a hidden door that the gypsy hadn't seen during his trip down to the cabin the afternoon before, and the sickly-sweet smell of old blood rose in a cloud to meet them. Tobyn's stomach bounced in agitation, but his teeth pricked at his upper lip. Something in him was responding to that scent. He wished it would keep quiet.

Cain lead the way down a trio of rickety, haphazard steps and into the vampire equivalent of a wine cellar. In wooden racks, dozens of bottles of ruby liquid waited, gleaming in the dim light from the corridor lamps. Neither vampire needed more illumination to see the room; night vision was wonderfully increased by the Change. Cain selected a pair of bottles and tossed one to Tobyn, who barely managed to catch it in time. The cork pulled free with a sluicing pop, and Tobyn peered dubiously into the container. Cain chuckled as he took a hearty swig.

"It's cold, yes, and mixed with water, but it'll keep you fed," he told Gemini. "Human donors gave that willingly, so don't let your morality—whatever that may be—get offended. Some of us Prime do have a sense of right and wrong. Besides," he added with a smile, "I could hardly steal all of this without being caught."

Tobyn raised an eyebrow as his only comment, then took a hesitant sip. The cold blood splashed against his tongue, and shivers of disgust raced up and down his spine even as the Other spasmed with delight. Cain watched dispassionately as Tobyn's natures warred over the merits of the drink, forcing swallow after swallow down his throat.

The gypsy vampire grimaced mightily as he recorked the bottle with a shudder. "Oh, this is awful."

"You'll find it's better if you warm it by a fire," Cain suggested. "Personally, I've gotten used to it this way."

"I don't know how. Haven't you got any taste buds left, or did those die along with you?"

Cain chuckled, seemingly unflappable. "Now, don't get churlish, little one." He took another drink, then offered Tobyn a cigarette. The gypsy declined, and Cain lit up for himself, blowing a gray streak at the bottles beside him. "I don't know how it is with your kind. Do you die, as we do, or do you simply continue on?"

"We Change," Tobyn said simply; it felt strange to speak of his sort of vampire as 'we.' Concern for Ara filled him, and he tried to put it off by taking another sip.

Cain wouldn't give up. "Change how?"

"Look, captain, I'm very grateful to you for helping us this way, but I'm not fool enough to think that you're doing it for free. Both Tristan and Isabella are very rich, and I'm certain you're well paid for your pains. I am under no obligation to entertain you with my life story."

"Not even for the sake of friendship?"

"I have as many friends as I want."

"Ah, but not as many as you need." O'Herlighy crossed his arms, hugging his bottle to his chest. "You see, my little toad, you will need a great many friends to survive in the outside world, as will I, once news gets out that it was my ship that ferried you away from France. Entertaining me with your life story is the least you can do, since just knowing you is enough to get me killed these days. I want to know who I've deserted my safe harbor for."

"I'm sure Isabella and Tristan told you all about it."

"Not all. Some, granted, but not all."

With a sigh, Tobyn slid down to sit on the floor, his own supply of liquid held between his knees, and began to tell the tale.

O'Herlighy appeared only after the women were asleep each night, pulling Tobyn down into the hold for their long talks over cold blood. He told Tobyn more than Gemini told him, and it was useful information; he talked about Ireland, and what to expect of the people and the weather. He explained the best ways to exchange French and Spanish money for pounds, always a tricky business when the English and the French were at war—and the English and French seemed to always be at war. He shared the gossip of the ship, from the rumors the sailors were telling each other about their passengers to the men's opinions of Tobyn's female companions. Most valuable of all, though, he shared his knowledge of the outside world, the political forces that moved vampires of all degrees through the lands outside of Tobyn's usual range. For the first time, Tobyn heard of Russian vampires who sailed from St. Petersburg to Oslo and down into Britain, trading in valuables and humans enslaved as donors, mindless and wasted as the unfortunates in Dumas' pantry, and of the English vampire set who moved among the royalty in the court at Windsor Castle. The royal family and the aristocracy, it seemed, were well aware of their friends' special needs, and it was the very allure of the oh-so-improper and unscientific vampires that held their sect in such high esteem among the English well-to-do. Tobyn longed to see London as soon as he heard the stories, knowing that his special status would make him the toast of the town. More than anything else, Tobyn liked being the center of attention...when that attention was positive.

What he longed for most, though, was to get off of the *Kerry Belle*. If it wasn't bad enough that he was surrounded by a crew whose language he spoke only intermittently at best, his sea sickness was a constant source of complaint. His thirst, a bothersome thing that made itself doubly known in the presence of the watered-down blood, was not satisfied, and he found himself nostalgic for Tristan's employed donors. Let Cain drink the cold stuff if he liked; if Tobyn ever got an estate of his own, he swore that the first people he would hire would be men and women who would offer their throats for pay.

Tobyn's concerns were increased by his sister's behavior, as well, which was becoming more and more erratic and bizarre as time went on. By the end of their third day on the ship, Ara wandered the decks singing to herself, smiling at all of the sailors with the innocence of a child. By the end of the week, her lucid moments were few and far between, and she spent most of her time rocking in her seat and babbling about what seemed to her twin to be utter nonsense. Even mind-to-mind she was unclear on the concept of reality.

Sela stood guard over both of them, keeping Ara's wandering contained and protecting Tobyn from sunlight and the curious. She didn't have much to say, which in a way was a worry for him, too. He wondered what was going on inside her head.

They reached the port on a gray afternoon, and Tobyn couldn't leave the ship fast enough. With Sela guiding Ara firmly along, he made connections with their transportation and they were on their way. An interminable coach ride took them from the port to Tristan's waiting estate. The house was large, but not as huge as the mansions and *chateaux* Tobyn had seen in France and Italy. The rough stone walls were gray-brown and slick with mist, looking like natural outgrowths of the green land that surrounded them. The house rose against the rain-gray sky like a cliff face, its edges crumbling and indistinct where the limestone facing had fallen away from the native rock that formed the walls.

Ireland was a kaleidoscope in green through the coach windows. Every blade of grass, every leaf on every tree was a different shade, and the constant mist washed over the land, softening it, blurring edges and making everything look sleepy.

The coachman smiled to the trio as he struggled their trunks down from the top of the rack. "Welcome to the Raven's Nest," he said, speaking French that Tobyn nearly blessed him for after a full day of hearing nothing but Irish accents that lost him completely. "Tristan took the liberty of explaining your special circumstances, so everything here has been taken care of. I'm James Donnell, and I'll be to you what the Serrano family has been to Doña Isabella."

"Tobyn Gemini," he introduced himself, shaking James' hand. "Araminah Gemini and Sela Reyes."

"A pleasure, ladies," the affable Irishman nodded to them. "I'll be overseeing the household staff, hiring, paying, coordinating. You won't have a worry in the world." He grinned. "At least, not in this world."

Ara began to wander off, distracted by a sparrow, and Tobyn grabbed her skirt's waistband to pull her back. "Thank you, James," he said quietly. "We should go in."

Donnell took a heartbeat to study Araminah, his thoughts clear to the gypsy vampire. *Beautiful, but out of her mind. Too bad.* Shaking his head, the Irishman smiled to his new employer. "Follow me."

The Raven's Nest was warmer inside than Tobyn had expected it to be, and more sparsely furnished. Somehow, the relative lack of furnishings made it feel more welcoming to him; he didn't have to endure the nervousness that came with fragile riches and things he could not identify.

James built up the fire in the front hall as Sela sat Ara in a chair and fussed over her like a mother with a child. Tobyn watched them silently for a moment, then went to James' side.

"I want to have the final word on who you hire," he informed Donnell. "There are particular concerns I have that you might not understand."

"Fine," James nodded, brushing off his hands. "I thought we'd concentrate on finding a permanent cook and a few donors for you first off. Then we'll worry about maids and stable hands. Will the ladies need dressers or handmaids?"

Tobyn glanced back at his vacuously smiling sister and her solemn companion. "Maybe a nursemaid."

James followed his gaze. "What's wrong with her, if you don't mind my asking?"

"She's Changing."

"How long has she been this way?"

"Just under a week. The Change is working on her very quickly."

The Irishman scratched his neck. "This is the first time one of your kind...the first time you've created a nightchild, isn't it?"

Tobyn began to wonder exactly how free Tristan had been with his information. "Yes, it is."

"So there's no way of knowing what's going to happen."

"That's right."

James whistled softly. "We'll keep an eye on her, make sure no harm comes to her. She's in a vulnerable way, isn't she?" He indicated Sela. "What about her? You Changing her?"

"No." His quick answer brought a slow, sideways look from Sela, who turned away as soon as Tobyn noticed her attention. How could he explain that he'd never meant to start making Ara into a vampire? He doubted if James or anyone would understand. It seemed that everyone merely assumed that he was driven to overpopulate the world with his kind. Whatever drove the Prime and the Brethren, Tobyn didn't know; he only knew that there were moments when he wouldn't wish his brand of existence on anyone.

The other man clapped him on the shoulder. "Come on. I'll give you a tour of your new home."

As the men left the room, Sela sat beside Ara and listened to her incoherent babbling. She was lonely. Tobyn was with her again, and she knew that he loved her still, but she could feel the distance between them. How quick he'd been to take the name Gemini away from her! As before, her husband was more dependent, more involved with Araminah than with her. Now that Ara was becoming a night creature like Tobyn, that would be another advantage that his sister had over his wife. In time,

Tobyn and Ara would be immortal together, the laughing, incestuous king and queen of some midnight empire while Sela rotted into dust.

She closed her eyes wearily as Ara rattled about the fire. She'd come so far and endured so much, and all for nothing. For as along as Ara was around and a vampire like Tobyn, then Sela stood no chance of winning her husband back to her side where he belonged. The simple answer would be to stop Ara from Changing, but Sela could think of no way short of murder to do that, and she simply wasn't capable of taking Ara's life.

There had to be a way for her to keep Tobyn, a simple way that she could manage without strain. She just hadn't found it yet.

Time passed quickly in the sedate safety of the Raven's Nest. Tobyn turned his attention to staffing the house, employing young men and women from the area, and listening to James read the letters from Tristan and Isabella. The Prime and the Brethren were at one another's throats again, Dumas by necessity being called off of his hunt for Tobyn. The extra breathing space was greatly appreciated, for with the war at its height, Tobyn was free to learn and rest and guard over his sister's Change without fear of attack.

Sela spent her days babysitting Araminah, who seemed caught up in another world and moving among angels. Her daily babbling was increasingly made up of nonsense, and both Sela and Tobyn began to harbor fears that when the Change was over her sanity would not return. Many nights were spent in solemn conversation, trying to decide what to do if Ara's mortality fled and took her reason with it. Neither of them could countenance ending her life, although secretly Sela hoped that Tobyn would overcome that hesitation if and when the time came.

Winter in Ireland was cold and wet, with blistering winds whistling in from the sea. The weather was hard on the three Spanish-born gypsies, none of whom ventured outside the warm front hall if they could help it. But the overcast days went easy on Tobyn's eyes, and his waking daylight hours were more comfortable than any he had ever known.

Confinement indoors was warm and safe, granted, but it was also stultifyingly boring. Around her care-taker duties, Sela devoted her time and energy to learning how to run a household like the Raven's Nest smoothly and efficiently. If this was to be the life her husband would lead, then she would be a fit wife for him, able to manage all of his affairs and keep the home fires burning without incident. She learned by watching James and quizzing their new housekeeper and cook, a dour, matronly woman named Fiona Kelly. She also learned by doing. By Christmas, Sela was personally overseeing all of the elaborate holiday preparations as well as the day-to-day details of the house.

She wasn't the only one learning from their Irish hosts. Tobyn and James locked themselves away in the library for hours at a stretch, and the gypsy vampire worked hard at lessons in English, reading, writing, book keeping and politics. James had decided that if conditions were going to force Tobyn to create an empire of his own, then he had better know how to run it. To that end, the first book that Tobyn read from cover to cover in English was *The Prince* by Machiavelli. That book spoke to something deep inside of Tobyn, and his understanding of the words written so many years ago was on many levels. It was simple, really, as Gemini saw it. Be fair, but be strong. Listen to people, understand them, use them if you had to—but never abuse them. And always, always get what you want. Beg, cheat, lie, borrow or steal to get what you want, but all was fair for as long as nobody ever caught you at it. Play the left against the right and play them both against the middle but don't ever look as if you were doing it.

Every time he thought about it, he had to smile. All of those years that he'd dealt with the *kris* in his caravan, he'd had no idea that he was being Machiavellian. He'd have made the Italian proud.

After one of his late night study sessions, he returned to his private rooms to enjoy a little solitude while the rest of the household slept. He locked the door behind himself and walked slowly into the main room where a fire waited, burning brightly in welcome. His brain was full of words and ideas and he was so distracted that it took several minutes before he noticed that Sela was waiting by the hearth.

"Hello, Tobyn," she greeted softly, not looking up from the flames. The flickering light played along the high planes of her pretty face, cascading down her raven hair. He felt suddenly very much in love with her.

"Hello. What brings you here?"

"I wanted to spend some time with my husband," she told him quietly, her voice husky. "Is there anything wrong with that?"

"No, nothing."

"And before you ask, Ara is all right. I left her being watched by Fiona."

He smiled edgily, hearing an odd harshness in her voice. "I wasn't going to ask. If you're here, then she's just fine."

"God forbid that I should ever do something for me without meeting her needs first."

"Sela, what's the matter?"

"You tell me."

He frowned, completely lost yet again by feminine logic. "What?"

"You tell me. What's the matter with me?"

Tobyn was utterly confused. Perhaps he hadn't learned his Machiavelli well enough after all. "Nothing is the matter with you. What the hell are you talking about?"

"There must be something." She rose and gestured wildly. "Is it my face? Not pretty enough? Or maybe my hair displeases. Or is it that my body isn't desirable to you anymore? Is that it? Too used?"

"There is nothing wrong with you, Sela!" he exclaimed. "You're very pretty, your hair is fine, and you're still a beautiful woman."

"Then why don't you want me?"

He blinked at her. "You've lost me."

After taking a deep breath, she explained, standing stock-still. "You claimed me from Antonio almost five months ago. Since that time, there's not a single night you've shared my bed. Why?" She looked him in the eye. "You're a man with intense desires, Tobyn. You've been going somewhere for loving, and it hasn't been here to me."

"I...it's not—"

"It hasn't been to Ara, because she's in no condition to even know what you'd be doing to her. Is it the donors?" Her lower lip trembled. "I am your wife. I should be helping you, not someone else." She shook her head. "I know that you love Ara more than you love me, and—"

"Sela, no! What I feel for you is different, but it's not less! Where are you getting this idea?"

Tears traced her cheeks. "You haven't touched me once. You haven't even tried. You probably haven't even wanted to." She looked away. "I just want to know why you took me from the *kumpania* if you only wanted me for Ara's maid. You could have hired someone for that."

He grasped her shoulders and forced her to look at him. "I got you away from there because I love you. I couldn't bear the thought of you being in my uncle's bed, hurt and abused. And, if you really want to know, I've been going to the donors because I thought you'd prefer not to be touched for a while. If you want me, woman, you come and get me. I won't force anything on you."

She looked him in the eye. "Which of us do you want more, me or Araminah?"

"Don't make me choose," he said with a shake of his head. "I can't do that."

"Sooner or later, you'll have to." She freed herself from his grip with a dignified shrug. "But not tonight. Tonight, I want you to prove to me that you love me without exception." She took his hands. "I'm coming to get you, Tobyn."

He pulled her close and touched her face gently. She looked like herself again, recovered from the effects of her marriage to Antonio. She smelled wonderful, womanly and inviting, as she kissed him with a passion she'd never shown before. This was her night, and he was content to let her take control, letting her guide and direct their lovemaking every step of the way. He found it exciting to have a woman in command.

When it was over only a few hours before dawn, he fell asleep, holding her in his arms. She watched him carefully, studying the minute play of dreams across his beautiful face. She wanted him all to herself, now. The days of her sharing him, understanding about his odd relationship with his twin, were far behind her. He was her husband, he belonged to her. There could be no other claims on him, no gaps between their lives and souls.

Dawn came and locked him into helpless slumber, and she waited for its grip to hold him fast. When she was sure he could not move or even wake, she went to the bedside where he kept his knife.

"Nothing will separate us now," she told him in a whisper. "Forgive me."

She pressed the point of his knife into his skin, puncturing his exposed chest and drawing blood. His body trembled almost with instinctive fear, but she wasted no time. Before the wound could heal, she bent to him and drank.

She had never tasted wine like this. It was sweet and warm, and it touched and fulfilled a need she had never known she had. It went farther, touched more, and the deeper it went, the more she needed. She could never get enough, she wanted to keep drinking forever...

Abruptly, she was knocked aside, sent reeling from Tobyn and his blood by a sharp blow. Ara stepped between Sela and the prone vampire, her hair unruly, her green eyes wide with fever. She pointed an accusing finger at Sela.

"Thief," she hissed. "Mirror glass between us. I saw you do it. Killer bitch lying bird! Your colors are all wrong." She retreated blankly a step at a time until she was curled around her naked brother. "I saw you do it."

Sela picked herself up and decided that it would be good for her to leave. She dressed quickly, frightened by Ara's angry glare, and raced for the door. What she found there stopped her in her tracks.

The door was still bolted on the inside.

She whirled to stare at the other woman. "How did you get in?" The windows were closed and locked against the winter's cold, and they were on the third floor where there were no balconies. There were no other doors to Tobyn's chambers. She backed away from Ara, who watched her like a suspicious cat. "How did you get in?!"

"Mirror glass between us," she said by way of answer, "and everything is air and water. I can see through you, bitch witch."

"The witch is you," Sela whispered, afraid. With a trembling hand, she threw aside the bolt, then ran from the room.

Ara watched her go with a self-satisfied smirk. "Run away, bitch witch thieving bird-cat-canary. Your colors are all wrong. Bitch bird. I saw you do it."

Twenty-Six

When Tobyn finally awoke at sunfall, enraged with thirst and betrayal, Sela was safely locked away in her room by James. The Irishman and his right hand, Fiona, supplied the ravenous vampire with a steady stream of donors, pulling them away before they could be seriously harmed and replacing them with fresh throats until Tobyn's needs were satisfied.

In the quiet after the last donor was led away and returned to her bed, a blissful smile on her pale face, James turned to Tobyn. "Sela told me everything that happened last night," he announced without preamble. "Do you want to drive her out?"

He was angry almost beyond endurance. "I want to break her damned spine over my knee," Gemini snarled. He sighed heavily and fought himself back under control. "No. She can stay. If she starts to Change—and there's no reason to assume that she won't—then she'll need the shelter. But you tell her to steer clear of me, understand? She had no right to steal that from me, and I am furious."

"I'll tell her." He sat back. "She said that Ara knocked her aside..."

"Good thing, or I'd be dry tonight. She'd have taken too much. She was already starting to."

"Tobyn, how did your sister get into the room? The door was still locked on the inside."

"Or so she claims."

"You wouldn't doubt her if you saw how shaken she is."

Tobyn smiled tightly. "She's shaken? Good. I hope she's terrified."

Donnell took a deep breath. This wasn't easy, but he'd never expected it to be. Vampires were sometimes a surly lot, especially when their power was stolen so underhandedly. He supposed that it must be the only way a mortal could rape a blood-drinker. How did that sit with Tobyn's pride, he wondered?

He turned back to the question. "She would have nothing to gain from making up such a fable—"

"Except distracting us from what she'd done."

"I believe her, Tobyn."

"The more fool you." The vampire closed his eyes and leaned his head against the back of the chair. He actually considered what Donnell was saying. "Maybe Ara is developing some kind of mind over matter. What was that Greek word?"

"Telekinesis."

"That's the one."

"But why lock the door again?"

"Why does she try to climb out the window after the birds? Why does she talk to people who aren't there and never sees those who are?" He shook his head. "Nothing she does makes sense. I wouldn't put it past her to relock the door."

"She was intent on saving you," James pointed out. "She wouldn't waste the time."

He let out a brief exclamation of disgust and exasperation. "What are you suggesting, then? That she walked through the door like a ghost?"

"Not exactly."

"Then what, exactly?"

The vampire's acid tone and black mood were getting to him. He rose. "I might talk to her. Maybe she can explain it to me."

"In her current state, I doubt if she could even tell you what her name is."

James paused at the door. "You think she's crazy."

"Isn't it obvious?"

"Well, maybe...maybe what she's seeing and talking to is real."

Tobyn snorted. "Now you're losing your mind."

"Quite the contrary. I'm opening it." He opened the door. "And maybe people get called crazy because they make too much sense. Think about it."

"Just go away, James," he ordered in heavily-accented English. "Just go away and leave me alone."

James obeyed, knowing his friend well enough to know that even if Tobyn didn't want to, he'd puzzle the question through until he found an answer.

Colors.

They swirled around her, rainbows dancing, and it dazzled her eyes. She held out her hands, trying to catch the solid colors that led her from her bed. She had to follow them, she had to see where they would take her.

Smiling to herself, humming to match the sounds the colors made, Ara pushed her covers aside and answered the call. The blues circled her, and she pirouetted in reply. Maybe they could talk this way...

The green lights in the mirror beckoned to her again, and she danced to the vanity. Inside the glass, she could see mist whirling and parting, pictures coming together and then scattering like dust before the wind. She saw Sela in her room, sitting silently at the window; she saw Fiona in the kitchen, helping with the bread. She saw James leaving Tobyn to sulk and pout, and she saw men and women she didn't know doing things she could never understand. They held objects she could not identify, metal things with flashing lights and moving parts. Handsome men whose faces seemed familiar and whose eyes she could not catch walked inside the green mist. She reached out toward them and let out a startled exclamation when her fingertips bounced off of the solid matter of mirror-glass instead of warm masculine flesh.

Her disappointment was brief, and the cool blue returned, washing over her like water. She swam in it, felt it with her mind, let it guide her. She felt strangely like she was coming home, and that at any moment a loving mother would appear to welcome her back into the fold. She laughed and sang a child's song. The blue hummed in reply.

Something solid came between her and the seductive, swirling colors. She blinked, touched it again, and identified it as a door. That was no real obstacle. With a slight smile, she wished herself to the corridor where she wanted to be, following after the colors and leaving a locked door in her wake.

James caught her before she could go more than six steps away from her room. He threw his arms around her to serve the combined purpose of stopping her, warming her, and covering her. It wouldn't do to have Tobyn's sister wandering about in the nude, no matter how appealing that thought was now that he'd seen her.

"Hold up, Araminah." She reached out for the empty air over his shoulder, whimpering like a lost puppy, one out-stretched hand grasping at nothing. "Shh, Ara! What are you seeing?"

"I have to follow."

He shook his head. "No, no. You have to stay here."

"No," she groaned, straining. The way she was squirming and the feel of her was doing horrible things to his self-control, and it was becoming increasingly difficult for him to keep his hands to the neutral positions they occupied.

Behave, he told himself sternly, wishing that all portions of his anatomy were as easily controlled as his hands. "Come, Ara. We'll get you dressed and in bed. Fiona!"

The housekeeper appeared a moment or two later, brushing flour from her hands. Her eyes widened when she saw Araminah. "Miss! Mr. Donnell, I'm so sorry. I'll take care of her at once."

"Let me know when you've got her dressed," he requested. "I need to talk to her."

Fiona knew men. She looked him in the eye, took in the flush on his cheeks, and pursed her lips. "It will wait until morning, Mr. Donnell. Good night."

She did not add that she would be there as chaperone, but James heard it clearly. He nodded once, smiled sheepishly. "Tomorrow, then."

The matron led Ara away, the gypsy woman looking over her shoulder as the dancing colors disappeared through a little round hole in the wall that only she could see.

"They wanted me to follow," she whispered, near tears.

"I know, dear," Fiona said, patting her hand. "You can do that in the morning."

"They'll be gone in the morning," she sighed. "They were so pretty."

Fiona paused at the locked door, then said quietly to her charge, "You need to rest, Ara dear. I think you should go back in and unlock the door so that I can put you to bed."

The young woman smiled and sing-songed, "All right." She closed her eyes and in an instant was gone.

The Irish matron glanced around the hallway, nervous although she knew no one had seen. She knew Ara's secret, and she would have been happier if she'd never known at all about the strange things that the gypsy woman could do.

"They used to burn witches in the courtyard," she muttered to herself, making a twitchy Sign of the Cross before the latch turned on the inside of the door. Fiona put her superstitions and religious fears aside and became practical again. There was work to be done, and she had many locks to change. It wouldn't do to have doors standing about with only Ara able to get past them.

~⁓ᴏᴖᴏᴗ⁓

It was long after midnight and the household was asleep, even the indefatigable James. Tobyn wandered through the dark silence, listening to the thrum of heartbeats in the house and pacing the floors. Nothing in this added up. As he pondered Sela's surprising and, in Tobyn's way of thinking, unforgivable act, he could find no sense or logic in the night.

How had Araminah entered a locked room without opening the door? He tried to put aside his automatic denial of the act as impossible. If it had happened, and he would momentarily accept that it had, then how?

Think, Tobyn. What travels through walls?

Sound went through walls, and bullets and sometimes knives. Thoughts could go through walls, especially along his twin link with Ara. No matter when or where, if one of them was hurt or in trouble, the other always knew and could respond with word or action. And there, perhaps, lay his first clue. Ara had entered his room to save him from being drained dry by Sela. To save him. Perhaps it was an extension of the twin link they had. If thoughts could go through walls, sent from one to the other, then spirits could, as well. Everyone knew that ghosts walked through walls. Ara could have sent her soul to his aid. And while she was at it, why not take her body along?

And if she could do it, then why couldn't he?

//Ara,// he Sent, trying to envision her lying against the white linen of her sheets. *//Ara.//* He tried to see himself standing next to her bed, looking down at her, hearing her steady breathing, feeling the crush of carpeting beneath his boots...

Something in his mind popped, and for a moment he was unable to breathe, unable to even think. Then, abruptly, he was in the very spot he had imagined, trembling with exertion and excitement. He laughed aloud, incredulous, as he stared at his sleeping sister.

"I did it," he whispered.

Ara stirred sleepily. "Tobyn?"

He sat beside her on the bed and took her hand. "Yes, love?"

"Go take the red back. This room is supposed to be blue. You did it wrong." She rolled over and hugged her pillow to her chest as she sprawled on her stomach. "Go 'way."

The vampire studied the room, trying to fathom what she was babbling about. James had sounded convinced that her insanity was really a result of seeing more of reality; it sounded hopelessly stupid, but Tobyn had seen other hopelessly stupid truths. Making another leap of faith, he studied the room, this time looking with *chovihano* eyes.

There was a swirling in the air, a disturbance where he had appeared. Now that he was really Looking, he could See that the room at large had a different feeling than that swirl, a feeling that was somehow...blue. And the swirl felt strangely red.

Sickness could be contained and pulled out of the body by the power of a healer's mind. He had seen Ara do it countless times, had witnessed it in his childhood as Beti healed. He himself had done it, but in a more limited way. He wondered if he could treat the swirl the same way and heal the room, in a manner of speaking.

"Why not?" he asked himself out loud. "I've already done one impossible thing. I might as well try for two."

It was difficult. First the swirling had to be stilled, then gathered up into a little scarlet bundle. When it was diminished in size that way, he could see a tiny blot of red and glowing black. It looked like a rip in a curtain. He wondered briefly what was on the other side, considered finding out the hard way, then decided just to push his little ball of red through and patch up the hole. The endeavor took a great deal of energy and several minutes of intense concentration before he got it right, but in the end the red was gone and the rip in reality's fabric was so well-patched that it could no longer be seen.

He sighed in self-satisfaction. "My boy, you are fantastic, an absolute phenomenon," he told himself in English, imitating a comment James had made during a tutoring session. He turned to look at his sister and watched her sleeping for a moment. She was beautiful, and he was tempted to wake her so he'd have a good reason to stay, but his experiment was incomplete. He still had to go back.

For the return trip, he pictured the chair in the library where he did all of his heaviest thinking. He Saw it, tried to feel it, strained to smell the faint smokiness of the embers on the hearth. It took concentration and effort and more time in the confusing half-state between Here and There, but finally he dropped into the chair with an all-but-audible pop and indulged in a triumphant laughing fit.

The noise attracted the attention of half of the staff on the main floor, and they appeared in the library wearing their nightclothes and puzzled expressions. James came in, took a look at the dizzily giggling Gemini, then sent the others back to their rooms with muttered assurances. When they were gone, James turned to Tobyn.

"What is so funny?"

Tobyn struggled to be able to breathe long enough to answer. "I did it. I did what Ara did. My God, James! What a tool!"

Donnell shook his head, perplexed. "What are you talking about? What did you do?"

With a loopy laugh, Tobyn pointed to the empty chair at James' side...and disappeared. A long moment later, he was seated there, still laughing, wiping tears from his eyes. The Irishman gaped, and it was only with difficulty that his companion did not laugh harder.

To show off more completely, Tobyn "popped" to several different places around the room. His last teleportation left him gasping for air on the settee.

"This is incredible," James said at last, moving over to sit beside Tobyn.

"Yes, it is. It's also damned exhausting." He took a deep breath and let it out in a rush. "There are some kinks yet, but nothing I can't work out with practice. Oh, James, what a tool! The Prime and the Brethren might be able to fly, but they can't do this. Just think of all the things this will enable me to do!"

"Such as?"

Gemini's blue eyes sparkled with malice. "Such as destroy Dumas."

"And start a war before you're ready for it?"

The Irishman's practicality threatened to dampen his enthusiasm. He refused to let it. Waving one hand dismissively, he said, "They'd never find me. I'll pop in and kill him and pop out. I'll do it during the day when he's helpless. They'll never even know it was me."

"You're assuming that you'll be able to find him."

"I will."

"How do you know?"

Tobyn sighed. "Because I will, that's all. I think Ara did it the first time because she followed our link. Maybe I can do the same with Dumas."

James looked frankly skeptical. "You have a bond with him?"

"Perhaps, distasteful though it is. He is my creator, so to speak. If you follow Tristan's terminology, he's my father. That is a blood link, almost literally, that I can follow to his lair at noon and destroy him." His face was hard and his voice icy as he stated flatly, "He owes me a great deal."

"But you're so different from him..." James shook his head. "What if the link isn't there? If it were there, don't you think Dumas would have followed it to destroy you for himself by now?"

Tobyn shrugged. "Maybe he doesn't have the ability to sense it. Maybe he doesn't believe, and so he can't do things like that. And maybe it only goes one way."

"All right, fine," James said. "What if you can only go to places you know well, like this room?" He caught Tobyn's gaze. "It's far too big a risk."

"It's mine to take."

"And if something should go wrong, what then? Who'll take care of your sister and your wife?"

His reply came quick. "You will."

"Ah, but not forever."

The idea chilled him and he shook it off. He would not allow shadows of what might be deny him his revenge, or the pleasure of plotting it, not when the tools he needed were in his hands. He rose, scowling.

"Go back to bed, James. You aren't being helpful."

"And you aren't being realistic. You don't know enough yet to—"

"Go to bed," he ordered. "You'll see tomorrow when I bring you Dumas' head on the end of my knife."

Affronted, Donnell rose and went to the door, where he paused long enough to take a parting shot. "Tomorrow you'll wish you'd listened to me."

⤳⤳⤳

Tobyn spent the rest of the night practicing his new maneuver, popping from room to room in the Raven's Nest until sunrise and exhaustion claimed him. James collected him from the library chair where he had fallen and put him safely to bed, where the vampire stayed long after the mandatory three hours' torpor had left him. Even well into the following night, Tobyn slept, wrapped in the grip of a profound fatigue that affected him to his very soul. James and Sela, cautious and silent, kept vigil at Tobyn's bedside while he slept through the following dawn and into night again.

Finally, three days after his discovery, Tobyn stirred, his blue-tinged lips moving slightly in a failed whisper. James, pragmatic as ever, sent Sela away and called for donors. A procession of eight young men and women came and went, and still Tobyn's thirst was unquenched. Tobyn stared up at James with glassy eyes as the last of the donors on hand was led away.

"More," the gypsy requested pitifully. "I need more."

"There are no more," Donnell told him.

"Yes!"

Fiona appeared at the side of the bed, concern on her wide face. "Perhaps one of us..."

"No," James objected. "We are not donors."

"This is no time to be caught up in titles, Mr. Donnell!" she scolded. "The lad needs help and attention, and while I can't say I'm pleased with what I've seen here in this house since I took my position, I also can't say that I'd be willing to turn my back. These may be demons, but still it's not a Christian thing to do."

"Christian!" James objected. "Madam, I—"

"More," Tobyn begged. "Please."

Fiona began to answer the call, and James pushed her aside with a disgusted sigh. "You don't know what it's like, Madam, and if you're concerned with being Christian, I think it's best that you don't learn."

"There's no danger," she stated.

"Just to your morality." He removed his cravat and pulled open his collar. "Go back to the kitchen, Fiona. I'll take care of things up here."

With an offended grunt, the woman grudgingly obeyed. Tobyn clutched at James' shoulders and mumbled at him in Romany, somehow being childlike and seductive at once. James closed his eyes and let Tobyn take his blood, making no effort to break out of the hold the vampire had him in. The effect was immediate and predictable. The Irishman's body responded energetically to the sensual feeling of being fed upon, and just as James had passed the point of fighting the pleasure and was urging it onward to its tantalizingly visible peak, Tobyn fell back with a sated sigh and drifted into unconsciousness again.

James slid off of the bed and onto the floor with a groan, his heart pounding in his ears, his body objecting to his abandonment.

"Are you all right?"

He was unprepared for the softly-spoken question. He started and turned to face the doorway, but no one was there. Ara repeated her question from the window seat.

"Are you all right?"

James swallowed hard as she rose from her perch. Her night clothes were loose and open, offering tempting glimpses of breast and leg as she moved closer. Her green eyes were wide and somewhat unfocussed as she knelt at his side.

In a husky voice, he asked, "What are you doing here?"

"There was so much red in this room," she said, looking around slowly. "I had to come and see what was wrong."

"You should not be here."

"He fed from you? He needs to feed a lot. He shouldn't do this." She shook her head and turned her eyes back to James. "I hope he learns his lesson. Red is bad. You have to use blue."

Donnell was fighting with himself. He wanted to pull away and he wanted to pull her closer. He wanted to rescue his integrity with a long walk in the cold night air, but he also wanted to succumb to the demands his body was making for the woman beside him.

Ara ran her hands through his hair. "Poor boy," she cooed in French, "poor boy. You don't know what they're doing over there, do you?"

He tried to hear her, but all he could do was savor the scent of her skin and the feeling of her hands upon his face. He wanted her so badly, and he had come so close with Tobyn... "Who?"

"Over there, in the mirror." She pointed, then dropped her hand. "They're gone now. I don't know who they are." James groaned and started to pull away, and Ara's gaze fell on his lap. "Oh."

His problem became all the worse with her awareness of it. They froze as they were, James staring at the softness revealed by Ara's nightclothes, Ara staring at the bulge in James' trousers. The moment galvanized him, his mind gave in to the demands his body was making and to the promise of this woman's nearness, and with a primal cry of desperation that the James of waking daylight would never have claimed, he seized her shoulders and bore her down to the carpet.

He took her until morning painted the room with unforgiving sunshine. Ashamed, he dressed without looking at her as she slowly braided a lock of hair that had fallen into her face.

"Poor James," she sighed, carefully arranging her hair. "Poor James."

"Get up," he ordered gruffly.

She did not hear him. Rocking, singing to herself, she sat in the middle of her disarrayed garments, clothes that James had never taken the time to relieve her of. "Poor James. Started something, couldn't stop it."

"Be quiet, please, I beg you." The scent of their union was still in the air, and it made him ill. Unable to bear the scene of his guilt a moment longer, he turned to go.

Fiona stood in the doorway, her hands folded before her, her mouth a line of disapproval. He froze in his tracks. "I see now why you feel the way you do about Christians, Mr. Donnell," she told him. "May God forgive you."

Without a word, he brushed past her and left the room. The matron went to Ara and gathered her up, pulling the nightgown over her exposed body, covering the faint bruises that were beginning to rise on her hips and arms.

"Poor James," Ara repeated, looking at Fiona. "He's done himself no favors here."

"That's true enough," Fiona agreed. "If it weren't for you, I'd be leaving this place. But you need some caring, don't you, my dear?" She pulled Ara to her feet and wrapped a comforting arm around the younger woman's shoulders. "Come along, little one. Let Mama take care of you now."

~~⚬~~

Fiona bathed Ara and put her into bed for a much-needed rest, then sought James in the study. The man was pacing like a caged tiger, staring at the sea beyond the windows, making nervous gestures with his hands as if he were pleading his case to an invisible judge. She watched him silently for a moment, then cleared her throat.

James stopped short, his eyes cast down onto the carpet at his feet. "I expect that you'll be leaving now."

"No, indeed, Mr. Donnell."

"Not even after what's happened?"

"Especially not after all that." She folded her hands again. "Someone has to protect that girl."

He turned to her. "I swear that I never intended—"

"You've been intending it since you first saw her in the corridor, and don't think that I don't know it. But I don't believe you'd have done anything of the sort without a great deal of extraordinary influence."

"Tobyn's feeding," he agreed, eager for a decent excuse for his indecent behavior.

"Nothing will make right the thing you did, Mr. Donnell, but I am willing to let it by this once on the grounds that nothing in this house has ever gone quite the way things in a decent Christian household should. Living with...with this type of creature can put a strong heart to the test. I believe that you were tested."

He turned anxious eyes to her. "You think badly of me now, don't you?"

"I believe that you were tested, and that you failed," she replied. "I believe that you abused a girl who was in no condition to understand what you were asking of her, a girl who is your very own employer's sister. I also believe that, left to yourself, you can be trusted, but with so many unusual people and things here, I cannot leave you alone."

"You aren't leaving?"

"No, sir. I wanted to tell you that." She drew herself up taller. "I'll be moving my things into Miss Ara's rooms. There won't be a moment when I'll let her out of my sight."

He grimaced. "You're keeping her safe from me."

"Exactly." She nodded her head once. "Good day, Mr. Donnell. Luncheon will be served promptly at one o'clock."

"Fiona," he called, stopping her as she was leaving. "Please...don't tell Tobyn what happened."

"Mr. Donnell, I cannot confess your sins for you." She nodded again. "I think you understand."

"Thank you, Fiona."

She turned to go and stopped again, this time sparing a moment to say, "You know, Mr. Donnell, once is a sin, but twice is a crime. And crimes are to be reported." She looked at him. "I think you understand that as well."

"Yes, I do, Madam. Thank you indeed."

Without a word, she left him to his guilt.

⁓✺⁓

Tobyn was able to leave his bed on the third day after his overdose of popping, and his mind was so focused upon honing his new toy that he never noticed the strain in James' eyes. Fiona spoke little to either man, and she spent almost all of her time no further from Ara than arm's length. Sela remained in hiding in her rooms.

Slowly, gradually, Tobyn began to pace his practicing. When he was strong again, he only teleported twice, keeping his range to places within the same room. At the end of two weeks, he had worked up to five 'pops' a night to all corners of the Raven's Nest. He was beginning to feel very confident and strong in his new ability, very self-fulfilled, when he noticed that something was wrong with James.

They were sitting in the library going over the household expenditure records and drinking a truly dreadful white wine that had come in from Germany a few days before. Tobyn watched the mortal's pale face and the lines around his mouth for a long time, studying them by candlelight, before he asked, "What's the matter, James?"

Donnell looked up. "Hmm?"

"What's the matter? You aren't acting yourself."

He faltered. "I'm busy trying to read this ledger. Your handwriting still isn't the best."

"It's something more than that." He cocked his head and guessed. "It's got to do with Ara, hasn't it?"

James almost dropped his pen. "Wh-what makes you say that?"

"Well, I know how you fancy her, and I also know that she's getting more and more...well, she's losing what little was left of her mind. I think about it a lot. I thought you might be, too."

He was not fooled by the false ingenuousness of the gypsy vampire's tone. Tobyn sounded innocent, which was the first clue that he was trying to manipulate the situation.

"Sort of. I was just thinking that she's Changing awfully fast. Didn't you say it took you two years?"

"Yes." He sat back. "Ara's only been Changing for about fourteen months. Not quite the same. You think she's going to make her Change soon, too, don't you?"

"That's what you've been thinking, when you're not plotting your wars?"

"Exactly. I want to know your opinion."

"I think I'm very interested in seeing what she's like when she has a mind." He scribbled a few computations, then said, "Tobyn...what if she doesn't regain her mind? What if she stays this way?"

The vampire's face darkened with a scowl. "Then I guess we get a house pet with a very long life expectancy."

"You'd let her continue that way? Mad as she is?"

"She's my sister. I love her."

"But won't she be a burden on you?"

Their eyes met, both of them guardedly hiding their thoughts. "What are you suggesting, James? That I kill her?"

"No, not exactly."

"Then what?"

"If she gets to be too much a trouble for you... well..."

"Give her to you?"

Silence hung between them. "Perhaps," James finally admitted.

"So she can be your toy."

"Not a toy."

"Do you love her, James? Or do you only want to fuck her?"

Donnell winced at the word. "I—I don't know...I..."

Tobyn laughed. "You're dying now, aren't you? How dare I apply so shocking a term to such a gentleman as yourself!" He leaned forward with a grin, his eyes still locked with the Irishman's. "What's the matter, James? Have I hit too close to the bone on this one? Is the immaculate James Donnell truly a man after all?"

"What do you want me to say, Tobyn? That I want your sister? That she attracts me? Then, fine, I'm saying it. I'd be a fool not to be drawn to her." He glared at the chuckling vampire. "Stop laughing! This isn't funny."

"Yes, it is. You're answering all my questions." He rose. "You see, I've been forming theories about you, my friend. I've never seen you with any women, you never avail yourself of the donors—who, I might add, are nothing if not willing—and you never say anything the least bit off color about anyone. To be honest, I was starting to wonder if you liked boys."

James bristled. "I simply choose to keep my private affairs private."

"That's not a problem. I don't care what you do in your bedroom, but I do like to be able to predict who you're doing it with. I don't think you're the violent type." James looked away, and Tobyn was having too much fun embarrassing him to properly read the shame that crept across the Irishman's face. "And I also think that you're a little too hot-blooded to be Mr. Happy Celibate for all these months. Call me nosy."

"Fine. You're nosy."

"Thank you. Now it's your turn to guess about me."

"Frankly, Tobyn, your sexual proclivities don't interest me."

"Ooh, listen to the little aristocrat! You know, James, you do a lovely Puritan impression, but I think that I know exactly what string controls you. And now I know that my sister is the one who pulls it."

James glared at him. "Is that it? You want to control me?"

"If you're going to be working for me," he answered promptly, "yes. I want to control the world."

There was little to no humor in the gypsy's voice, and it left James cold, especially since he had no doubt that, sooner or later, Gemini could do it.

∝∽∾∾∝

Ara stirred beneath her coverlet with a gasp of pain. Her eyes were clear and wide as she clutched her abdomen, feeling the twisting cramps descend on her like a fallen angel. She was sweating, hot, and she wouldn't have been surprised to find her blood boiling beneath her parchment-pale skin. Another cramp hit and it felt like all of her innards were rearranging themselves at once. She moaned pitiably.

On the other side of the room, sleeping on a sofa, Fiona heard the low pain sound. Rising and blinking sleep from her eyes, she moved closer. "What is it, child? What's wrong? Are you sick?"

A strange, sweet scent struck through her like a knife, and Ara groaned in the grip of a sudden surging response. Her breathing was too fast, she was hyperventilating; she felt as if her lungs were a wild horse and she was only along for a ride she could not control. The room was spinning as she squeezed her eyes closed.

"Oh...God..."

Her mouth hurt. Her skin ached as if it were stretching too far over limbs that were contorting as she writhed. Fiona grasped her, trying to hold her still and steady.

A distant drum beat called Araminah's attention away, and her eyes were silver when she opened them again. Her lips pulled back from angry fangs and she sprang on Fiona with a growling hiss, seizing the woman's throat and inexpertly slashing into the vein. Fiona managed one reedy cry before her life flooded onto Ara's tongue. She was dead within moments.

She pulled on the vein, dragging the last drops to the surface, then threw the Irishwoman's body aside like a rag doll. Moonlight glistened against the blood that streaked her chin as she tossed her hair and screamed like a caged tiger.

∽⧸∾◦ϵ◦

In the library, they heard.

Tobyn was on his feet like a shot, racing for his sister's room, and James was at his heels. They burst into the bed chamber, expecting the worst and finding it.

Ara was kneeling in the center of the bed, spattered with blood from her novice kill, her eyes wild and silver-spotted. She reached her arms out for James, her wicked teeth showing white against her scarlet-stained lips.

"Tobyn..." he said, uncertain.

"Wait."

The male vampire strode forward and took Ara's hands in his own, his eyes staring deeply into hers. She pulled at him, trying to bring him nearer, but he resisted, his scant superior age giving him strength above her madness. She whimpered beneath his gaze, then sank lower to the mattress until she was lying on her stomach, softly moaning. Tobyn offered her his wrist, and she clutched him like a drowning man. James hovered at the end of the bed as Tobyn swayed, eyes closed, lost to her drinking.

"Tobyn," he said at last, frightened by seeing the gypsy man start to falter. "Tobyn!"

Gemini blinked, then broke away from his sister's greed. She slumped onto the bed, breathing heavily, her face pressed into the blankets. Tobyn wiped her mouth with his sleeve.

"She'll be all right," he said shakily, not wanting to admit how weak he was. "I think she needs more, but she'll be safe for you now."

His voice was small. "For me?"

"Do you see anyone else here? Of course for you!" He stepped away. "Do it, James. I need to see the donors."

Tobyn lurched from the room, and Donnell hesitantly went to kneel at Ara's side. She lay still, her beautiful face lax, her head cradled on her arm. He stroked her hair away from her brow, let his fingers tangle in it, and felt the mad desire for her rise in him again. She moved one delicate hand to slowly cover his, then opened her eyes. They were green once more, and showed more sanity than he had seen in them before...but less than he would have liked.

"James," she said softly, her voice a sigh. "Poor James."

"Ara..."

She pulled him down to her, and he joined her on the bed, stretched out across the bloody mattress. Neither of them noticed the mess as she began to drink from him, slowly, her tongue moving like a caress against his skin. He moaned and crushed her to him, and she did not resist. She was making love to the blood and the feeling of feeding; nothing else was getting through to her. She did not feel him sliding her nightgown over her shoulders, did not feel his hands laying claim to her breasts. All she knew was the blood, the rhythm of his pulse, and the dizzying excitement that grew as he pushed into her. They were both lost.

And when it was over, they both wept.

Twenty-Seven

Sela brought a bowl of soup into Ara's bedroom after the new vampire had slept off the exhaustion of her Change. She was unprepared for the tight, drawn look around the female Gemini's mouth, and the shadows in her green eyes were unsettling. Ara accepted the bowl without comment, shifting to lean more comfortably against her pillows with the covers drawn up to her chest. She sipped silently for a moment, and Sela felt compelled to speak.

"I was hoping you'd be all right," she said lamely, her voice strained even to her own ears. "After everything that happened, I wasn't certain that you'd be—"

"I'm all right, Sela," she said flatly. "Stop worrying."

"Have you spoken to Tobyn?"

Ara glanced at her. "Yes. He slept here last night." Quickly, she added, "He only slept."

"I wasn't going to say anything. I just wondered...how is he?" She leaned closer. "Did he mention me at all?"

The stern look deepened. "Not at all." She put the bowl aside. "You shouldn't have done what you did, Sela, but I can't say I blame you. I know what he means to you. I just don't know that any man is worth...this."

"Tobyn is."

"I don't know."

"That's just because you had a hard Change."

"Hard?" Ara laughed sharply. "It wasn't hard for me. I haven't got a right to complain. That right is Fiona's."

Sela shook her head. "You can't hold yourself responsible for what happened—"

"Can't I? I killed her, Sela. I tore her throat out and swallowed her blood. I carry that guilt." She looked away as tears rose in her eyes. "This is so wrong. I wish..."

"You wish it had never happened? Or perhaps you wish that Tobyn had never chosen to bring you over?" Now Sela's tone was harsh and angry. "How can you regret this? You have taken without thinking what I had to steal."

"If you want it so damned bad, I hope it makes you very happy," Ara hissed. "I don't want it. I never wanted it, not really."

"That's not what I've heard. Tobyn told James—"

"Don't talk to me about James!"

The fury behind the *chovihani's* voice put Sela into stunned silence, and she sat on the edge of the bed, staring at Ara, as the door opened and Tobyn and James strolled in. Tobyn saw his wife sitting there and stiffened, his eyes going cold. Without a word, he turned on his heel and stalked out. James hovered on the threshold, caught in indecision, then entered further.

"Araminah," he said in a level tone. "Are you well?"

She looked up at him, icy and controlled. "As well as I can be, under the circumstances. What do you want?"

"I was only concerned about you. Your brother and I were checking in on your condition. He wanted to speak to you before he..." He trailed off, biting back what he had been meaning to say.

Ara wouldn't let him evade. "Before he what, James?"

He didn't miss the way his name was a curse on her lips, and he didn't blame her. He looked away. "Before he left for a business trip."

"Business trip? What business does my brother have that would take him away now?" She gestured toward the window with one hand while the other almost subconsciously tugged the bedclothes higher. "It's winter here."

He smiled helplessly and directed his comments to Sela, who was staring toward the door. "He's learning book keeping, you know, and he's been managing the Raven's Nest's investments. He's making quite a lot of money." Donnell sighed and took Sela's hand. "I think this has gone on long enough. Shall I speak to him for you, madam?"

"Would you? You're his best friend now...he'd listen to anything you said," she urged hopefully.

James nodded. "I shall do my best. I hate to see women in distress." Ara snorted rudely, and James ignored her to the best of his ability. "Good day, ladies."

"That's our Mr. Donnell," Ara told his back, "always the perfect gentleman."

James hesitated but did not respond. Instead, he squared his shoulders and strode out in Tobyn's wake.

※

He found Tobyn in the library, stalking angrily through the room. "Keep her away from Ara," he ordered as James walked in. "I don't trust her. I don't trust what she'll do."

"You aren't being very forgiving," Donnell said gently. "It's been a long time."

"She'll be immortal. We have time."

"Sela needs you to understand."

"I need you to keep your mind on the business at hand." He turned to his friend. "James, I want you to be my lieutenant when this war starts. I want to bring you over."

James blinked and sank, staring, onto the nearest flat surface, which happened to be an end table. "What?"

"I want to make you a vampire, like me and like Ara and like Sela will be. I want you to be one of us. I trust no one as much as I trust you." He saw Donnell's brow twitch, and he frowned. "What's wrong, James? Don't you want this?"

The Irishman took a deep breath as a thousand possibilities raced through his head. "Yes and no."

Tobyn smiled. "Good. I wouldn't give it to you if you didn't find it frightening. Nobody who really wants this should have it. This power would be too easy to abuse."

James crossed his arms over his chest and looked away. "And you trust me not to be abusive?"

"Absolutely. I trust you with everything. You're my second in command, you know."

"I thought that would be Ara."

"Oh, she's just a woman. She can't lead. She can be queen," he acceded.

"I don't think she'll be content with just that."

Tobyn sighed. "Well, it's a little too soon to see what Ara will be content with. She's been relentlessly nasty since she woke up yesterday, and I don't know what her problem is. I know it's not an easy thing, and I know that what happened with Fiona must upset her, but she'll get over it. She's resilient. She's had to be." He shook his head. "She needs to acclimate, that's all. Then she'll be good as new." He sat at the desk. "Tell me, James. Will you take my offer?"

"We'll see," he murmured, even while he knew that he would eventually say 'yes.'

The vampire grinned. "Excellent. Now then, your first duty as my lieutenant is to keep watch over this place and hold the fort, as it were, while I'm away. I've got a big day planned for tomorrow, and you'll need to be here keeping things in order until I can get back."

"I can't believe that you're actually planning on going through with this. You really believe that you can 'pop' in on Dumas, murder him, and be done with it all so easily?"

"I certainly do. Listen, I can trace him now. I've spent enough time and energy these past few weeks on honing the link that I can find him no matter where he goes...as long as he doesn't change too much. Sometimes it fluctuates, like he's stronger on some days and easier to find, and some days he's weak and almost invisible—"

"And you think you can find him in the daylight when he's sleeping. Won't he completely elude your link then?"

Tobyn scowled. "So I'll go for him at night."

"It's a fool's risk. He'll have his court around him. He always does."

"Not always. Not if he's at his *chateau*. He was almost always alone there." Tobyn spread his hands in an expansive gesture. "James, this is such a wonderful opportunity...I can't let it go. Not now. I have to seize what I want, take it while I can. Don't tell me you've never felt the same way."

He thought about the beautiful vampire upstairs and rubbed his forehead. "Sometimes it isn't good to simply take."

"Nonsense. Sometimes it's the only way." He leaned forward, his elbows on his knees. "What do you say, James? Will you stay and care for my sister and Sela while I'm away?"

"Aha! You said her name, and you want her cared for. That means you don't hate her after all."

He sighed. "James, I never said I hated her. I said I was angry with her."

"Do you still love her?"

They stared at one another for a moment. "Maybe."

"Then talk to her."

He groaned. "Change the subject, my friend. You're getting boring."

"All right, fine. But it would be best." He poked at the carpet with his boot. "Will you leave in the day or in the evening?"

Tobyn considered. "As you pointed out, finding Dumas in the day will be difficult, and at this point, I have to be honest and admit that I'm less than professional at this 'popping' business. I don't want to take the chance of getting lost in between here and there." He sighed. "I guess I'll leave in the evening, but early. Dusk. Dumas will be awake, but groggy, and the majority of his court will be too young or too weak to be out of their beds or coffins or whatever at that hour."

"I wish you'd reconsider."

"You are boring me," Tobyn warned.

"I thought I was supposed to be your lieutenant. Isn't part of my job to be keeping you under control?"

"No. I don't want to be controlled, James. I want to be supported."

"That I'll do. But I won't support you in something I consider foolhardy."

Tobyn looked at him for a long time. "Will you defy me, try to stop me?"

The silence stretched, and James looked away. "I won't undermine your decisions, if that's what you mean."

"Good." He rose. "I'll be leaving at dusk tomorrow. I don't know how long I'll be gone, but in the meantime, you know how to care for the women. Ara will be more than self-sufficient. She's very independent. Sela I don't know about."

"She'll be better if you talk to her."

"I'm going to talk to Ara instead right now." He started toward the door, then stopped. "James, I want you to take blood tonight. I want to make sure that you're Changing before I go, just in case I don't come back."

"I can't take it from you. That would weaken you too much before your 'pop.'"

"Then take it from Ara."

James stiffened. "What makes you think she'd be willing to give it to me?"

"That's why I'm going to talk to her. I can convince her."

"Don't...don't force her to do anything she doesn't want to do," he said hesitantly, although the idea of being that close to her again had already made his heart beat faster.

"I won't. I never force Ara. I might convince her, but I won't force her."

"Good. Thank you."

Tobyn snickered. "You're in love with her, aren't you?"

He shrugged helplessly. "I'd be hard pressed not to be attracted, wouldn't I?"

"Oh, but this is more than an attraction. This sounds like an addiction."

"Don't say that."

"I think making you immortal will be very interesting, if only to see what happens between you two."

"Don't do this if it's just an experiment," James snapped. "I am not here solely for your amusement."

"I know that!" Tobyn shook his head. "You take me far too seriously. You have to learn when I'm joking and when I'm not. You also have to learn how to have a little fun with life. I'm not really a megalomaniac. It's just so easy to convince you that I am."

Tobyn strolled out again, and James watched him go, unsure if the gypsy had ever teased about anything in his life.

~✧~

Ara looked up guardedly when Tobyn returned to her room, and her twin wondered, not for the first time, what had happened to make her so angry. He sat beside her on the mattress, considerate enough of her mood that he did not try to touch her. He doubted if she would appreciate the contact.

"Where are you going?" she asked. "He said that you had a business trip."

"I'm going to find Dumas," he told her honestly, "and I'm going to kill him."

She frowned. "How? Do you know where he is?"

"I can find him."

"Well, you aren't going alone."

"Yes, I am. But don't worry. I have a secret way to get there."

She arched a slender brow. "Secret way? What are you babbling about?"

"I'll 'pop.'"

She shook her head. "You're crazy."

"I know." He sighed and settled closer to her. "But I just can't let a chance like this get away from me. Do you have any idea what that...creature has done, what pain he's caused all of us?" His blue eyes were haunted and he dropped the façades for her. "He hurt me very badly, Ara, and it's because he hurt you that this has happened. You know that I never wanted to bring you into this life. You're a healer, and so gentle. I know that killing is tearing you apart. It tore me to bits, and I'm not as nice as you are. I'd never want you to suffer, love, and he made you suffer. The only way I could think of to stop your pain and to keep you with me was to Make you." He shook his head. "I'm sorry, Ara. My selfishness caused this, too. I just couldn't bear to lose you."

"Oh, Tobyn, I know that." She embraced him, finding some comfort in the vulnerability that he was finally sharing. "But it's happened, now, and I can't see any reason to be angry with you for it. I can see that it goes back to Dumas."

"There are so many things," he said, suddenly finding it difficult to breathe as tears began to come. "He ruined everything for me, Ara. He Changed me into something I don't want to be. He destroyed any chance we had to live happily in the *kumpania*, and I know you didn't like it there, but I was happy to be a gypsy. God, Ara, it was everything I was! And he took it away from me. He raped me, body, mind, and spirit, and I have to make him pay for that." He clutched her close. "He's still hurting me, just by living. He's turned you and Sela into fugitives, he's forced me into starting an army and a war when I don't want to fight on a scale that huge...he has to pay!"

"I agree," she whispered, "but not this way. Tobyn, please. Don't go into this alone."

"I got into this alone at the start, if you remember." He drew himself up and locked his emotions down again. "I can end it alone, too."

"Please," she begged, holding his hands in her own. "I'm afraid for you. And I don't want to be left here."

"You'll be safe," he assured her. "I'm leaving James in charge. He's going to take care of everything."

She froze. "James?"

"Yes. He's going to be my lieutenant, I've decided. He can fight alongside me."

"I don't like him," she whispered.

"Oh, you just don't know him. He's a very decent fellow when you talk to him."

She shook her head. "Decent? I don't think you know him as well as you say you do."

"Give him a chance, Ara. For me." He smiled wistfully at her, and for a moment he looked very much like a lost and lonely little boy. "I need all the friends I can find, and he's the best friend I've had in years."

Araminah could not resist her brother when he looked like that, and she was sure that on some level Tobyn knew it. Even while she kicked herself for being gullible, she acquiesced. "All right, Tobyn. Whatever you want."

"Do you promise?" he asked, desperate for certainty.

"I promise. Anything you want, love."

"Good!" He squeezed her hands. "I want James to take blood tonight. Are you strong?"

"I'm all right," she said slowly, beginning to wish she hadn't agreed to humor him. "Why?"

He took a deep breath, knowing that he was about to ask a great deal. "Because I'll need all of my strength for tomorrow night, and I want him to take blood...from you."

She pulled away. "You're insane!"

"You promised." He heard himself sounding like a whiny child, and he amended, "Ara, it's not that I want to push you, it's just that there are so few people in this world that I think we can trust. James is the only one I trust this much. He's helped me more than I can tell you over the past months, and he's taught me so much...I need him beside me, Ara. I need his guidance. I wouldn't ask this if it weren't important." He took her hands again. "Ara, I'm thinking in big terms now, since we have no other choice. He's a smart man, a practical man. He'd be an excellent person to help me run an army. He understands politics and finances and tactics and all of the things that generals need to know. And he's going to be my foremost general." He met her eyes. "Ara, please. This goes beyond you and me. This goes to eternity."

She stared at him, warring with herself. The idea of voluntarily getting into physical contact with that man sickened her, but at the same time, a little voice was singing to her that perhaps none of what had happened had really been James' fault. That little voice, a nagging gadfly if ever Ara had encountered one, urged her to give the Irishman a second chance. *It's so important to Tobyn,* she thought, and her decision was made. With a deep sigh, she nodded.

"All right. But let me sleep first. I want to be sure that I'm strong."

"Are you still not well?" he asked, his brow puckering. "Ara, if you're not up to this—"

"I will be, tonight. Just let me sleep." She tried to smile. "I'll do it. I promised."

He kissed her on the cheek and smiled. "I knew I could count on you. I depend on you so much, Ara."

She smiled back wanly. "I know."

✦

It was well after midnight, in the strange hours of the early morning before sunrise when the light seemed to be filtered through stained glass. Tobyn brought James to Ara's rooms and found her, up and dressed in a solemn black gown, stoking the fire in the hearth. Her dark curls were pulled back in a scarlet ribbon, streaming down her back, and her face was composed and icily calm when she turned around. James swallowed hard, nervous and shaky and feeling like he was either falling in love or coming down with pneumonia.

"Welcome," Ara said simply. "Come and sit by the fire."

Tobyn led James to the trio of chairs she had set up in the semicircle of heat. James sat slowly in the middle seat as the twins took up position on both sides of him. Ara pulled a long, slender knife from the pocket of her gown, and in the firelight its silver point looked deadly. She twirled it in her hand.

"This won't take long," Tobyn promised. "I'll be here to chaperone." They both looked at him strangely, and he wondered what connotations his words had to elicit such unreadable emotions. He cleared his throat. "I'll make sure he doesn't take too much."

"Good. I don't think I have that much to spare," she said with a small smile. "Are you ready for this, James?"

He was glad to hear that she no longer spat his name, and while he knew it was solely for Tobyn's benefit that she was even in the room at all, he let himself enjoy the moment. "Yes."

"All right." She offered the blade to Tobyn. "Here. I don't think I have the nerve to do it myself."

"You have all the nerve you need," he said, shaking his head. Silently, he added, *//You've always been the stronger of us.//*

//Don't forget that when you get to be king,// she replied. *//Nobody likes an arrogant monarch.//*

He smiled. *//Nobody but the Prime.//*

Donnell cleared his throat. "What do I have to do?"

She looked at him calmly, cool as a princess carved in marble. "When I make a wound, you have to drink the blood that comes. And do it quickly, because I will heal very fast."

He nodded. "All right."

Ara looked to Tobyn, and he nodded his silent support to her. Slowly, she rolled up her sleeve and exposed the tender skin on the inside of her left arm. She took a deep breath, readied the blade, and viciously slashed the veins open.

James had to get on his knees to take the blood, but he fell eagerly, like a supplicant at the shrine of a saint. He licked the ruby liquid as it streamed from the gash, letting his hunger take control as the power of the Change began to worm its way into his soul. He pulled her closer, tighter, and sucked at her wound until she cried out in alarm. Tobyn grabbed his shoulders and hauled him away from his sister, a frown of deep concern on his face.

He looked up into Ara's shaken face. "Are you all right?"

"Yes," she gasped, breathless from a dizzying combination of pleasure and pain. She pressed her hand over the spot where the wound had been, touching the new flesh that had healed into place.

James blinked groggily after several minutes, then slowly got up from the floor where he had sprawled. He wiped at his mouth and looked down at the red stain on his fingertips.

"Oh, my."

Tobyn chuckled. "Are you all right?"

"Time will tell, won't it?"

"That it will." He gathered his friend up. "Come on. Let's put you to bed." As he escorted Donnell out of the room, he looked back at his sister as she sat in a silence that was almost majestic. *//Thank you.//*

//Anything for you, Tobyn.//

He slept only as long as he needed to, eager as he was to exact his vengeance on Dumas. When he emerged from his rooms in the early afternoon, he found James, pale but energetic and seemingly recovered from his ordeal the night before, waiting for him. The look on his face made Tobyn sigh.

"What do you want?" he asked, neither rude nor polite.

"To ask you again to reconsider."

"You are tiresome, my friend. There is nothing more to discuss. I am going, and that's final."

James fell into step with him as he went to rummage through the kitchen. "Sela wants to talk to you."

"When I get back."

"Tobyn—"

"Later."

Their eyes met, and the Irishman did not flinch. "Now. She's your wife, for God's sake. Don't you care what she has to say, why she did it?"

Tobyn's voice was as brisk as his steps as he trotted down the stairs. "She did it because she loves me and couldn't bear the thought of not being with me forever, right?"

"That's right. And what's wrong with that?"

Gemini stopped short and looked at James in silence. Finally, he said, "She could have asked."

"And you'd have said no."

He hated it when James was right. With a sigh, he relented. "All right. Where is she?"

"In the garden, by the roses."

"Is it sunny?"

"Overcast."

Tobyn nodded. "Fine. I'll talk to her. Where's my coat?"

"I'll get it." He grasped his friend's shoulder before he turned to go. "Thank you."

James returned a moment later with Tobyn's coat and his wide-brimmed hat. Wordlessly, the vampire armed himself against the daylight and went out to the garden. The carefully-landscaped plots of growing things were pretty enough in the summer, he supposed, when they bloomed in colors and variety, but right now they were boring and dead. He strode with purpose along the geometric pattern of the tiles, wondering what in the world Sela was thinking to sit outside in the cold by a clump of winter-blighted roses.

She was huddled miserably beneath her shawl when he turned the corner to face her. Her slender hands, pale, clutched each other on her lap, and her head was bowed. He could hear the uneven rhythm of her breath and knew that she was crying.

He stepped closer. "Sela."

He never anticipated her reaction. She started violently, then cringed and held up her hands in an instinctive defense. Her quiet crying gained a voice, and she turned her face away, clearly expecting him to hit her.

"Sela, no. Shh." He took her hands gently in his own and sat beside her, disturbed by her fear. "Sela, look at me."

She turned slowly and gave him the briefest of glances. He took her face in his hands and looked into her teary eyes, feeling overcome with tenderness and a need to help. She trembled beneath his touch. "I'm so sorry," she finally gasped out. "So sorry..."

"Hush, love. It's all right."

She stared at him. "You're not still angry?"

"I was furious." He stopped her from pulling away. "Stop shrinking from me, Sela. I'm not my uncle, and I'm not furious anymore."

She timidly covered his hands with her own. "Do you understand? James told me that he'd explain..."

"I think I do. And it doesn't make it all right, and I think you've made a terrible mistake, but we can't undo it. Done is done, and it's time to make the best of things." He smiled softly. "I sound like my grandmother."

"She was a wise woman."

"Yes, she was."

They were quiet for a moment, sitting together on their stone bench, holding hands. Sela found the courage to look him in the eye. "Do you still love me, Tobyn, even though I've done this thing?"

He answered her with a kiss. He poured everything he felt for her into that touch, pulling her to him with arms both strong and gentle. She leaned against him, then sighed happily when their lips parted. They hugged one another for what seemed a very long time.

"I couldn't lose you," she breathed in his ear. "I'm not sorry I did it."

"I'm sorry you had to steal it from me," he told her honestly, "but I think I'm glad you'll stay with me now."

"Now and forever," she promised. "We have forever."

He pulled away and rose. "Come inside, Sela. It's cold out and I'm famished."

His tender moments never lasted for very long, she noted, but at least he had them. Smiling at him, she took his hands and followed him back into the Raven's Nest.

⤙⤚⤙⤚

Throughout the meal, Sela was edgy and unpredictable, one moment happy, the next agitated and skittish. Tobyn spent hours trying to keep her calm. Finally he succeeded in reassuring her just as sunset was painting the western sky. He would have very little time before Dumas awoke.

He left his wife with James, who begged Tobyn with his eyes alone to stop his plan before it started. Tobyn ignored him.

In the quiet of the library, he settled into his favorite chair and tried to Sense where his Maker might be. It took a bit of time and searching, but he was finally able to locate the slender line that connected the Frenchman's soul to his. Tobyn tightened his grip on his knife and pushed into the murky barrier between the Raven's Nest and Michel Dumas.

He felt like he was frozen in ice that wasn't cold. He could neither move nor breathe, and his panicky mind demanded that he do both. His chest tightened and he began to feel afraid. Then he emerged on the other side, standing only a few inches away from Dumas, face to face.

The shock on the French vampire's face was priceless, but Tobyn abruptly realized that he was in no position to savor the moment. He stood in the center of a circular room, deep and dark, with a smell like decay in the air. Behind Dumas were a trio of other vampires, members of the Prime; behind Tobyn stood a semi-circle of creatures in the robes of the Brethren.

He had made a serious tactical error.

"Shit."

Dumas seized his arms, a look of triumph replacing the surprise on his face. Tobyn kicked at the other's groin like a street fighter and threw himself frantically back into the strange between-space, unprepared and totally without direction.

Around him he could See colors he had no names for, and landscapes utterly alien to him. This was not the between-space he had traveled through before.

"Jesus Christ, where am I?" He turned slowly, like swimming in jelly. Around him he could Feel energy building, coherent and directed, all but solid. Dozens of separable energies swarmed around him, and he could hear laughter and voices colliding. It sounded like a party.

What is this?

It's solid, corporeal.

Is it alive?

Can we use it?

Tobyn could feel cold, slimy fingers on his shoulders, and he shuddered. Better to run to something known and bad than to stay with something unknown and infinitely worse; he gathered up the last of his strength and hurled himself back the way he'd come.

After the popping sound left his ears, he found himself lying on his back between the Prime and the Brethren, gulping for air, his knife hopelessly lost. The leader of the Brethren stepped forward and crouched beside him, her beautiful face brightened by a wide smile that was just shy of maniacal.

"Tobyn Reyes, I presume. Is this the one, Dumas?"

"It is."

The gypsy was too exhausted to do more than stare at the woman. "Welcome to Rome, Señor Reyes. I am Marita of the Brethren. You are Dumas' little abomination."

He managed to crack a smile and gasp out pluckily, "That's me."

"You are also my enemy," she pronounced. "You have murdered our Brothers and Sisters, and you have fraternized with a known criminal, Duncan McIntyre."

Breathing was easier now, so he used it for bravado. "My sister fraternized. I just talked to the man."

"It is enough." She motioned for two of her companions, who pulled him off of the floor and tied him to a chair that someone kindly supplied. "And you exist as something no one can quite identify. Is it enough."

Dumas spoke up, and beneath the affected aristocratic disinterest Tobyn could hear honest concern. "Enough for what, madam?"

"Enough for trial by sunlight."

The Brethren erupted into wild cheers and applause while the Prime turned expectant eyes onto their leader. The Frenchman spared a glance at Tobyn, who had begun to giggle unsteadily, then said, "This is an absurd interruption in these proceedings. The creature is my responsibility. Hand him over to me and we can continue our treaty-making."

"Oh, no!" Tobyn said quickly. "Please, I'd rather have the sun than be given back to him." He was planning to dramatize his point, but his own laughter cut him off.

Beside Dumas, Elisa Dieter said, "He is mad."

"It may be so," Marita agreed, "But, mad or not, he has broken Brethren laws and must accept Brethren punishment. I will not give him to you, Dumas."

The Prime scowled. "You would jeopardize this fragile accord for him? Is exacting your punishment worth continued warfare with us?"

The leader of the Brethren smiled thinly. "Yes, it is worth it. It is the duty of my kind to punish sinners and mete out the judgment of the Lord. This creature is evil, a demon spawned by demons." She pointed at Tobyn, who was easing off of his spasm of laughter and bravely trying not to smile. "He kills mortals, vampires, the good and the evil without discretion or selectivity. He must be destroyed. We must do it. That is the way of things." She folded her arms. "And may I remind you that you are in an extremely poor bargaining position? You are on Brethren soil."

Dumas was torn. Conflicting emotions danced in his eyes, and he blurted, "Give Tobyn to me and the Prime will withdraw from Rome entirely. It will be yours."

Murmurs followed in the wake of his desperate offer. Marita, dark head tilted, her pale eyes as crafty as a cat's, said, "You really want him quite badly, don't you?"

The admission came easily. "Yes."

"Why?" she challenged. "What drives you? Do you love him?"

"At one time," he replied, looking into Tobyn's face with a hurt solemnity that sobered the gypsy, "I thought I did."

"And that is a sin as well. The Lord punishes those with the Greek disease. Homosexuality." She spat when she said it. "It is wrong and punishable by sunlight."

"He was my creation," Dumas pressed, ignoring Elisa's efforts to silence him. "Give him to me and I will destroy him."

"Bastaris," Tobyn observed, adding his two cents' worth.

"Silence!" Marita shook her head. "No. You want it too much, Dumas. I will allow you and your Prime companions to leave Rome safely, but I will keep Reyes and this city."

"Unacceptable!"

"It is my final offer. I urge you to take it."

The Frenchman's face colored with rage he could not release. He bowed slightly, militarily crisp, and glared at the unflinching Marita. "Then there is no reason for me to continue this charade. There will be no accord between our people." He held out a hand, and one of his seconds placed his coat in it. Dumas tugged the garment over his shoulders. "Keep Reyes, then; do what you will to him. But Rome shall never be yours. This is war, Marita, and I swear here and now that I will live to see the end of the Brethren."

One of her guards took a menacing step toward the Prime, but Marita stopped him with a delicate wave of her hand. "Then so be it, Michel Dumas. War to the death of us all."

The Prime could not bear to look at Tobyn again. With a curt order, he turned and led his party out of the bargaining room. Tobyn tugged at his bonds experimentally; they did not respond in the least. He sighed and watched Elisa watching him until she was forced to turn and go. He hated her, especially for the look of triumph on her face. She quite enjoyed the thought of his upcoming demise.

Marita pulled a flat wooden bench over and sat on it, facing him, her hands primly folded in her lap. Her gaze was intensely scrutinizing, and Tobyn refused to be intimidated by it. Lifting his chin, he stared back at her, examining her in return.

Finally, she smiled. "Brave little thing, aren't you?"

"Yes."

"And you're not mad at all, are you?"

"No, just a little annoyed."

Marita chuckled. "It's almost a shame to kill you come morning. You could be an interesting friend."

"Well, you'd better do me in anyway," he advised with mock concern. "I've been a very bad boy."

"So you have. And so you'll die. But it's not that bad, really. You'll be serving a very important function. The Brethren haven't had a good execution in years."

"Poor things. They must be feeling very deprived."

Their shared smiles were not friendly. "You will put on a good show, won't you?"

"I'll try."

"Oh, good." She leaned closer. "Tell me, how did you get here?"

"I popped," he said with a shrug.

"You what?"

"Popped."

"How?"

He smiled. "I don't know. I just did."

"Why haven't you done it again to escape?"

"I tried. It didn't work." He shrugged again. "I'm still figuring it out."

Marita sat silently pondering this, wondering if it was something that she could somehow achieve as well. They sat that way for over an hour, staring at each other and trying to guess the other's thoughts.

She spoke up after the long silence. "You won't tell me how?"

"No."

She sighed. "A shame. We could have learned much from one another."

"Perhaps, but if you're just going to kill me anyway, isn't that a waste of time?"

"Not for me."

One of her compatriots approached, his eyes dark and wary as he studied the passive-faced Gemini. He bent to whisper into Marita's ear, and she listened with weary disinterest. For the leader of a fanatical group, Tobyn decided, she wasn't much of a fanatic. She just seemed bored.

As she listened to her underling, Tobyn took the time to consider her. She was strikingly beautiful, milky-skinned and lynx-eyed like some oriental princess from a fable. She seemed reasonable enough, and yet she bore the air of someone who could not be trusted, of a woman who was dangerous and slightly unhinged. He thought she was interesting.

Marita dismissed the other member of the Brethren and turned to her reluctant guest. "I'm afraid that your friend Dumas is making a nuisance of himself and business elsewhere calls me away. I fear that our farewell must be short and all too soon. It was a pleasure to meet you." She nodded to her waiting Brethren. "Take him out when the sun is about to rise and tie him to the gate. Signore Reyes, I regret that our brief acquaintance must end this way. Adieu."

"*Hasta la vista*," he grinned.

"I do not believe that we shall meet again."

His grin widened. "Don't be too sure."

With a wry smile, she half-bowed to him before she walked away. Her lieutenant took a militant stance, arms crossed over his bullish chest, no humor at all in his face. Tobyn regretted the exchange of companions. Marita was far more diverting than this ugly living mountain.

He tried to evaluate his power reserves, hoping to perhaps 'pop' back to the Raven's Nest, but he was a bit too drained. He had no desire to get caught by his energy-being friends, and he could only benefit from the Prime and Brethren believing that he was dead. While he was 'dead,' Sela and James could Change in safety and solitude until he knew what to do next. It stood to reason that if the Prime and the Brethren were busy ripping each other to bits, then he and his army could skate in and pick up the pieces...just as soon as he had an army.

Proliferation of his kind would be slow, but he believed it could be done. It would take careful management to keep both the timing and the people involved under control, but he could do it. What was more, having more of his kind about him would only improve his position. He disliked being called an "abomination;" perhaps, if he headed an army capable of hurting both existing groups, then he would earn a little respect.

His army needed a good name and good organization. He thought about it long and hard while he stared at his guard and tried to make the other man nervous. The obvious answer appeared to him. His army would be called the Kris, and it would be divided into *kumpanias*. It would be led according to the rules of Romany politics, but Tobyn would be the king. All of the *kumpanias* would answer to him and him alone, and independent action would be allowed to run rampant.

It was beautiful. And all he had to do was walk away from his execution in the morning.

As luck had it, his goon companion mistimed the execution. By the time he'd untied Tobyn from the chair, pulled him unresisting through the stinking, labyrinthine corridors of the Brethren catacombs, and reached the doors to the outside world, sunlight was beginning to touch the eastern sky. Frantic to avoid the burning rays that were already prickly to his skin, the Brother rudely shoved Tobyn out the door instead of taking the time to tie him to the blackened post that the gypsy presumed was the usual execution site. The Brother locked the door securely behind him, keeping Tobyn out. Gemini, overcome by the dawn, landed on his face on the ground, locked into a deep, death-like sleep, a smile on his face.

When he awoke at noon, he picked himself up, dusted himself off, and considered the closed door. If he'd had a hat, he would have doffed it to his enemies-cum-liberators. He smiled, pleased to make fools of the Brethren so easily, and, careful to keep his eyes out of the light, he turned and started the long walk back to Ireland.

He had work to do.